The Translator and Editor

MICHAEL R. KATZ is the Dean of Language Schools and Schools Abroad, and Professor of Russian at Middlebury College. Formerly, Professor Katz was director of the Center for Post-Soviet and East European Studies, chairman of the Department of Slavic Languages, and professor of Russian at the University of Texas at Austin. He previously taught at Williams College. He is the author of *The Literary Ballad in Early Nineteenth-Century Russian Literature* and *Dreams and the Unconscious in Nineteenth-Century Russian Fiction.* He has translated and edited the Norton Critical Edition of Fyodor Dostoevsky's *Notes from Underground* and *Tolstoy's Short Fiction.* He has also translated Alexander Herzen's *Who Is to Blame?*, N. G. Chernyshevsky's *What Is to Be Done?*, Dostoevsky's *Devils*, Druzhinin's *Polinka Saks*, and Artsybashev's *Sanin.*

A NORTON CRITICAL EDITION

Ivan Turgenev
FATHERS AND SONS

THE AUTHOR ON THE NOVEL
THE CONTEMPORARY REACTION
ESSAYS IN CRITICISM

Translated and Edited by
MICHAEL R. KATZ

MIDDLEBURY COLLEGE

W • W • NORTON & COMPANY • *New York* • *London*

Copyright © 1996, 1994 by W. W. Norton & Company

Printed in the United States of America

First Edition

The text of this book is composed in Electra
with the display set in Bernhard Modern.
Composition by PennSet, Inc.
Manufacturing by Courier, Westford.

Library of Congress Cataloging-in-Publication Data
Turgenev, Ivan Sergeevich, 1818–1883.
[Otsy i deti. English]
Fathers and sons / Ivan Turgenev ; translated and edited by
Michael R. Katz.
p.   cm. — (Norton critical edition)
Includes bibliographical references.
1. Fathers and sons—Fiction.   2. Russia—Social life and
customs—1533–1917—Fiction.   3. Russia—Social
conditions—1801–1917—Fiction.   I. Katz, Michael R.   II. Title.
III. Series.
PG3420.O8E5   1995
891.73′3—dc20   95-5395
ISBN 0-393-96752-2

W. W. Norton & Company, Inc., 500 Fifth Avenue, New York, N.Y. 10110
www.wwnorton.com

W. W. Norton & Company Ltd., Castle House, 75/76 Wells Street,
London W1T 3QT

8 9 0

Contents

Preface

In the preface to the first Norton Critical Edition of *Fathers and Sons*, the editor began as follows:

> Translating Turgenev's novel poses many problems, beginning with the title. The literal translation is *Fathers and Children*. But "sons" in English better implies the notion of spiritual and intellectual generations conveyed by the Russian *deti* (vii).

Perhaps that is the case, or has become the case as a result of English usage. During the preparation of this Norton Critical Edition of Turgenev's classic, I considered changing the title to the more literal *Fathers and Children*. Just when I had persuaded my eminently reasonable editor of the wisdom (and marketability) of this alteration, I myself had a change of heart. In spite of the explicit sexism of the accepted English title, *Fathers and Sons*, I decided for reasons of tradition and euphony to retain Ralph Matlaw's choice, but to address the role of women in the novel through the inclusion of several articles in the critical apparatus that deal directly with the subject, including one of my own written for this occasion entitled *"Fathers and Sons* (and Daughters)." It is to my own daughter that my work on this new edition of Turgenev's novel is dedicated.

The background material begins with Turgenev's reflections on the controversy aroused by the publication of this novel in 1862. Entitled "Apropos of *Fathers and Sons*," the piece was first published in the author's "Literary and Autobiographical Reminiscences" (1869). It provides an interesting account of the genesis of the work, as well as a poignant portrait of his consternation at the critical storm it provoked. This essay is followed by a selection from Turgenev's letters where the reader can follow the process of creation, writing, and revision, as well as the author's attempts to respond to specific questions and objections raised by his critics. The section called "The Contemporary Reaction" provides a representative sample of the diversity of critical opinion by the most influential writers of Turgenev's own day; these excerpts should be read in conjunction with the author's letters and his own *apologia* that precedes them.

The "Essays in Criticism," the majority of which are new in this edition, are organized around several themes: (1) the issue of translation, addressed in a brief excerpt from an essay by Edmund Wilson; (2) political concerns, including Turgenev's liberalism (variously defined as "civic responsibility" and "hesitation"), his view of revolution, his attitude toward nihilism; (3) literary aspects, including the author's use of imagery, his depiction of time, the role of women, the portrayal of love, the conflict of generations, the impact of science, the use of discourse; and finally (4) Turgenev's "influence," to which both Donald Fanger and Robert L. Jackson address themselves in different ways.

Throughout these critical essays the reader will find a complex interweaving of local, specific issues characteristic of mid-nineteenth-century Russian literature and culture, as well as a discussion of broader, universal themes pertaining to the human experience. More than anything else, this mix guarantees that Turgenev's *Fathers and Sons* will continue to be read and enjoyed as a masterpiece of world literature.

The "Essays in Criticism" are followed by "Ivan Turgenev: A Chronology" as well as by a "Selected Bibliography," which provides a list of suggestions for further reading.

The Text of
FATHERS AND SONS

Translated by Michael R. Katz

Fathers and Sons[1]

Dedicated to the memory of
Vissarion Grigorevich
BELINSKY[2]

I

"Well, Peter, still no sign of them?" asked the gentleman on the twentieth of May 1859,[3] as he came out onto the low porch of a carriage inn on *** highway.[4] The man, in his early forties, wearing a dust-covered coat, checked trousers, and no hat, directed the question to his servant, a chubby young fellow with whitish down on his chin and small dull eyes.

The servant, about whom everything—the turquoise ring in his ear, styled multicolored hair, ingratiating movements, in a word, everything—proclaimed him to be a man of the new, advanced generation, glanced condescendingly down the road and replied, "No, sir, no sign of them."

"No sign?" repeated the gentleman.

"No sign," replied the servant a second time.

The gentleman sighed and sat down on the bench. Let's acquaint the reader with him while he's sitting there, feet tucked under him, gazing thoughtfully around.

His name is Nikolai Petrovich Kirsanov. He owns a fine estate, located twelve miles or so from the carriage inn,[5] with two hundred serfs, or, as he describes it, since negotiating the boundaries with his peasants and establishing a "farm,"[6] an estate with about five thousand acres of land. His father, a general who fought in 1812,[7] was a semiliterate, coarse Russian, not in the least malicious, who worked hard all his life—first in command of a brigade, then a division—and who always lived in

1. A literal translation of the Russian title (*Otsy i deti*) would be "Fathers and Children"; this version has been retained for reasons of tradition and euphony.
2. Vissarion Belinsky (1811–48) was the most influential literary critic of his day, a staunch Westernizer, and an enthusiastic supporter of Turgenev.
3. The novel is set before the emancipation of the serfs, which took place in February 1861.
4. Russian literary convention typically omits place names and abbreviates surnames (e.g., Princess Kh. and Princess R.).
5. An establishment where travelers could procure fresh horses and find food and lodging.
6. Kirsanov wishes to be seen as a progressive landowner who's taken steps to improve conditions for the peasants on his estate.
7. The year Napoleon initiated his disastrous military campaign against Russia.

the provinces, where, as a result of his rank, he came to play quite an important role. Nikolai Petrovich was born in the south of Russia, just like his older brother, Pavel, about whom more later, and was brought up at home until the age of fourteen, surrounded by underpaid tutors, free-and-easy but obsequious adjutants, and other regimental and staff people. His mother, a member of the Kolyazin family, called *Agathe* as a girl, then Agafokleya Kuzminishna Kirsanova as a general's wife, belonged to a group of "lady commandants"; she wore splendid caps and silk dresses that rustled, was the first one in church to approach the cross, spoke a great deal and in a loud voice, allowed her children to kiss her hand in the morning, and gave them her blessing at night—in a word, she lived life just as she pleased. In his role as the general's son, Nikolai Petrovich—not only was he undistinguished by bravery, but he'd even earned a reputation as something of a coward—was required, just like his brother, Pavel, to enter military service; but he managed to break his leg the very day he received news of his commission, and, after spending two months in bed, retained a slight limp for the rest of his life. His father gave up on him and allowed him to enter the civil service. He brought him to Petersburg as soon as he turned eighteen and enrolled him in the university. By the way, just about the same time, his brother became an officer in a guards regiment. The two young men shared an apartment under the distant supervision of a cousin on their mother's side, Ilya Kolyazin, an important man. Their father returned home to his division and his spouse, and only upon occasion would he send his sons large quarto sheets of gray paper covered with a sweeping clerkly scrawl. On the bottom of these sheets appeared the words "Piotr Kirsanoff, Major-General," painstakingly surrounded by flourishes. In 1835 Nikolai Petrovich left the university with a candidate's degree;[8] in the same year General Kirsanov, involuntarily retired after an unsuccessful review, arrived in Petersburg with his wife to take up residence. He was just about to move into a house near the Tauride Garden and join the English Club when he died suddenly from a stroke. Agafokleya Kuzminishna followed soon afterward: she couldn't get used to the dull life in the capital—she was consumed by the ennui of retirement. In the meantime Nikolai Petrovich, during his parents' lifetime, and to their considerable dismay, had managed to fall in love with the daughter of a certain Prepolovensky, a low-ranking civil servant and the previous owner of their apartment. She was an attractive and, as they say, progressive young woman: she used to read serious journal articles published in the section called "Science." He married her right after the period of mourning, and, forsaking the Ministry of Crown Domains[9] where his father had secured him a position, he led a blissful

8. The lowest academic rank, roughly equivalent to the bachelor's degree.
9. The branch of the tsarist government created to oversee property belonging to the Romanov family.

life with his Masha, first in a country cottage near the Forestry Institute; later in town, in a small, comfortable apartment, with a clean staircase and a chilly living room; and finally, in the country, where he settled down once and for all and where, a very short time afterward, his son, Arkady, was born. The couple lived very happily and peacefully: they were hardly ever apart, read together, played pieces for four hands at the piano, sang duets; she planted flowers and looked after the poultry; every so often he went off hunting and busied himself with estate management, while Arkady kept on growing—also happily and peacefully. Ten years passed like a dream. In 1847 Kirsanov's wife died. He hardly survived the blow and his hair turned gray in the course of a few weeks; he was hoping to go abroad to distract himself a bit . . . but then came the events of 1848.[1] He returned to the country against his will and, after a rather long period of inactivity, occupied himself with the reorganization of his estate. In 1855 he brought his son to the university; he spent three winters there with him in Petersburg, going almost nowhere and trying to make the acquaintance of Arkady's young companions. The last winter he was unable to come—and now we see him in May 1859, completely gray, stout, and somewhat stooped; he's waiting for his son, who just received his candidate's degree, as he himself had some time before.

The servant, out of a sense of propriety, or perhaps because he didn't want to remain under his master's eye, had gone to the gate and lit his pipe. Nikolai Petrovich bent his head and began staring at the decrepit porch steps; nearby, a large mottled young chicken strutted with a stately gait, treading firmly with its big yellow legs; a scruffy cat, curled up in a most affected manner against the railing, observed the chicken with hostility. The sun was scorching; a smell of warm rye bread wafted from the dark passage of the carriage inn. Our Nikolai Petrovich fell into a reverie. "My son . . . a graduate . . . Arkasha . . ." constantly ran through his head; he tried to think about something else, but the same thoughts returned. He recalled his late wife . . . "She didn't live to see it!" he whispered gloomily . . . A plump, blue-gray dove flew down onto the road and went off to drink from a puddle near the well. Nikolai Petrovich stared at it, but his ear had already caught the sound of approaching wheels . . .

"Seems they're coming, sir," announced the servant, darting in from the gate.

Nikolai Petrovich jumped up and fixed his gaze on the road. A coach appeared, drawn by a troika of posthorses harnessed three abreast; in the coach could be seen the band of a student cap and the familiar profile of a beloved face . . .

"Arkasha! Arkasha!" cried Kirsanov and ran down waving his arms

1. A series of unsuccessful revolutionary uprisings in Western Europe that led to a period of extreme reaction in Russia.

. . . A few moments later his lips were pressed against the beardless, dusty, sunburnt cheek of the young graduate.

II

"Let me shake myself off first, Papa," said Arkady in a voice a bit hoarse from the road, but still strong and youthful, as he cheerfully responded to his father's caresses. "I'm getting you all covered with dust."

"Never mind, never mind," Nikolai Petrovich replied, smiling tenderly, and twice brushed off the collar of his son's overcoat and his own jacket. "Let me have a look at you, then, let me have a look," he said stepping back; then he set off in haste toward the carriage inn, calling out, "This way, over here, bring the horses at once."

Nikolai Petrovich seemed much more excited than his son; he seemed to have become a little flustered, grown timid as it were. Arkady stopped him.

"Papa," he said, "let me introduce you to my friend Bazarov, about whom I've written so often. He's kindly agreed to pay us a visit."

Nikolai Petrovich turned around quickly and, advancing toward a tall man in a long, loose garment with tassels who had just climbed out of the coach, warmly shook his bare, ruddy hand, which hadn't been immediately extended.

"I'm very glad," he began, "and grateful you've decided to visit us; I hope that . . . may I ask your name and patronymic?"[2]

"Evgeny Vasilev," replied Bazarov in a lazy but steadfast voice; turning down the collar of his loose garment, he showed Nikolai Petrovich his entire face. Long and thin, with a broad forehead, a nose that was flat at the top but sharp at the tip, large greenish eyes, and drooping side whiskers of a sandy color, it was enlivened with a serene smile and reflected both self-confidence and intelligence.

"I hope, dear Evgeny Vasilich, you won't be bored here," continued Nikolai Petrovich.

Bazarov's thin lips moved slightly, but he made no reply and merely raised his cap. His dark blond hair, long and thick, didn't conceal the prominent bulges in his capacious skull.

"Well then, Arkady," Nikolai Petrovich began again, turning to his son, "shall we have the horses harnessed at once, or do you want to rest a little?"

"We'll rest at home, Papa; have the horses harnessed."

"At once, at once," agreed the father. "Hey, Peter, do you hear? Get a move on, lad, faster."

Peter, who in his role as enlightened servant hadn't gone up to kiss the young master's hand and had merely nodded to him from a distance, once again withdrew beyond the gate.

---

2. A middle name formed by adding a suffix to the father's first name; it is often contracted in conversation and therefore appears in various forms in the text.

"I'm here with a small carriage, but there's a troika of horses for your coach as well," said Nikolai Petrovich with some concern, while Arkady had a drink of water from an iron dipper brought by the woman in charge of the carriage inn, and Bazarov lit his pipe and walked over to the driver, who was unharnessing the horses. "But our carriage only seats two, and I don't know how your friend will . . ."

"He'll go in the coach," Arkady said, interrupting him in a low voice. "Please don't stand on ceremony with him. He's a splendid fellow, very simple—you'll see."

Nikolai Petrovich's coachman led out the horses.

"Well, get a move on, bushy beard!" Bazarov said, addressing the driver.

"Hear that, Mityukha," said another driver who was standing nearby, hands thrust into the rear slit of his sheepskin coat. "Hear what the gentleman called you? You bushy beard, you."

Mityukha merely shook his hat and pulled the reins off the sweaty shafthorse.[3]

"Let's go, let's go, lads, give them a hand," cried Nikolai Petrovich. "There'll be money for vodka!"

In a few minutes the horses were harnessed; father and son got into the carriage; Peter climbed onto the box; Bazarov jumped into the coach, buried his head in a leather cushion—and both vehicles set off.

III

"So, here you are, a graduate at last, and you've come home," said Nikolai Petrovich, touching Arkady first on the shoulder, then on the knee. "At long last!"

"How's Uncle? In good health?" asked Arkady, who, in spite of the genuine, almost childlike rapture that filled him, wanted to shift the subject of conversation as quickly as possible from high emotion to everyday matters.

"In good health. He wanted to come and meet you, but, for some reason, he changed his mind."

"Did you have to wait long?" asked Arkady.

"Almost five hours."

"Dear Papa!"

Arkady turned quickly to his father and planted a loud kiss on his cheek. Nikolai Petrovich chuckled softly. "What a splendid horse I have for you!" he said. "You'll see. And your room's been wallpapered."

"Is there a room for Bazarov?"

"We'll find one for him, too."

"Papa, please, be nice to him. I can't tell you how much I value his friendship."

"Have you known him long?"

3. Shafthorses run within the shafts on a Russian troika; tracehorses, outside.

"Not very."

"That explains why I didn't meet him last winter. What's he studying?"

"His main subject is natural science. But he knows everything. Next year he hopes to qualify as a doctor."

"Ah! He's a student in the medical faculty," observed Nikolai Petrovich and fell silent. "Peter," he called, extending his arm, "are those our peasants over there?"

Peter glanced in the direction his master was pointing. A few carts harnessed with unbridled horses were running swiftly along a narrow country lane. In each cart there were one or two peasants wearing unbuttoned sheepskin coats.

"Yes, sir, they are," replied Peter.

"Where're they going, to town or what?"

"To town, I suppose. The tavern," he added contemptuously and leaned slightly toward the coachman, as if in search of support. But he didn't even budge: the coachman was a man of the old school and didn't share the latest views.

"I've had a lot of trouble with the peasants this year," said Nikolai Petrovich, turning to his son. "They don't pay their quitrent.[4] What can one do?"

"Are you satisfied with your hired laborers?"

"Yes," said Nikolai Petrovich through his teeth. "But they're being provoked, that's the problem; and they still make no real effort. They spoil the harness. But they've done the ploughing well. It'll all work out in the end. Are you taking an interest in farming now?"

"There's no shade here; that's unfortunate," observed Arkady, without answering the last question.

"I've installed a large awning on the north side of the house just above the balcony," said Nikolai Petrovich. "Now we can have dinner outside."

"It'll look too much like a summer cottage . . . but that doesn't really matter. Then again, the air here's so fresh! It smells so good! You know, it seems to me the air doesn't smell as good anywhere else in the world as it does right here! And the sky's . . ."

Arkady stopped suddenly, cast a furtive glance behind him, and fell silent.

"Of course," Nikolai Petrovich observed, "you were born here, so everything must seem special to you . . ."

"Come, Papa, it really doesn't matter where a person's born."

"Still . . ."

"No, it doesn't make any difference whatsoever."

Nikolai Petrovich cast a sidelong glance at his son; the carriage traveled on for half a mile or so before their conversation resumed.

"I don't remember whether I wrote you," Nikolai Petrovich began, "your former nanny, Egorovna, passed away."

---

4. The system of land cultivation under which serfs farmed the landowner's estate and paid him an annual sum of money known as the quitrent (*obrok*).

"Really? Poor old thing! And is Prokofich alive and well?"

"Alive and well and hasn't changed in the least. He grumbles just as much as ever. In general, you won't find any major changes in Marino."

"Do you still have the same steward?"

"That's the one thing I have changed. I decided not to keep any of the freed serfs who used to be house servants, or, at least, not to assign them any duties carrying responsibility. [Arkady pointed to Peter.] *Il est libre, en effet*,"[5] Nikolai Petrovich said in a low voice, "but he's just a valet. Now I have a steward who's a townsman; he seems to be a sensible fellow. I pay him a salary of two hundred and fifty rubles a year. However," added Nikolai Petrovich, wiping his forehead and brow with his hand, which was always a sign of some inner embarrassment, "I just said you wouldn't find any changes in Marino . . . That's not quite true. I consider it my duty to prepare you, although . . ."

He hesitated a moment and then went on in French.

"A stern moralist would consider my candor inappropriate; but, in the first place, it's impossible to conceal, and, in the second, you know I've always maintained particular views regarding the relationship between a father and son. At my age . . . In a word, this . . . this young woman about whom you've probably heard something or other . . ."

"Fenechka?" Arkady asked casually.

Nikolai Petrovich blushed.

"Please don't say her name too loud . . . Well, yes . . . she's now living with me. I've moved her into the house . . . there were two little rooms. But it can all be changed."

"Goodness, Papa, whatever for?"

"Your friend will be staying with us . . . It's awkward . . ."

"As far as Bazarov's concerned, please don't worry about it. He's above all that."

"Well, and what about you?" Nikolai Petrovich said. "The rooms in the little wing aren't very nice—and that's a pity."

"Goodness, Papa," Arkady interrupted. "It's as if you're apologizing; you should be ashamed."

"Of course I should," replied Nikolai Petrovich, blushing even more.

"Enough of that, Papa, enough, please!" Arkady said with a tender smile. "What's there to apologize for?" he thought; a feeling of indulgent tenderness toward his gentle father, combined with a sensation of secret superiority, filled his soul. "Stop it, please," he repeated, involuntarily enjoying an awareness of his own maturity and freedom.

Nikolai Petrovich glanced at him through the fingers of his hand, with which he was continuing to wipe his forehead, and felt a pang in his heart . . . But he blamed himself for it immediately.

"Now we've reached our own fields," he said after a long silence.

"Is that our forest up ahead?" asked Arkady.

---

5. "As a matter of fact, he's free" (French).

"Yes. But I've sold it. It'll be chopped down this year."

"Why did you sell it?"

"I needed the money; besides, that land's to be given to the peasants."

"Who don't pay their quitrent?"

"That's their business, but they'll pay someday."

"Too bad about the forest," said Arkady and began looking around.

The area in which they were traveling couldn't be described as picturesque. Field after field stretched as far as the horizon, first gently ascending, then descending; here and there were little woodlands and winding ravines covered in sparse low-lying shrubs that called to mind their characteristic representation on ancient maps in the time of Catherine the Great.[6] They came upon little streams with cleared banks, tiny ponds with fragile dams, little villages with low peasant huts under dark roofs often missing half their thatch, small crooked threshing barns with walls of woven brushwood and gaping doorways beside abandoned threshing floors, and churches, some made of brick with the plaster falling off, others of wood with slanted crosses and overgrown cemeteries. Arkady's heart gradually sank. And, as luck would have it, the peasants they passed were all in tatters and riding pathetic nags; the roadside willows stood, bark torn and branches broken, like beggars in rags; emaciated, shaggy cows, mere bags of bones, gnawed greedily on the grass growing along ditches. They seemed to have been snatched recently from some ravenous, deadly claws—and, called into being by the pitiful sight of these enfeebled animals, there arose in the midst of this fine spring day the white specter of joyless, endless winter with its blizzards, frosts, and snows . . . "No," thought Arkady, "this land isn't very rich; it strikes one neither by its prosperity nor by its industriousness; it's impossible, impossible for it to stay like this; reforms are essential . . . but how to implement them, where to begin? . . ."

These were Arkady's thoughts . . . and while he pondered, spring was making itself felt. Everything around glittered golden green, everything—trees, bushes, and grass—waved gently and expansively, shining under the soft breath of the warm breeze; everywhere skylarks poured out their song in endless, resonant streams; lapwings called as they circled over low-lying meadows, then darted silently across tussocks of grass; rooks strutted about, appearing black and beautiful against the tender green of the low spring corn; they disappeared into the rye, which was already turning white, and only occasionally did their heads reappear amidst the smoky gray waves. Arkady gazed and gazed, his thoughts diminishing gradually and then disappearing altogether . . . He threw off his overcoat and looked at his father with such a young boy's joyous face that his father embraced him once again.

"It's not much further now," said Nikolai Petrovich. "We've only to

6. Empress of Russia (1729–96), who ruled from 1762 until her death. She greatly extended the boundaries of the empire and was also a great patron of the arts.

climb this little hill and then the house'll be visible. We'll get along splendidly, Arkasha; you'll help me run the estate, if you don't find it too boring. We should become much closer, get to know each other better, don't you agree?"

"Of course," said Arkady. "What a splendid day it is!"

"In honor of your arrival, my dear. Yes, spring's in full bloom. But I do agree with Pushkin—you recall the lines from *Eugene Onegin*:

> How sad your coming is to me,
> Spring, oh spring, the time of love!
> What . . .[7]

"Arkady!" Bazarov's voice rang out from the coach. "Give me a match, will you? I've nothing to light my pipe."

Nikolai Petrovich fell silent, and Arkady, who'd begun listening to him not without a certain astonishment, but not without sympathy, hastened to pull a silver matchbox from his pocket and sent it over to Bazarov with Peter.

"You want a cigar?" Bazarov shouted again.

"Sure," replied Arkady.

Peter returned to the carriage and handed him his matchbox and a fat, black cigar, which Arkady lit immediately, spreading such a strong and acrid smell of cheap tobacco around himself that Nikolai Petrovich, who'd never been a smoker, turned away, though unobtrusively so as not to offend his son.

A quarter of an hour later both carriages stopped in front of the porch of a new wooden house painted gray and covered with a red iron roof. This was Marino, also known as New Wick, or, as the peasants used to call it, Landless Farmstead.

IV

No crowd of servants came pouring onto the porch to meet the masters; only one twelve-year-old girl appeared, and after her a young fellow emerged from the house who resembled Peter; dressed in gray livery with white buttons bearing a coat of arms, he was Pavel Petrovich Kirsanov's servant. He silently opened the door of the carriage and unfastened the apron of the coach. Nikolai Petrovich, his son, and Bazarov proceeded through a dark, almost deserted hall, behind the door of which a young woman's face appeared momentarily; they entered a drawing room furnished in the latest style.

"Here we are at home," said Nikolai Petrovich, removing his cap and shaking his head. "Now the most important thing's to have supper and get some rest."

7. A quotation from chapter 7, stanza 2 of *Eugene Onegin*, a novel in verse (pub. 1825–31) by the most famous Russian poet, Aleksandr Pushkin (1799–1837).

"It wouldn't be a bad idea to have something to eat," observed Bazarov, stretching himself and sinking down on the sofa.

"Yes, yes, let's have supper, as soon as possible," Nikolai Petrovich said and began stamping his feet for no apparent reason. "Here comes Prokofich just in time."

A man aged sixty entered, white-haired, thin, and dark, in a brown frock coat with brass buttons and a pink scarf tied around his neck. He grinned, went up to kiss Arkady's hand, and, after bowing to the guest, withdrew to the door and stood with both hands behind his back.

"Here he is, Prokofich," began Nikolai Petrovich. "He's come back to us at long last . . . Well? What do you think of him?"

"He's looking well, sir," said the old man and grinned again, but knit his thick brows immediately. "Do you wish me to serve supper, sir?" he asked pretentiously.

"Yes, yes, please do. Perhaps you'd like to go to your room first, Evgeny Vasilich?"

"No, thank you very much, there's no reason. But have them bring my suitcase up, if you would, and this coat of mine," he added, taking off his loose-fitting garment.

"Very well. Prokofich, take his coat. [Prokofich, as if confused, picked up Bazarov's "coat" and holding it above his head, walked out on tiptoe.] And you, Arkady, do you want to go to your room for a minute?"

"Yes, to wash up," Arkady replied and headed toward the door, but at that moment a man of medium height, dressed in a dark English suit, fashionable low cravat, and patent leather shoes, entered the drawing room—Pavel Petrovich Kirsanov. He appeared to be about forty-five: his closely cropped gray hair shone with a dark luster, like new silver; his face, sallow, but without wrinkles, unusually regular and pure of line, as if carved by a light and delicate chisel, revealed traces of remarkable beauty; his bright, black almond-shaped eyes were particularly exquisite. The entire figure of Arkady's uncle, elegant and well-bred, retained a youthful gracefulness and a striving upward, away from the earth, which in most cases is lost after a man leaves his twenties behind.

From the pocket of his trousers Pavel Petrovich removed his beautiful hand with long pink fingernails—a hand that seemed even more beautiful in contrast to the snowy whiteness of his cuff fastened with one large opal—and extended it to his nephew. After completing this preliminary European-style "handshake," he then kissed him three times in the Russian manner; that is, he brushed his perfumed mustache against his nephew's cheek three times and said, "Welcome."

Nikolai Petrovich introduced him to Bazarov: Pavel Petrovich bowed his elegant figure slightly and smiled slightly, but didn't extend his hand and even put it back into his pocket.

"I thought you wouldn't come today," he began in a pleasant voice, swaying gently, shrugging his shoulders, and showing his magnificent white teeth. "Did something happen to you along the way?"

"Nothing happened," replied Arkady. "We just tarried a bit. But now we're hungry as wolves. Do make Prokofich hurry, Papa, and I'll be right back."

"Wait, I'll go with you," cried Bazarov, suddenly jumping up from the sofa. Both young men left the room.

"Who's that?" asked Pavel Petrovich.

"Arkady's friend, a very bright fellow according to him."

"Is he going to stay here with us?"

"Yes."

"That hairy creature?"

"Well, yes."

Pavel Petrovich tapped his nails on the table.

"I imagine that Arkady *s'est dégourdi*,"[8] he observed. "I'm glad he's come home."

They talked very little during supper. Bazarov especially said almost nothing at all, but ate a great deal. Nikolai Petrovich related various episodes from his life as a farmer, as he put it, and talked about impending government measures, committees, deputies, the need to introduce machinery, and so on. Pavel Petrovich paced slowly back and forth in the dining room (he never ate supper) and occasionally sipped a goblet filled with red wine and even less frequently uttered some remark, or rather exclamation, such as "Ah! Aha! Hmm!" Arkady related some Petersburg news, but felt a certain awkwardness that usually overtakes a young man who's just ceased being a child and who's returned to the place where others are used to seeing and regarding him as such. He dragged out his speech for no reason, avoided using the word "Papa," and once even replaced it with "Father," pronounced, it's true, between his teeth; with excessive carelessness he poured much more wine into his glass than he really wanted and then drank it all. Prokofich didn't take his eyes off him and merely chewed his lips. After supper everyone immediately went their separate ways.

"Your uncle's a bit of an eccentric," Bazarov said to Arkady, sitting down next to his bed in his dressing gown and smoking a short pipe. "Such dandyism in the country, just think! And his fingernails, what fingernails, they could be put on display!"

"But you don't know," Arkady replied, "what a social lion he was in his own day. Sometime I'll have to tell you his story. He was quite a handsome man and used to turn women's heads."

"So that's it! Does it for old time's sake. Pity there's no one out here to charm. I kept looking at him: he has such astonishing collars, as if

---

8. "Has grown smarter" (French).

made of stone, and his chin's so exquisitely shaved. Arkady Nikolaich, don't you think it's a bit absurd?"

"Perhaps, but he's really a fine person."

"An archaic phenomenon! But your father's a splendid fellow. He wastes his time reading poetry and hardly understands estate management, but he's a good sort."

"My father's pure gold."

"Did you see how shy he is?"

Arkady nodded his head, as if he himself weren't shy.

"It's quite astonishing," Bazarov continued, "these aging romantics! They'll expand their nervous systems to the breaking point . . . then, all equilibrium will be destroyed. Anyway, good night! There's an English washstand in my room and the door doesn't lock. Nevertheless, one must encourage it all—English washstands, that's real progress!"

Bazarov left and Arkady was overcome by a joyous feeling. It's very pleasant to fall asleep in one's own house, in a familiar bed, under a blanket made by loving hands, perhaps his nanny's, those affectionate, kind, untiring hands. Arkady remembered Egorovna, sighed, and wished her eternal peace . . . He didn't pray for himself.

Both he and Bazarov soon fell fast asleep, but other people in the house were unable to sleep for some time. His son's return had excited Nikolai Petrovich. He lay down in bed, but didn't blow the candle out and, resting his head on his arm, thought long and hard. His brother sat up in his study long past midnight in a broad Hambs[9] armchair before the fireplace in which some embers were glowing dimly. Pavel Petrovich hadn't gotten undressed; he'd only exchanged his patent leather shoes for some red Chinese slippers without heels. In his hands he held the latest issue of *Galignani*,[1] but he wasn't reading; he stared fixedly into the fire where a bluish flame flickered, first dying down, then flaring up . . . God knows where his thoughts wandered, but it wasn't only to the past; the expression on his face was intense and gloomy, which doesn't happen when a man's absorbed only in recollections. And in the little back room sitting on a large trunk, wearing a light blue sleeveless jacket, a white kerchief thrown over her dark hair, was a young woman, Fenechka; she was either listening or dozing or looking through the open door, behind which a child's cot could be seen and the even breathing of a sleeping child could be heard.

V

The next morning Bazarov woke up before everyone else and left the house. "Hey!" he thought, glancing around, "this place isn't much to look at." When Nikolai Petrovich divided the estate with his peasants,

9. A French furniture maker (1765–1831) who lived in Petersburg.
1. A liberal newspaper, *Galignani's Messenger*, published in English in Paris.

he'd been obliged to build his new manor house on a plot consisting of some ten acres of completely flat and barren land. He constructed the house and outbuildings, laid out a garden, and dug a pond and two wells; but the young trees hadn't taken, too little water collected in the pond, and that in the wells had a brackish taste. Only one small arbor of lilacs and acacias did fairly well; they sometimes had tea or ate dinner out there. In a few minutes Bazarov had covered all the paths in the garden, looked over the cattle sheds and stables, and come upon two local lads whose acquaintance he made at once; he set off with them to a small marsh, about a mile from the manor house, to search for frogs.

"What do you need frogs for, sir?" one of the boys asked.

"I'll tell you what for," Bazarov replied; he had a special flair for inspiring trust in members of the lower class, although he never indulged them and always treated them in an offhanded manner. "I'll cut the frogs open and look inside to see what's going on; since you and I are just like frogs, except that we walk on two legs, I'll find out what's going on inside us as well."

"What do you want to know that for?"

"So I don't make any mistakes if you get sick and I have to make you better."

"Are you a doctor, then?"

"Yes."

"Vaska, you hear, the gentleman says you and me are just like frogs. How do you like that?"

"I'm afraid of them, of frogs," observed Vaska, a lad about seven, with hair as pale as flax, a gray smock with a stand-up collar, and bare feet.

"What are you afraid of? You think they bite?"

"Come on now, just wade into the water, you philosophers," said Bazarov.

Meanwhile, Nikolai Petrovich had also awakened and set off to see Arkady, whom he found already up and dressed. Father and son went onto the terrace under the awning; next to the railing on the table, between large bouquets of lilacs, a samovar was already bubbling. A young girl appeared, the one who'd been the first to greet the travelers on the porch the night before. She announced in a thin voice, "Fedosya Nikolaevna isn't feeling well and can't come; she told me to ask if you'll pour the tea yourself or should she send Dunyasha?"

"I'll pour it myself," Nikolai replied hurriedly. "Arkady, do you take your tea with cream or lemon?"

"Cream," answered Arkady; after a brief silence, he inquired, "Papa?"

Nikolai Petrovich looked at his son in embarrassment.

"What?" he asked.

Arkady lowered his eyes.

"Forgive me, Papa, if my question seems inappropriate," he began, "but you yourself, with your candor yesterday, invited mine . . . you won't get angry, will you? . . ."

"Go on."

"You give me the courage to ask . . . Is it perhaps that Fen . . . isn't it because I'm here that she won't come out to pour the tea?"

Nikolai Petrovich turned away slightly.

"Perhaps," he said at last, "she supposes . . . she's ashamed . . ."

Arkady cast a quick glance at his father.

"There's no reason for her to be ashamed. In the first place, you're well aware of my way of thinking [Arkady very much enjoyed uttering these words]; in the second place, why should I want to inhibit your life or habits in the least? Besides, I'm sure you couldn't have made a bad choice; if you've invited her to live here with you under one roof, she must deserve it. In any case, a son has no right to judge his father, especially me, especially a father such as you, who's never restricted my freedom in any way."

Arkady's voice was shaky at first: he perceived himself as magnanimous, but at the same time realized he was delivering something of a lecture to his father. But the sound of one's own words makes a powerful impact, and Arkady uttered his last words forcefully, even with emphasis.

"Thank you, Arkasha," Nikolai Petrovich began in a hollow voice, his fingers once again running over his brow and forehead. "Your assumptions are, in fact, accurate. Of course, if this young woman wasn't worth . . . This is no frivolous fancy. I find it awkward to talk about it with you; but you can understand why she finds it hard to come out with you here, especially the first day after your arrival."

"In that case, I'll go see her myself," cried Arkady with a new rush of magnanimous feeling, and he jumped up from his chair. "I'll explain to her there's nothing to be ashamed of in front of me."

Nikolai Petrovich also stood up.

"Arkady," he began, "do me a favor . . . how can you . . . there . . . I haven't told you . . ."

But Arkady, who wasn't listening to him anymore, rushed away from the terrace. Nikolai Petrovich looked after him and sank down on his chair in confusion. His heart began pounding . . . Did he imagine at that moment the inevitable strangeness of future relations between him and his son? Was he aware that his son might have shown him more respect if he'd never mentioned the subject? Did he reproach himself for his own weakness? It's hard to say. All these emotions were present, but in the form of sensations—and not very distinct ones at that; the flush didn't leave his face and his heart kept pounding.

There was a sound of hurried footsteps and Arkady returned to the terrace.

"We've become acquainted, Father!" he exclaimed with an expression of tender and good-natured triumph on his face. "Fedosya Nikolaevna really doesn't feel well today and will come out later. But why didn't you tell me I have a brother? I'd have gone in last night to cover him with kisses, as I did just now."

Nikolai Petrovich wanted to say something, to stand up and open his arms wide . . . Arkady threw himself into his father's embrace.

"What's this? Embracing again?" resounded the voice of Pavel Petrovich behind them.

Father and son rejoiced equally in his appearance at this moment; there are certain touching situations from which one nevertheless wants to escape as quickly as possible.

"Why are you so surprised?" Nikolai Petrovich began cheerfully. "I've been waiting ages for him to return . . . I haven't even had time to get a good look at him since yesterday."

"I'm not at all surprised," Pavel Petrovich replied. "I have nothing against embracing him myself."

Arkady went up to his uncle and once again felt the touch of his fragrant mustache against his cheek. Pavel Petrovich sat down at the table. He was wearing an elegant morning suit in the English style; his head was graced with a small fez. This fez and a casually knotted tie hinted at the freedom of country life, but the stiff collars of his shirt—true, not white, but striped, as befits morning attire—stood up as inexorably as ever against his well-shaved chin.

"Where's your new friend?" he asked Arkady.

"He's not home; he usually gets up early and goes off somewhere. The main thing is not to pay him too much attention: he doesn't like ceremony."

"Yes, that's obvious." Pavel Petrovich began, without hurrying, to spread some butter on his bread. "Is he going to stay here long?"

"Possibly. He stopped by on his way home to see his father."

"Where does his father live?"

"In our province, about sixty miles from here. They have a small estate. He used to be a regimental doctor."

"Yes, yes, yes . . . I've been asking myself where I'd heard the name Bazarov before . . . Nikolai, remember, in Father's division there was a doctor named Bazarov?"

"I think there was."

"Precisely, precisely. So that doctor was his father. Hmm!" Pavel Petrovich twitched his mustache. "Well, and what exactly is this Mr. Bazarov?" he asked slowly and deliberately.

"What is Bazarov?" Arkady grinned. "Would you like me to tell you, Uncle, what he really is?"

"If you please, Nephew."

"He's a nihilist."[2]

"How's that?" asked Nikolai Petrovich, while Pavel Petrovich raised

2. Note the way each character defines the term: Nikolai is neutral; Pavel, antagonistic; Arkady, approving.

his knife in the air with a piece of butter on the end of the blade and remained motionless.

"He's a nihilist," repeated Arkady.

"Nihilist," said Nikolai Petrovich. "That's from the Latin *nihil*, nothing, as far as I can tell; therefore, the word signifies a person who . . . acknowledges nothing?"

"Say, rather, who respects nothing," Pavel Petrovich put in, and once again set about spreading his butter.

"Who approaches everything from a critical point of view," observed Arkady.

"Isn't it all the same thing?" asked Pavel Petrovich.

"No, it isn't all the same thing. A nihilist is a person who doesn't bow down before authorities, doesn't accept even one principle on faith, no matter how much respect surrounds that principle."

"And is that a good thing?" Pavel Petrovich interrupted.

"That depends, Uncle. For some people, it's good; for others, it's not."

"So that's how it is. Well, I can see it's not our cup of tea. We're people of another age, we assume that without *principles*[3] [Pavel Petrovich articulated this word softly, in the French manner; Arkady, on the contrary, pronounced it *prínciples*, accenting the first syllable], without *prínciples* accepted, as you say, on faith, it's impossible to take a step, to draw a breath. *Vous avez changé tout cela,*[4] God grant you health and the rank of general;[5] we'll merely stand by and admire you, you gentlemen . . . how is it?"

"Nihilists," Arkady replied clearly.

"Yes. Before there were Hegelists,[6] and now we have nihilists. We'll see how you'll fare in a void, a vacuum; and now, Brother, Nikolai Petrovich, please ring for the servants because it's time for me to drink my cocoa."

Nikolai Petrovich rang and called, "Dunyasha!" But instead of Dunyasha, Fenechka came out onto the terrace. She was a young woman, about twenty-three years old, all fair and soft, with dark hair and eyes, full, red, childlike lips, and sweet little hands. She was wearing a neat cotton print dress; a new light blue scarf was resting softly on her rounded shoulders. She was carrying a large cup of cocoa, and, placing it in front of Pavel Petrovich, she became flustered: warm blood rushed in a crimson wave under the delicate skin of her attractive face. She dropped her eyes and stood near the table, resting lightly on her fingertips. She seemed ashamed that she'd come, yet at the same time seemed to feel she had a right to come.

---

3. Pavel uses the French word, while Arkady prefers the Russian borrowing.
4. "You've changed all that" (French).
5. A quotation from act 2 of the famous comedy *Woe from Wit* (1824) by A. S. Griboedov (1795–1829).
6. A derogatory reference to the followers of the German idealist philosopher Friedrich Hegel (1770–1831), usually called "Hegelians."

Pavel Petrovich knitted his brows sternly, while Nikolai Petrovich appeared embarrassed.

"Hello, Fenechka," he muttered through his teeth.

"Hello, sir," she replied in a low, but pleasant voice; with a sideways glance at Arkady, who was smiling at her in a friendly manner, she quietly withdrew. She walked with a slight waddle, but even that suited her.

Silence prevailed on the terrace in the course of the next few moments. Pavel Petrovich sipped his cocoa and suddenly raised his head.

"Here's our Mr. Nihilist come to grace us with his presence," he said in a low voice.

Bazarov was indeed coming through the garden, stepping over flowerbeds. His linen coat and trousers were spattered with mud; clinging marsh weed was twined around the crown of his old round hat; in his right hand he held a small sack; in it was something alive and moving. He approached the terrace rapidly and, nodding his head, said, "Hello, gentlemen. Excuse me for being late to tea; I'll be right back. I must take care of these captives of mine."

"What do you have there, leeches?" asked Pavel Petrovich.

"No, frogs."

"Do you eat them or breed them?"

"They're for experiments," replied Bazarov with indifference and went into the house.

"He plans to cut them up," Pavel Petrovich observed. "He doesn't believe in principles, but he believes in frogs."

Arkady looked at his uncle with pity, and Nikolai Petrovich shrugged his shoulders on the sly. Pavel Petrovich felt his witty remark had fallen flat, and began talking about the estate and the new steward who'd come to see him the night before to complain that the worker Foma "was deboshing" and had gotten out of hand. "Some Aesop[7] he is," he said among other things. "He passes himself off everywhere as a worthless fellow; he lives like a fool and will die the same way."

VI

Bazarov returned, sat down at the table, and began drinking his tea hurriedly. Both brothers watched him in silence, while Arkady glanced stealthily first at his father, then at his uncle.

"Did you go far from here?" Nikolai Petrovich asked at last.

"There's a little marsh not too far away, near the aspen grove. I startled half a dozen snipe there; you might want to go shooting, Arkady."

"You're not a hunter?"

"No."

"Is it physics you're studying?" Pavel Petrovich took a turn asking.

7. Traditional Greek author of animal fables, said to have been a slave on the island of Samos in the sixth century B.C.

"Yes, physics; natural sciences in general."

"They say the Teutons have enjoyed great success in that field of late."

"Yes, the Germans are our teachers in this regard," Bazarov replied casually.

Pavel Petrovich used the word *Teutons* instead of *Germans* for the sake of irony; no one, however, took any notice.

"Do you have such a high opinion of the Germans?" Pavel Petrovich asked with studied courtesy. He was beginning to feel a secret irritation. His aristocratic nature was disturbed by Bazarov's free-and-easy manner. This son of a doctor was not only unintimidated, but even replied abruptly and unwillingly; and, in the sound of his voice, there was something rude, almost insolent.

"Their scientists know what they're doing."

"Indeed. Well, and you probably have a much less flattering opinion of Russian scientists?"

"Perhaps I do."

"That's very praiseworthy self-effacement," Pavel Petrovich said, sitting up straight and throwing his head back. "But how is it that Arkady Nikolaevich told us just now you don't acknowledge any authorities? You don't believe in them?"

"Why should I acknowledge them? And what am I to believe in? They tell me what it's all about, I agree, and that's all there is to it."

"Do the Germans tell you what it's all about?" uttered Pavel Petrovich; his face took on such a detached, remote expression, as if he'd entirely withdrawn to some cloudy height.

"Not all of them," replied Bazarov with a short yawn; it was obvious he didn't want to continue the discussion.

Pavel Petrovich glanced at Arkady, as if wishing to say to him: "Polite, this friend of yours, isn't he?"

"As far as I'm concerned," he began again, not without some effort, "sinner that I am, I don't regard Germans with much favor. I'm not even talking about Russian Germans: it's well known what sort of creatures they are. Even German Germans aren't to my liking. Previously, there were some acceptable ones; they had their—well, there was Schiller, also Goethe . . . My brother here's especially fond of them . . . But now all they have is chemists and materialists . . ."

"A decent chemist is twenty times more useful than any poet," Bazarov interrupted.

"Is that so?" muttered Pavel Petrovich and, as if about to doze off, he raised his eyebrows slightly. "So you don't acknowledge art?"

"The art of making money or curing hemorrhoids!"[8] cried Bazarov with a contemptuous laugh.

---

8. Bazarov's joke probably refers to two translated works popular in Russia during the 1840s.

"Quite so, quite so. You do like to joke. Then you must reject everything? Let's assume so. That means you believe only in science."

"I've already explained that I don't believe in anything; besides, what is science—science in general? There are sciences, just like there are trades and vocations; but science in general doesn't exist."

"Very good, sir. And do you hold the same negative attitude concerning other conventions accepted in human society?"

"What's this, an interrogation?" asked Bazarov.

Pavel Petrovich paled slightly . . . Nikolai Petrovich considered it his obligation to intervene in the conversation.

"Some other time we'll talk about this subject in greater detail with you, my dear Evgeny Vasilich; we'll learn your opinions and express our own. For my part, I'm very glad you're studying the natural sciences. I've heard Leibig[9] has made some astonishing discoveries concerning the fertilization of fields. You could assist me in my agronomical work: you could give me some useful advice."

"I'm at your disposal, Nikolai Petrovich; but we have a long way to go to reach Leibig! First we need to study the alphabet and only later learn how to read books; we haven't even begun our ABCs."

"Well, I see you really are a nihilist," thought Nikolai Petrovich. "Nevertheless, I hope you'll allow me to consult you on occasion," he added aloud. "And now, Brother, I think it's time for us to chat with the steward."

Pavel Petrovich stood up from the table.

"Yes," he replied, without looking at anyone, "it's unfortunate to have lived these last five years out here in the country, far away from such great intellects! You become a fool in no time at all. You try not to forget what you've been taught, but then—all of a sudden—it turns out all to be nonsense; you're told that sensible people don't bother about that stuff anymore and that you are, so to speak, an old fogy. What's to be done? It's obvious that young people really are cleverer than we are."

Pavel Petrovich turned slowly on his heels and slowly withdrew; Nikolai Petrovich followed him.

"Well, is he always like that?" Bazarov asked Arkady coolly, as soon as the door closed behind the two brothers.

"Listen, Evgeny, you treated him too harshly," observed Arkady. "You offended him."

"Yes, and am I supposed to pander to them, these provincial aristocrats? Why, it's all vanity, society habits, foppishness. Well, he should've carried on his career in Petersburg, if that was his inclination . . . But, to hell with him! I've found a rather rare example of a water bug, *Dytiscus marginatus*, do you know it? I'll show it to you."

9. Baron Justus von Leibig (1803–73) was a German chemist and one of the founders of scientific agronomy.

"I promised to tell you his story," Arkady began.

"The story of the bug?"

"Enough of that, Evgeny. My uncle's story. You'll see he's not the sort of man you think he is. He's more deserving of compassion than mockery."

"I won't argue with that; but why're you so concerned about him?"

"One must be fair, Evgeny."

"How does that follow?"

"No, listen . . ."

And Arkady told him the story of his uncle. The reader will find it in the next chapter.

VII

Pavel Petrovich Kirsanov was educated first at home, like his younger brother, Nikolai, and subsequently in the Corps of Pages.[1] From childhood he was distinguished by his good looks; in addition, he was self-assured, somewhat sarcastic, and amusingly acrimonious—he couldn't help being liked. He began to appear everywhere as soon as he became an officer. He was lionized by many people, indulged himself, even played the fool, and put on airs; but this too suited him. Women were crazy about him, and men called him a dandy and envied him in secret. He lived, as has already been said, in the same apartment with his brother, whom he loved dearly, even though he didn't resemble him in the least. Nikolai Petrovich had a slight limp; small, pleasant, but rather gloomy features; small, dark eyes, and soft, sparse hair. He was fond of inactivity, also liked to read, and he shunned society. Pavel Petrovich rarely spent an evening at home; he was known for his audacity and agility (he was making gymnastics fashionable among young people in society) and had read a total of some five or six books in French. At the age of twenty-eight he'd already earned the rank of captain; a brilliant career lay ahead of him. Suddenly everything changed.

At that time in Petersburg society, there occasionally appeared a woman who's not been forgotten to this day, a certain Princess R. She had a well-educated and decent, but foolish, husband and no children. She would leave unexpectedly to go abroad, then return unexpectedly to Russia; in general, she led a strange life. She had a reputation as a frivolous coquette and devoted herself eagerly to all sorts of pleasures, dancing until she collapsed, laughing and joking with young people whom she received before dinner in a dimly lit drawing room; but at night she wept and prayed, finding no solace anywhere, often pacing her room until early morning, wringing her hands in anguish or sitting, cold and pale, over her Psalter. Day would come, and once again she was transformed into a society lady; she'd go out, laugh, chatter, and

---

1. An exclusive military school in Petersburg that enjoyed the tsar's patronage.

literally throw herself at anything that could afford her the least bit of pleasure. She had an astonishing figure; her braid of yellow hair, heavy as gold, fell below her knees, but no one would've called her beautiful. Her only good feature was her eyes, not really her eyes themselves—they were small and gray—but their gaze, quick and deep, uncaring to the point of audacity, pensive to the point of despondency—enigmatic. Something extraordinary shone in that gaze even when her tongue was uttering the emptiest phrases. She dressed elegantly. Pavel Petrovich met her at a ball, danced a mazurka with her in the course of which she uttered not one sensible word, and fell passionately in love with her. Accustomed to victory, he soon achieved his goal with her, too; but the ease of his victory didn't dampen his enthusiasm. On the contrary, he became even more agonizingly, more intimately attached to this woman, in whom there remained, even when she surrendered herself to him entirely, something secret and inaccessible, which no one could penetrate. God knows what was hidden away in her soul! She seemed to be in the power of some mysterious forces, unknown even to her; they toyed with her as they wished; her limited intellect couldn't withstand their whims. All her behavior presented a series of incongruities; she wrote the only letters that could've aroused her husband's justified suspicions to a man whom she hardly knew, and her love always retained a measure of sadness; she no longer laughed or joked with the man she'd chosen; she listened to him and looked at him in bewilderment. Sometimes, usually all of a sudden, this bewilderment would change into cold horror; her face would assume a wild, deathly expression; she'd lock herself up in her bedroom, and her maid, putting her ear to the keyhole, could hear her smothered sobs. On more than one occasion, upon returning home from a tender meeting with her, Kirsanov would experience that lacerating and bitter annoyance that overwhelms one's heart after a definitive failure. "What more do I want?" he'd ask himself, and his heart would ache. Once he gave her a present of a ring with a sphinx carved on a stone.

"What's this?" she asked. "A sphinx?"

"Yes," he replied, "and you're that sphinx."

"I am?" she asked, slowly raising her enigmatic gaze to him. "You know, that's very flattering," she added with a meaningless smile, and her eyes gazed at him with an equally strange look.

Pavel Petrovich found it difficult even when Princess R. was in love with him; but when she cooled, and that happened rather soon, he almost lost his mind. He was racked with pain and jealousy, gave her no peace, and followed her around everywhere; she was sick and tired of his persistent pursuit and left for abroad. He retired, in spite of entreaties by friends and pleas by superiors, and set out in search of the princess; he spent four years in foreign parts, first pursuing her, then deliberately losing sight of her; he was ashamed of himself, indignant at his own weakness . . . but nothing helped. Her image, an incomprehensible, almost meaningless, but enchanting image, had penetrated his soul too deeply. In Baden once again he somehow became as close to her as before; it seemed she'd never loved him so passionately . . . but a month later it was all over: the flame had flared up for the last time and gone out forever. Foreseeing an inevitable separation, he wanted to remain her friend at least, as if friendship with such a woman were possible . . . She left Baden quietly and thereafter constantly avoided meeting Kirsanov. He returned to Russia, tried to pick up his former life, but was unable to settle into his old routine. Like someone deranged, he wandered from place to place; he still appeared in society and maintained all the habits of a man about town; he could boast of two or three new conquests; but he no longer expected anything much from himself or other people and undertook no new ventures. He grew old, his hair turned gray; spending his evenings at the club, peevishly bored, arguing indifferently amidst bachelor society became essential to him, and this, as is well known, is a bad sign. Needless to say, he didn't even consider getting married. Ten years passed, colorlessly, fruitlessly, quickly, terribly quickly. Nowhere but in Russia does time pass so swiftly; they say it flies by even more quickly in jail. Once at dinner in the club Pavel Petrovich learned of Princess R.'s death. She'd died in Paris, in a condition bordering on insanity. He stood up from the table, paced the room for a long time, and then stopped next to the cardplayers, as if rooted to the spot; but he didn't go home any earlier than usual that evening. A little while later he received a parcel addressed to him: it contained the ring he'd given the princess. She'd drawn a pair of crossed lines over the sphinx and asked that he be informed that the cross was the solution to her enigma.

This occurred at the beginning of 1848, at the same time Nikolai Petrovich, having lost his wife, was setting off for Petersburg. Pavel Petrovich had hardly seen his brother since Nikolai had settled in the country: Nikolai's wedding had coincided with the beginning of Pavel's acquaintance with the princess. Having returned home from abroad, Pavel went to visit his brother with the intention of spending a month or two, to share his happiness, but he could stand no more than a week of it. The difference in the two brothers' situations was too great. By 1848 this difference had diminished: Nikolai Petrovich had lost his wife and Pavel Petrovich, his memories; after the princess' death he tried not to think about her anymore. But Nikolai was left with the feeling of a life well-spent, and his son was growing up before his very eyes; Pavel, on the other hand, a lonely bachelor, was entering into that troubled, twilight phase of life when regrets resemble hopes, and hopes, regrets, when youth has passed, but old age has not yet set in.

This time proved more difficult for Pavel Petrovich than for anyone else: when he'd lost his past, he'd lost everything.

"I won't invite you to come to Marino now," Nikolai Petrovich once said to him (he'd given that name to the village in honor of his late wife, Marya). "You were bored there even when my wife was still alive; now I think you'd die of boredom."

"I was still foolish and finicky," replied Pavel Petrovich. "Since then I've grown calmer, if not wiser. Now, on the contrary, if you'll allow me, I'm ready to settle down with you for good."

Instead of an answer Nikolai Petrovich embraced him; but a year and a half elapsed after this conversation before Pavel Petrovich actually decided to make good on his intention. On the other hand, once he settled in the country, he never left it again, even during the three winters Nikolai Petrovich spent with his son in Petersburg. He began reading, more and more in English; in general he arranged his entire life on the English model, rarely saw his neighbors, and came out only for the elections,[2] where, for the most part, he remained silent, only occasionally teasing and frightening landowners of the old school with his liberal witticisms; nor did he associate with representatives of the younger generation. Both the former and the latter considered him "arrogant"; both groups respected him for his superb aristocratic manners and the rumors surrounding his conquests; for the fact that he dressed so elegantly and always stayed in the best room of the best hotel; for the fact that he usually dined well, and once had even dined with Wellington at Louis Philippe's table;[3] for the fact that he always carried around a genuine silver dressing case and a portable bath; that he always smelled of some extraordinary, astonishingly "genteel" scent; that he played whist in a masterly fashion and always lost; and finally, they respected him for his incorruptible honesty. Women regarded him as a charming melancholic, but he didn't keep company with ladies . . .

"So you see, Evgény," said Arkady, finishing his story, "how unfair you were to judge my uncle! I'm not even talking about the fact that on more than one occasion he's rescued my father from misfortune, given him all his money—perhaps you don't know, but their estate's never been divided[4]—he's glad to help anyone and, by the way, always stands up for the peasants; true, when he speaks to them he frowns and sniffs his eau de cologne . . ."

"His nerves, no doubt," Bazarov interrupted him.

"Perhaps, but he has a very kind heart. And he's by no means stupid. He's given me some very useful advice . . . especially . . . especially concerning relations with women."

---

2. The nobles in each province and district met every three years to elect officials called "marshals," who represented their interests as well as participated in local administration.
3. The duke of Wellington (1769–1852) was the English commander at the battle of Waterloo (1815), where Napoleon was finally defeated; Louis Philippe (1773–1850), king of France (1830–48), was deposed as a result of the revolution in Paris in 1848.
4. According to Russian law, each of the two brothers inherited half the father's estate; the Kirsanovs chose to maintain joint ownership of the entire property.

"Aha! He scalds himself on boiling milk and then tries to cool down someone else's hot water. We know the type!"

"Well, in a word," continued Arkady, "he's profoundly unhappy, believe me; it's a sin to despise him."

"Who despises him?" Bazarov objected. "Still I say that a man who stakes his whole life on a woman's love and, when that one card gets beaten, turns sour and sinks to the point where he's incapable of doing anything at all, then that person is no longer a man, not even a male of the species. You say he's unhappy: you ought to know; but all his foolishness still hasn't gone out of him. I'm certain that he earnestly regards himself as a worthwhile person because he reads *Galignani* once a month and saves an occasional peasant from corporal punishment."

"But remember his education, the age he lived in," observed Arkady.

"Education?" Bazarov broke in. "Every man should educate himself—just as I've done, for instance . . . And as regards the age— why should I depend on it? Let it rather depend on me. No, my friend, it's all that lack of discipline, shallowness! And what about those mysterious relations between a man and a woman? We physiologists understand all that. You just study the anatomy of the eye: where does that enigmatic gaze come from that you talk about? It's all romanticism, nonsense, rubbish, artifice. Let's go have a look at that beetle."

The two friends went off to Bazarov's room, which was already pervaded by a strong medicinal-surgical odor, mixed with the smell of cheap tobacco.

VIII

Pavel Petrovich wasn't present for long during his brother's conversation with the steward, a tall, thin man with a sugary, consumptive voice and deceitful eyes, who replied to all of Nikolai Petrovich's questions by saying, "Certainly, sir, everyone knows that, sir," and who tried to depict peasants as drunkards and thieves. The new system of estate management, introduced only recently, squeaked like an ungreased wheel, creaked like homemade furniture fashioned from unseasoned wood. Nikolai Petrovich didn't lose heart, but would frequently heave a sigh or sink into a reverie: he felt it wouldn't work without money, and he knew that almost all his money had been spent. Arkady was telling the truth: Pavel Petrovich had helped his brother on several occasions; seeing Nikolai struggling and racking his brains more than once, trying to think of a way out, Pavel would walk slowly up to the window and, thrusting his hands into his pockets, mutter through his teeth: "*Mais je puis vous donner de l'argent*"[5]—and he'd give him some money; but on this day he had none to give and preferred to withdraw. Annoyances stemming from running the household depressed him; it

5. "But I can give you some money" (French).

always seemed to him that Nikolai Petrovich, in spite of his zeal and love for hard work, didn't set about things in the right way, although he was unable to specify the exact nature of Nikolai's failings. "My brother isn't practical enough," he said to himself, "and he's being deceived." Nikolai Petrovich, on the other hand, had a high opinion of Pavel's practicality and always asked him for advice. "I'm a gentle man, weak, and have spent my life in the country," he used to say. "But you've benefited from living among so many people, you know them so well: you have an eagle eye." Pavel Petrovich merely turned away in response to these words, but did nothing to disabuse his brother of this opinion.

Leaving Nikolai Petrovich in his study, he headed along the corridor dividing the front part of the house from the rear, and, when reaching a low door, paused to reflect, then tugged at his mustache, and knocked.

"Who's there? Come in," Fenechka's voice rang out.

"It's I," Pavel Petrovich replied and opened the door.

Fenechka jumped up from the table where she'd been sitting with her child and, handing him to the girl, who carried him right out of the room, hurriedly adjusted her kerchief.

"Excuse me for disturbing you," Pavel Petrovich said without looking at her. "I only wanted to ask . . . today, it seems, they're going into town . . . Have them buy me some green tea."

"Certainly, sir," replied Fenechka, "how much would you like?"

"Half a pound will do, I think. I see you've made some changes in here," he added, casting a quick glance around, his eyes gliding past Fenechka's face. "Those curtains," he said, seeing she didn't understand him.

"Yes, sir, curtains; Nikolai Petrovich was kind enough to give them to me; they've been here for some time."

"But I haven't been here for some time. It's very nice here now."

"Thanks to Nikolai Petrovich," Fenechka whispered.

"Do you like it better here than in the wing where you were before?" asked Pavel Petrovich politely, but without the slightest smile.

"Of course, it's better here, sir."

"Who's been given your place?"

"The laundresses are there now."

"Ah!"

Pavel Petrovich fell silent. "He'll leave now," thought Fenechka, but he didn't, and she stood there before him as if rooted to the spot, her fingers fidgeting weakly.

"Why did you have your child taken away?" Pavel Petrovich said at last. "I love children: show him to me."

Fenechka blushed with embarrassment and joy. She was afraid of Pavel Petrovich: he almost never spoke to her.

"Dunyasha," she cried, "please bring Mitya here. [Fenechka used formal address[6] with everyone in the house.] But wait a minute; I have to get him dressed."

Fenechka headed for the door.

"It doesn't matter," said Pavel Petrovich.

"I'll be right back," Fenechka replied and left quickly.

Pavel Petrovich remained alone and this time looked around with special attention. The small, low-ceilinged room in which he found himself was very clean and comfortable. It smelled of a freshly painted floor, as well as of camomile and melissa. Along the walls stood chairs with backs in the shape of lyres; they'd been bought by the late general in Poland, during one of his campaigns; in one corner was a little bed under a muslin canopy, next to a trunk with forged clamps and a rounded lid. In the opposite corner, a lamp was burning in front of a large dark icon of St. Nikolai the miracle worker;[7] a tiny porcelain egg on a red ribbon fastened to the saint's gold halo hung over his chest; there were jars of last year's preserves on the windowsills, carefully arranged, glistening bright green; on their paper lids Fenechka had written in large letters: "Guzbery." Nikolai Petrovich was particularly fond of gooseberry jam. From the ceiling on a long cord hung a cage containing a short-tailed siskin; it chirped continuously, hopping around, its cage constantly shaking and rocking: hempseeds were being scattered on the floor with a light tapping sound. On the wall between two windows, above a small washstand, hung some rather poor photographs of Nikolai Petrovich in various poses taken by an itinerant artist; there was also a photograph of Fenechka that was a complete failure: a face without eyes and a forced smile staring out of a dark frame—it was impossible to make out anything else—and above Fenechka, General Ermolov[8] in a Circassian cloak was frowning menacingly toward distant Caucasian mountains, peering out from under a little silk pincushion that had fallen over his forehead.

About five minutes passed; from the next room came the sounds of bustling and whispering. Pavel Petrovich picked up a greasy book from the washstand, an odd volume of Masalsky's *Streltsy,*[9] and flipped over a few pages . . . The door opened and Fenechka entered with Mitya in her arms. She'd dressed him in a red shirt with a lace collar, combed his hair and washed his face: he was breathing heavily, his whole body straining, and he was waving his little arms around just the way all healthy babies do; but the fancy shirt obviously had an effect on him: a feeling of pleasure was reflected in his plump little face. Fenechka had fixed her own hair as well, and had arranged her kerchief better,

6. Russian distinguishes between informal (*ty*) and formal address (*vy*); cf. French *tous* and *vous*.
7. A patron saint in Russia venerated as the "miracle worker."
8. A. P. Ermolov (1772–1861) was a famous Russian general, hero of the war of 1812, and commander of the Russian army in the Caucasus; Circassians are a Moslem people inhabiting the greater Caucasus.
9. A lengthy historical novel (1832) by K. P. Masalsky (1802–61) about the musketeers formed by Ivan the Great in the sixteenth century and disbanded by Peter the Great at the end of the seventeenth century.

although she really could've stayed the way she was. In fact, is there anything on earth more charming than a beautiful young mother with a healthy child in her arms?

"What a chubby little fellow," Pavel Petrovich said indulgently and tickled Mitya's double chin with the tip of the long nail on his index finger; the child stared at the siskin and started to laugh.

"This is your uncle," said Fenechka, leaning over him and shaking him slightly, while Dunyasha quietly set a lighted aromatic candle on the windowsill, after placing a half-copeck piece under it.

"How old is he?" Pavel Petrovich asked.

"Six months; he'll be seven soon, on the eleventh."

"Isn't it eight, Fedosya Nikolaevna?" Dunyasha interrupted, not without timidity.

"No, seven; how could that be?" The child began laughing again, stared at the trunk, and suddenly grabbed hold of his mother's nose and mouth with his whole hand. "You mischief maker," said Fenechka without moving her face away from his fingers.

"He looks like my brother," said Pavel Petrovich.

"Who else should he look like?" wondered Fenechka.

"Yes," Pavel Petrovich continued, as if talking to himself, "there's an unmistakable resemblance." He looked at Fenechka carefully, almost mournfully.

"This is your uncle," she repeated, almost whispering.

"Ah! Pavel! So this is where you are!" Nikolai Petrovich's voice suddenly rang out.

Pavel Petrovich turned quickly and frowned; but his brother was looking at him so joyously, with such gratitude, he couldn't help but return a smile.

"What a fine little lad you have here," he said and looked at his watch. "I called in to see about my tea . . ."

And, assuming an air of indifference, Pavel Petrovich left the room at once.

"Did he come on his own?" Nikolai Petrovich asked Fenechka.

"Yes, sir; he knocked and came in."

"Well, and has Arkasha been here again?"

"No, he hasn't. Shall I move back to the wing of the house, Nikolai Petrovich?"

"What for?"

"I wonder if it might be better for the time being."

"N—no," Nikolai Petrovich stuttered and wiped his forehead. "It should've been done before . . . Hello, you little kid, you," he said with sudden animation and, drawing close to the child, kissed his cheek; then he bent over a little and put his lips to Fenechka's hand, which appeared white as milk against Mitya's red shirt.

"Nikolai Petrovich! What are you doing?" she asked, lowering her

eyes, then quietly raising them . . . Her expression was lovely when she
looked up at him from under her brows, chuckling affectionately and
a little foolishly.

Nikolai Petrovich had made Fenechka's acquaintance in the following
way. Once, about three years ago, he happened to spend a night at an
inn in a remote district town. The cleanliness of his room and freshness
of the bed linen made a pleasant impression on him. "Perhaps the
mistress is German?" he wondered; but the mistress turned out to be
Russian, a woman about fifty, neatly dressed, with a good-looking,
intelligent face and a measured way of speaking. He struck up a conversation with her at tea; he liked her very much. At that time Nikolai
Petrovich had just settled into his new manor house and, not wishing
to keep serfs on as house staff, he was looking for hired laborers; the
mistress, for her part, complained about the small number of travelers
who came to town and about hard times; he suggested she come to work
for him as a housekeeper; she agreed. Her husband had long since died,
having left her only a daughter, Fenechka. Two weeks later Arina Sa-
vishna (that was the new housekeeper's name) arrived at Marino together
with her daughter and settled in the lodge. Nikolai Petrovich's choice
turned out to be successful. Arina introduced order into the household.
No one said anything much about Fenechka, who'd just turned seventeen,[1] and she was rarely seen: she lived quietly, modestly, and only
on Sundays Nikolai Petrovich would notice the delicate profile of her
fair face in the parish church, sitting somewhere off on one side. A year
or so passed.

One morning Arina came into his study and, after bowing deeply as
usual, asked him if he could help her daughter, who had a spark from
the stove in her eye. Like all homebodies, Nikolai Petrovich was able
to care for the sick and had even ordered a collection of homeopathic
remedies. He had Arina bring the patient to him at once. Upon learning
that the master was summoning her, Fenechka grew very frightened,
but followed her mother. Nikolai Petrovich led her up to the window
and held her head in his hands. After examining her swollen red eye
closely, he prescribed and prepared a lotion, and, tearing his own handkerchief into small pieces, showed her how to apply it. Fenechka listened
to him and wanted to leave. "Kiss the master's hand, you silly girl,"
Arina said to her. Nikolai Petrovich didn't allow her to kiss his hand,
and, feeling somewhat embarrassed, kissed her bent head, on the part
of her hair. Fenechka's eye got better soon, but the impression she'd
made on Nikolai Petrovich didn't fade quickly. He kept dreaming of this
pure, tender, timid upturned face; he could feel her soft hair under the

---

1. Turgenev's text lists different ages for Fenechka. Above (p. 18), she is said to be "about twenty-
three"; here, she is said to have been seventeen "about three years ago."

palms of his hands, see those innocent, slightly parted lips through which her moist, pearly white teeth glistened in the sunshine. He began paying more attention to her in church and tried to speak with her. At first she shunned him and once, toward evening, meeting him on a narrow footpath through a field, she turned off into the tall, thick rye, overgrown with wormwood and cornflowers, so as not to be seen by him. He spotted her head through the golden network of rye, from which she peered out like a little animal, and called to her affectionately, "Hello, Fenechka! I won't bite you!"

"Hello, sir," she whispered without leaving her hiding place.

Gradually she grew used to him, but was still timid in his presence, when suddenly her mother, Arina, died from cholera. What was to become of Fenechka? She'd inherited her mother's love of order, common sense, and propriety; but she was so young and lonely; Nikolai Petrovich was such a kind, modest man . . . There's no need to tell the rest.

"So my brother just dropped in on you?" Nikolai Petrovich asked. "Knocked and entered?"

"Yes, sir."

"Well, that's fine. Let me give Mitya a swing."

And Nikolai Petrovich began tossing him about, almost up to the ceiling to the child's great delight and the mother's considerable discomfort, who at every toss stretched out her own arms to catch his bare little legs.

Meanwhile Pavel Petrovich returned to his elegant study, its walls covered with attractive dark gray wallpaper and weapons displayed on a colorful Oriental rug, walnut furniture upholstered in dark green velveteen, a Renaissance-style bookcase made of dark, old oak, bronze statues on a magnificent writing desk, and a fireplace . . . He threw himself onto the sofa, put his hands behind his head, and sat there motionless, staring at the ceiling almost in despair. Whether he wanted to hide from the walls that which was being reflected in his face, or for some other reason, he got up, drew the heavy curtains across the windows, and threw himself down on the sofa again.

IX

Bazarov also made Fenechka's acquaintance that same day. He and Arkady were out walking together in the garden, and he was explaining to him why some of the trees, especially the young oaks, hadn't taken.

"You should plant more silver poplars here, and firs, and perhaps lindens, after you increase the loam. Now that arbor's done well," he added, "because it's all acacia and lilac—they're good boys and don't need much care. Bah! Why, there's someone over there."

In the arbor sat Fenechka with Dunyasha and Mitya. Bazarov stopped, while Arkady nodded to Fenechka as if they were old friends.

"Who's that?" Bazarov asked as soon as they'd gone past. "What a pretty girl!"

"Who're you talking about?"

"It's obvious: there was only one pretty girl."

Arkady, not without embarrassment, explained to him in a few words who Fenechka was.

"Aha!" muttered Bazarov. "Your father certainly has good taste. I like him, your father, I really do. He's a good man. But I must make her acquaintance."

"Evgeny!" Arkady called after him in fear. "Be careful, for heaven's sake."

"Don't worry," replied Bazarov. "I've got lots of experience; I've been around, you know."

He took off his cap as he approached Fenechka.

"Allow me to introduce myself," he began with a polite bow. "I'm a friend of Arkady Nikolaevich and a humble man."

Fenechka stood up from the bench and looked at him in silence.

"What a splendid child!" continued Bazarov. "Don't worry, I haven't given anyone the evil eye. Why are his cheeks so red? Is he cutting new teeth?"

"Yes, sir," Fenechka replied. "He's cut four new teeth already, and now his gums are swollen again."

"Let me have a look . . . You don't have to be afraid. I'm a doctor."

Bazarov picked up the child, who, to both Fenechka's and Dunyasha's surprise, offered not the least resistance and showed no fear.

"I see, I see . . . It's nothing; everything's in order: he'll have good teeth. If anything happens, just let me know. Are you in good health?"

"Yes, thank God."

"Thank God—that's the best thing of all. And you?" he added, turning to Dunyasha.

Dunyasha, a very stern young woman inside the house, but a real giggler outside, merely snorted in reply.

"Well, fine. Here's your little warrior back."

Fenechka took the child in her arms.

"He behaved so well with you," she said in a low voice.

"All children behave well with me," replied Bazarov. "I have a way with them."

"Children can tell who loves them," Dunyasha observed.

"Exactly," Fenechka agreed. "There're some people Mitya'd never go to."

"Will he come to me?" asked Arkady, who, having stood apart for some time, now approached the arbor.

He tried to get Mitya to come to him, but Mitya threw his head back and started whining, which upset Fenechka a great deal.

"Later, after he's grown used to me," Arkady said indulgently, and the two friends left.

"What did you say her name was?" asked Bazarov.

"Fenechka . . . Fedosya," replied Arkady.

"And her patronymic? One must know that, too."

"Nikolaevna."

"*Bene.*[2] I like the fact that she wasn't too shy. Other people might hold that against her. What nonsense! Why be shy? She's a mother— so she's right not to be shy."

"She is right," observed Arkady, "but as for my father . . ."

"And he's right," Bazarov interrupted.

"Well, no, I don't think so."

"Perhaps you don't like the idea of having an extra heir?"

"You should be ashamed to attribute such ideas to me!" Arkady replied heatedly. "It's not from that point of view I consider my father wrong; I think he should marry her."

"Oho!" Bazarov said serenely. "How very generous we are! So you still attach significance to marriage; I never expected that from you."

The friends took several steps in silence.

"I've seen your father's entire establishment," Bazarov began again. "The cattle are poor, the horses, run-down. The buildings are in bad shape and the workers look like confirmed loafers; the steward's either a fool or a thief, I still can't tell which."

"You're being rather harsh today, Evgeny Vasilevich."

"And the good little peasants are taking your father for all he's worth. You know the saying, 'The Russian peasant would devour God Himself.' "

"I'm beginning to agree with my uncle," said Arkady. "You really do have a poor opinion of Russians."

"What difference does that make? The only good point about a Russian is that he has a very low opinion of himself. What's important is that two times two makes four; all the rest's nonsense."

"And is nature nonsense?" asked Arkady, looking thoughtfully across the multicolored fields, gently and beautifully illuminated by the setting sun.

"Nature's nonsense too in the sense you understand it. Nature's not a temple, but a workshop where man's the laborer."

At that moment the slow, drawn-out notes of a cello reached them from the house. Someone was playing Schubert's *Erwartung*[3] with feeling, although with an inexperienced touch, and the sweet melody flowed through the air like honey.

"What's that?" Bazarov asked in astonishment.

"It's my father."

2. "Fine" (Latin).
3. "Expectation" (1815) is a lyrical song by the romantic Austrian composer Franz Schubert (1797–1828).

"Your father plays the cello?"

"Yes."

"How old's your father?"

"Forty-four."

Bazarov suddenly burst out laughing.

"What're you laughing at?"

"Imagine! A forty-four-year-old man, a *pater familias*,[4] living in such-and-such district—and plays the cello!"

Bazarov continued laughing; but Arkady, as much as he revered his mentor, this time didn't even smile.

X

About two weeks passed. Life in Marino flowed along in the usual way: Arkady lived a life of luxury while Bazarov worked. Everyone in the house had gotten used to him, his offhand manner, his laconic and abrupt way of speaking. Fenechka in particular felt so comfortable with him that one night she even summoned him: Mitya was having convulsions. He came and, in his usual manner, half-joking, half-asleep, spent two hours sitting with her and helping the child. On the other hand, Pavel Petrovich came to despise Bazarov with all the strength he could muster: he considered him arrogant, impudent, a cynic, and a plebian; he suspected that Bazarov didn't respect him, that he might even despise him—Pavel Kirsanov! Nikolai Petrovich was afraid of the young "nihilist" and had some doubts about his influence on Arkady; but he listened to him eagerly and attended his experiments in chemistry and physics willingly. Bazarov had brought along a microscope and spent hours using it. The servants also grew accustomed to him, even though they made fun of him: they felt that he was almost one of them, not a master. Dunyasha giggled with him gladly and would give him sidelong, meaningful glances as she ran by "like a little quail"; Peter, an extremely vain and stupid man whose brow was eternally furrowed under the strain, a man whose entire merit consisted in the fact that he looked respectful, could read haltingly, and frequently brushed his jacket—even he would smirk and brighten up as soon as Bazarov paid him any attention; the peasant boys ran after the "doktur" like little puppies. Only old man Prokofich didn't like him, served him his food at the table with a gloomy expression, referred to him as a "swindler" and a "knave," and asserted that with his side whiskers he looked just like a pig in a poke. Prokofich, in his own way, was just as much of an aristocrat as Pavel Petrovich.

The best time of year arrived—the first days of June. The weather was magnificent; true, there was a distant threat of cholera, but the inhabitants of the province had managed to accustom themselves to its

4. "The father of a family" (Latin).

visitations. Bazarov would get up very early and head off two or three miles, not for a stroll—he couldn't stand strolls without a purpose—but to collect grasses and insects. Sometimes he took Arkady along with him. On their return they usually got into an argument; Arkady was usually demolished, even though he spoke far more than his comrade.

Once for some reason they lingered quite a while; Nikolai Petrovich went out to meet them in the garden and, upon approaching the arbor, suddenly overheard the rapid footsteps and voices of the two young men. They were walking on the other side of the arbor and couldn't see him.

"You don't know my father well enough," said Arkady.

Nikolai Petrovich hid.

"Your father's a good man," Bazarov said, "but he's antiquated; his song's been sung."

Nikolai Petrovich listened more intently . . . Arkady made no reply.

The "antiquated" man stood there without moving for a few minutes and then slowly made his way home.

"A few days ago I looked over and he was reading Pushkin," Bazarov continued meanwhile. "Tell him, if you would, that it's of no use. After all, he's no longer a young boy: it's time to toss that rubbish aside. Just imagine the desire to be a romantic in this day and age! Give him something more substantial to read."

"What should I give him?"

"Well, I think Büchner's *Stoff und Kraft*[5] to begin with."

"I think so, too," Arkady observed approvingly. "*Stoff und Kraft* is written in a popular style . . ."

"So you see," Nikolai Petrovich said to his brother after dinner that same day while sitting in his study, "you and I've become antiquated; our song's been sung. Well, what of it? Perhaps Bazarov's even right; but, I must confess, one thing hurts: this was precisely when I'd hoped to become closer to Arkady. Now it turns out I've been left behind while he's moved ahead, and we can't understand each other."

"How is it he's moved ahead? How's he so different from us?" Pavel Petrovich exclaimed impatiently. "It's that *signor*, that nihilist who's been stuffing his head full of these things. I hate that so-called doctor; in my opinion, he's simply a charlatan; I doubt he knows that much about physics, even with all his frogs."

"No, Brother, don't say that: Bazarov's clever and he knows his stuff."

"His conceit's repulsive," Pavel Petrovich said, interrupting him.

"Yes," said Nikolai Petrovich. "He is conceited. But there seems to be no way around that; here's what I don't understand. I seem to do all I can to keep up with the times: I've made arrangements for my peasants, established a farm, with the result that I'm called a "Red" throughout

5. The actual title of the famous work by the German philosopher and physician Ludwig Büchner (1824–99) is *Kraft und Stoff* (Force and matter) (1855). This controversial book, which provided a materialist interpretation of the universe, was first translated into Russian in 1860.

the province; I read, study, and try to respond in general to the require-ments of our day—but they say my song's been sung. You know, Brother, I'm beginning to think perhaps it really has been sung."

"Why so?"

"Here's why. Today I was sitting and reading Pushkin . . . as I recall, it happened to be *The Gypsies* . . . [6] Suddenly Arkady comes up to me and silently, with an expression of such tender compassion, very gently, as if I were a little child, takes my book away and places another one in front of me, a German one . . . he smiles and then leaves, carrying away my Pushkin."

"You don't say! What book did he give you?"

"Here it is."

Nikolai Petrovich took from the back pocket of his frock coat a copy of the notorious treatise by Büchner in its ninth edition.

Pavel Petrovich turned it over in his hands.

"Hmm!" he muttered. "Arkady Nikolaevich's worried about your ed-ucation. Well, have you tried to read it?"

"I have."

"And, what do you think?"

"Either I'm stupid or it's all rubbish. I must be stupid."

"You haven't forgotten your German?" asked Pavel Petrovich.

"I understand German."

Pavel Petrovich once again turned the book over in his hands and glanced at his brother from under his brows. They were both silent.

"Oh, by the way," Nikolai Petrovich began, obviously eager to change the subject of conversation. "I received a letter from Kolyazin."

"Matvei Ilich?"

"Yes. He's come to town to inspect the province. He's a person of consequence now and writes that, as a relative, he wants to see us and has invited us and Arkady to town."

"Are you going?" asked Pavel Petrovich.

"No. What about you?"

"I'm not going either. Why drag myself thirty miles for no good reason at all. Mathieu wants to show himself to us in all his glory: to hell with him! The whole province'll be singing his praises—he can do without us. What a great honor: a privy councillor! If I'd continued in the civil service, engaged in such drudgery, why I'd be an adjutant-general by now. Besides, you and I are antiquated people."

"Yes, Brother; clearly it's time to order our coffins and lay our arms across our chests," Nikolai Petrovich observed with a sigh.

"Well, I won't give up so easily," his brother muttered. "We'll still have a skirmish with that doctor fellow; I feel it coming."

The skirmish occurred that very day at evening tea. Pavel Petrovich entered the living room ready for battle, irritable and determined. He

6. A narrative poem (1824) by Pushkin that treats the themes of passion and freedom in the context of gypsy life.

merely waited for a pretext to attack his enemy; but for a long time no pretext presented itself. In general Bazarov said very little in the presence of the "little old Kirsanov men" (as he called the two brothers), but that evening he was in a bad mood and sat in silence drinking cup after cup of tea. Pavel Petrovich burned with impatience; at last his wishes were fulfilled.

The conversation turned to one of the local landowners. "He's trash, a lousy little aristocrat," Bazarov observed indifferently; he'd met him in Petersburg.

"Allow me to inquire," Pavel Petrovich began, his lips trembling, "in your understanding are the words *trash* and *aristocrat* synonymous?"

"I said 'lousy little aristocrat,' " replied Bazarov, lazily sipping his tea.

"Indeed you did, sir; but I'm assuming you hold the same opinion of 'aristocrats' that you do of 'lousy little aristocrats.' I consider it my obligation to inform you that I do not share that opinion. I dare say everyone knows me to be a liberal who advocates progress; but that's precisely why I respect aristocrats—genuine ones. Remember, my dear sir [at these words Bazarov raised his gaze to Pavel Petrovich's face], remember, my dear sir," he repeated bitterly, "the English aristocrats. They don't retreat one iota from their rights, and consequently, they respect the rights of others; they demand the fulfillment of obligations owing to them, and consequently, fulfill their own obligations. The aristocracy gave England its freedom and supports it."

"We've heard that tune many times," Bazarov replied, "but what do you hope to prove by that?"

"By *that* I hope to prove, my dear sir [When he was angry, Pavel Petrovich deliberately mispronounced the words *this* and *that*, although he knew he was violating the rules of grammar. This whim of his was left over from the reign of Alexander I.[7] The notables of that time, in the rare instances when they spoke their native language, mispronounced *this* and *that*, as if to say, "We're genuine Russians, and at the same time, we're grandees who're allowed to ignore schoolboy rules of grammar"], by *that* I hope to prove that without a sense of one's own worth, without respect for oneself—in aristocrats these feelings are very well-developed—there's no secure foundation for social . . . *bien public*,[8] for the social structure. Personality, my dear sir, that's the main thing; human personality must be solid as a rock because everything's built upon it. I know very well, for example, that you find my habits amusing, my apparel, even my neatness, but all this comes from my own sense of self-respect, a sense of duty, yes, sir, duty. I live in the country, the backwoods, but I don't let myself go, I respect the human qualities in myself."

"Allow me, Pavel Petrovich," said Bazarov, "you say you respect

---

7. Alexander (1777–1825) ruled Russia from 1801 until his death, during which time France continued to exert a strong cultural and linguistic impact on Russian society.
8. "Public welfare" (French).

yourself, yet you sit here with your arms crossed; what use is that to the *bien public*? You'd be better off not respecting yourself, but doing something."

Pavel Petrovich grew pale.

"That's a completely different question. There's no need for me to explain to you at this time why I sit here with my arms crossed, as you so kindly put it. I merely want to say that aristocratism is a principle, and in these times only immoral or frivolous people can live without principles. I said this to Arkady the day after he arrived here and I say it again. Isn't that so, Nikolai?"

Nikolai Petrovich nodded his head.

"Aristocratism, liberalism, progress, principles," Bazarov was saying meanwhile, "just think, how many foreign . . . and useless words! A Russian has no need of them whatsoever."

"What, then, in your opinion, does he need? According to you, we stand outside humanity, beyond its laws. For heaven's sake, the logic of history demands . . ."

"What good's that logic? We can get along without that, too."

"How so?"

"Just so. You, I trust, don't need logic to put a piece of bread in your mouth when you're hungry. What do we need all these abstractions for?"

Pavel Petrovich wrung his hands. "After that I don't understand you. You insult the Russian people. I don't see how it's possible to reject principles and rules! On what basis can you act?"

"I've already told you, Uncle, we don't accept any authorities," Arkady intervened.

"We act on the basis of what we recognize as useful," Bazarov replied. "Nowadays the most useful thing of all is rejection—we reject."

"Everything?"

"Everything."

"What? Not only art and poetry . . . but even . . . it's too awful to say . . ."

"Everything," Bazarov repeated with indescribable composure.

Pavel Petrovich stared at him. He hadn't expected this, and Arkady even blushed from delight.

"But allow me," Nikolai Petrovich began. "You reject everything, or, to put it more precisely, you destroy everything . . . But one must also build."

"That's not for us to do . . . First, the ground must be cleared."

"The present condition of the people demands it," Arkady added pompously. "We must respond to these demands; we have no right to give in to the satisfaction of our personal egoism."

Apparently Bazarov didn't like this last phrase; it smacked of philosophy, that is, romanticism, since Bazarov referred to all philosophy as romanticism; but he considered it unnecessary to correct his young disciple.

"No, no!" Pavel Petrovich exclaimed with a sudden burst of emotion. "I don't want to believe that you gentlemen really know the Russian people and represent their needs and aspirations! No, the Russian people isn't as you imagine it to be. It holds tradition sacred; it's a patriarchal people and can't live without faith . . ."

"I won't argue with that," Bazarov said, interrupting. "I'm even ready to agree that you're correct *in this regard.*"

"But if I'm right . . ."

"It still doesn't prove anything."

"Precisely, it doesn't prove anything," Arkady repeated with the certainty of an experienced chess player who's foreseen an apparently dangerous move by his opponent and therefore isn't in the least perturbed.

"What do you mean it doesn't prove anything?" asked the astonished Pavel Petrovich. "Then you're going against your own people?"

"What if that were true?" cried Bazarov. "The people believe that when they hear thunder, it's the prophet Elijah riding across the sky in his chariot. What then? Am I supposed to agree with that? Besides, they're Russian and I'm Russian, too, aren't I?"

"No, after what you've just said, you're not Russian! I can't acknowledge you as Russian."

"My grandfather ploughed the earth," Bazarov replied with arrogant pride. "Ask any of your peasants which of us—you or me—he recognizes as his fellow countryman. You don't even know how to talk to them."

"While you speak to them and despise them at the same time."

"So what, if they deserve to be despised? You condemn my course, but whoever said it was accidental, that it wasn't occasioned by that same national spirit in whose name you protest?"

"Is that so? Much we need nihilists!"

"Needed or not—it's not for us to decide. Why, you don't consider yourself useless."

"Gentlemen, gentlemen, please, let's not get personal!" Nikolai Petrovich exclaimed, rising to his feet.

Pavel Petrovich smiled and, placing his hand on his brother's shoulder, made him sit down again.

"Don't worry," he said. "I won't forget myself precisely because of that feeling of self-worth that was so cruelly mocked by Mister . . . by Mister Doctor. Allow me to ask," he continued, addressing Bazarov once more, "do you perhaps think your doctrine is something new? If so, you're quite mistaken. The materialism you preach has been in fashion more than once before and has always turned out to be insubstantial . . ."

"Another foreign word!" Bazarov interrupted. He was beginning to get angry and his face turned a particular rough coppery color. "In the first place, we're not preaching anything; that's not our custom . . ."

"Then what are you doing?"

"I'll tell you what we're doing. Previously, in recent times, we acknowledged that our civil servants take bribes, that we lack roads, commerce, true justice . . ."

"Well, yes, so, you're denouncers—that's what it seems to be called. I agree with many of your denunciations, but . . ."

"Then we realized that talking, simply talking all the time about our open sores isn't worth the trouble, that it leads only to being vulgar and doctrinaire; we saw that even our intelligent men, our so-called progressives and denouncers, served no purpose at all, that we were preoccupied with a lot of nonsense, arguing over some form of art, unconscious creativity, parliamentarianism, legal profession, and the devil knows what else, while it was really a question of our daily bread, when we were being oppressed by the most primitive superstitions, when all our joint stock companies were collapsing merely as a result of a lack of honest men, while the emancipation, about which the government was so concerned, will hardly do any good because our peasants are happy to steal from themselves, as long as they can get stinking drunk in the tavern."

"Yes," Pavel Petrovich said, interrupting him, "I see: you've become convinced of all this and now have decided not to do anything serious about it."

"We've decided not to do anything serious about it," Bazarov repeated grimly.

He was suddenly annoyed with himself for having been so expansive with this gentleman.

"And merely curse everything?"

"And curse everything."

"And this is called nihilism?"

"And this is called nihilism," Bazarov repeated again, this time with particular rudeness.

Pavel Petrovich wrinkled his face slightly.

"So that's how it is!" he said in a strangely serene voice. "Nihilism is supposed to relieve all our ills, and you, you're our saviors and heroes. But then why do you abuse others, even those very denouncers? Aren't you doing a lot of talking, too, just like all the rest?"

"We're guilty of many sins, but not that one," Bazarov said through his teeth.

"Well, then? Are you taking action or what? Are you preparing to take action?"

Bazarov made no reply. Pavel Petrovich gave a little shudder, but then gained control of himself.

"Hmmm! To act, destroy . . . ," he continued. "But how can one destroy without even knowing why?"

"We destroy because we're a force," Arkady observed.

Pavel Petrovich looked at his nephew and smiled.[9]

"Yes, a force—one that doesn't need to account for itself," Arkady said and sat up straighter.

"You unfortunate lad!" cried Pavel Petrovich; he was positively unable to restrain himself any longer. "If only you'd consider what it is you're supporting in Russia with your vulgar maxim! Why, it's enough to try the patience of a saint! A force! There's force in a wild Kalmuck[1] and a Mongol—but what's the good of that to us? Our road's one of civilization, yes, sir, yes, my kind sir; its fruits are dear to us. And don't you tell me these fruits are insignificant: the worst dauber, *un barbouilleur*,[2] a ballroom pianist who gets five copecks to play for an entire evening, all of them are more useful than you because they're representatives of civilization, not some primitive Mongol force! You imagine you're progressive, but you're only fit to sit in some Kalmuck's cart! A force! Just you remember once and for all, you mighty gentlemen, that there're only four and a half of you, while there're millions of others who won't let you trample their most sacred beliefs underfoot and who'll crush you!"

"If they crush us, so be it," said Bazarov. "But we'll see what we shall see. There aren't as few of us as you think."

"What? Do you seriously think you can take on, cope with a whole people?"

"Moscow, you know, burned down from a candle that cost only one copeck," replied Bazarov.

"Yes, I see. First there's almost Satanic pride, then ridicule. That's how our young people amuse themselves, that's what wins the inexperienced hearts of young lads! There, just look, one of them's sitting there next to you; why, he almost worships you. Look at him. [Arkady turned away and frowned.] And this infection's already spread quite far. I've heard that in Rome our artists won't set foot in the Vatican. They consider Raphael[3] a fool because, they say, he's an authority; and they themselves are disgustingly impotent and sterile; their imagination goes no further than *Girl at the Fountain*[4] no matter how hard they try! And that girl's very poorly depicted. According to you, they're fine fellows, isn't that so?"

"According to me," Bazarov objected, "Raphael isn't worth a damn and they're no better than he is."

"Bravo! Bravo! Listen, Arkady . . . that's the way contemporary young

9. In the original version of the novel, Pavel Petrovich replies to Arkady, "A fine thing, force—without any content."
1. The Kalmucks (or Kalmyks) were an Asian people and a branch of the Mongols.
2. "Dabbler" (in writing or painting) (French).
3. Major Italian Renaissance painter (1483–1520).
4. This does not refer to any specific painting, but merely indicates a total lack of talent among young Russian artists.

people should express themselves! Just think, how can they resist following you? Previously, young people were required to study; they didn't want to be viewed as ignorant, so they worked whether they wanted to or not. But now all they have to say is, 'Everything on earth's nonsense!'—and that's all there is to it. Young people are delighted. The fact is that before they were simply blockheads, but these days they've suddenly become nihilists."

"Now your vaulted sense of self-dignity has betrayed you," Bazarov observed phlegmatically, while Arkady flared up, his eyes flashing. "Our argument's gone too far . . . I think it's better to stop here. I'll be prepared to agree with you later," he said standing up, "when you present me with a single institution of contemporary life, either in the family or in the social sphere, that doesn't deserve absolute and merciless rejection."

"I can present you with millions of such institutions," cried Pavel Petrovich, "millions of them! Why, there's the peasant commune,[5] for example."

A cold smirk distorted Bazarov's lips.

"Well, as far as the peasant commune's concerned," he said, "you really ought to talk to your brother. I think he's found out by now what sort of thing the commune is, with its collective responsibility, sobriety, and other such customs."

"The family, then, the family as it exists among our peasants!" cried Pavel Petrovich.

"I suggest you'd better not look into that question in too much detail either. No doubt you've heard about a father-in-law's rights with his daughter-in-law?[6] Listen to me, Pavel Petrovich, give yourself some time to think about it; it's difficult to come up with something on the spot. Sort through all the levels of our society and think carefully about each; meanwhile Arkady and I will . . ."

"You must ridicule everything," Pavel Petrovich interrupted.

"No, we must dissect frogs. Let's go, Arkady; good-bye, gentlemen!"

The two friends left. The brothers remained alone and at first merely looked at one another.

"There," began Pavel Petrovich at last, "there's our contemporary young people for you! There they are—our heirs!"

"Heirs," repeated Nikolai Petrovich with a mournful sigh. During the course of the entire argument, he sat as if on tenterhooks, stealthily casting painful glances at Arkady from time to time. "Do you know what I remembered, Brother? Once I had an argument with our late mother: she was shouting and didn't want to listen to me . . . Finally, I told her she couldn't understand me; I said we belonged to two different generations. She was terribly offended, and I thought to myself: what's to be done? It's a bitter pill—but one must swallow it. Well, now our

5. *Mir*, a form of peasant self-government that is regarded as uniquely Russian.
6. That is, to have sexual relations with his son's wife.

turn's come, and our heirs can say to us: 'We belong to a different generation; swallow that pill.' "

"You're being much too generous and modest," Pavel Petrovich objected. "On the contrary, I'm sure you and I are far more in the right than these young fellows, although perhaps we express ourselves in rather archaic language, *vielli*,[7] and lack that arrogant self-assurance . . . The haughtiness of these young people nowadays! You ask one of them, 'Which wine would you like, red or white?' 'It's my custom to prefer red!' he answers in a bass voice and with such a pompous expression, as if the entire universe were observing him at that very moment . . ."

"Would you care for some more tea?" Fenechka inquired, sticking her head in the door: she'd decided not to enter the living room as long as she heard voices arguing there.

"No, you can tell them to take the samovar away," Nikolai Petrovich replied and stood up to meet her. Pavel Petrovich abruptly said *bon soir*[8] to him and retired to his study.

XI

Half an hour later Nikolai Petrovich went into the garden to his favorite pavilion. He was sunk in gloomy meditation. This was the first time he'd become aware of any distance between him and his son; he felt that with each passing day this distance would increase. Consequently, those winters in Petersburg when he'd spent endless days studying the latest works had all been in vain; in vain had he listened in on those young people's conversations; in vain had he rejoiced when he managed to insert a word or two into their heated discussions. "My brother says we're right," he thought, "and, setting aside all vanity, it also seems to me that they're farther from the truth than we are; but at the same time, I feel they have something we lack, some advantage over us . . . Youth? No, it's not only youth. Perhaps their advantage consists in the fact that there're fewer traces of gentry mentality left in them than in us?"

Nikolai Petrovich hung his head and wiped his hand across his face.

"But to reject poetry?" he thought again, "to have no feeling for art, nature . . . ?"

He looked around, as if wishing to understand how it was possible to have no feeling for nature. It was almost evening; the sun was hidden behind a small grove of aspens that stood about half a verst[9] from the garden: its shadow stretched endlessly across motionless fields. A little peasant on a white nag was trotting along a dark, narrow path next to the grove; he was clearly visible, all of him, including the patch on his shoulder, even though he was in the shadows; the horse's hooves could

7. "Old-fashioned" (Italian).
8. "Good evening" (French).
9. A unit of linear measure (3,500 feet).

be seen plainly rising and falling in a pleasant fashion. The sun's rays, for their part, made their way into the grove; penetrating the thickets, they bathed the aspen trunks in such warm light that they began to resemble pine trees, and their leaves looked almost dark blue, while above them stretched the pale blue sky, slightly reddened by the sunset. The swallows were flying very high; the wind had died down completely; some tardy bees were lazily and sleepily buzzing amidst the lilac blossoms; a swarm of midges hung over a single outstretched branch. "My God, how nice it all is!" thought Nikolai Petrovich, and just as his favorite lines of poetry were about to come to his lips, he remembered Arkady and his *Stoff und Kraft*—and remained silent; but he continued sitting there, giving way to melancholy and the comforting play of solitary reflection. He loved to dream; country life had fostered this tendency in him. It was not all that long ago he'd engaged in such dreaming while waiting for his son at the carriage inn; but since then such a change had occurred, and their relations, which had at that time been so unclear, had now become quite well-defined . . . how well-defined they were! He thought once again about his late wife, not as he'd known her through many years, not as a good, domestic housewife, but rather as a young girl with her slim figure, her innocent, inquisitive look, and her tightly knotted braid over her slender, childish neck. He remembered seeing her for the first time. He was still a student then. He'd met her on the stairs of the apartment where he lived; accidentally bumping into her, he turned around to apologize, but could mutter only, *"Pardon, monsieur,"* while she bent her head, started laughing, and suddenly, as if frightened, scurried away. At the bend in the stairs, she glanced back at him quickly, assumed a serious look, and blushed. Then he recalled his first timid visits, half-words, half-smiles, and the embarrassment, sadness, upheavals, and finally the breathless rapture . . . Where had it all gone? She became his wife; he was happy as few people on earth ever are . . . "But," he thought, "those first, sweet moments, why can't a person live an eternal, immortal life in them?"

He didn't try to clarify his own thoughts, yet felt he wanted to preserve that blessed time with something stronger than memory; he wanted to feel once more the presence of his Marya, experience her warmth and breath, and he could already imagine above him . . .

"Nikolai Petrovich," Fenechka's voice rang out nearby. "Where are you?"

He shuddered. He felt neither pain nor shame . . . He'd never even allow the possibility of comparison between his wife and Fenechka, but regretted that she'd come to look for him. Her voice summoned him back at once: his gray hair, his age, his present . . .

The magical world he'd already entered, arising from dim mists of the past, was shaken and then vanished.

"Over here," he replied. "I'm coming. You go on ahead." "There they are, those traces of gentry mentality" flashed through his mind. Fenechka looked into the pavilion and glanced at him in silence, then disappeared; meanwhile he was surprised to notice that night had fallen while he was sitting there dreaming. Everything around him had grown dark and quiet, and Fenechka's face appeared before him, so small and pale. He stood up, wanting to return home, but the emotions stirring in his heart couldn't be calmed; he began pacing slowly around the garden, first gazing sadly at the ground under his feet, then raising his eyes to the sky, where swarms of stars were already twinkling. He paced a great deal, until he was quite exhausted, but his agitation, a vague, searching, mournful agitation, couldn't be appeased. Oh, how Bazarov would've made fun of him, if only he'd known what he was feeling at that moment! Arkady too would judge him harshly. He, a forty-four-year-old man, an agronomist and landowner, with tears welling up in his eyes, senseless tears; this was a hundred times worse than playing the cello.

Nikolai Petrovich continued to pace and couldn't resolve to return home, to that peaceful and comfortable nest that looked at him so invitingly with all its illuminated windows; he was unable to part with the darkness, the garden, the fresh air in his face, and his grief, his agitation. . . .

At a bend in the path he met Pavel Petrovich.

"What's wrong?" he asked Nikolai Petrovich. "You're pale as a ghost; you must be ill. Why don't you go to bed?"

Nikolai Petrovich explained his state of mind briefly, then moved on. Pavel Petrovich walked to the end of the garden, also grew thoughtful, and also raised his gaze to the sky. But nothing was reflected in his handsome dark eyes except the stars. He hadn't been born a romantic, and his fastidiously dry and passionate soul, with its touch of French misanthropy, didn't even know how to dream . . .

"Do you know what?" Bazarov said to Arkady that very evening. "I've just had a splendid idea. Today your father said he's received an invitation from your illustrious relative. Your father isn't going; why don't you and I set off for ∗∗∗; you know, that gentleman's invited you, too. You see how fine the weather is now; let's go for a ride and have a look at the town. We'll spend five or six days there, and that's that!"

"Will you come back here afterward?"

"No, I'll have to go see my father. You know, he's only about thirty versts from ∗∗∗. I haven't seen him or my mother for a long time; one must console the old folks. They're good people, especially my father; he's so amusing. I'm all they have."

"Will you stay there long?"

"I don't think so. I'll probably get bored."

"Will you come to see us on your way back?"

"I don't know . . . we'll see. Well, so, how about it? Shall we go?"

"All right," Arkady replied lazily.

In his heart and soul he was delighted with his friend's proposal, but he considered it his obligation to conceal his emotions. It was not for nothing he was a nihilist!

The next day he left with Bazarov for ***. The young people in Marino regretted their departure; Dunyasha even shed a few tears . . . but the old folks breathed a sigh of relief.

XII

The town of ***, to which our friends were heading, came under the jurisdiction of a youngish governor who was both a progressive and a despot, as happens all too often in Russia. During the first year of his administration, he managed to quarrel not only with the marshal of the nobility, a retired captain of the horse guards who ran a stud farm and entertained frequently, but also with his own subordinates. The squabbles arising from this situation finally grew to such proportions that the ministry in Petersburg found it necessary to dispatch a trusted personage to investigate the entire matter on the spot. The authorities' choice fell upon Matvei Ilich Kolyazin, son of the Kolyazin whose patronage the Kirsanov brothers once enjoyed. He was also "youngish," that is, recently turned forty, but already aspiring to an important government position and sporting stars on both sides of his chest. It's true that one was a foreign decoration, and not all that distinguished. Just like the governor he'd come to review, he was considered a progressive and, being a person of consequence already, didn't resemble the majority of such people. He thought very highly of himself; his vanity knew no bounds, but he behaved simply, looked approvingly, listened indulgently, and laughed so generously that at first glance he might even be taken for a "good fellow." However, on important occasions, he knew quite well how to throw his weight around, as the saying goes. "Energy is essential," he used to say at such times, *"l'énergie est la première qualité d'un homme d'état";*[1] but for all that, he was usually made a fool of, and any relatively experienced civil servant could wrap him around his little finger. Matvei Ilich used to express his great respect for Guizot[2] and tried to impress each and every person with the idea that he didn't belong to the ranks of ordinary officials and backward bureaucrats and that he didn't neglect any important aspect of social life . . . Such phrases were most customary to him. He even followed the development of contemporary literature, though with casual condescension, it's true: in the same way a grown man who meets a line of young boys on the street will sometimes fall in behind it. In essence, Matvei Ilich hadn't progressed much beyond

1. "Energy is the primary quality of a statesman" (French).
2. François Guizot (1787–1874), a French statesman and historian.

those statesmen of Alexander I, who, to prepare themselves for an evening at Madame Svechina's[3]—living in Petersburg at the time—would read a page or two of Condillac[4] that very morning; but his methods were different, more up-to-date. He was a shrewd courtier, a great schemer, and nothing more; he didn't know a thing about business and had zero intelligence; but he knew how to handle his own affairs: no one could outsmart him there, and that was the most important thing.

Matvei Ilich received Arkady with the generosity—we might even say, playfulness—characteristic of an enlightened higher official. However, he was surprised to learn that the relatives he'd invited had chosen to remain in the country. "Your father always was a bit of an eccentric," he observed, playing with the tassels of his magnificent velvet dressing gown. Suddenly turning to a young civil servant attired in a smart uniform, he exclaimed with a worried expression, "What?" The young man, whose lips were stuck together as a result of his prolonged silence, rose to attention and regarded his superior with perplexity. But, after so confounding his subordinate, Matvei Ilich no longer paid him any attention. Our higher officials are quite fond of confounding their subordinates; the means to which they resort for accomplishing this goal are rather diverse. The following method, among many others, is rather popular, "quite a favorite," as the English would say: the high official suddenly ceases to understand even the simplest words, feigning total deafness. He asks, for example, "What day is it?"

He's informed most respectfully: "Today's Friday, Your Exc-c-cellency."

"Eh? What? What's that? What did you say?" the high official repeats in annoyance.

"Today's Friday, Your Exc-c-cellency."

"How's that? What? What's Friday? Which Friday?"

"Friday, Your Exc-c-c-c-cellency, the day of the week."

"So, you've decided to teach me a lesson, have you?"

Matvei Ilich was just this sort of higher official, even though he was considered a liberal.

"I advise you, my friend, to pay a visit to the governor," he said to Arkady. "You understand, I'm urging you to do this not because I subscribe to old-fashioned ideas about the need to pay one's respects to the authorities, but simply because the governor's a decent chap; besides, you probably want to make the acquaintance of local society . . . After all, you're not a bear, I hope? And, the day after tomorrow he's giving a grand ball."

"Will you be there?" asked Arkady.

3. Sofiya Svechina (1782–1859) was a popular Russian writer and proponent of fashionable religious mysticism.
4. Étienne Bonnot de Condillac (1715–80) was a French philosopher who developed a theory of sensationalism.

"He's giving it for me," said Matvei Ilich, almost pityingly. "Do you know how to dance?"

"I do, rather badly."

"That's a shame. There're some pretty girls around here and a young man should be ashamed if he doesn't know how to dance. Once again, I'm not saying this in support of any old ideas; by no means do I assume that a man's intelligence resides in his feet, but Byronism[5] is rather ridiculous, *il a fait son temps*."[6]

"But, Uncle, it's not because of Byronism that I . . ."

"I'll introduce you to our local young ladies, I'll take you under my wing," Matvei Ilich said, interrupting him and giving a self-satisfied chuckle. "You'll find it warm here, eh?"

The servant entered and informed him that the chairman of the provincial revenue department had arrived, an old man with sugarsweet eyes and wrinkled lips, who loved nature deeply, especially on a summer's day, when, in his own words, "every little bee takes a little bribe from every little flower . . ." Arkady left.

He found Bazarov at the inn where they were staying and spent a long time persuading him to visit the governor. "There's no way out!" said Bazarov at last. "If we've come this far, we might as well go through with it. We wanted to have a look at the landowners—well, then, let's have a look at them!" The governor received the young people cordially, but didn't ask them to sit down and remained standing himself. He was constantly fussing and hurrying; in the morning he'd put on a snug uniform and an extremely tight necktie; he never had time to finish eating or drinking, and was always giving orders. In the province he was nicknamed Bourdaloue,[7] not after the reknowned French preacher, but after the Russian word *burda*—"slops." He invited Kirsanov and Bazarov to the ball and a few minutes later invited them again, taking them for brothers and referring to them as the Kaisarovs.

They were just returning home from the governor's, when suddenly a rather short man jumped from a passing carriage; wearing a Slavophile jacket,[8] shouting, "Evgeny Vasilich!" he threw himself at Bazarov.

"Ah! It's you, Herr Sitnikov," said Bazarov, continuing along the sidewalk. "What brings you here?"

"Just imagine, it's pure chance," he replied; turning to his carriage, he waved his hand five times or so and shouted, "Follow us, follow us! My father has some business here," he continued, jumping over a ditch, "so he asked me . . . I learned of your arrival today and have already

---

5. A romantic worldview and lifestyle based on the life and works of the great English romantic poet Lord Byron (1788–1824).
6. "It's had its day" (French).
7. Louis Bourdaloue (1632–1704) was a French Jesuit preacher and famous orator whose works were translated into Russian.
8. An affected "native" style of dress, worn to demonstrate nationalist feeling. The Slavophiles, as opposed to the Westernizers, sought to preserve the originality of Russian culture.

been to your room . . . [In fact, when the friends returned to their room they found a visiting card with bent corners and Sitnikov's name, in French on one side, Cyrillic on the other.] I hope you're not just coming from the governor's?"

"Don't hope: that's exactly where we were."

"Ah! Well, in that case, I'll visit him, too . . . Evgeny Vasilich, introduce me to your . . . to him . . ."

"Sitnikov, Kirsanov," Bazarov grumbled without stopping.

"I'm very flattered," began Sitnikov, walking sideways, grinning, and hurriedly pulling off his overly elegant gloves. "I've heard so much about . . . I'm an old friend of Evgeny Vasilich and can even say—his disciple. I owe him my regeneration . . ."

Arkady looked at Bazarov's disciple. A restless and vacant expression appeared on the small, though pleasant features of his pampered face; his little eyes, looking as if they'd been squeezed into his face, stared intently and uneasily, and he laughed nervously, in an abrupt, wooden manner.

"Would you believe it?" he went on. "When Evgeny Vasilevich first told me that one needn't acknowledge any authorities, I felt such delight . . . it was as if I suddenly saw the light! 'There,' I thought, 'at long last I've found a man!' By the way, Evgeny Vasilevich, you really must drop in on a certain lady who's completely capable of understanding you, for whom your visit will be a real treat; I think you may've heard something about her."

"Who is it?" Bazarov asked unwillingly.

"Kukshina, Eudoxie, Evdoksiya Kukshina. She's a remarkable character, *émancipée* in the true sense of the word, a progressive woman. Do you know what? Let's drop in on her together right now. She lives only a little way from here. We'll have some lunch there. You haven't had lunch yet, have you?"

"Not yet."

"Well, splendid. She's separated from her husband, you understand, and is completely independent."

"Is she good-looking?" Bazarov asked, interrupting him.

"N . . . no, one couldn't say that."

"Then why the devil are you taking us to see her?"

"Ah, you're making fun . . . She'll treat us to a bottle of champagne."

"So that's it! Now I see what a practical fellow you are. By the way, is your father still tax farming?"[9]

"Yes, indeed," Sitnikov replied quickly, emitting a shrill laugh. "Well then? Shall we go?"

"I don't really know."

---

9. Individuals hired by the state to collect liquor taxes often managed to increase their personal wealth in the performance of their official duties.

"You wanted to have a look at people, go on," Arkady said in a low voice.

"What about you, Mr. Kirsanov?" Sitnikov resumed. "You come too; we won't go without you."

"How can we all descend on her at once?"

"Never mind! Kukshina's a marvelous person."

"Will there really be a bottle of champagne?" asked Bazarov.

"Three of them!" cried Sitnikov. "I swear to it!"

"Swear on what?"

"My own head."

"It'd be better to swear on your father's moneybags. Well, let's go."

XIII

The small nobleman's house built in the Moscow style where Avdotya (or Evdoksiya) Nikitishna Kukshina lived, stood on one of the recently burnt-out streets in the town of ***; it's a well-known fact that our provincial towns burn down every five years or so. At the door, above a visiting card nailed at an angle, was a bell handle; in the entryway visitors were greeted by someone who wasn't exactly a servant, but not quite a companion, wearing a cap—obvious signs of the mistress's progressive tendencies. Sitnikov asked whether Avdotya Nikitishna was at home.

"Is that you, Victor?" a shrill voice rang out from the next room. "Come on in."

The woman in the cap disappeared at once.

"I'm not alone," Sitnikov replied, boldly removing his jacket, under which he was wearing something like a jerkin or sackcoat, and casting a brazen glance at Arkady and Bazarov.

"Never mind," answered the voice. "*Entrez.*"[1]

The young men went in. The room in which they found themselves looked more like a study than a drawing room. Papers, letters, thick Russian journals, for the most part with their pages uncut, lay strewn about on dusty tables; cigarette butts were scattered everywhere. On a leather-covered sofa a lady was half-reclining; she was still young, had fair hair, a bit disheveled, and was wearing a silk dress, not altogether tidy, with large bracelets on her short arms, a lace kerchief on her head. She got up from the sofa; casually pulling a velvet cape trimmed with yellowed ermine over her shoulders, she said languidly, "Hello, Victor," and shook Sitnikov's hand.

"Bazarov, Kirsanov," he said abruptly, imitating Bazarov.

"Welcome," replied Kukshina and, fixing Bazarov with her round eyes between which was a forlorn, turned-up, very little red nose, she added, "I know you," and she shook his hand, too.

1. "Come in" (French).

Bazarov frowned. There was nothing ugly in the small, unprepossessing figure of this emancipated woman, but the expression on her face made a bad impression on the viewer. One felt inclined to ask: "What's the matter? Are you hungry? Bored? Afraid? Why so tense?" Just like Sitnikov, she was always anxious. She spoke and moved in a rather casual, though awkward, manner: she obviously considered herself a good-natured, simple creature; at the same time, no matter what she did, it always seemed that she didn't want to be doing that. Everything she did appeared to be done on purpose, as children say, that is, neither simply nor naturally.

"Yes, yes, I know you, Bazarov," she repeated. (She had the habit, like many of our provincial and Moscow ladies, of calling men by their surname from the moment she met them.) "Would you like a cigar?"

"A cigar's all well and good," said Sitnikov, who was already sprawling in an armchair and sticking one leg up in the air, "but do give us some lunch; we're awfully hungry. And have them open a bottle of champagne for us."

"You sybarite," muttered Evdoksiya and began laughing. (When she laughed, the gums above her upper teeth showed.) "Isn't it true, Bazarov, he's a sybarite?"

"I love the comforts of life," Sitnikov intoned pompously. "That doesn't prevent me from being a liberal."

"Yes, it does, it does prevent you!" cried Evdoksiya, but she still gave her maid orders for lunch and a bottle of champagne. "What do you think?" she asked, turning to Bazarov. "I'm certain you share my opinion."

"Well, no," Bazarov replied. "A piece of meat's better than a piece of bread, even from the chemical point of view."

"Do you study chemistry? It's my passion. I've even invented a new resin."

"A resin? You?"

"Yes, me. Do you know what it's for? To make dolls' heads that won't break. I'm also practical. But it's not quite finished. I must still read Leibig.[2] By the way, have you read Kislyakov's article about women's labor in the *Moscow News*?[3] Do read it. You must be interested in the women's question. And in schools, too? What's your friend studying? What's his name?"

Madame Kukshina scattered her questions one after another with casual disregard, without waiting for answers; it's just the way spoiled children talk to their nannies.

"My name's Arkady Nikolaevich Kirsanov," Arkady replied, "and I'm not studying anything."

2. See above, p. 21, n. 9.
3. A newspaper published between 1756 and 1917. The author's name, Kislyakov (lit. "sourpuss"), is probably invented.

Evdoksiya burst out laughing.

"How nice! Well, do you smoke? Victor, you know I'm angry with you."

"What for?"

"I'm told you've begun singing the praises of George Sand.[4] She's a retrograde woman and nothing more! How can one compare her to Emerson?[5] She has no ideas whatever about education, physiology, nothing. I'm sure she's never even heard of embryology, and in our day and age—what can one do without it? [Evdoksiya even threw up her hands.] Ah, what a splendid article Elisevich[6] wrote on this score. He's such a brilliant gentleman! [Evdoksiya constantly used the word *gentleman* instead of *man*.] Bazarov, come over here and sit down on the sofa next to me. Perhaps you don't know it, but I'm very much afraid of you."

"Why so? Allow me to inquire."

"You're a dangerous gentleman; you're such a critic. Oh, my God! It's so absurd, but I'm talking like a country landowner. In fact, I really am a landowner. I manage my own estate, and, just imagine, have a steward named Erofey—he's a wonderful character, just like Cooper's Pathfinder:[7] there's something so spontaneous about him! I've settled down here once and for all; the town's unbearable, isn't that so? But what's to be done?"

"It's a town like any other," Bazarov remarked coolly.

"Petty interests all the time, that's what makes it so awful! I used to spend winters in Moscow . . . but now my lawful spouse, Monsieur Kukshin, resides there. Besides, Moscow nowadays . . . well, I don't know—it's not quite the same as it was. I'm thinking about going abroad; last year I was just about to set off."

"To Paris, naturally?" asked Bazarov.

"Paris and Heidelberg."

"Why Heidelberg?"

"Good Lord, because Bunsen's[8] there!"

Bazarov could find nothing to say in reply to this.

"Pierre Sapozhnikov . . . do you know him?"

"No, I don't."

"Good Lord, Pierre Sapozhnikov . . . why he's always at Lidiya Khostakova's."

4. French feminist writer (1804–76) whose eighty or so novels treat primarily women's issues, especially romantic love.
5. Ralph Waldo Emerson (1803–82), one of the United States's most influential writers and philosophers and founder of the transcendentalist movement.
6. A name probably invented by combining those of two radical journalists, G. Z. Eliseev and M. A. Antonovich, major contributors to *The Contemporary*.
7. James Fenimore Cooper (1789–1851), the first American novelist. His narratives about the frontier often idealized the life of the American Indian. *The Pathfinder* was published in 1840.
8. Robert Wilhelm Bunsen (1811–99), a German scientist, pioneer in the field of chemistry, and inventor of the Bunsen burner.

"I don't know her either."

"Well, he's the one who agreed to accompany me. Thank God, I'm free, I have no children . . . What was that I just said? *'Thank God'*! Well, it doesn't matter."

Evdoksiya rolled a cigarette with her tobacco-stained fingers, licked the edge of it with her tongue, sucked on it, and then lit it. The maid entered carrying a tray.

"Ah, here's our lunch! Would you like something to eat? Victor, open the bottle; that's in your line of work."

"Yes, it is, it is indeed," muttered Sitnikov, once again emitting a shrill laugh.

"Are there any pretty women around here?" asked Bazarov, as he downed a third glass.

"There are," replied Evdoksiya, "but they're all so empty-headed. For example, *mon amie*[9] Odintsova isn't bad looking. It's a pity her reputation's so . . . That wouldn't matter, though, but she has no independent views, no breadth, nothing of that sort. We must reform the entire educational system. I've given it some thought already; our women are very badly educated."

"You can't do anything with them," Sitnikov said. "One ought to despise them, and I do, absolutely and completely! [The possibility of despising someone and expressing that feeling was a most pleasant sensation for Sitnikov; he attacked women most of all, never suspecting that in a few months he'd be groveling before his wife, simply because she'd been born a Princess Durdoleosova.] Not a single one of them could understand our conversation; not one even deserves being talked about by serious men like us!"

"But they've no need to understand our conversation," said Bazarov.

"Who're you talking about?" Evdoksiya interrupted.

"Pretty women."

"What? Then you must share Proudhon's[1] opinion?"

Bazarov drew himself up arrogantly.

"I don't share anyone's opinion: I have my own."

"Down with authorities!" cried Sitnikov, delighted with the chance to express himself incisively in the presence of the man before whom he fawned.

"But Macaulay[2] himself," Kukshina started to say.

"Down with Macaulay!" thundered Sitnikov. "Are you going to defend those silly females?"

"Not those silly females, but women's rights, which I've sworn to defend with my last drop of blood."

---

9. "My friend" (French).
1. Pierre Joseph Proudhon (1809–65), radical French social theorist, founder of anarchism, and opponent of feminism.
2. Thomas Babington Macaulay (1800–59), famous English historian and essayist.

"Down with them!" But Sitnikov stopped there. "I don't reject them," he said.

"No, I can see you're a Slavophile!"[3]

"No, I'm not, although, of course . . ."

"No, no, no! You *are* a Slavophile. You're a proponent of the *Domostroi*.[4] You should carry a whip in your hand!"

"A whip's a fine thing," observed Bazarov, "but we're down to the last drop . . ."

"Of what?" asked Evdoksiya.

"Champagne, most esteemed Evdoksiya Nikitishna, champagne—not your blood."

"I can't listen with indifference when women are attacked," continued Evdoksiya. "It's awful, just awful. Instead of attacking them, you ought to read Michelet's *De l'amour*.[5] It's wonderful! Gentlemen, let's talk about love," added Evdoksiya, lowering her arm languorously onto the rumpled cushion of the sofa.

There suddenly followed a moment of silence.

"No, why talk about love?" Bazarov asked. "But you just said something about Odintsova . . . That's what you called her, right? Who is that lady?"

"She's lovely, simply lovely," squeaked Sitnikov. "I'll introduce you to her. She's clever, rich, and a widow. Unfortunately, she's still not very enlightened: she needs to become better acquainted with our Evdoksiya. I drink to your health, Eudoxie! Let's clink glasses! '*Et toc, et toc, et tin-tin-tin! Et toc, et toc, et tin-tin-tin!!*' "[6]

"Victor, you're a naughty boy."

Lunch lasted a very long time. The first bottle of champagne was followed by a second, then a third, even a fourth . . . Evdoksiya chattered without stopping; Sitnikov echoed her. They talked a great deal about the meaning of marriage—whether it was a prejudice or a crime, whether people are born equal or not, and the nature of individualism. It finally reached the point that Evdoksiya, flushed from all the wine she'd drunk, banging her blunt nails on the keys of an out-of-tune piano, began singing in a hoarse voice, first some gypsy songs, then Seymour Schiff's romance "Grenada lies slumbering,"[7] while Sitnikov tied a scarf around his head and imitated a dying lover at the words:

> And thy lips to mine
> In burning kiss entwine.

---

3. See above, p. 48, n. 8.
4. A product of sixteenth-century Russian culture, expounding a rigid system of household management.
5. *On Love* (1859), a work by the great French romantic historian Jules Michelet (1798–1874).
6. A line quoted from a song entitled "*L'ivrogne et sa femme*" (The drunkard and his wife) by the French lyrical poet Pierre Jean de Béranger (1780–1857).
7. A reference to a romance entitled "Night in Grenada" by K. A. Taranovsky, set to music by the pianist and composer Seymour Schiff.

Finally Arkady could stand no more. "Gentlemen, this has begun to resemble bedlam," he observed aloud.

Bazarov, who from time to time merely inserted a sarcastic word or two into the conversation—he was more interested in the champagne —yawned loudly, stood up, and, without saying good-bye to the hostess, walked out with Arkady. Sitnikov ran after them.

"So then, what do you think?" he asked, skipping obsequiously first to the right, then to the left. "I told you, didn't I: she's a remarkable person! If we only had more women like her! In her own way she's a highly moral phenomenon."

"What about *your* father's establishment? Is that also a moral phenomenon?" asked Bazarov, pointing to the tavern they were passing that very moment.

Sitnikov once again emitted a shrill laugh. He was very ashamed of his background and didn't know whether to feel flattered or offended by Bazarov's unexpected familiarity in addressing him.

XIV

A few days later there was a ball at the governor's house. Matvei Ilich was the real "hero of the occasion"; the Marshal of the Nobility[8] declared to each and every one that he'd come simply out of respect for the governor; while the governor, even at the ball, even while standing motionless, continued to "govern." The cordiality of Matvei Ilich's demeanor could only be equaled by his stateliness. He was nice to everyone—to some with a trace of antipathy, to others with a trace of respect. To ladies he appeared *"en vrai chevalier français,"*[9] and constantly broke into a strong, sonorous, solitary laugh, appropriate for a dignitary. He slapped Arkady on the back and loudly called him "my little nephew"; to Bazarov, who was attired in a rather old dress coat, he gave an absentminded, but condescending sidelong glance, and an indistinct, but affable grunt, from which one could only make out the words "I" and "terribly"; he extended a finger or two to Sitnikov and smiled, but he'd already turned away; even to Kukshina, who appeared at the ball wearing no crinolines whatever, a pair of dirty gloves, and a bird of paradise in her hair, even to Kukshina he said, *"Enchanté."*[1] There were hordes of people and no lack of dancing partners; the civilians tended to crowd along the walls, but the military men danced enthusiastically, especially one who'd spent six weeks in Paris, where he'd learned various devil-may-care exclamations such as, *"Zut," "Ah, fichtrre," "Pst, pst, mon bibi,"*[2] and so on. He pronounced them perfectly, with genuine Parisian *chic*; yet at the same time he said, *"si j'aurais"*

8. See above, p. 25, n. 2.
9. "Like a true French cavalier" (French).
1. "Delighted" (French).
2. Various nonsensical exclamations in French.

instead of *"si j'avais,"* and used the word *"absolument"* in the sense of "certainly."[3] In brief, he expressed himself in that Great Russo-French dialect that the French love to mock when they have no need to assure us that we speak their language like angels, *"comme des anges."*

Arkady danced badly, as we already know, while Bazarov didn't dance at all. They both stood in a corner; Sitnikov joined them there. Having assumed a look of contemptuous scorn and letting venomous remarks fall where they may, he looked around insolently and seemed to be enjoying himself immensely. Suddenly his expression changed and, turning to Arkady, he said as if with some embarrassment, "Odintsova's just arrived."

Arkady turned around and saw a tall woman in a black dress standing near the door of the room. He was struck by her dignified bearing. Her bare arms lay gracefully alongside her slender figure; light sprays of fuchsia hung tastefully from her shiny hair onto her slanting shoulders; from under a slightly protruding white forehead her bright eyes peered out serenely and quietly—it was precisely serenely, not pensively, and her lips curled into a scarcely noticeable smile. Some sort of tender, gentle strength emanated from her face.

"Are you acquainted with her?" Arkady asked Sitnikov.

"Intimately. Do you want me to introduce you?"

"Please . . . after this quadrille."

Bazarov also turned his attention to Odintsova.

"And who might that be?" he asked. "She doesn't resemble the other hags."

Waiting until the end of the quadrille, Sitnikov led Arkady to Odintsova. He was hardly intimately acquainted with her: he became confused as he spoke, and she regarded him with some astonishment. But her face assumed a cordial expression when she heard Arkady's surname. She asked if he was Nikolai Petrovich's son.

"Precisely."

"I've met your father on two occasions and have heard a great deal about him," she continued. "I'm very glad to make your acquaintance."

At that moment an adjutant came rushing up and asked her to dance a quadrille. She agreed.

"So you dance?" Arkady inquired politely.

"I do. Why did you think I didn't? Do I seem too old to you?"

"I beg your pardon, how could I . . . In that case, allow me to ask you for the mazurka."

Odintsova smiled indulgently.

"If you wish," she said and looked at Arkady, not exactly as a superior, but as married sisters regard their much younger brothers.

Odintsova was a little older than Arkady; she'd already turned twenty-

---

3. Matvei Ilich makes mistakes in his French grammar here, saying "if I should have" (conditional) instead of "if I had" (imperfect). He also makes mistakes in his French diction, using the adverb *absolutely* to mean "certainly."

nine, but in her presence he felt like a schoolboy, a student, as if the difference in their ages was much greater. Matvei Ilich came up to her with an imposing air and obsequious phrases. Arkady moved aside, but continued watching her; he didn't take his eyes off her all during the quadrille. She chatted just as casually with her partner as with the dignitary; she quietly turned her head and eyes, and laughed softly once or twice. Her nose was a little broad, like almost all Russian noses, and her complexion was not entirely clear; nevertheless, Arkady was sure he'd never met such a lovely woman. He couldn't get the sound of her voice out of his ears; the very folds of her dress seemed to hang in a special way, more gracefully and elegantly than all the rest, and her movements were particularly smooth, yet natural at one and the same time.

Arkady felt some timidity in his heart when, at the first sounds of the mazurka, he sat down next to his partner; preparing to engage her in conversation, he merely passed his hand through his hair, unable to think of anything to say. But he didn't feel timid or agitated for very long; Odintsova's serenity was communicated to him as well. Within a quarter of an hour he was telling her all about his father, his uncle, life in Petersburg, and in the country. Odintsova listened with polite attention, gently opening and closing her fan; his chatter was interrupted when she was asked to dance quadrilles; Sitnikov, by the way, asked her twice. She'd come back, sit down again, pick up her fan, and wouldn't even be breathing more rapidly; meanwhile Arkady would resume his chatter, suffused with happiness by being so near her, talking to her, looking into her eyes, at her beautiful forehead, at her pleasant, imposing, intelligent face. She said very little, but her words revealed her knowledge of life; from several of her remarks Arkady gathered that this young woman had already managed to feel and think a great deal . . .

"Who was that man you were just with," she asked him, "when Mr. Sitnikov introduced you to me?"

"Oh, so you noticed him?" Arkady asked in turn. "He has a fine face, doesn't he? His name's Bazarov; he's a friend of mine."

Arkady began telling her about "his friend."

He spoke about him in such detail and with such enthusiasm that Odintsova turned and looked at him very carefully. Meanwhile the mazurka was coming to an end. Arkady felt sad at having to part from her: he had so enjoyed spending nearly an hour with her! True, during the whole time he constantly felt she was indulging him, that he ought to feel grateful to her . . . but young hearts aren't burdened much by this feeling.

The music ended.

"*Merci*," Odintsova said and stood up. "You promised to visit me; bring your friend with you. I'd be very curious to meet a man who's bold enough not to believe in anything."

The governor went up to Odintsova and announced that supper was served and, with a preoccupied look, offered her his arm. As she left she turned around to smile and nod to Arkady for the last time. He bowed deeply and watched her go (her figure seemed so graceful to him, draped in the grayish sheen of black silk!); he thought, "By this time she's forgotten entirely about my existence," and in his soul he felt a sense of exquisite humility . . .

"Well, so?" Bazarov asked Arkady, as soon as the latter had returned to the corner. "Did you enjoy yourself? One gentleman here just told me she's quite a woman—*ooh là là*; then again, that gentleman seems to be a bit of a fool. Well, what do you think, is she—*ooh là là*, or not?"

"I don't quite understand what you mean," replied Arkady.

"Is that so! What innocence!"

"In that case I really don't understand that gentleman. Odintsova is very nice—no doubt, but her behavior's so cold and severe that . . ."

"Still waters run deep, you know!" Bazarov interrupted. "You say she's cold. That provides special flavor. You like ice cream, don't you?"

"Perhaps," muttered Arkady. "I can't judge such things. She wants to make your acquaintance and has asked me to bring you along to meet her."

"I can just imagine how you described me! However, you did very well. Take me along. Whoever she may be—simply a provincial lioness or 'an emancipated woman' like Kukshina—she still has the nicest pair of shoulders I've seen in a long time."

Arkady was offended by Bazarov's cynicism, but—as is often the case—reproached his friend for something other than what he disliked in him . . .

"Why are you so unwilling to allow women to be freethinkers?" he asked in a low voice.

"Because, my little friend, as far as I've observed, the only female freethinkers are ugly monsters."

Their conversation ended here. Both young men left right after supper. Kukshina, in a nervously spiteful way, but not without timidity, began laughing after they left: her vanity was deeply offended by the fact that neither of them had paid her any attention. She stayed at the ball later than everyone else; at three o'clock in the morning she was still dancing a polka-mazurka in the Parisian style with Sitnikov. The governor's fête concluded with this edifying spectacle.

XV

"Let's see what species of Mammalia this person belongs to," Bazarov said to Arkady the next day as they both climbed the stairs of the hotel where Odintsova was staying. "My nose tells me something's not quite right."

"I'm surprised at you!" cried Arkady. "What? You, you, Bazarov, clinging to such narrow-minded morality, that . . ."

"What a strange fellow you are!" Bazarov said, cutting him off abruptly. "Don't you know in our language, when we say 'not quite right,' that means 'quite all right'? In other words, there's something to be gained. Wasn't it you who said today that she married peculiarly, although, in my opinion, marriage to a wealthy old man—isn't peculiar at all; on the contrary, it's very sensible. I don't believe all those rumors heard in town; but I do like to think, as our educated governor says, that they're well-founded."

Arkady made no reply and knocked on the door of the room. A young servant dressed in livery led the two friends into a large room, badly furnished, like all rooms in Russian hotels, but well supplied with flowers. Odintsova soon appeared in a simple morning dress. She seemed even younger in the light of the springtime sun. Arkady introduced Bazarov to her and was secretly astonished to notice that he seemed embarrassed, while Odintsova remained completely serene, just as she had yesterday. Bazarov was aware of his embarrassment and became annoyed. "Well, I'll be! Afraid of a woman!" he thought. Sprawling in an armchair just as Sitnikov had, he began talking in an exaggeratedly casual manner, while Odintsova never took her clear eyes off him.

Anna Sergeevna Odintsova was the daughter of Sergei Nikolaevich Loktev, known as a handsome man, a speculator and gambler, who, after hanging on for fifteen years or so and becoming famous in both Petersburg and Moscow, ended up by losing everything. He was forced to settle in the country, where he soon died, leaving a tiny inheritance to his two daughters, Anna, who was twenty, and Katerina, twelve. Their mother, who'd come from an impoverished line of Princes Kh., passed away in Petersburg, when her husband was at the peak of his powers. After her father's death, Anna's situation became very difficult. The splendid education she'd received in Petersburg hadn't prepared her to assume responsibility for the household and estate—or for life in the remote countryside. She knew absolutely no one in the entire neighborhood, and there was no one to turn to. Her father had managed to avoid all contact with his neighbors; he despised them and they, him, each in his own way. She didn't lose her head, however, and promptly summoned her mother's sister, the Princess Avdotya Stepanovna Kh., a nasty, arrogant old woman, who, after taking up residence in her niece's house, appropriated all the best rooms for herself, growled and grumbled from morning to night, and wouldn't even go out for walks in the garden unless accompanied by her one servant, a gloomy footman in worn, pea-green livery with light blue braid, and a three-cornered hat. Anna patiently endured all her aunt's whims, gradually assumed responsibility for her sister's education, and, it seemed, had already reconciled herself to the idea of wasting away in the remote countryside.

. . . But fate had decreed otherwise for her. A certain Odintsov happened to notice her; he was a very wealthy man, about forty-six years old, eccentric, hypochondriac, portly, ponderous, and sour, but neither stupid nor mean; he fell in love with her and proposed marriage. She agreed to become his wife; he lived with her almost six years and, when he died, left her all his property. For about a year after his death Anna Sergeevna didn't leave the country; then she went abroad with her sister, but only to Germany; she grew bored and returned to live on her beloved estate of Nikolskoe, about forty versts from the town of ***. There she had a magnificent, splendidly furnished house and a lovely garden with a conservatory: the late Odintsov had denied himself nothing. Anna Sergeevna rarely went into town; when she did, it was only on business and she never stayed long. She wasn't loved in the province; there was a great deal of fuss over her marriage to Odintsov, and all sorts of unbelievable stories circulated about her: it was claimed she'd helped her father with his cardsharping, had good reasons for going abroad, and had to conceal some unfortunate consequences[4] . . . "You know what I mean," the indignant narrators would conclude their tale. "She's gone through fire and water," they used to say about her; and a well-known local wit would add, "And through copper pipes as well."[5] All these rumors reached her, but she didn't pay any attention to them: she had an independent and rather resolute character.

Odintsova was seated, leaning against the back of an armchair, and, with one hand resting on the other, was listening to Bazarov. Contrary to his normal behavior, he spoke a great deal and made an obvious effort to interest his interlocutor, which also surprised Arkady. He couldn't tell whether Bazarov had achieved his goal. It was hard to guess from Anna Sergeevna's face what sort of impression he was making: her face retained one and the same expression—cordial and elegant; her lovely eyes shone with attention, but that attention was completely composed. Bazarov's affectation in the first moments of their meeting had an unpleasant effect on her, like a foul odor or a shrill sound; but she understood at once that he was embarrassed, and even found that flattering. Vulgar mediocrity was the only thing that repulsed her, and no one could accuse Bazarov of that. Arkady continued to be surprised all that day. He expected Bazarov would talk to an intelligent woman like Odintsova about his convictions and views: she'd declared her desire to meet a man "bold enough not to believe in anything." But instead, Bazarov talked about medicine, homeopathy, and botany. It turned out Odintsova hadn't been wasting her time in solitude: she'd read several good books and expressed herself in excellent Russian. She directed the conversation to music, but when she learned that Bazarov didn't acknowledge art, she quietly returned to the subject of botany, although Arkady

4. Perhaps an unwanted pregnancy.
5. The pregnancy might have ended in an illegal abortion.

was just about to launch into a disquisition on the significance of folk melodies. Odintsova continued to treat him as if he were her younger brother: she seemed to value his youthful generosity and good nature— but nothing more. Their conversation lasted a little over three hours— it was unhurried, free-ranging, and animated.

At last the friends stood up and began to take their leave. Anna Sergeevna looked at them cordially, extended her beautiful white hand to each, and, after reflecting a moment, said with some hesitation, but with a pleasant smile, "Gentlemen, if you're not afraid of being bored, do come visit me in Nikolskoe."

"If you like, Anna Sergeevna," cried Arkady, "I'd consider it a great honor . . ."

"And you, Monsieur Bazarov?"

Bazarov merely bowed—and Arkady was surprised for one last time: he noticed his friend had blushed.

"Well?" he said to him on the street. "Do you still think she's—*ooh là là?*"

"Who knows? Just see how frigid she's made herself!" Bazarov replied. After a brief silence he added: "She's a duchess, a regal personage. All she needs is a train out behind her and a crown on top of her head."

"Our duchesses don't speak Russian that well," Arkady observed.

"She's been through many changes, my dear boy; she's tasted the common bread."

"All the same, she's lovely!" said Arkady.

"What a delectable body!" continued Bazarov. "Perfect for the dissecting table."

"Stop it, Evgeny, for God's sake! That's unspeakable."

"Well, don't get angry, my little one. What I meant was—she's first-rate. We'll have to pay her a visit."

"When?"

"Why not the day after tomorrow? What's there to do here? Drink champagne with Kukshina? Listen to your relative, that liberal official? . . . We'll leave the day after tomorrow. By the way—my father's small estate isn't too far from there. This Nikolskoe's along the *** road, isn't it?"

"It is."

"*Optime.*[6] There's no need to dawdle; only fools and know-it-alls do that. I tell you: she has a delectable body!"

Three days later the two friends were on their way to Nikolskoe. The day was bright and not too hot, the well-fed little posthorses trotted along smoothly, gently switching their twisted and braided tails. Arkady looked at the road and smiled without knowing why.

"Congratulate me," Bazarov cried suddenly, "today, June twenty-

6. "Perfect" (Latin).

second, is my guardian angel's day.[7] Let's see how he takes care of me. My parents expect me home today," he added, lowering his voice . . . "Well, they'll wait. What difference does it make?"

XVI

Anna Sergeevna's estate stood on the slope of a bare hill, not far from a yellow stone church with a green roof, white columns, and a fresco over the main entrance depicting the "Resurrection of Christ" in the "Italian" style.[8] A swarthy warrior wearing a helmet and reclining in the foreground was particularly noteworthy for his rounded contours. Behind the church a large village extended for some distance in two rows of cottages with chimneys visible here and there over thatched roofs. The manor house was built in the same style as the church, known here as Alexandrine;[9] the house was also painted yellow, had a green roof, white columns, and a gable with a coat of arms. The provincial architect had erected both buildings with the approval of the late Odintsov, who couldn't stand any frivolous or extemporaneous innovations, as he referred to them. The house was flanked on both sides by dark trees in an old garden; an avenue of pruned firs led to the entrance.

Our friends were met in the hall by two tall footmen in livery; one ran off to fetch the butler immediately. The butler, a portly man wearing a black frockcoat, appeared at once and directed the guests up a carpeted staircase to a special room already provided with two beds and all the prerequisites for their toilette. It was clear that order prevailed in this house: everything was clean and sweet-smelling, just like in a minister's reception room.

"Anna Sergeevna requests that you come see her in half an hour," the butler informed them. "Is there anything you require at present?"

"Nothing at present, most esteemed sir," replied Bazarov. "Would you be so kind as to bring me a glass of vodka?"

"Yes, sir," replied the butler, somewhat bewildered, and left, his boots squeaking.

"What grand style!" observed Bazarov. "That's what it's called by your sort, isn't it?"

"A fine duchess she is," Arkady retorted. "At the first acquaintance she invites such mighty aristocrats as you and me to come visit her."

"Especially me, a future medic, a medic's son, and a sexton's grandson . . . Did you know I'm the grandson of a sexton? Like Speransky,"[1] he

---

7. The birthday of one's patron saint, also known as one's name day.
8. That is, presumably, Renaissance style.
9. Pertaining to the reign of Alexander I; see above, p. 37, n.7.
1. Mikhail Mikhailovich Speransky (1772–1839), a leading statesman and liberal reformer under Alexander I. He was the son of a village priest and one of the first to rise to a position of great power from such humble origins.

added, pursing his lips after a brief silence. "Still, she has pampered herself; oh, how this lady's pampered herself! Maybe we should put on our frockcoats?"

Arkady merely shrugged his shoulders . . . but he too felt slightly embarrassed.

Half an hour later Bazarov and Arkady entered the drawing room. It was a spacious, lofty room, furnished rather elegantly, but without any particular taste. Heavy, expensive furniture stood in the usual formal arrangement along walls covered in brown paper with a gold design; the late Odintsov had ordered the wallpaper from Moscow through his friend and agent, a wine merchant. Over the middle sofa hung a portrait of a corpulent, fair-haired man who seemed to be looking down at the guests inhospitably. "That must be *him*," whispered Bazarov to Arkady, and, wrinkling up his nose, added, "Maybe we should get out of here?" But at that very moment the mistress appeared. She was wearing a light beige dress; her hair was combed smooth behind her and lent a girlish expression to her clear, fresh face.

"Thank you so much for keeping your word," she began. "You must stay a while: it really isn't too bad here. I'll introduce you to my sister; she plays the piano very well. That won't make any difference to you, Monsieur Bazarov; but it seems that you, Monsieur Kirsanov, love music; besides my sister, I also have an old aunt living here with me, and a neighbor of ours sometimes comes over to play cards: that's our entire society. And now, let's sit down."

Odintsova uttered this entire short speech with particular precision, as if she'd learned it all by heart; then she turned to Arkady. It turned out that her mother had known Arkady's mother and had even been aware of her love for Nikolai Petrovich. Arkady began talking about his late mother with enthusiasm; meanwhile, Bazarov set about examining picture albums. "What an unassuming fellow I've become," he thought.

A beautiful borzoi with a blue collar came running into the drawing room, paws tapping the floor, followed by a girl about eighteen,[2] with black hair and dark skin, a roundish, but pleasant face, and small dark eyes. In her hands she held a basket filled with flowers.

"Here's my Katya," said Odintsova, nodding her head toward her.

Katya made a slight curtsey, took up a position next to her sister, and began sorting the flowers. The borzoi, whose name was Fifi, went up to each visitor in turn, wagging her tail, and thrust her cold nose into their hands.

"Did you pick them all yourself?" Odintsova asked.

"I did," Katya replied.

"Is Auntie coming to tea?"

"She is."

2. Turgenev's text lists different ages for Katya: here she is "about eighteen"; above (p. 59) she is described as eight years younger than Anna, who is said to be twenty-nine.

When Katya spoke, she smiled very sweetly, both timidly and openly, and glanced up in an amusingly stern way. Everything about her was still green and fresh: her voice, the light down on her face, her pink hands with white circles on her palms, and her slightly narrow shoulders . . . She was constantly blushing and hastily catching her breath.

Odintsova turned to Bazarov.

"You're looking at those pictures out of politeness, Evgeny Vasilich," she began. "They really don't interest you. Come and join us and let's argue about something or other."

Bazarov moved closer.

"What shall we talk about?" he asked.

"Whatever you like. I must warn you, I love to argue."

"You?"

"Yes. Does that surprise you? Why?"

"Because as far as I can tell, you have a cold, serene manner; one must have passion to argue."

"How did you manage to find me out so soon? In the first place, I'm impatient and insistent—just ask Katya; in the second, I get excited very easily."

Bazarov looked at Anna Sergeevna.

"Perhaps; you know best. So, you'd like to have an argument—by all means. I was examining some views of Saxony in your album, and you observed that such an activity couldn't interest me. You said that because you assume I have no feeling for art whatsoever—yes, in fact I lack such feeling; but these views could've interested me from a geological point of view, for example, the formation of mountains."

"Excuse me; as a geologist you'd be more likely to resort to a book, a special work on the subject, rather than these drawings."

"A drawing can show me at one glance what might take ten pages in a book to describe."

Anna Sergeevna was silent for a moment.

"All the same, you haven't the least bit of artistic feeling?" she asked, resting her elbows on the table, and in so doing, brought her face close to Bazarov's. "How do you get along without it?"

"What good is it, may I ask?"

"Well, if only to know how to study and understand people."

Bazarov smiled.

"In the first place, one's life experience serves that purpose; in the second, I can tell you it isn't worth the trouble to study separate individuals. All people resemble each other, in soul as well as body; each one of us has a brain, spleen, heart, and lungs, all made similarly. So-called moral qualities are also shared by everyone: small variations don't mean a thing. A single human specimen's sufficient to make judgments about all the rest. People are like trees in a forest; no botanist would study each birch individually."

Katya, who was arranging her flowers without hurrying, raised her eyes to Bazarov in perplexity; meeting his swift and careless glance, she blushed to her ears. Anna Sergeevna shook her head.

"Trees in a forest," she repeated. "Then in your opinion there's no difference between a stupid person and a clever one, between a good person and a bad one?"

"Yes, there is. Just like between a sick person and a healthy one: the lungs of a consumptive patient aren't in the same condition as your lungs and mine, although they're built similarly. We know more or less what causes physical ailments; moral illnesses result from bad upbringing, all the nonsense that gets stuffed into people's heads from childhood, in a word, the deformed condition of society. If you correct society, you won't have any more illness."

Bazarov said all this with a look on his face as if he were thinking: "You can believe me or not, it's all the same to me!" He was slowly stroking his long side whiskers while his eyes were roaming around the room.

"And you assume," Anna Sergeevna said, "that when society is cured, there won't be any more stupid or bad people?"

"At least in a properly organized society it won't make any difference whether a person's stupid or clever, bad or good."

"Yes, I understand; everyone will have the same spleen."

"Precisely, madame."

Odintsova turned to Arkady.

"What's your opinion, Arkady Nikolaevich?"

"I agree with Evgeny," he replied.

Katya looked at him from under her brows.

"You amaze me, gentlemen," Odintsova said, "but we'll talk with you further. As for now, I see that Auntie's coming for tea; we must spare her ears."

Anna Sergeevna's auntie, the Princess Kh., a short, slender woman with a face pinched like a fist and nasty, steady eyes under a gray wig, came in. Scarcely greeting the guests, she lowered herself into a large velvet-covered armchair, in which no one else had any right to sit. Katya placed a little bench under her feet; the old woman didn't thank her and didn't even glance up; she merely placed her hands underneath the yellow shawl covering almost her entire feeble body. The princess loved the color yellow: she was also wearing a cap with bright yellow ribbons.

"Did you have a good rest, Auntie?" Odintsova inquired, raising her voice.

"That dog's in here again," the old woman muttered in reply. Noticing that Fifi had made a few hesitant steps in her direction, she cried, "Shoo, shoo!"

Katya called Fifi and opened the door for her.

Fifi gladly ran out in the hope that someone would take her for a walk, but when left alone on the other side of the door, she began scratching and whining. The princess frowned and Katya was about to leave . . .

"I think tea's ready," Odintsova announced. "Gentlemen, if you please; Auntie, let's go have tea."

The princess stood up from her armchair and was the first to leave the drawing room. Everyone followed her into the dining room. A servant boy in livery pulled an armchair stacked with cushions away from the table with a loud scrape—she sank into this chair, which was also reserved exclusively for her use; Katya was pouring tea and handed her the first cup decorated with a coat of arms. The old woman put some honey into the cup (she considered it sinful and expensive to drink tea with sugar, even though she never spent a copeck on anything); she suddenly asked in a hoarse voice, "What does *Preence* Ivan write?"

No one answered her. Bazarov and Arkady quickly surmised that no one paid her any attention, although she was treated with respect. "It's all *for the sake of appearance* they keep her, because she comes from a princely line," thought Bazarov . . . After tea Anna Sergeevna suggested they go for a walk; but it began to drizzle and everyone, except for the princess, returned to the drawing room. The neighbor who loved to play cards arrived; his name was Porfiry Platonych. He was a portly, gray-haired man with short, pointy legs that looked as if they'd been sharpened, and he was very polite and entertaining. Anna Sergeevna, who chatted mostly with Bazarov, asked him whether he'd like to play an old-fashioned game of preference[3] with them. Bazarov agreed, saying he really needed to prepare himself in advance for a career as a country doctor.

"Be careful," remarked Anna Sergeevna, "Porfiry Platonych and I will beat you. And you, Katya," she added, "play something for Arkady Nikolaevich; he loves music, and we'll listen, too."

Katya went to the piano unwillingly; Arkady, although he really did love music, followed her unwillingly. Odintsova seemed to be sending him away; like every young man of his age, he felt in his heart the welling up of a vague, painful sensation, resembling the forebodings of love. Katya raised the cover of the piano and, without looking up at Arkady, asked in a low voice, "What would you like me to play?"

"Whatever you like," Arkady replied indifferently.

"What kind of music do you prefer?" Katya repeated, without changing her position.

"Classical," replied Arkady in the same tone of voice.

"Do you like Mozart?"

"Yes."

Katya took out Mozart's Sonata-Fantasia in C Minor. She played very

---

3. A card game similar to whist.

well, although her rendition was a bit stiff and dry. Without taking her eyes off the music and pressing her lips together firmly, she sat upright and motionless; only at the end of the sonata did her face flush and a little curl of hair fall down over her dark brow.

Arkady was particularly struck by the last part of the sonata, that part where, in the midst of the enchanting gaiety of a carefree melody, there suddenly burst forth strains of such mournful, almost tragic grief . . . But the reflections aroused in him by the sounds of the Mozart didn't refer to Katya. Looking at her, he merely thought: "This young lady doesn't play too badly, and she's not bad-looking either."

After finishing the sonata, Katya, without lifting her hands from the keyboard, asked, "Is that enough?" Arkady declared that he dare not trouble her further and began chatting with her about Mozart. He asked whether she'd chosen that sonata herself, or someone had recommended it to her. Katya answered him in monosyllables: she was *hiding*, having retreated into herself. When this happened, she didn't emerge very quickly; her face would assume a stubborn, almost dull-witted expression. She wasn't exactly shy, merely distrustful and a little intimidated by her sister, who'd provided her with an education, and who, of course, had no suspicion of all this. Arkady wound up calling Fifi, who'd come back in; to maintain appearances, he began petting the dog's head with a gracious smile. Katya returned to her flowers.

Meanwhile, Bazarov kept losing round after round. Anna Sergeevna played cards like a master; Porfiry Platonych could also hold his own. Bazarov wound up losing a sum of money that, though insignificant, was still not altogether pleasant for him. During supper Anna Sergeevna once again turned the conversation to botany.

"Let's go for a walk tomorrow morning," she said to him. "I want to learn the Latin names of the wildflowers and all their characteristics."

"Why do you want to know the Latin names?" asked Bazarov.

"Order is needed in all things," she replied.

"What a splendid woman Anna Sergeevna is," exclaimed Arkady, when left alone later with his companion in the room reserved for them.

"Yes," answered Bazarov, "that lady has a head on her shoulders. And she's been around as well."

"In what sense do you mean that, Evgeny Vasilich?"

"In a good sense, my dear boy, Arkady Nikolaevich, in a good sense! I'm sure she also does a fine job managing her estate. But she's not the splendid one—it's her sister."

"What? That swarthy girl?"

"Yes, that swarthy girl. She's so fresh, unspoiled, timid, taciturn, anything you like. That's someone to take an interest in. You could make anything you like of her; while the other one's an old warhorse."

Arkady said nothing in reply to Bazarov, and each of them lay down to sleep with his own thoughts.

That evening Anna Sergeevna also thought about her guests. She liked Bazarov—the absence of flirtatiousness and the very harshness of his judgments. She saw something novel in him, something she'd never encountered before, and was curious.

Anna Sergeevna was a rather strange creature. Without any prejudices, without even any strong convictions, she never yielded to anyone or deviated from her path. She saw a great deal very clearly, took an interest in many things, but nothing completely satisfied her; she scarcely desired complete satisfaction. Her mind was both inquisitive and indifferent at the same time: her doubts never subsided into oblivion or expanded to anxiety. If she hadn't been so rich and independent, she might have thrown herself into the struggle, might have come to know real passion . . . But she had an easy life, though boring at times, and continued passing day after day, without hurrying and only occasionally getting agitated. The colors of the rainbow would sometimes dance before her eyes, but she was always relieved when they faded and had no regrets. Her imagination even exceeded the boundaries of what's considered permissible according to the laws of conventional morality; but even then her blood flowed as quietly as ever in her charmingly graceful and tranquil body. Sometimes, upon emerging from a fragrant bath, all warm and soft, she'd fall to musing about the insignificance of life, its sadness, travail, and evil . . . Her soul would be filled with unexpected boldness and seethe with noble aspiration; but a draught of wind would blow in from a half-opened window and Anna Sergeevna would retreat into herself, complain, and feel almost angry; the only thing she needed at that moment was for the nasty wind to stop blowing on her.

Like all women who never managed to fall in love, she longed for something without knowing precisely what it was. Strictly speaking, she didn't want anything, although it seemed to her she wanted everything. She could hardly stand the late Odintsov (she married him out of calculation, although she probably wouldn't have agreed to become his wife if she hadn't considered him a good man), and she harbored a secret disgust for all men whom she considered to be nothing more than slovenly, ponderous, flaccid, feebly tiresome creatures. Once while abroad she met a handsome young Swede with a chivalrous expression and honest blue eyes under a broad forehead; he made a strong impression on her, but that didn't prevent her from returning to Russia.

"This doctor's a strange man!" she thought, lying in her magnificent bed on lace cushions under a light silk coverlet . . . Anna Sergeevna had inherited from her father a share of his penchant for luxury. She'd loved her sinful, but kindhearted father very dearly, and he'd adored her, joked with her in a friendly way as with an equal, and trusted her entirely, consulted her. She could scarcely remember her mother.

"That doctor's strange!" she repeated to herself. She stretched, smiled, put her hands behind her head, then ran her eyes over a few pages of a silly French novel, threw down the book—and fell fast asleep, feeling all clean and cool, in sweet, fragrant bed linen.

The next morning right after breakfast Anna Sergeevna set off botanizing with Bazarov and returned before dinner; Arkady didn't go anywhere and spent about an hour with Katya. He wasn't bored with her, and she offered to repeat yesterday's performance of the sonata; but when at last Odintsova returned and he saw her, his heart instantly felt a pang . . . She was coming through the garden at a somewhat tired pace; her cheeks were red, her eyes shining brighter than usual under her round straw hat. She was twisting the thin stem of a wildflower in her fingers, her light shawl had slipped down to her elbows, and the broad gray ribbons of her hat were clinging to her chest. Bazarov walked alongside, in a confident, carefree manner, as always, but the expression on his face, although cheerful and even affectionate, was not at all to Arkady's liking. After muttering through his teeth, "Hello!" Bazarov headed to his room, while Odintsova shook Arkady's hand absentmindedly and also walked right past him.

"Hello?"[4] wondered Arkady. "As if we hadn't seen each other already today?"

XVII

Time (as is well known) sometimes flies by like a bird, while at other times it crawls like a worm; but a person is particularly fortunate when he doesn't even notice whether it's passing swiftly or slowly. In precisely this way Arkady and Bazarov spent about two weeks at Odintsova's. This was facilitated in part by the order she'd established in her house and in her life. She adhered to it very strictly and forced others to submit as well. Everything in the course of a day was done at a certain time. At exactly eight o'clock in the morning everyone assembled for tea; between tea and breakfast each person did as he wished; the mistress herself was busy with the steward (the estate was run on the quitrent system),[5] with the butler, and the main housekeeper. Before dinner everyone gathered again to converse or read; evenings were devoted to walks, cards, or music; at half past ten Anna Sergeevna retired to her room, gave orders for the following day, and went to bed. Bazarov didn't care for this regimented, somewhat imperious punctuality in everyday life; "it's as if everything moved along rails," he said. The footmen in livery and the formal butlers offended his democratic sentiments. He believed that if things had gone that far, it was fitting to dine entirely in the English style—frockcoats and white ties. Once he aired his views on this subject to Anna Sergeevna. She behaved in such a way so that everyone, without a moment's hesitation, would express his opinions to

4. Russians typically greet each other only once a day.
5. See above, p. 8, n. 4.

her. She heard him out and replied: "From your point of view, you're correct—perhaps, in this case, I am an aristocratic lady; but in the country it's impossible to live with disorder; the boredom would be overwhelming." And she continued in her own ways. Bazarov complained, but it was precisely because "everything moved along rails" that he and Arkady lived so comfortably in Odintsova's house.

Nevertheless, a change had occurred in both young men since the first days of their stay at Nikolskoe. Bazarov, toward whom Anna Sergeevna was obviously well-inclined, though she rarely agreed with him, began to display unprecedented signs of anxiety: he was easily irritated, spoke unwillingly, looked angry, and couldn't sit still, as if he felt provoked; meanwhile Arkady, who'd decided all by himself that he was in love with Odintsova once and for all, began to give way to quiet despondency. This feeling, however, didn't prevent him from drawing closer to Katya; it even helped him establish affectionate, friendly relations with her. "*She* doesn't appreciate me! So be it! . . . But this kind creature doesn't reject me," he thought, and his heart once again experienced the sweetness of magnanimous emotion. Katya vaguely understood that he was seeking some consolation in her company; but she didn't deny either him or herself the innocent pleasure of a half-bashful, half-trusting friendship. They didn't talk much in Anna Sergeevna's presence: Katya always retreated under her sister's sharp gaze, while Arkady, as is typical for a person in love when in the presence of his beloved, couldn't pay attention to anything else; but he was only happy with Katya. He felt he wasn't exciting enough to interest Odintsova; he became timid and confused when left alone with her. Nor did she know what to say to him: he was too young for her. On the other hand, Arkady felt at home with Katya; he treated her indulgently, didn't prevent her from expressing those impressions aroused in her by music or reading tales, verse, and other trifles, without noticing or realizing himself that these very *trifles* interested him as well. For her part, Katya didn't prevent him from feeling despondent.

Arkady felt comfortable with Katya; Odintsova, with Bazarov; therefore it often happened that the two couples, after spending some time together, would each go their separate ways, especially during their walks. Katya *adored* nature, and Arkady loved it, though dared not admit it; Odintsova was rather indifferent to it, just like Bazarov. The almost constant separation of the two friends had its consequences: relations between them began to change. Bazarov stopped talking to Arkady about Odintsova and even ceased mocking her "aristocratic ways"; it's true, he continued to praise Katya as before, merely advising Arkady to restrain her sentimental tendencies, but his praise was hurried, his advice, dry; in general he talked with Arkady much less than before . . . as if avoiding him, feeling ashamed of something . . .

Arkady noticed all this, but kept his opinions to himself.

The real cause of all this "newness" was the feeling in Bazarov inspired by Odintsova—a feeling that tormented and enraged him, one that he'd have denied immediately with scornful laughter and cynical abuse, had anyone ever remotely suggested the possibility of what was actually taking place. Bazarov was a great lover of women and feminine beauty, but love in the ideal sense, or, as he expressed it, in the romantic sense, he called rubbish or unforgivable stupidity; he considered chivalrous feelings something akin to deformity or disease and had expressed his amazement more than once: why hadn't Toggenburg[6] been locked away in an asylum with all those minstrels and troubadors? "If you like a woman," he used to say, "try to gain your end; if that's impossible—well, never mind, turn your back on her—there's plenty of fish in the sea." He liked Odintsova: the rumors circulating about her, the freedom and independence of her thought, her indisputable fondness for him—all this, it seemed, was in his favor; but he soon realized that with her he wouldn't "gain his end"; to his own amazement, however, he lacked the strength to turn his back on her. His blood caught fire as soon as he thought about her; he could've easily coped with his blood, but something else had taken root in him that he'd never been able to admit, something he'd always mocked, something that irritated his pride. In conversations with Anna Sergeevna he expressed even more strongly than before his careless contempt of everything romantic; but when left alone he acknowledged with indignation the romantic in himself. At such times he headed for the woods and walked with long strides, breaking any branches that got in his way, cursing both her and himself under his breath; or else he took to the hayloft in the barn and, stubbornly closing his eyes, forced himself to sleep, which, naturally, he couldn't always do. He imagined those chaste arms wrapping around his neck, those proud lips responding to his kisses, those clever eyes coming to rest on his with tenderness—yes, tenderness—and his head would start spinning; for a moment he'd forget where he was until his indignation would flare up once again. He caught himself having all sorts of "shameful" thoughts, as if the devil were teasing him. Sometimes it seemed to him that a change was also taking place in Odintsova, that something special had appeared in her expression, that perhaps . . . But at this point he usually stamped his foot or clenched his teeth and shook a fist in his own face.

Meanwhile, Bazarov wasn't entirely mistaken. He'd appealed to Odintsova's imagination; he interested her and she thought about him a great deal. She wasn't bored in his absence and didn't wait for him to come, but his appearance enlivened her at once; she willingly remained alone with him and gladly conversed with him, even when he angered her or offended her taste, her elegant habits. It was as if she wished to test him and come to know herself.

6. The romantic hero of a literary ballad (1797) by the German writer Friedrich von Schiller (1759–1805), entitled *"Ritter Toggenburg"* (The knight Toggenburg).

Once while walking with her in the garden, he suddenly announced in a sullen voice that he intended to leave soon and visit his father in the country . . . She turned pale, as if something had caused her great pain, so much pain that she herself was surprised and thought for a long time afterward about what it might mean. Bazarov had informed her of his impending departure with no intention of testing her or to see what might happen: he never "fabricated." That morning he'd talked with his father's steward, Timofeich, who used to take care of him. This Timofeich, an experienced and clever old man with faded yellow hair, a weather-beaten reddish face, and tiny teardrops in his squinting eyes, had appeared before Bazarov unexpectedly, wearing his shortish coat of thick blue-gray cloth, tied with a leather belt, and tarred boots.

"Ah, hello, old man," cried Bazarov.

"Good day, Evgeny Vasilevich, sir," the old fellow began with a broad grin, so that his whole face was covered in wrinkles.

"What're you doing here? Have they sent for me, or what?"

"For goodness sake, sir, how could we?" Timofeich muttered (recalling the strict orders he'd received from his master before departure). "I was on my way to town on the master's business and heard you were here, sir, so I turned in along the way, that is—to have a look at you, sir . . . how could we think of disturbing you?"

"Come on now, don't lie," Bazarov said, interrupting him. "The road to town doesn't pass anywhere near here."

Timofeich hesitated and made no reply.

"Is father well?"

"Thank God, sir."

"And mother?"

"And Arina Vlasevna, glory be to God."

"I suppose they're waiting for me?"

The old man leaned his small head to one side.

"Ah, Evgeny Vasilevich, I'll say they're waiting, sir! So help me God, my heart aches just looking at your parents."

"Well, all right, all right! Don't carry on. Tell them I'll be there soon."

"Yes, sir," Timofeich replied with a sigh.

As he left the house, he pulled his cap down over his head with both hands, climbed into the dilapidated racing carriage left at the gate, and set off at a trot, not toward town.

That evening Anna Sergeevna was sitting in her room with Bazarov, while Arkady was pacing the hall listening to Katya's playing. The princess had retired to her own room upstairs; she couldn't stand guests in general, especially these "new wild-looking ones," as she called them. In the public rooms she merely sulked; but in her own room, in her maid's presence, she expressed her irritation in such abusive language, that her cap would bounce up and down on her head together with her wig. Odintsova had heard all about this.

CHAPTER XVII

"Why do you plan to leave us?" she began. "What about your promise?"

Bazarov was startled.

"What promise, madam?"

"You've forgotten. You offered to give me lessons in chemistry."

"What's to be done, madam? My father's waiting for me; it's impossible for me to remain here any longer. Besides, you can read Pelouse et Frémy, *Notions générales de chimie*;[7] it's a good book and very clearly written. You'll find everything you need in it."

"Don't you remember: you assured me a book could never replace . . . I forget exactly what you said, but you know what I mean . . . do you remember?"

"What's to be done, madam?" Bazarov repeated.

"Why must you leave?" Odintsova repeated, lowering her voice.

He looked at her. She'd rested her head on the back of the armchair and folded her arms, bare to the elbow, across her chest. She seemed pale in the light of one lamp covered by a perforated paper shade. Her ample white dress hid her completely beneath its gentle folds; her legs were crossed, and the ends of her feet could hardly be seen.

"Why stay?" replied Bazarov.

Odintsova turned her head slightly.

"What do you mean, why? Aren't you enjoying yourself here? Perhaps you think you won't be missed?"

"I'm sure about that."

Odintsova was silent.

"You're wrong. Besides, I don't believe you. You couldn't have said that seriously." Bazarov continued sitting there without moving. "Evgeny Vasilevich, why don't you say something?"

"What can I say? In general it's not worth missing people, especially me."

"Why so?"

"I'm an unimaginative, uninteresting man. I don't even know how to converse."

"You're fishing for compliments, Evgeny Vasilevich."

"That's not one of my habits. You know, don't you, the elegant side of life is inaccessible to me, that side you value so highly."

Odintsova bit the corner of her handkerchief.

"Think whatever you like, but I'll be bored after you leave."

"Arkady will be here," Bazarov remarked. Odintsova shrugged her shoulders slightly.

"I'll be bored," she repeated.

"Really? In any case, you won't be bored for long."

"Why do you think that?"

"Because you yourself told me you're bored only when your normal

7. *General Principles of Chemistry,* a work published in Paris in 1853 by Theophile Pelouse (1807–67) and Edmond Frémy (1814–94).

routine's disturbed. You've organized your life with such infallible precision, there's no room in it for boredom or depression . . . no painful feelings."

"You think I'm infallible . . . that is, I've organized my life in such a way?"

"I'll say! Here's an example: in a few minutes it'll be ten o'clock and I know full well you'll chase me out."

"No, I won't, Evgeny Vasilich. You may stay. Open that window . . . it's stuffy in here."

Bazarov stood up and pushed the window. It flew open with a loud noise . . . He hadn't expected it to move so easily; besides, his hands were trembling. The soft, dark night peered into the room with its almost black sky, its lightly rustling trees, and the fresh aroma of pure, free air.

"Lower the curtain and sit down," Odintsova said. "I'd like to talk to you before you leave. Tell me something about yourself; you never talk about yourself."

"I try to converse about useful matters, Anna Sergeevna."

"You're so modest . . . But I'd like to find out something about you, your family, your father—for whom you're forsaking us."

"Why does she say such things?" Bazarov wondered.

"All that isn't the least bit interesting," he said aloud, "especially for you; you and I are somber people . . ."

"And, in your opinion, I'm an aristocrat?"

Bazarov raised his eyes and looked at Odintsova.

"Yes," he replied with exaggerated abruptness.

She smiled.

"I see you don't know me very well, even though you're sure all people resemble one another and it's not worth studying them. Sometime I'll tell you the story of my life . . . but first you must tell me yours."

"I don't know you well," replied Bazarov. "Perhaps you're right; perhaps it's true that every person's a mystery. Take you, for example: you avoid society, feel oppressed by it—yet you've invited two students to visit you here. Why, with your intellect and beauty, do you choose to live in the country?"

"What? How did you put that?" Odintsova asked briskly. "With my . . . beauty?"

Bazarov frowned.

"It doesn't matter," he muttered. "I wanted to say that I really don't understand why you've settled down in the country."

"You don't understand . . . But you must explain it to yourself somehow."

"Yes . . . I suppose you choose to remain in one place because you've spoiled yourself, because you love comfort and convenience a great deal, and you're indifferent to all the rest."

Odintsova smiled again.

"You really don't want to believe I can be carried away?"

Bazarov glanced at her from under his brow.

"By curiosity, perhaps; but nothing else."

"Really? Well, now I can understand why we've become friends; you're just like me."

"Become friends . . ." Bazarov repeated hollowly.

Bazarov stood up. A lamp burnt dimly in the darkened, fragrant, solitary room; through the curtain, which billowed occasionally, the irritating freshness of night air flowed in and mysterious whispering could be heard. Odintsova didn't move a muscle, but a secret excitement was gradually overtaking her . . . It was communicated to Bazarov. He suddenly felt he was all alone with a beautiful young woman . . .

"Where're you going?" she asked slowly.

He made no reply and sank onto a chair.

"So, you consider me a placid, pampered, spoiled creature," she continued in the same voice, without taking her eyes off him. "While all I know about myself is I'm very unhappy."

"Unhappy! Why? Surely you can't attribute any significance to those idle rumors?"

Odintsova frowned. She was annoyed at the way he understood her.

"Those rumors don't even amuse me, Evgeny Vasilevich, and I'm too proud to let them disturb me. I'm unhappy because . . . I have no desire, no will to live. You're looking at me incredulously and thinking: here's an 'aristocrat' speaking, all dressed up in lace, sitting on a velvet armchair. I'm not hiding anything: I love what you call comfort, and at the same time I have little desire to live. Explain that contradiction as best you can. Besides, in your eyes it's all romanticism."

Bazarov shook his head.

"You're healthy, independent, rich; what else is there? What do you want?"

"What do I want?" Odintsova repeated and sighed. "I feel very tired and old; it seems as if I've been living for a long time. Yes, I'm old," she added, gently pulling the ends of her mantilla over her bare arms. Her eyes met Bazarov's and she blushed slightly. "There're so many memories behind me: life in Petersburg, wealth, then poverty, my father's death, marriage, then a trip abroad, just as it should be . . . Many memories, but nothing to remember, while ahead of me—a long, long path, but no goal . . . I really don't want to go on."

"Are you that disenchanted?" Bazarov asked.

"No," Odintsova replied slowly and deliberately, "but I'm not satisfied. It seems that if I could form a strong attachment to something . . ."

"You want to fall in love," Bazarov said, interrupting her, "but you can't: that explains your unhappiness."

Odintsova began examining the sleeves of her mantilla.

"Is it true I can't fall in love?" she asked.

"Hardly! But I wouldn't have called that unhappiness. On the contrary, a person to whom it happens is more deserving of pity."

"What happens?"

"Falling in love."

"How do you know that?"

"By hearsay," Bazarov replied angrily.

"You're flirting," he thought, "you're bored and teasing me because you've nothing better to do, while I . . ." His heart was about to burst.

"Besides, perhaps you're too demanding," he said, leaning his whole body forward and playing with the fringe on the chair.

"Perhaps. In my opinion, it's either all or nothing. A life for a life. You take mine, you give up yours, without regrets, without turning back. Or else, why bother?"

"Well," remarked Bazarov, "those are fair conditions. But I'm surprised that up to now . . . you haven't found what you're looking for."

"Do you think it's easy to surrender yourself completely to whatever you want?"

"Not easy if you begin to reflect, waiting and assigning value to yourself, that is, appreciating yourself; but if you don't reflect, then it's easy to surrender yourself."

"How can you help but appreciate yourself? If I have no value, then who needs my devotion?"

"That's not really my business; it's someone else's job to determine my value. The main thing is, you must know how to surrender yourself."

Odintsova leaned forward in her chair.

"Don't talk like that," she began, "as if you've experienced it all."

"Incidentally, Anna Sergeevna: you should know that all this isn't in my line."

"But you'd know how to surrender yourself?"

"I don't know; I don't want to boast."

Odintsova didn't say anything and Bazarov fell silent. The sounds of the piano reached them from the drawing room.

"Why's Katya playing so late?" Odintsova inquired.

Bazarov stood up.

"Yes, it really is late and time for you to get some rest."

"Wait, where are you going? . . . I have one more thing to say to you."

"What's that?"

"Wait," she whispered.

Her eyes rested on Bazarov; she seemed to be scrutinizing him closely.

He walked around the room, then all of a sudden approached her, hurriedly said, "Good-bye," squeezed her hand so hard she almost cried, and left the room. She brought her crushed fingers to her lips, blew on them, and then, suddenly, stood up abruptly from her chair and headed to the door with rapid steps, as if wishing to call Bazarov back . . . The maid came into the room carrying a pitcher on a silver tray. Odintsova stopped, told her to go away, sat down again, and once more sank into thought. Her braid became undone and curled around her shoulder like a dark snake. A lamp remained lit for a long time in Anna Sergeevna's room, and she remained motionless for a long time, only occasionally rubbing her hands, which were being lightly nipped by the cold night air.

Meanwhile, two hours later, Bazarov returned to his room, his boots damp from the dew, looking disheveled and dismal. He found Arkady at the writing table with a book in his hands, his jacket buttoned up to his neck.

"You still haven't gone to bed?" he asked, as if annoyed.

"You were with Anna Sergeevna a long time today," Arkady said, without replying to his question.

"Yes, I was with her all the while you and Katya Sergeevna were playing the piano."

"I wasn't playing," Arkady began and then fell silent. He felt tears welling up in his eyes and didn't want to cry in front of his sarcastic friend.

XVIII

The next day when Odintsova appeared at tea, Bazarov sat leaning over his cup for some time, then suddenly looked up at her . . . She turned to him as if prodded; her face seemed to have become paler overnight. She soon returned to her own room and reappeared only at breakfast. The weather that morning was rainy, so there was no possibility of an outing. Everyone gathered in the drawing room. Arkady picked up the latest issue of a journal and began reading aloud. The princess's face expressed surprise at first, as was her custom, as if he were doing something indecent; then she began glaring at him angrily; he didn't pay her any attention.

"Evgeny Vasilevich," said Anna Sergeevna, "come to my room . . . I want to ask you something . . . Yesterday you mentioned a particular manual . . ."

She stood up and headed for the door. The princess looked around as if to say: "Look, see how amazed I am!" Once more she glared at Arkady, but he raised his voice and, exchanging glances with Katya, who was sitting next to him, continued reading.

Odintsova reached her study with hurried steps. Bazarov followed her quickly, without raising his eyes, merely catching the whispering and rustling sounds of her silk dress as it glided ahead of him. Odintsova lowered herself into the same armchair where she'd been sitting the night before, while Bazarov took up the same position he'd occupied yesterday.

"So what was the name of that book?" she began after a brief silence.

"Pelouse et Frémy, *Notions générales . . .*" Bazarov replied. "In addition, I can recommend Ganot, *Traité élémentaire de physique expérimentale*.[8] The drawings are clearer in that work, and in general the text's more . . ."

Odintsova stretched out her hand.

"Evgeny Vasilich, forgive me, but I didn't ask you here to discuss textbooks. I wanted to renew the conversation we began yesterday. You left so suddenly . . . Will it bore you?"

"I'm at your service, Anna Sergeevna. But what were we talking about yesterday?"

Odintsova threw a sidelong glance at Bazarov.

"It seems we were talking about happiness. I was telling you about myself. By the way, I just mentioned the word *happiness*. Tell me why it is that even when we're enjoying music, for example, or a pleasant evening, conversation with sympathetic people, why does all that seem more like an intimation of some immeasurable happiness that exists somewhere or other, rather than actual happiness, that is, the kind we ourselves possess? Why is this so? Perhaps you've never experienced this feeling?"

"You know the saying, 'The grass is always greener,' " replied Bazarov. "Besides, you yourself told me yesterday you weren't satisfied. It's true, though, such thoughts never enter my head."

"Perhaps you find them ridiculous?"

"No, but they never enter my head."

"Really? You know I'd really like to know what you do think about."

"What? I don't understand you."

"Listen, for some time now I've been wanting to have a frank conversation with you. There's no need to tell you—you know it all too well—you're not an ordinary sort of person; you're still young—your whole life's ahead of you. What're you preparing yourself for? What sort of future awaits you? I mean to say—what goal do you hope to achieve, where are you headed, what do you have in mind? In short, who are you and what are you?"

"You surprise me, Anna Sergeevna. You know I'm studying natural science, and as for who I am . . ."

"Yes, who are you?"

"I've already told you I'm a future district doctor."

Anna Sergeevna made an impatient movement.

"Why do you say that? You don't believe it. Arkady could answer me like that, but not you."

"What's Arkady got to do with this . . . ?"

"Stop it! Is it really possible you could be satisfied with such a modest

8. *Elementary Treatise of Experimental Physics*, a work published in Paris in 1851 by A. Ganot (1804–87).

occupation? Aren't you always maintaining that for you medicine doesn't exist? You—with your ambition—a district doctor! You're just saying that to escape from me, because you don't trust me. But you know, Evgeny Vasilich, I've managed to figure you out: I was poor and ambitious like you; I may have gone through the same trials as you."

"That's all splendid, Anna Sergeevna, but you must forgive me . . . In general I'm not accustomed to such frank pronouncements and there's such a distance separating you and me . . ."

"What kind of distance? Are you going to tell me once again that I'm an aristocrat? Enough of that, Evgeny Vasilich; I thought I'd proved to you that . . ."

"Yes, and besides that," Bazarov said, interrupting her, "why do you have such a desire to think and talk about the future, which, for the most part, doesn't depend on us? If the chance of doing something turns up, then fine; if not, then at least I can be content that I didn't prattle on about it needlessly."

"You call a friendly conversation 'prattle'? . . . Perhaps you don't consider me as a woman worthy of your confidence? Why, you despise all of us."

"I don't despise you, Anna Sergeevna, and you know that."

"No, I don't know anything . . . but let's suppose: I understand your disinclination to talk about your future; but as for what's transpiring within you now . . ."

" 'Transpiring!' " repeated Bazarov. "As if I were some state or society! In any case, it's not at all interesting; besides, is it really possible for a person always to say what's 'transpiring' within him?"

"I don't see why it isn't possible to say everything you have in mind."

"Can *you*?" Bazarov asked.

"I can," Anna Sergeevna replied after a brief hesitation.

Bazarov bowed his head.

"You're more fortunate than I."

Anna Sergeevna looked at him questioningly. "As you wish," she continued. "Something still tells me we've not come together in vain, that we'll become good friends. I'm sure that your—how shall I say?— your reticence, reserve will eventually disappear."

"So you've noticed my reserve . . . how else did you put it . . . my reticence?"

"I have."

Bazarov stood up and went over to the window.

"And you'd like to know the reason for my reserve; you'd like to know what's transpiring within me?"

"Yes," Odintsova repeated with some apprehension that she didn't quite comprehend.

"And you won't get angry?"

"I won't."

"You won't?" Bazarov stood with his back to her. "Then you should
know that I love you, stupidly, madly . . . Now see what you've
extracted."

Odintsova stretched out both her arms, while Bazarov pressed his
forehead against the window. He was breathing hard; his whole body
was trembling visibly. But it was not the trembling of youthful timidity
or the sweet fretting over a first declaration of love that overcame him:
it was passion struggling within him—powerful and painful—passion
that resembled malice and was perhaps even related to it . . . Odintsova
was both afraid of him and felt sorry for him.

"Evgeny Vasilich," she said with a touch of unintended tenderness
in her voice.

He turned around quickly, threw her a devouring look—and, seizing
both her hands, suddenly drew her to his chest.

She didn't free herself from his embrace immediately; but a moment
later she was standing far away in the corner, looking at Bazarov from
there. He rushed toward her.

"You've misunderstood me," she whispered in hurried alarm. It
seemed that if he took another step, she'd scream . . . Bazarov bit his
lips and left the room.

Half an hour later the maid brought Anna Sergeevna a note from
Bazarov; it consisted of only one line: "Must I leave today—or may I
stay until tomorrow?" "Why leave? I didn't understand you—you didn't
understand me," Anna Sergeevna replied, and thought to herself: "I
didn't even understand myself."

She didn't appear until dinner and kept pacing her room, arms behind
her back, stopping from time to time in front of the window or the
mirror, slowly wiping her handkerchief over her neck where she still
seemed to feel a burning spot. She kept asking herself what had compelled her to "extract," as Bazarov had put it, his candor; hadn't she
suspected something of that sort? . . . "I'm to blame," she muttered
aloud, "but I couldn't have foreseen it." She became pensive and then
blushed, remembering Bazarov's almost savage face as he threw himself
at her . . .

"Or else?" she suddenly said aloud, stopped, and tossed back her curls
. . . She looked at herself in the mirror; her head thrown back, a
mysterious smile on her half-closed, half-open lips, and at that moment
her eyes seemed to tell her something she found embarrassing . . .

"No," she decided once and for all, "God knows where it might have
led; one mustn't fool around with this kind of thing; serenity is still better
than anything else on earth."

Her composure wasn't shaken, but she felt sad, even shed a few tears,
not knowing why, but not from any insult inflicted on her. She didn't
feel insulted: instead she felt guilty. Under the influence of various vague
emotions, an awareness of life passing by, a desire for novelty, she'd

forced herself to reach a certain point, to look beyond it—and there she glimpsed not even an abyss, but emptiness . . . or formless hideousness.

XIX

No matter how great Odintsova's self-control, how distanced she was from every sort of prejudice, she still felt uncomfortable at dinner in the dining room. But the meal passed rather smoothly. Porfiry Platonych arrived and told various anecdotes; he'd just returned from town. Among other things, he said that the governor, Bourdaloue,[9] had issued a special order to all his subordinates to wear spurs, just in case he should have to dispatch them on horseback in a great hurry. Arkady was conversing with Katya in a low voice and diplomatically attending to the princess. Bazarov was stubbornly and morosely silent. Two or three times Odintsova glanced—directly, not stealthily—at his face, which was stern and irritable, his eyes downcast, signs of contemptuous resolution visible in every feature, and she thought, "No . . . no . . . no . . ." After dinner she went into the garden with all the assembled guests; noticing that Bazarov wished to speak with her, she took several steps to one side and stopped. He drew near, but even then didn't raise his eyes and said in a hollow voice, "I must apologize, Anna Sergeevna. You must be furious with me."

"No, I'm not angry, Evgeny Vasilich," replied Odintsova, "but I am chagrined."

"So much the worse. In any case, I've been punished enough. My position, as you'll doubtless agree, is ridiculous. You wrote, 'Why leave?' I can't stay and don't care to. I'll be gone by tomorrow."

"Evgeny Vasilich, why are you . . ."

"Leaving?"

"No, that's not what I wanted to say."

"You can't bring back the past, Anna Sergeevna . . . sooner or later this was bound to happen. Therefore, I must leave. I can imagine only one condition under which I could stay, but that condition can never be. Excuse my audacity, but you don't love me and never will, isn't that so?"

Bazarov's eyes glittered for an instant from under his dark brows.

Anna Sergeevna didn't reply. "I'm afraid of this man" flashed through her mind.

"Farewell, madame," Bazarov said, as if guessing her thought, and headed back to the house.

Anna Sergeevna walked behind him slowly and, after calling Katya, took her by the hand. She didn't part from her until evening. She didn't play cards and kept laughing frequently, in marked contrast to her pale and worried look. Arkady didn't understand and kept an eye on her as

9. See above, p. 48 and n. 7.

young people tend to do, that is, constantly wondering what it all meant. Bazarov locked himself in his room, but came down for tea. Anna Sergeevna wanted to say a kind word or two to him, but didn't know where to begin . . .

An unexpected coincidence rescued her from the difficult situation: the butler announced Sitnikov's arrival.

It's difficult to convey in words exactly how the young progressive came bursting into the room like a quail. He'd decided, with his characteristic impudence, to set out for the country and visit a woman he hardly knew and who'd never invited him, but with whom, according to his various sources of information, many of his intelligent and intimate friends were staying. Still, he felt timid through and through; instead of using all the apologies and greetings he'd prepared in advance, he mumbled some nonsense to the effect that Evdoksiya, that is, Kukshina, had sent him to inquire about Anna Sergeevna's health and that Arkady Nikolaevich had always sung the highest praises of . . . At this point he hesitated and became so confused he sat on his hat. However, when no one turned him away and Anna Sergeevna even introduced him to her aunt and sister, he quickly recovered and began chatting merrily. The appearance of mediocrity is sometimes a useful thing in life: it soothes strings that have been stretched too taut and it sobers emotions that have become too self-confident or forgetful, suggesting their own close proximity to the mediocre. With Sitnikov's arrival everything became somehow duller—and simpler; everyone even ate a heartier supper and toddled off to bed half an hour earlier than usual.

"Now I can repeat to you," Arkady said, as he got into bed, to Bazarov, who was undressing, "something you once said to me: 'Why are you so depressed? Did you just carry out some sacred duty?' "

For some time now an artificially casual banter had been established between the two friends, a sure sign of secret dissatisfaction or unstated suspicion.

"Tomorrow I'm going home to see my old man," Bazarov replied.

Arkady raised himself up and rested on his elbow. He was both surprised and, for some reason or other, delighted.

"Ah!" he said. "Is that why you're depressed?"

Bazarov yawned. "If you know too much, you'll grow old too soon."

"What about Anna Sergeevna?" continued Arkady.

"What about Anna Sergeevna?"

"I mean, will she really let you go?"

"I'm not her hired hand."

Arkady became pensive, while Bazarov lay down and turned his face to the wall.

A few moments of silence passed.

"Evgeny!" cried Arkady suddenly.

"What?"

"I'm going with you tomorrow."

Bazarov made no reply.

"But I'll head for home," Arkady continued. "We can travel together as far as the Khokhlovsky settlement, and there you can get fresh horses from Fedot. I'd like to meet your parents, but I'm afraid to trouble them and you. You'll come back to us later, won't you?"

"I've left my things there," Bazarov answered, without turning over.

"How come he doesn't ask me why I'm leaving, and just as suddenly as he is?" wondered Arkady. "Come to think of it, why am I leaving and why is he?" he continued his reflections. He couldn't answer his own question satisfactorily, and his heart filled with bitterness. He felt it would be hard for him to part from this life to which he'd grown so accustomed; but it would also be awkward for him to stay on alone. "Something's happened between them," he said to himself. "Why should I hang around here in her presence after he's gone? She'll get sick and tired of me once and for all; I'll lose what little remains." He began to think about Anna Sergeevna, but then someone else's features gradually eclipsed the image of the lovely young widow.

"I also feel sorry for Katya!" Arkady said softly into his pillow, on which a tear had already fallen . . . Suddenly he tossed back his hair and said aloud, "Why on earth did that idiot Sitnikov turn up here?"

At first Bazarov stirred in his bed, then replied, "My boy, I can see you're still a fool. Sitnikovs are indispensable to us. Understand this: I need dolts like him. Not God, but man makes pot and pan!"

"Oho!" Arkady thought; it was then and only for a moment that the broad expanse of Bazarov's conceit was revealed to him. "Are you and I gods, then? That is, if you're a god, I must be a dolt?"

"Yes," repeated Bazarov gloomily, "you're still a fool."

Odintsova displayed no particular surprise the next day when Arkady told her he'd be leaving with Bazarov; she seemed absentminded and tired. Katya gave him a silent, serious look; the princess even made the sign of the cross under her shawl, so he couldn't see it; on the other hand, Sitnikov was completely disconcerted. He'd only just come down to breakfast wearing a fashionable new outfit, this time not in the Slavophile style; the previous evening he'd astonished the servant assigned to him by the amount of linen he'd brought along. And now, all of a sudden, his comrades were deserting him! He took a few dainty steps, then rushed around like a hunted hare at the edge of the woods—and suddenly, almost in fear, almost in a wail, announced that he too intended to leave. Odintsova made no attempt to detain him.

"I have a very smooth carriage," the young man added, turning to Arkady. "I can give you a ride. Evgeny Vasilich can take your coach, so it'll be even more comfortable."

"But wait a minute, it's out of your way and quite far to my place."

"Never mind, it's no trouble; I've lots of time. Besides, I have some business in that area."

"Tax farming?" asked Arkady, rather too contemptuously.

But Sitnikov was so desperate he didn't even laugh as usual. "I assure you the carriage is extremely smooth," he muttered, "and there's room for everyone."

"Don't offend Mr. Sitnikov by refusing," Anna Sergeevna said . . .

Arkady glanced at her and lowered his head in agreement.

The guests departed after breakfast. Saying good-bye to Bazarov, Odintsova stretched out her hand and said, "We'll see each other again, won't we?"

"As you wish," replied Bazarov.

"In that case, we will."

Arkady was the first to emerge onto the porch; he climbed into Sitnikov's carriage. The butler rendered polite assistance, but Arkady would gladly have hit him or else burst into tears. Bazarov took his place in the coach. Having reached the Khokhlovsky settlement, Arkady waited until Fedot, the proprietor of the coaching inn, had harnessed the fresh horses; then, going up to the coach, he said to Bazarov with his previous grin, "Evgeny, take me with you; I want to visit your house."

"Get in," Bazarov replied through his teeth.

Sitnikov, who'd been walking around whistling boldly near the wheels of his carriage, merely gaped in surprise when he heard these last words. Arkady coolly removed his things from the carriage and climbed in next to Bazarov. Bowing politely to his former traveling companion, he cried, "Let's go!" The coach started up and soon vanished from sight . . . Sitnikov, completely bewildered, looked at his coachman, but he was busy flicking his whip above the tail of the tracehorse.[1] Then Sitnikov jumped into his carriage and, after bellowing at two passing peasants, "Put on your caps, you idiots!" drove back to town, where he arrived very late and where, at Kukshina's the following day, he didn't mince his words about those two "repulsive, arrogant, stupid louts."

Sitting next to Bazarov in the coach, Arkady squeezed his hand warmly and for a long time said nothing. Bazarov seemed to understand and appreciate both the gesture and the silence. He hadn't slept at all the previous night, hadn't smoked, and had hardly eaten anything for the last few days. His spare profile stood out glumly and sharply from under the cáp pulled way down on his head.

"Well, my boy," he said at last, "give me a cigar, will you? Have a look: is my tongue yellow?"

"It is," replied Arkady.

"Well, yes . . . and the cigar doesn't taste very good. The machine's falling apart."

"You've really changed of late," observed Arkady.

"Never mind! We'll recover. One thing's a nuisance—my mother's so tenderhearted: if your belly doesn't swell and you don't eat ten times

1. See above, p. 7, n. 3.

a day, she gets very upset. But my father's all right; he's been around, had his ups and downs. No, I can't smoke," he added, tossing the cigar onto the dusty road.

"Is it about twenty-five versts to your estate?" asked Arkady.

"Yes. But you can ask this sage here."

He pointed to the peasant sitting on the box, one of Fedot's workers.

But the sage replied, "How in 'ell should I know—versts ain't counted 'ereabouts," and continued in a low voice to abuse the shafthorse for "kickin' with his headpiece," by which he meant jerking his head.

"Yes, yes," said Bazarov, "let it be a lesson to you, my young friend, an instructive example. The devil only knows what sort of nonsense it all is! Every man hangs by a thread, an abyss can open up beneath him at any moment, he can create all sorts of unpleasantness for himself, spoil his whole life."

"What are you hinting at?" asked Arkady.

"I'm not hinting at anything. I'm saying plainly that you and I behaved very foolishly. What's to explain? But as I've already observed in the hospital, a person who gets angry at his own illness is sure to overcome it."

"I don't quite understand you," Arkady said. "It seems to me you've nothing to complain about."

"Since you don't quite understand me, let me inform you of the following: in my opinion, it's better to break rocks on a roadway than to let a woman gain control of even the tip of one's little finger. That's all . . ." Bazarov almost uttered his favorite word *romanticism*, but restrained himself and said, "nonsense." "You won't believe me now, but let me say this: you and I fell into the society of women and found it very pleasant; forsaking society of that sort is just like splashing yourself with cold water on a hot day. Men have no time to waste on such trifles. A man must be fierce, says a splendid Spanish proverb. Why, you," he added, turning to the peasant sitting on the box, "you know-it-all, do you have a wife?"

The peasant turned his dull and weak-sighted face to the two friends.

"A wife? Sure, I do. Why not?"

"Do you beat her?"

"My wife? Anything can happen. I don't beat her for no reason."

"Splendid. And does she beat you?"

The peasant tugged at the reins.

"What a thing to say, sir. You do like to have a joke . . ." He was obviously offended.

"You hear, Arkady Nikolaevich? You and I were given a beating . . . that's what it means to be educated men."

Arkady gave a forced laugh, but Bazarov turned away and didn't open his mouth all the rest of the way.

Those twenty-five versts seemed like fifty to Arkady. But then, on the slope of a gently rising hill at long last there appeared a small village where Bazarov's parents lived. Next to it, in a grove of young birch trees, they could see a small manor house with a thatched roof. Two peasants wearing caps stood in front of the first hut and traded insults. "You're a big pig," one said to the other, "worse than a little piglet." "And your wife's a witch," the other retorted.

"From the lack of restraint in their mode of address," Bazarov observed to Arkady, "and by the playfulness of their expressions, you can tell my father's peasants aren't overly oppressed. Here he comes himself onto the porch of the house. He must've heard the bells. That's him, that's him—I recognize his figure. Hey! how gray he's become, the poor old fellow!"

XX

Bazarov leaned out of his carriage, while Arkady poked his head around his comrade's back and saw on the little porch of the manor house a tall, gaunt man with disheveled hair and a thin aquiline nose, dressed in an old, unfastened military jacket. He stood there, legs wide apart, smoking a long pipe, his eyes squinting from the sun.

The horses stopped.

"Home at last," said Bazarov's father, continuing to smoke, although the pipe was bobbing up and down in his fingers. "Well, get out, get out, let me give you a hug."

He began embracing his son . . . "Enyusha, Enyusha,"[2] a trembling woman's voice exclaimed. The door flew open and on the threshold appeared a squat, short old woman, wearing a white cap and a short colorful blouse. She cried out, swayed a bit, and certainly would've collapsed if Bazarov hadn't caught her. Her plump arms were instantly entwined around his neck, her head pressed to his chest, and there was complete silence. The only sound was that of her intermittent sobbing.

Old man Bazarov was breathing deeply and squinting even more than before.

"Well, enough, enough, Arisha! Stop it," he said, exchanging glances with Arkady, who was standing near the carriage while even the peasant sitting on the box had turned away. "That's not necessary at all! Please, stop it."

"Ah, Vasily Ivanych," the old woman muttered, "it's been so long, my dear, darling boy, my Enyushenka . . ." and, without letting him go, moved her gentle, tender, tear-stained face away, looked at him with her blissful, comical eyes, and once again fell on him.

"Well, yes, of course, it's all in the nature of things," Vasily Ivanych said, "but we'd better go inside. Look, a guest has come with Evgeny.

---

2. One of several affectionate diminutive forms of Evgeny used by his mother (cf. below "En-yushenka" and "Enyushechka").

Forgive me," he added, turning to Arkady, and shuffled one foot a little. "You understand, it's a woman's weakness; well, and a mother's heart . . ."

But his own lips and eyebrows were also twitching, his chin trembling . . . obviously he was trying to control his emotions and appear almost indifferent. Arkady bowed.

"Let's go in, Mother, really," said Bazarov and led the weakened old woman into the house. After sitting her in an armchair, he gave his father another quick hug and then introduced Arkady to him.

"Delighted to make your acquaintance," said Vasily Ivanovich. "You mustn't be too hard on us: everything here's very plain and simple, like the military. Calm down, Arina Vlasevna, do me a favor. Why so fainthearted? What will our distinguished visitor think?"

"Sir," the old woman said through her tears, "I haven't the honor of knowing your first name and patronymic . . ."

"Arkady Nikolaich," Vasily Ivanych prompted her solemnly in a loud whisper.

"Forgive a stupid old woman like me." She blew her nose and, leaning her head first to the right, then to the left, carefully wiped one eye after the other. "You'll excuse me. Why, I thought I might even die before ever getting to see my da-a-arling little boy again."

"Now you've seen him, madame," Vasily Ivanovich inserted. "Tanyushka," he said, turning to a barefoot girl of thirteen, wearing a bright red cotton dress, timidly peeking in at the door. "Bring the mistress a glass of water—on a tray, you hear? And you, gentlemen," he added with old-fashioned playfulness, "allow a retired old veteran to invite you into his study."

"Just let me hug you once more, Enyushechka," Arina Vlasevna moaned. Bazarov leaned over to her. "What a handsome man you've become!"

"Well, handsome or not," observed Vasily Ivanovich, "still a man, as they say, *ommfay*.[3] Now I hope, Arina Vlasevna, having satisfied your maternal heart, you'll begin to worry about satisfying the appetites of your dear guests because, as you know, even nightingales can't live on fairy tales alone."

The old woman stood up from her chair.

"Right away, Vasily Ivanych, the table will be set, I'll run to the kitchen myself and have the samovar heated. Everything'll be ready, everything. I haven't seen him for three years, haven't served him any food or drink. Do you think it's been easy?"

"Well, go on then, little housewife, get busy, don't disgrace us; meanwhile, gentlemen, I invite you to follow me. Here's Timofeich come

---

3. *Homme fait*: "a real man" (French).

to pay his respects to you, Evgeny. He's happy, too, the old dog, I can tell. What? Happy, aren't you, you old dog? Please follow me."

Vasily Ivanovich bustled on ahead, shuffling and scraping his worn-out slippers.

His entire abode consisted of six little rooms. One of them, where he led our friends, was called the study. A thick-legged table, piled high with papers black from dust, looking as if they'd been smoked, occupied all the space between the two windows; on the walls hung Turkish guns, whips and sabers, two maps, some anatomical drawings, a portrait of Hufeland,[4] a monogram made of hair in a black frame, and a mounted diploma; a leather sofa, worn and torn in places, stood between two enormous cupboards of Karelian birchwood; the shelves were crowded with books, boxes, stuffed birds, jars, and vials in disarray; in one corner stood some broken electric gadget.

"I warned you, my dear guest," Vasily Ivanych began, "we live here, so to speak, in a bivouac . . ."

"Stop it! Why are you apologizing?" Bazarov said, interrupting him. "Kirsanov knows full well we're no Croesuses[5] and you don't own a palace. Where will we put him, that's the question?"

"Yes, of course, Evgeny; there's an excellent room in the wing next to me: he'll be fine there."

"So you've added a wing, have you?"

"Yes, sir; where the bathhouse is, sir," Timofeich inserted.

"That is, next to the bathhouse," Vasily Ivanovich added hurriedly. "It's summer now . . . I'll go over there right away and arrange things myself; meanwhile, Timofeich, you bring their things. Evgeny, you'll take my study, of course. *Suum cuique*."[6]

"That's my father! An amusing old man and very kind," Bazarov added as soon as Vasily Ivanovich had left. "Just as eccentric as your father, but in a different way. He chatters a great deal."

"And your mother seems to be a wonderful woman," Arkady remarked.

"Yes, lacking all guile. Just see what kind of dinner she'll fix us."

"They weren't expecting you today, sir; no beef's been delivered," said Timofeich, who'd just dragged in Bazarov's case.

"We'll manage without beef; where nothing is, nothing can be had. Poverty, they say, is no sin."

"How many serfs does your father own?" Arkady asked suddenly.

"The estate belongs to my mother, not him; if I remember correctly, they have fifteen serfs."

"Twenty-two in all," Timofeich observed with some dissatisfaction.

---

4. Chistoph Wilhelm Hufeland (1762–1836), a well-respected German physician famous for his treatise entitled *On Extending the Human Life Span* (1796).
5. Croesus, the last king of Lydia (c. 560–546 B.C.), ruled a large part of Asia Minor. He had a reputation among the Greeks for incredible wealth.
6. "To each his own" (Latin).

They heard slippers shuffling, and Vasily Ivanovich appeared once again.

"Your room'll be ready for you in a little while," he exclaimed triumphantly. "Arkady . . . it's Nikolaich, isn't it? Here's a servant for you," he added, pointing to a closely cropped young boy wearing a blue caftan with worn-out elbows and someone else's boots. "His name's Fedka. Once more, I repeat, though my son forbids it, you mustn't expect too much. But he knows how to fill a pipe. You smoke, don't you?"

"Mostly cigars," Arkady replied.

"That's very sensible of you. I prefer cigars, too, but it's extremely difficult to obtain them in remote areas like this."

"Stop bemoaning your fate," Bazarov said, interrupting him again. "Why don't you sit here on the sofa and let me get a good look at you."

Vasily Ivanovich laughed and sat down. He looked a great deal like his son, but his brow was lower and narrower, his mouth somewhat wider, and he was constantly in motion, shrugging his shoulders as if his coat cut him under the arms, blinking, coughing, wiggling his fingers, while his son was marked by his casual immobility.

"Bemoaning my fate!" repeated Vasily Ivanovich. "Evgeny, don't think I'm trying to win our guest's sympathy by telling him we live in the boondocks. On the contrary, I'm of the opinion that for a thinking man there's no such thing as boondocks. At least I try, as far as possible, not to let any grass grow under my feet, as they say, not to fall behind the times."

Vasily Ivanovich pulled from his pocket a new yellow handkerchief that he'd managed to pick up when he ran to Arkady's room; waving it in the air, he continued, "I'm not even alluding to the fact that I, for example, not without considerable sacrifice on my part, put my peasants on the quitrent system and have given them land for sharecropping.[7] I considered this my duty; common sense dictates as much in this case, although other landowners don't even dream of such a solution. I'm talking about science, education."

"Yes. I see you have here the 1855 edition of *The Friend of Health*,"[8] remarked Bazarov.

"An old comrade sends it to me out of friendship," Vasily Ivanovich said hurriedly, "but even we, for example, have some idea of phrenology," he added, turning, however, more to Arkady and pointing toward the cupboard housing a small plaster head divided into numbered squares. "We've heard about Schönlein[9] and Rademacher[1] as well."

7. The technical term is *métayage*: a system of land cultivation under which peasants farmed the landowner's estate in return for a share of the crop.
8. A newspaper for doctors published in Petersburg from 1833 to 1869.
9. Johann Lukas Schönlein (1793–1864), a German doctor and professor of medicine.
1. Johann Gottfried Rademacher (1772–1849), a German doctor and follower of Philippus Paracelsus (1493?–1541), Swiss physician and alchemist who advocated the use of specific remedies for specific diseases.

"Do people out in this province of ours still believe in Rademacher?" Bazarov inquired.

Vasily Ivanovich cleared his throat.

"In this province of ours . . . Of course, you gentlemen know better; how could we possibly keep up with you? Why, you've come along to replace us. In my own time some humoralist named Hoffmann[2] and some vitalist called Brown[3] seemed ridiculous to us, but they too had their day. Someone new has taken Rademacher's place and you idolize him; but in twenty years or so, perhaps, they'll probably be making fun of him."

"I'll say this to console you," said Bazarov. "Nowadays we make fun of medicine in general and don't bow down before anyone."

"How can that be? Don't you want to become a doctor?"

"Yes, but one thing doesn't prevent the other."

Vasily Ivanovich poked his middle finger into his pipe, where a small amount of burning ash still remained.

"Well, perhaps, perhaps—I don't want to argue. Besides, what am I? A retired army doctor, *voyla-too*;[4] and now I've become an agronomist. I served in your grandfather's regiment," he said, turning once again to Arkady. "Yes, sir; yes, sir; I've seen quite a bit in my time, I have. I've been in society, known all sorts of people! I myself, the man you see before you now, have shaken hands and felt the pulse both of Prince Wittgenstein[5] and Zhukovsky![6] They were in the southern army, on the fourteenth of December,[7] you understand [here Vasily Ivanovich pursed his lips knowingly]. I knew each and every one of them. But my work lay elsewhere: know your lancet, and that's that! Your grandfather was a well-respected man, a true soldier."

"Confess, he was a real blockhead," Bazarov said lazily.

"Oh, Evgeny, don't say things like that! Mercy! . . . Of course, General Kirsanov wasn't one of those who . . ."

"Well, never mind him," Bazarov said, interrupting him. "As I was approaching the house, I was glad to see your birch grove; it's taken nicely."

Vasily Ivanovich grew animated.

"Just wait 'til you see my little garden! I planted each and every tree myself. There are fruit trees, berries, all sorts of medicinal herbs. No

2. Friedrich Hoffmann (1660–1742), a German doctor and humoralist who believed that illness was the result of an imbalance in the body's fluids or "humors."
3. John Brown (1735–88), an English doctor and vitalist who maintained that life is sustained by a vital principle distinct from all physical and chemical forces.
4. *Voilá tout:* "that's all" (French).
5. Prince Peter Wittgenstein (1768–1842), a field marshal in the Russian army who participated in the War of 1812 against Napoleon and commanded the southern army from 1818 to 1828.
6. Vasily Zhukovsky (1783–1852), a leading preromantic poet and translator.
7. A reference to the rebellion staged in Petersburg on December 14, 1825, by the members of the Society of Decembrists, a group of army officers.

matter how smart you young fellows are, old man Paracelsus[8] spoke the truth when he said: *in herbis, verbis et lapidibus*[9] . . . You know, I don't practice anymore, but two or three times a week I'm obliged to relive the past. Folks come to me for advice—I can't chase them away. Sometimes the poor come for my help. There aren't any doctors around here. Imagine, one of my neighbors, a retired major, also treats patients. So I asked whether he'd ever studied medicine . . . They reply, 'No, he hasn't; he does it more out of philanthropy . . . ' Ha, ha! Philanthropy! Eh? That's something! Ha, ha! Ha, ha!"

"Fedka! Fill me a pipe!" Bazarov said harshly.

"There used to be another doctor around here who once visited a patient," Vasily Ivanovich continued in some desperation, "but the patient was already *ad patres*;[1] the servant wouldn't let the doctor in, saying it was no longer necessary. The doctor hadn't expected that, was embarrassed and asked, 'Did your master hiccup before he died?' 'Yes, sir.' 'Did he hiccup a great deal?' 'A great deal.' 'Well, that's good,' he said and turned to leave. Ha, ha, ha!"

The old man was the only one laughing; Arkady managed to smile. Bazarov merely inhaled on his pipe. The conversation went on like this for about an hour; Arkady was able to slip away temporarily to his little room, which did turn out to be attached to the bathhouse, but was very clean and comfortable. At last Tanyusha came in and announced that dinner was served.

Vasily Ivanovich was the first to stand up.

"Let's go, gentlemen! Forgive me if I've bored you. Perhaps the mistress will satisfy you better."

Dinner, even though hastily prepared, turned out to be very good, even sumptuous; only the wine could be found wanting: it was almost dark sherry, purchased by Timofeich from a merchant he knew in town. It tasted not quite like copper, not quite like resin; the flies were also a bother. On ordinary days a servant boy used to chase them off by waving a large green branch; but on this occasion Vasily Ivanovich had sent him away for fear of being condemned by the younger generation. Arina Vlasevna had had time to dress up; she'd put on a tall cap with silk ribbons and a light blue patterned shawl. She began to cry once again as soon as she set eyes on her Enyusha, but her husband didn't even have to admonish her: she quickly wiped away her tears so as not to stain her shawl. Only the young people ate: the master and mistress had eaten their dinner some time before. Fedka served the meal, obviously encumbered by unfamiliar boots; he was aided by a woman named Anfisushka, who had a masculine face and only one eye, who performed the duties of housekeeper, poultry keeper, and laundress. All during

8. See above, p. 89, n. 1.
9. "In herbs, words and minerals" (Latin).
1. "To [one's] fathers," i.e., dead (Latin).

dinner Vasily Ivanovich paced the room with a completely happy, even blissful expression, talking about his serious misgivings concerning Napoleon's policies and the complexity of the Italian question.[2] Arina Vlasevna paid no attention to Arkady, failing to regale him with her hospitality. She supported her round face on her small closed fist. Her full, cherry red lips and the moles both on her cheeks and over her brows imparted a good-natured expression to her face. She never took her eyes off her son and sighed constantly; she desperately wanted to know how long he was going to stay, but was afraid to ask. "Well, what if he says only two days," she thought, and her heart almost stopped. After the main course Vasily Ivanovich disappeared for a minute and returned with an opened half-bottle of champagne. "Here," he exclaimed, "even though we live in the boondocks, we still have ways to celebrate special occasions!" He filled three goblets and a little wineglass, toasted the health of their "inestimable visitors," immediately downed his glass military style, and forced Arina Vlasevna to drink hers to the very last drop. When time came for preserves, Arkady, who didn't care for sweets, thought it his duty to sample four different kinds, all freshly made, all the more so since Bazarov flatly refused and promptly lit up a cigar. Tea was served—with cream, butter, and biscuits; then Vasily Ivanovich led them all into the garden to admire the beauty of the evening. Walking past a bench he whispered to Arkady, "This is where I love to sit and philosophize while watching the sun set: it suits an old hermit like me. Over there I planted a few of the trees beloved by Horace."

"What kind of trees?" Bazarov asked, overhearing.

"Why acacias . . . of course."

Bazarov began to yawn.

"I suppose it's time our travelers were nestled in the arms of Morpheus," observed Vasily Ivanovich.

"That is, it's time for bed!" Bazarov interjected. "That's a fair judgment. It *is* time."

Saying good night to his mother, he kissed her forehead; she embraced him and stealthily crossed him three times behind his back. Vasily Ivanovich accompanied Arkady to his room and wished him "the same kind of refreshing repose I enjoyed when I was your tender age." As a matter of fact, Arkady slept very well in his little room attached to the bathhouse: it smelled of mint, and two crickets took turns chirping soporifically behind the stove. Vasily Ivanovich left Arkady and returned to his study. Perching on the sofa at his son's feet, he hoped to have a nice chat with him, but Bazarov sent him away at once, saying that he wanted to sleep; but he didn't fall asleep until morning. Eyes wide open, he stared vindictively into the darkness: childhood memories had no

2. Italy's struggle for independence from Austria and for national unification was frequently discussed in the Russian press during the 1850s.

power over him; however, he still hadn't managed to rid himself of recent bitter impressions. Arina Vlasevna first prayed to her heart's content, then had a very long chat with Anfisushka, who stood as if rooted to the spot before her mistress, her solitary eye fixed on her, conveying in a mysterious whisper all her observations and speculations about Evgeny Vasilevich. The old woman's head was spinning from joy, the wine, and cigar smoke; her husband tried speaking with her, but gave up.

Arina Vlasevna was a genuine Russian noblewoman of the old school; she should have lived some two hundred years earlier, in the days of old Muscovy.[3] She was very devout and emotional, believing in all sorts of omens, fortune-telling, charms, and dreams; she believed in holy fools, house spirits, forest spirits, unlucky meetings, the evil eye, folk remedies, Maundy salt,[4] and the imminent end of the world; she believed that if on Easter Sunday the candles didn't go out during the midnight service, there'd be a good buckwheat harvest, and if a person looked at a mushroom, it wouldn't grow any bigger; she believed the devil liked to be near water, and that every Jew carried a bloodstain on his chest; she was afraid of mice, snakes, frogs, sparrows, leeches, thunder, cold water, drafts of air, horses, goats, redheaded people, and black cats; she regarded crickets and dogs as unclean animals; she didn't eat veal, pigeon, crayfish, cheese, asparagus, artichokes, rabbit, or watermelon because a cut watermelon reminded her of the head of John the Baptist; and she couldn't mention oysters without shuddering. She loved to eat, but maintained strict fasts; she slept ten hours out of every twenty-four and didn't go to bed at all if Vasily Ivanovich had a headache; she'd never read a single book, except for *Alexis, or the Cottage in the Forest*,[5] and she wrote only one—at most two—letters a year; but she certainly knew how to run a household, dry produce, and make preserves, even though she never touched anything with her own hands and in general preferred to remain seated in one place. Arina Vlasevna was very kind and, in her own way, not at all stupid. She understood that there were some people on earth who were supposed to give orders and other, simple folk who were supposed to take orders, so she showed no aversion to servility or prostrations; but she always treated subordinates politely and kindly, never let a begger go away empty-handed, and never condemned anyone outright, although she was partial to a little gossip from time to time. In her youth she'd been very attractive, played the clavichord, and spoken a little French; but over the course of considerable wandering with her husband, whom she'd married against her will, she'd put on weight and forgotten both her music and her French. She loved and

3. Ancient name of the Russian state.
4. A folk remedy for various ailments consisting of thickened kvass (traditional Russian beverage) mixed with salt and brewed on the Thursday of Easter week.
5. A sentimental novel (1788) by the French writer Ducray-Duminil (1761–1819), which was translated into Russian three times and became very popular in the early nineteenth century.

feared her son incredibly; she left the running of the estate to Vasily Ivanovich—and refused to interfere in any way: she used to groan, wave her handkerchief, and raise her eyebrows higher and higher in horror as soon as her husband began talking about the impending reforms and his own machinations. She was apprehensive, constantly anticipating some great misfortune, and used to cry whenever she thought about anything sad . . . Such women are now becoming much harder to find. God knows whether that's a good or a bad thing!

XXI

After getting out of bed, Arkady opened the window—the first thing he saw was Vasily Ivanovich. Dressed in an Oriental robe fastened at the waist with a very large handkerchief, the old man was digging energetically in his garden. He noticed his young guest; resting on his shovel, he exclaimed, "Good health to you! Did you sleep well?"

"Splendidly," replied Arkady.

"Here I am, you see, just like Cincinnatus,[6] preparing a bed for some late turnips. The time has come—thank the Lord!—when everyone should provide his own sustenance with his own hands. There's no need to rely on others; one must do one's own work. It seems Jean-Jacques Rousseau[7] was right. Half an hour ago, my good sir, you'd have seen me in a completely different situation. An old country woman was complaining of the gripes—that's her language; we call it dysentery; I . . . how can I best explain it? . . . I gave her a dose of opium; for another woman, I extracted a tooth. I offered her some ether . . . but she refused. All this I do *gratis—anamater.*[8] It's no wonder I do it: I'm a plebian, after all, *homo novus*[9]—not from a well-established family like my better half . . . Would you like to come out here in the shade and get a breath of fresh air before morning tea?"

Arkady went out to join him.

"Welcome once again!" Vasily Ivanovich said, raising his hand in military salute to the greasy skullcap covering his head. "I know you're used to luxury and pleasure, but even great men of the world aren't averse to spending a little time beneath a cottage roof."

"Good heavens," cried Arkady, "as if I were a great man of the world? Nor am I used to luxury."

"Pardon me, pardon me," Vasily Ivanovich objected with a kindly grimace. "Even though I've now been consigned to the archive, I've been around a bit too—I can tell a bird by its flight. I'm also something

---

6. Lucius Cincinnatus (519?–348 B.C.), legendary Roman patrician and statesman who retired to his farm after defeating various enemies of the Roman state.
7. Swiss-French philosopher and political theorist (1712–78), who, among many other things, advocated the virtues of the simple life and physical labor.
8. *Gratis*: "free" (Latin). *En amateur*: "as an amateur" (French).
9. "New man" (Latin).

of a psychologist and physiognomist. I daresay, if I hadn't had that talent, I'd never have made it—I'd have been lost, an insignificant man like me. I can say without compliments: the friendship between you and my son makes me very happy. I've just seen him; it's his custom, as you probably know, to get up very early and explore the area. Allow me to ask, have you known my Evgeny for long?"

"Since last winter."

"I see. Allow me to ask—but, perhaps you'd care to sit down? Allow me to ask, as a father in all candor, what do you think of my Evgeny?"

"Your son is one of the most remarkable men I've ever met," Arkady replied spiritedly.

Vasily Ivanovich's eyes suddenly opened wide, his cheeks flushed slightly. The shovel slid from his hands.

"So, you expect . . ." he began.

"I'm convinced," Arkady said, interrupting him, "a great future awaits your son and he'll make your name famous. I've been certain of that since our first meeting."

"What . . . what was that?" Vasily Ivanovich could hardly speak. An ecstatic smile parted his broad lips and remained fixed there.

"Would you like to know how we met?"

"Yes . . . and in general . . ."

Arkady began to tell the story and talked about Bazarov with more energy and enthusiasm than he had that evening when he danced the mazurka with Odintsova.

Vasily Ivanovich listened with great attention, blew his nose, twisted his handkerchief in both hands, coughed, ruffled his hair—and, at long last, couldn't stand it: he leaned over to Arkady and kissed him on the shoulder.

"You've made me absolutely happy," he said, still smiling broadly. "I must tell you . . . I idolize my son; as for the old woman: you know how mothers are! But I never express my feelings in his presence because he doesn't like it. He objects to all emotional outbursts; many people condemn him for such severity of character and consider it a sign of arrogance or lack of feeling; but it's not appropriate to judge people like him by ordinary standards, isn't that right? Someone else in his place, for example, would've been a constant drag on his parents. In our case, would you believe it, from the day he was born he's never taken an extra copeck from us, so help me God!"

"He's an unselfish man, an honest man," Arkady observed.

"Unselfish, indeed. What's more, Arkady Nikolaich, not only do I idolize him, but I'm also proud of him. My greatest ambition is that one day the following words will appear in his biography: 'Son of a simple regimental doctor, but one who was able to recognize his son's talents early and spared no expense for his education . . .' " The old man's voice broke off.

Arkady squeezed his hand.

"What do you think?" Vasily Ivanovich asked after a brief silence. "He won't achieve the fame you expect for him in medicine, will he?"

"Of course it won't be medicine, but even in that field he'll prove to be one of our most important scholars."

"In what then, Arkady Nikolaich?"

"It's hard to say now, but he'll be famous."

"He'll be famous!" repeated the old man and sank into thought.

"Arina Vlasevna summons you to tea," said Anfisushka, walking past with an enormous dish of ripe raspberries.

Vasily Ivanovich gave a start.

"Will there be chilled cream with the raspberries?"

"Yes, sir."

"Make sure it's chilled! Don't stand on ceremony, Arkady Nikolaich, do have some. Why hasn't Evgeny come?"

"I'm here," Bazarov's voice rang out from Arkady's room.

Vasily Ivanovich turned around quickly.

"Aha! You wanted to see your friend. You're late, *amice*;[1] he and I've already had a nice long chat. Now it's time for tea: your mother's calling us. By the way, I have to speak with you."

"What about?"

"There's a peasant here suffering from icterus . . ."

"You mean jaundice?"

"Yes, chronic and very obstinate icterus. I've prescribed centaury and St. John's wort,[2] made him eat carrots, given him soda; but all these are *palliative* measures; he needs something more effective. Even though you make fun of medicine, I'm sure you can give me some useful advice. We'll talk about it later. Now let's go have tea."

Vasily Ivanovich jumped up briskly from the bench and began singing something from the opera *Robert le Diable*:[3]

A law, a law, let's make a law,
To live for hap . . . for hap . . . for happiness.

"What remarkable vigor!" Bazarov observed, moving away from the window.

It was midday. The sun was burning behind a thin layer of solid whitish clouds. Everything was silent, only the cocks crowed boisterously in the village, arousing in any listeners a strange sensation of drowsiness and ennui; somewhere high above the treetops could be heard the unceasing plaintive screech of a fledgling hawk. Arkady and Bazarov lay in the shade of a small haystack, having spread several armfuls of dry, rustling, though still green, fragrant hay.

1. "Old fellow" (Latin).
2. Two plants believed to have medicinal properties.
3. A very popular five-act opera, *Robert the Devil* (1831), by the dramatic composer Giacomo Meyerbeer (1791–1864).

"That aspen over there," Bazarov began, "reminds me of my child-hood. It's growing at the edge of a pit left from a brick shed; back then I was convinced that both the pit and the aspen possessed magical powers: I was never bored near them. At the time I didn't understand that I wasn't bored because I was still a child. Well, now I've grown up, and the magic doesn't work anymore."

"How much time did you spend here all together?" asked Arkady.

"A couple of years in a row; then we moved around. We led a life of wandering, trudging around towns for the most part."

"Has this house been here long?"

"Yes. My maternal grandfather built it."

"Who was he, that grandfather of yours?"

"The devil only knows. Some second-major or other; he served under Suvorov[4] and kept talking about a march across the Alps. He was probably lying."

"So that's why a portrait of Suvorov hangs in your drawing room. I love little houses like yours; they're so old and cozy, and they have a special smell."

"It's from lamp oil and sweet clover," said Bazarov, yawning. "As for the flies in these sweet little houses—ugh!"

"Tell me," began Arkady after a brief silence, "were your parents strict with you when you were a child?"

"You see what sort of parents I have. They're not strict."

"Do you love them, Evgeny?"

"I do, Arkady!"

"They love you very much!"

Bazarov was silent for a while.

"Do you know what I'm thinking?" he said at last, placing his hands behind his head.

"No, what?"

"I'm thinking: my parents have a pretty good life! At sixty my father manages to keep busy, talks about 'palliative' measures, sees patients, treats his peasants generously—in a word, has a fine time. And my mother's all right: her day's full of all sorts of activities, 'oohs' and 'ahs,' she's no time to think; while I . . ."

"While you?"

"While I think: here I lie under a haystack . . . The tiny space I occupy is so small compared to the rest of space, where I am not and where things have nothing to do with me; and the amount of time in which I get to live my life is so insignificant compared to eternity, where I've never been and won't ever be . . . Yet in this atom, this mathematical point blood circulates, a brain functions and desires something as well . . . How absurd! What nonsense!"

---

4. Count Alexander Suvorov (1729–1800), a famous Russian field marshal whose last achievement was a well-executed retreat across the Swiss Alps during the French Revolutionary Wars (1798–99).

"Let me say that what you're arguing can be applied to all people in general . . ."

"You're right," said Bazarov, interrupting him. "I was trying to say that they, that is, my parents, are occupied, and don't worry in the least about their own insignificance; they don't give a damn about it . . . While I . . . I feel only boredom and anger."

"Anger? Why anger?"

"Why? What do you mean, 'Why'? Have you forgotten?"

"I remember everything, but I still don't think you've any right to be angry. You're unhappy, I agree, but . . ."

"Hey! Well, Arkady Nikolaevich, I see you understand love like all our modern young men: 'Here chick, chick! Here, chick, chick!' But as soon as the chick starts to approach, you run like hell! I'm not like that. But enough of this. What can't be helped shouldn't even be talked about." He turned over on his side. "Look! Here's a heroic ant dragging away a half-dead fly. Go on, brother, pull! Don't pay any attention to her resistance; take advantage of the fact that as an animal you have the right not to feel any compassion, unlike us, self-destructive creatures that we are!"

"You shouldn't say that, Evgeny! When have you tried to destroy yourself?"

Bazarov raised his head. "That's the only thing I'm proud of. I haven't destroyed myself, and no woman's going to destroy me. Amen! Finished! You won't hear another word about it from me."

Both friends lay there for a while in silence.

"Yes," began Bazarov, "man's a strange being. When you look from the side or from a distance at the empty life our 'fathers' led, you think: what could be better? You eat, drink, and know you're acting in the most proper, judicious manner. But no; ennui overcomes you. You want to have contact with people, even if it's only to abuse them, you still want to have contact."

"You have to organize your life so that each moment is significant," Arkady declared thoughtfully.

"Look who's talking! The significant, even though false, perhaps, is sweet, though one can also become reconciled to the insignificant . . . but petty squabbles, that's the calamity."

"Petty squabbles don't exist for a man if he chooses not to acknowledge them."

"Hmmm . . . you've just uttered an *inverted commonplace*."

"What? What do you mean by that?"

"Here's what: to say, for example, 'enlightenment is useful' is a commonplace; but to say 'enlightenment is harmful' is an inverted commonplace. It seems more impressive, but in reality it's the same thing."

"Where does truth lie, on which side?"

"Where? I'll answer you like an echo, 'Where?' "

"You're in a melancholy mood today, Evgeny."

"Really? The sun must've gotten to me, and one shouldn't eat so many raspberries."

"In that case, it wouldn't be a bad idea to have a little snooze," Arkady observed.

"Perhaps; but don't look at me. Everyone's face looks stupid when they're asleep."

"Does it really matter what people think of you?"

"I don't know how to reply. A real man shouldn't care; a real man is someone you don't have to think about, but someone who should be obeyed or despised."

"That's strange! I don't despise anyone," said Arkady after some thought.

"Whereas I despise so many people. You're a tender soul, so wishy-washy, how could you despise anyone? . . . You're timid, and don't rely enough on yourself . . ."

"And you," Arkady said, interrupting him, "do you rely on yourself? Do you have such a high opinion of yourself?"

Bazarov was silent.

"When I meet a man who can hold his own next to me," he said with slow deliberation, "I'll change my opinion of myself. Despise! Why, just today, for example, as we were going past our bailiff Philip's cottage—the one that's so fine and white—you said, 'Russia will attain perfection when the poorest peasant has a house like that and each one of us should help bring that about . . .' Meanwhile, I've conceived a hatred for the poorest peasant—Philip or Sidor—those for whom I'm supposed to jump out of my skin and who won't even thank me for it . . . Besides, what the hell do I need his thanks for? So, he'll be living in a fine white hut while I'm pushing up burdock; well, then what?"

"Enough, Evgeny . . . listening to you today, one would have to agree willy-nilly with those who reproach us for not having any principles."

"You sound like your uncle. There aren't any general principles—you haven't even figured that out yet—there are only sensations. Everything depends on them."

"How so?"

"It just does. Take me, for example: I advocate a negative point of view—as a result of my sensations. I find it pleasant to negate, my brain is so organized—and that's that! Why do I like chemistry? Why do you like apples? As a result of our sensations. It's all the same thing. People will never get any further than that. Not everyone will tell you this, and I might not even tell you another time."

"What? Is honesty also a sensation?"

"Indeed it is."

"Evgeny!" began Arkady in a sad tone of voice.

"Yes? What is it? Don't you like that?" Bazarov cut in. "No, friend! Once you've decided to mow everything down—go ahead and don't spare yourself! . . . But we've philosophized enough. 'Nature induces the silence of sleep,' Pushkin said."

"He said nothing of the sort," Arkady replied.

"Well, even if he didn't, he could've and should've, as a poet. By the way, he must've served in the military."

"Pushkin was never a soldier."

"Really? But on every page he writes, 'To battle, to battle! For the honor of Russia!' "

"What sort of nonsense are you fabricating? That's slander, anyway."

"Slander? So what? What a word you've brought up to frighten me! Whatever slander you hurl at someone, you can always be sure he deserves twenty times worse."

"Let's go to sleep!" Arkady said in some annoyance.

"With pleasure," replied Bazarov.

But neither felt like sleeping. Some hostile feeling invaded the hearts of both young men. Five minutes later they opened their eyes and regarded each other in silence.

"Look," said Arkady suddenly, "a dry maple leaf's broken off and is falling to earth; its movements are like those of a butterfly in flight. Isn't it strange? What's saddest and dead resembles what's most joyous and alive."

"Oh, Arkady Nikolaich, my friend!" cried Bazarov. "One thing I ask of you: no fine talk."

"I talk the way I know how . . . Besides, that's despotism on your part. A thought entered my head: why shouldn't I express it?"

"Right; and why shouldn't I express my thought? I consider such fine talk indecent."

"What's decent then? Swearing?"

"Aha! I see you really do intend to follow in your uncle's footsteps. That idiot would be so pleased if he could hear you!"

"What did you call Pavel Petrovich?"

"I called him an idiot, just as he deserves."

"Why that's outrageous!" cried Arkady.

"Aha! That's family feeling showing itself," Bazarov said serenely. "My observation is that it's firmly rooted in people. A man's prepared to renounce everything, to part with all his prejudices; but to admit, for example, that his brother who steals handkerchiefs is a thief—that's way beyond his power. As a matter of fact, it's *my* brother, *mine*—even if he's not a genius—how could it be possible?"

"It wasn't family feeling at all, but a simple sense of justice," Arkady objected contentiously. "But since you don't understand that feeling, you lack that *sensation*, you can't make any judgments about it."

"In other words: Arkady Kirsanov is too exalted for my comprehension—I bow down and hold my tongue."

"Enough, please, Evgeny; we might end up really quarreling."

"Oh, Arkady! Do me a favor, let's have a real quarrel once and for all—to the bitter end, to the death."

"But if we do, we might wind up . . ."

"Fighting?" Bazarov cut him off. "So what? Here, in the hay, such idyllic surroundings, far from the world and other people's eyes—it wouldn't really matter. But you'd be no match for me. I'd grab you by the throat at once . . ."

Bazarov extended his long, tough fingers . . . Arkady turned around and prepared, as if in jest, to resist . . . But his friend's face appeared so malicious, his twisted grin and gleaming eyes contained such an earnest threat, that Arkady felt an instinctive fear . . .

"Ah! So this is where you've got to!" Vasily Ivanovich's voice rang out at that very moment, and the old army doctor appeared before the young men, dressed in a homemade linen jacket, wearing a homemade straw hat. "I've been looking all over for you . . . But you've chosen an excellent spot and you're engaged in a splendid pursuit. Lying on the 'earth,' looking up at the 'heavens' . . . You know, there's special significance in that."

"I look into the heavens only when I want to sneeze," muttered Bazarov and, turning to Arkady, added in a low voice, "Pity he interfered."

"Well, enough of that," Arkady whispered and squeezed his friend's hand surreptitiously. But no friendship can survive such confrontations for very long.

"I look at you, my young interlocutors," Vasily Ivanovich said meanwhile, shaking his head, resting his folded arms on a cleverly designed stick of his own making with a Turk's head for a handle, "I look at you and can't help admiring you. There's so much strength in you, youth in full bloom, ability, talent! You're simply—Castor and Pollux!"[5]

"So that's where he's got to—mythology!" Bazarov declared. "You can tell right away that in his own day he was a great Latinist! Don't I recall you once won a silver medal for a composition?"

"Dioscuri, Dioscuri!" repeated Vasily Ivanovich.

"That's enough, father, don't be so self-indulgent."

"Every once and a while it's allowed," muttered the old man. "Besides, I was looking for you, gentlemen, not to pay you any compliments; in the first place, I wanted to let you know we'll be eating soon; in the second place, I wanted to warn you, Evgeny . . . You're a clever lad, you understand people, and you understand women; therefore, you'll forgive them . . . Your mother requested a church service to celebrate your coming home. You mustn't think I'm asking you to be present at the service; it's already over; but Father Aleksei . . ."

"The cleric?"

5. Twin heroes and inseparable friends in Greek mythology, also called the Dioscuri; probably both sons of Zeus.

"Yes, the priest; he's going to . . . dine with us . . . I didn't expect it and advised against it . . . but that's how it turned out . . . he didn't understand me . . . Well, and Arina Vlasevna . . . Besides, he's very nice and reasonable."

"He won't eat my portion of dinner, will he?" Bazarov asked.

Vasily Ivanovich began laughing.

"For heaven's sake, what're you saying?"

"That's all I care about. I'm prepared to sit down at table with any man."

Vasily Ivanovich adjusted his hat.

"I knew beforehand," he said, "you're above any prejudice. Here I am, an old man, sixty-two years old, and I don't have any either. [Vasily Ivanovich didn't dare admit he'd also desired the church service . . . He was no less devout than his wife.] But Father Aleksei really wants to make your acquaintance. You'll like him, you'll see. He's not opposed to playing cards, and even . . . this is strictly *entre nous* . . . smokes a pipe."

"Is that so? After dinner we'll sit down to a game of cards and I'll clean him out."

"Ha, ha, ha! We'll see! I wouldn't be so sure about that!"

"Really? So you're harking back to the good old days?" Bazarov said with particular emphasis.

Vasily Ivanovich's bronze cheeks turned dark red. "You should be ashamed of yourself, Evgeny . . . That's all over and done with. Well, yes, I'm prepared to admit in front of this *gentleman* here that I had a certain passion in my youth—that's true; I certainly paid for it! But it's very hot. Allow me to sit down with you. I'm not disturbing you, am I?"

"Not in the least," replied Arkady.

Vasily Ivanovich lowered himself into the hay with a grunt.

"Your present berth reminds me, my dear sirs," he began, "of my military life in bivouacs, dressing stations, somewhere like this next to a haystack, and we were grateful for it." He sighed. "I've gone through a great deal, a very great deal in my time. For example, if you'll allow me, I'll tell you an interesting story about the plague in Bessarabia."[6]

"For which you received the St. Vladimir Cross?"[7] Bazarov broke in. "We've heard it, we've heard it . . . By the way, why aren't you wearing it?"

"I told you I have no prejudices," Vasily Ivanovich muttered (only the day before he'd removed the red ribbon from his jacket), and he set about relating the story of the plague. "Why, he's fallen fast asleep," he

---

6. Originally part of Roman Dacia, conquered by the princes of Moldavia in the fourteenth century and ceded to Russia in 1812.
7. Military decoration and order established by Catherine the Great in 1792 and named for the first Russian grand prince of Kiev.

whispered suddenly to Arkady, pointing to Evgeny and winking good-naturedly. "Evgeny! Wake up!" he added in a loud voice. "Let's go eat . . ."

Father Aleksei, a large, fine figure of a man with thick, carefully groomed hair and an embroidered belt around his violet-colored silk cassock, turned out to be a most clever and resourceful fellow. He was the first to extend his hand to Arkady and Bazarov, as if realizing in advance they had no desire to receive his blessing; in general he behaved in an unconstrained manner. He didn't belittle himself, nor did he offend others; incidentally, he enjoyed a chuckle over seminary Latin and rose to the defense of his bishop; he drank two glasses of wine, but refused a third; he accepted a cigar from Arkady, but didn't smoke it, saying he'd take it home with him. The only thing slightly unpleasant about him was that from time to time he'd slowly and carefully raise his hand to capture a fly on his own face and sometimes squash them there. He sat down at the green card table, an expression of moderate satisfaction on his face, and ended up winning two rubles fifty copecks in paper money from Bazarov: in Arina Vlasevna's house there was no notion whatever of reckoning in silver . . . [8] She sat next to her son as before (she didn't play cards), resting her cheek on her little fist as before, and stood up only to arrange for some new delicacy to be served. She was afraid of displaying any affection for Bazarov; he provided no encouragement and appreciated no displays. Besides, Vasily Ivanovich had urged her not to "disturb" him. "Young folks don't much like that," he explained to her. (It goes without saying what sort of dinner was served that day: Timofeich had galloped off at the crack of dawn in search of some special Circassian beef; the bailiff had set off in another direction to fetch turbot, ruff, and crayfish; for the mushrooms alone, the peasant women had received forty-two copecks in copper coins.) But Arina Vlasevna's gaze, directed constantly at Bazarov, expressed not only devotion and tenderness; it also reflected sorrow, combined with curiosity and fear, as well as a humble reproach.

Bazarov, however, was in no mood to analyze what precisely was reflected in his mother's gaze; he rarely addressed her, and when he did, it was only with a brief question. Once he asked for her hand to bring him "good luck"; she gently placed her soft little hand on his large, tough palm.

"Well," she asked after a little while, "did it help?"

"Made it worse," he replied with an offhand laugh.

"He takes far too many risks," Father Aleksei intoned, as if with sympathy, and stroked his fine beard.

"It's Napoleon's rule, good father, Napoleon's rule," Vasily Ivanovich put in and led with an ace.

8. A silver ruble was worth three and a half times a paper ruble.

"That's what got him sent to St. Helena,"[9] Father Aleksei replied and trumped the ace.

"Wouldn't you like some black currant drink, Enyushechka?" asked Arina Vlasevna.

Bazarov merely shrugged his shoulders.

"No!" he said to Arkady the next day. "I'm leaving tomorrow. It's boring here; I feel like working, but can't. I'll go back to your place in the country where I left all my things. At least there I can lock my door. Here my father keeps telling me, 'My study's at your service—no one'll bother you'; but he doesn't leave me alone for a moment. And it's awkward trying to keep him out. Then there's my mother. I can hear her sighing through the wall, but when I go out to see her—I have nothing to say to her."

"She'll be very upset," Arkady said, "and so will he."

"I'll return."

"When?"

"On my way back to Petersburg."

"I feel most sorry for your mother."

"Why? Has she been plying you with berries, or what?"

Arkady lowered his eyes.

"You don't know your own mother, Evgeny. She's not only a splendid woman, she's really very clever. This morning she chatted with me for half an hour, and it was very sensible and interesting."

"She was probably going on all about me."

"It wasn't only about you."

"You may be right; an outsider can see things more clearly. If a woman can keep up a conversation for half an hour, that's a good sign. But I'm still leaving."

"It won't be easy to break the news to them. They talk all the time about what we'll be doing two weeks from now."

"It won't be easy. I don't know what possessed me to tease my father today: he had one of his peasants on quitrent flogged the other day— that was the right thing to do; yes, yes, don't look at me with such horror! It was the right thing to do because the peasant's a thief and a terrible drunkard; but my father never expected I'd be apprised of the facts, as they say. He was very embarrassed; now it turns out I'll have to upset him again . . . Never mind! He'll survive."

Bazarov said, "Never mind!"—yet a whole day went by before he decided to tell Vasily Ivanovich of his intention. Finally, as he was saying good night to him in the study, he uttered with a forced yawn, "Oh, yes . . . I almost forgot to tell you . . . Have them send our horses to Fedot's tomorrow for the relay, will you?"

9. A British island in the Atlantic where Napoleon was exiled in 1815 and died in 1821.

Vasily Ivanovich was astounded.

"Is Mr. Kirsanov leaving us, then?"

"Yes, and I'm going with him."

Vasily Ivanovich recoiled from the blow.

"You're leaving?"

"Yes . . . I have to. Please arrange for the horses."

"All right," muttered the old man, "horses for the relay . . . all right . . . but . . . but . . . why?"

"I have to call in at his place for a little while. Then I'll come back here."

"Yes! For a little while . . . All right." Vasily Ivanovich took out his handkerchief and blew his nose, bending over almost to the ground. "Well, it . . . it'll all be done. But I thought you'd stay here . . . longer. Three days . . . It's, it's a little short after three years, a little short, Evgeny!"

"I tell you, I'll be back soon. I have to go."

"Have to . . . Well, then. Above all, one must do one's duty . . . So, you want the horses sent on? All right. Of course, Arina and I didn't expect this. She's just requested some flowers from our neighbor to decorate your room. [Vasily Ivanovich didn't even mention the fact that every morning at daybreak he stood, his bare feet in slippers, conferring with Timofeich, and, with trembling fingers, would take out one worn bank note after another, enjoining him to make various purchases, placing special emphasis on tasty delicacies and red wine, which, as far as he could tell, the young men really enjoyed.] The main thing is—freedom; that's my rule . . . you mustn't be hindered . . . you mustn't . . ."

He suddenly fell silent and headed for the door.

"We'll see each other again soon, Father, really."

But without turning around, Vasily Ivanovich merely gestured in despair and left the room. Returning to his bedroom, he found his wife in bed and began praying in a whisper so as not to wake her. But she woke up anyway.

"Is that you, Vasily Ivanych?" she asked.

"Yes, Mother!"

"Are you coming from Enyusha? You know, I'm afraid he may not be comfortable sleeping on the sofa. I told Anfisushka to give him your old traveling mattress and some new pillows; I'd have given him our feather bed, but I seem to recall he doesn't like sleeping on anything too soft."

"Never mind, Mother, don't worry. He's fine. Lord, have mercy on us sinners," he continued his prayers in a low voice. Vasily Ivanovich felt sorry for his old wife; he didn't want to tell her that night what was in store for her.

Bazarov and Arkady left the next day. From early morning the entire house was plunged in gloom; Anfisushka kept dropping dishes; even Fedka was confused and ended up taking off his boots. Vasily Ivanovich fussed more than usual: he was obviously trying to put on a good show. He spoke in a loud voice and stamped his feet, but his face looked haggard and he kept avoiding his son's eyes. Arina Vlasevna wept quietly; she'd have broken down completely and lost all control of herself, if her husband hadn't spent two hours early that morning trying to dissuade her. When after repeated promises to return not later than in a month's time, Bazarov finally managed to tear himself away from the embraces that held him and climb into the coach; when the horses set off, the harness bells began to ring, and the wheels began to turn; when there was nothing left to see, the dust lifted, and Timofeich, stooped and tottering as he walked, crawled back to his room; when the old folks were left alone in their own little house, which now suddenly seemed shrunken and decrepit, Vasily Ivanovich, who for several moments continued bravely waving his handkerchief good-bye on the back porch, sank down on a chair, his head dropped to his chest. "He's forsaken us, forsaken us," he muttered, "forsaken us; he was bored here. Now I'm alone, completely alone!" he repeated several times, holding up his hand each time with his index finger erect. Then Arina Vlasevna went over to him and, leaning her gray head against his, said: "What's to be done, Vasya? A son's a piece cut off. He's like a falcon: he comes and goes whenever he likes; while you and I are like mushrooms growing in the hollow of a log: we sit side by side and never budge. Except that I'll always be here for you, as you will for me."

Vasily Ivanovich took his hands away from his face and embraced his wife, his helpmate, more firmly than he'd ever done in his youth; she comforted him in his grief.

XXII

In silence, only occasionally exchanging small talk, our friends arrived at Fedot's. Bazarov wasn't entirely satisfied with himself; Arkady was dissatisfied with him. In addition, he felt in his own heart that groundless grief familiar only to those very young. The coachman changed the horses and, climbing onto the box, asked, "Where to? Right or left?"

Arkady shuddered. The road to the right led into town, and from there toward home; the road to the left led to Odintsova's.

He glanced at Bazarov.

"Evgeny," he asked, "to the left?"

Bazarov turned away.

"What sort of stupid idea is that?" he muttered.

"I know it's stupid," replied Arkady. "But what does that matter? It wouldn't be the first time, would it?"

Bazarov pulled his cap down over his forehead.

"As you like," he said at last.

"To the left!" cried Arkady.

The coach headed in the direction of Nikolskoe. But, having decided to do something stupid, the friends maintained an even more stubborn silence than before and even seemed angry.

By the very way in which the butler met them on the steps of Odintsova's house, the friends realized they'd acted unwisely in yielding so suddenly to a passing whim. Obviously they hadn't been expected. They had to sit in the drawing room for rather a long time looking rather foolish. At long last Odintsova entered. She greeted them with her usual politeness, was surprised by their hasty return, and, as far as one could tell from her unhurried gestures and speech, was none too pleased by it. They hastened to explain that they'd merely called in along the way and would have to set off for town in about four hours. She confined herself to a slight exclamation, asked Arkady to convey her regards to his father, and sent for her auntie. The princess appeared looking very sleepy, which lent her wrinkled, old face an even more spiteful expression. Katya wasn't feeling very well and didn't emerge from her room. Arkady unexpectedly realized that he wanted to see Katya as much as he did Anna Sergeevna herself. The next four hours were spent in insignificant discussion of this and that; Anna Sergeevna both listened and talked without smiling. Only at the moment of their departure did any of her former affection seem to stir in her heart.

"I'm feeling rather depressed at the moment," she said, "but don't pay it any attention; come back again in a little while—I say this to both of you."

Bazarov and Arkady answered her with a silent bow, climbed back into their carriage, and, without stopping anywhere, headed home, to Marino, where they arrived safely the following evening. During the entire journey, neither one nor the other even mentioned Odintsova's name. Bazarov, in particular, hardly opened his mouth; he kept looking off to one side, away from the road, with a kind of embittered intensity.

In Marino everyone was very pleased to see them. The prolonged absence of his son had begun to worry Nikolai Petrovich; he gave a shout and began swinging his feet and bouncing on the sofa when Fenechka came running in with sparkling eyes to tell him of "the young gentlemen's" arrival; even Pavel Petrovich felt a certain pleasant agitation and smiled condescendingly as he shook hands with the returning travelers. Discussion and questions followed; Arkady spoke most of all, especially during supper, which lasted until long after midnight. Nikolai Petrovich ordered several bottles of porter, which had just been delivered from Moscow, and drank so much his cheeks turned red as raspberries and kept emitting not quite a childish, not quite a nervous laugh. The general sense of merriment was communicated to the servants as well. Dunyasha ran back and forth like a madwoman and kept slamming doors; meanwhile Peter, even at three o'clock in the morning, was still trying to strum a Cossack waltz on the guitar. The strings emitted a plaintive, pleasant sound in the still air, but, with the exception of a few brief initial grace notes, nothing resulted from the educated valet's efforts: nature had denied him musical talent, along with talent for anything else.

Meanwhile life at Marino hadn't been proceeding too smoothly; things were going badly for poor Nikolai Petrovich. His difficulties with the farm increased with every passing day—cheerless, senseless difficulties. Problems with the hired workers had become intolerable. Some demanded payment of their accounts or an increase; others left, even after receiving their wages in advance; horses fell ill; harnesses were worn out in no time at all; tasks were performed carelessly; the threshing machine ordered from Moscow turned out to be useless because of its enormous weight; another machine was ruined the very first time it was used; half the cattle shed burned down because a blind old woman, one of the house serfs, went out to fumigate her cow in windy weather carrying a burning ember . . . true, according to the testimony of the old woman, the difficulty arose from the fact that the master had decided to introduce some newfangled cheeses and dairy products. The bailiff grew lazy and even began gaining weight, as every Russian does when he comes upon "a bed of roses." To show his zeal, when he would catch sight of Nikolai Petrovich from a distance, he'd throw a stick at a passing piglet or threaten a half-naked urchin, but for the most part he just slept. The peasants on quitrent didn't make their payments on time and stole firewood; almost every night the watchman caught—and sometimes seized by force—peasants' horses grazing in the "farm" meadows. Nikolai Petrovich tried to establish monetary fines for any damages, but the matter usually ended when the horses were returned to their owners after a day or two of grazing on the master's land. To top it all, the peasants began quarreling among themselves: brothers demanded the redivision of their property because their wives couldn't coexist under the same roof; a fight would suddenly break out, everyone would jump to their feet, as if at a given signal, and rush to the office steps, often in a drunken state, with bruised faces, asking to see the master, demanding justice and reprisals; an uproar and clamor would ensue, the women's shrill shrieking mingling with the men's cursing. It was necessary to separate the feuding factions, shouting until one became hoarse, knowing full well it was impossible to arrive at a just solution. There weren't enough hands for the harvest: a neighboring landowner with a most benign countenance had agreed to supply him with reapers for two rubles an acre, and then cheated him in a most unabashed way; his own peasant women demanded exorbitant wages, while the grain went to seed; they were behind schedule with the mowing and the Board of Guardians[1] was

1. Organ of local government concerned with issues of trusteeship, foundling hospitals, and credit operations, including the mortgaging of estates.

threatening and demanding immediate payment in full of all interest due . . .

"I've no strength left!" Nikolai Petrovich exclaimed in despair more than once. "I can't fight with them myself, my principles won't allow me to summon the local police, and one can't accomplish anything without the fear of punishment!"

"*Du calme, du calme,*"[2] Pavel Petrovich would reply to this, while he himself would hum, frown, and tug at his mustache.

Bazarov kept himself away from all these "squabbles"; besides, as a guest, it wasn't his place to interfere in other people's affairs. The day after their arrival in Marino he set to work on his frogs, infusoria,[3] and chemical compounds, spending all his time on them. Arkady, on the other hand, considered it his duty, if not to help his father, then at least to display some willingness to help. He listened to him patiently and once even offered some suggestions, not so much to have them followed, but rather to show interest. Managing the estate didn't arouse any revulsion in him: he even used to dream about agricultural activity with pleasure, but at the present time other thoughts were swarming in his head. To his own astonishment, Arkady constantly thought about Nikolskoe; previously he'd merely have shrugged his shoulders if anyone had told him he could be bored under the same roof with Bazarov, and whose roof at that—his father's! But he really was bored and yearned to get away. He tried taking long walks to the point of exhaustion, but that didn't help. While chatting with his father on one occasion, he learned that Nikolai Petrovich had in his possession several rather interesting letters written some time ago to his late wife by Odintsova's mother; Arkady wouldn't leave him alone until he produced those letters. Nikolai Petrovich was forced to rummage through twenty boxes and trunks to find them. After obtaining these half-decayed documents, Arkady seemed to calm down, as if he now had a goal. "I say this to both of you," he whispered over and over to himself. "That's what she herself said. I'll go, I'll go, damn it all!" But he recalled their last visit, the chilly reception, his previous awkwardness, and was overcome by timidity. The "what the hell" attitude of youth, a secret desire to try his luck, put his own powers to the test, without anyone's protection, finally won out. Scarcely ten days had passed since his return to Marino when, on the pretext of studying how the Sunday schools[4] were functioning, he galloped off to town and from there to Nikolskoe. Constantly urging the driver on, he proceeded like a young officer advancing into battle: he was afraid and cheerful, breathless with impatience. "The main thing's not to think," he repeated to himself. The driver happened to be something of a daredevil; he stopped in front of every tavern and

2. "Be calm" (French).
3. Microscopic organisms found in decayed organic matter and stagnant water.
4. Established to further adult literacy first in Petersburg and Kiev in 1859, then in other cities and towns.

asked, "One for the road?" Or "What about one for the road?"—and, after consuming *one for the road*, he didn't spare the horses. There, at last, the high roof of the familiar house . . . "What am I doing?" suddenly flashed through Arkady's mind. "But I can't turn back now!" The troika of horses rushed on ahead, the driver whooping and whistling at them. Now the little bridge thundered beneath their hooves and wheels, then the alley of trimmed pine trees drew closer and closer . . . A girl's pink dress flashed against the dark green, a young face peeked out from beneath the light fringe of a parasol . . . He recognized Katya and she, him. Arkady had the driver stop the galloping horses; he leapt out of the carriage and went toward her. "It's you!" she said, gradually blushing all over. "Let's go see my sister; she's out in the garden; she'll be very glad to see you."

Katya led Arkady into the garden. The meeting with her struck him as a particularly happy omen; he was delighted to see her, as if she were family. Everything seemed to be working out splendidly: no butler, no formal announcement. At a turn in the path he caught sight of Anna Sergeevna. She stood with her back to him. Hearing his footsteps, she turned around slowly.

Arkady began to feel embarrassed again, but the first words she uttered quickly put him at ease. "Hello, you fugitive!" she said in an even, affectionate tone of voice and moved to greet him, smiling and squinting from the sun and wind. "Where did you find him, Katya?"

"Anna Sergeevna," he began, "I've brought you something you never expected . . ."

"You've brought yourself," she said. "That's best of all."

XXIII

After seeing Arkady off with sarcastic expressions of regret and letting him know that he was not in the least deceived about the real purpose of his journey, Bazarov eventually went off on his own: he was possessed by a passion for work. He no longer argued with Pavel Petrovich, all the more so because the latter assumed an excessively aristocratic demeanor in his presence and expressed his opinions more with sounds than words. On only one occasion was Pavel Petrovich about to enter the fray against the *nihilist* concerning the controversial question of noblemen's rights in the Baltic provinces,[5] but he suddenly stopped, and declared with cold politeness, "However, we can't really understand each other; at least I lack the honor of understanding you."

"Certainly not!" exclaimed Bazarov. "Man's in a position to understand everything—how the ether vibrates as well as what transpires on the sun; but he's in no position to understand how another person can blow his nose differently from the way he blows his own."

5. German landowners living in these provinces (Lithuania, Latvia, and Estonia) opposed the emancipation of the serfs.

"What? Is that supposed to be clever?" asked Pavel Petrovich and stalked out.

However, he sometimes asked permission to be present at Bazarov's experiments, and once even brought his sweet-smelling face, washed with the finest of soaps, close to the microscope to see how transparent infusoria swallow green specks of dust and carefully chew them using some very efficient little devices in their throat. It was Nikolai Petrovich who, much more frequently than his brother, visited Bazarov; he'd have come every day to "study," as he used to say, if the business of managing his estate hadn't kept him away. He didn't get in the young scientist's way: he sat somewhere off in a corner of the room watching carefully, from time to time allowing himself to ask a discreet question. During dinners and suppers he'd attempt to direct the conversation to physics, geology, or chemistry, since all other subjects, even those pertaining to agriculture, not to mention politics, could lead to mutual dissatisfaction, if not to direct confrontation. Nikolai Petrovich surmised that his brother's loathing for Bazarov hadn't diminished in the least. An insignificant episode, one among many, confirmed this assumption. Cholera began to make an appearance here and there in the neighborhood and even "carried off" two people from Marino itself. One night Pavel Petrovich endured a rather severe attack. He suffered until morning, but refused to call for Bazarov's assistance; when he saw him the next day, in reply to his question "Why wasn't I sent for?"—he replied, still looking very pale, but already cleanly shaved and immaculately brushed, "Don't I recall your declaring that you don't believe in medicine?" So the days passed. Bazarov worked stubbornly and glumly . . . Meanwhile in Nikolai Petrovich's house there was one creature to whom if he could not exactly open his heart, he was always glad to chat . . . That creature was Fenechka.

He used to meet her most often in the early mornings, in the garden or courtyard; he never went to her room, and only once did she come to his door to ask whether or not she should bathe Mitya. Not only did she trust him and have no fear of him, she actually felt freer around him and even behaved more naturally with him than with Nikolai Petrovich. It's hard to say why this was so, perhaps because she sensed Bazarov's lack of any aristocratic vestiges, any air of superiority that both attracts and repels. In her eyes he was both an excellent doctor and a simple man. Unembarrassed by his presence, she'd attend to her baby; once, when she suddenly felt dizzy and got a headache, she'd even accepted a spoonful of medicine from his hand. In Nikolai Petrovich's presence she seemed to avoid Bazarov; she did that not out of cunning, but out of a sense of decency. She was more afraid of Pavel Petrovich than ever; some time ago he'd begun following her and would appear unexpectedly, as if out of nowhere, behind her back, wearing his English suit, standing there with his immobile, watchful face, his hands in his pockets. "It gives me the chills," Fenechka complained once to Dunyasha; the latter sighed in reply and thought about another "unfeeling" man. Bazarov, without even suspecting it, had become the *cruel tyrant* of her heart.

Fenechka liked Bazarov; but he liked her, too. Even his face would change when he talked with her: it took on a cheerful, almost gentle expression, and a playful attentiveness was combined with his usual casual attitude. Fenechka grew more attractive with every passing day. There comes a time in the life of young women when they suddenly begin to unfold and blossom like summer roses; such a time had come for Fenechka. Everything contributed to it, even the intense July heat, then at its most extreme. Dressed in a light white dress, she herself appeared lighter and whiter: she didn't tan in the sun, but the heat, from which she couldn't protect herself, would turn her cheeks and ears a light pink, suffuse her whole body with gentle indolence, and be reflected in the dreamy languor of her pretty little eyes. She could hardly do any work; her hands would slip down into her lap. She could scarcely walk and constantly sighed and complained with comic helplessness.

"You ought to go swimming more often," Nikolai Petrovich said to her.

He'd built a large bathing place, covered with a canopy, at one pond that hadn't dried up completely.

"Oh, Nikolai Petrovich! You die from the heat getting there and die again on the way back. And there's no shade in the garden."

"It's true, there's no shade," Nikolai Petrovich replied, wiping his brow.

Once, at about seven o'clock in the morning, as Bazarov was returning from an outing, he came upon Fenechka in a lilac arbor that had long since flowered, but was still thick and green. She was sitting on a bench, wearing a white kerchief on her head as usual; next to her lay a large heap of red and white roses still wet from the dew. He greeted her.

"Ah! Evgeny Vasilich!" she said, raising the edge of her kerchief a little so she could look at him, and in so doing bared her arm to the elbow.

"What are you doing here?" asked Bazarov, sitting down next to her. "Are you making a bouquet?"

"Yes, for the breakfast table. Nikolai Petrovich likes it."

"But it's still a long time until breakfast. What a pile of flowers!"

"I've gathered them now because it'll soon be too hot and I won't be able to go out. This is the only time I can breathe. I've grown weak from all this heat. I'm even afraid I might be ill."

"What an imagination! Let me check your pulse." Bazarov took her hand, looked for a vein that was beating evenly, but didn't even start counting. "You'll live a hundred years," he said, letting go of her hand.

"Oh, God forbid!" she cried.

"Why? Don't you want to live a long time?"

"A hundred years! I have a grandmother who was eighty-five—what a martyr she was! Dark, deaf, hunched over, coughing all the time; she was only a burden to herself. What sort of life is that?"

"So it's better to be young?"

"Of course."

"Why is it better? Tell me!"

"Why? Why, when you're young, you can do everything—come, and go, and fetch, and you don't have to ask anyone . . . What could be better?"

"It doesn't matter to me whether I'm young or old."

"You say it doesn't matter? You really can't mean that."

"Judge for yourself, Fedosya Nikolaevna. What good's my youth to me? I live alone, all on my own . . ."

"That depends on you."

"It doesn't all depend on me! Someone should take pity on me."

Fenechka glanced sidelong at Bazarov but didn't say anything.

"What book do you have there?" she asked after a little while.

"This one? It's a scientific book, very difficult."

"You're always studying. Isn't it boring? You must know everything already."

"Obviously not everything. Try to read a bit of it."

"I won't understand a thing. Is it in Russian?" Fenechka asked, taking the heavily bound volume into her hands. "It's so thick!"

"It's in Russian."

"I still won't understand a thing."

"I don't care if you understand it. I want to watch you read. When you do, the tip of your nose wiggles very sweetly."

Fenechka, who was trying to decipher in a low voice the article "On Creosote" she'd opened up to, started laughing and put the book aside . . . It slipped from the bench onto the ground.

"I also like it when you laugh," Bazarov said.

"Enough of that!"

"I like it when you talk. It's like a babbling brook."

Fenechka turned her head away. "Oh, you!" she said, sorting through the flowers with her fingers. "Why should you listen to me? You've talked with such clever women."

"Ah, Fedosya Nikolaevna! Believe me, all the clever women in the world aren't worth your little elbow."

"Well, whatever will you think of next?" whispered Fenechka, clasping her hands.

Bazarov picked up the book from the ground.

"It's a medical book; why did you throw it down?"

"Medical?" repeated Fenechka and turned to him. "Do you know what? Since you gave me those drops, remember? Mitya sleeps so soundly! I don't know how to thank you; you're really very kind."

"As a matter of fact, doctors have to be paid," Bazarov remarked with a smile. "Doctors are mercenary, you know."

Fenechka raised her eyes to look at Bazarov, eyes that seemed even darker from the whitish reflection on the upper part of her face. She didn't know whether he was joking or not.

"If you like, with pleasure . . . I'll have to ask Nikolai Petrovich about . . ."

"You think I want money?" Bazarov interrupted her. "No, I don't want any money from you."

"What, then?" asked Fenechka.

"What?" repeated Bazarov. "Guess."

"I'm not very good at guessing."

"Then I'll tell you; I want . . . one of those roses."

Fenechka started laughing again and even clapped her hands, so amusing did Bazarov's request seem to her. She laughed and at the same time felt flattered. Bazarov stared at her intently.

"Please, if you like," she said at last. Bending down to the bench, she began sorting through her roses. "What color do you prefer, red or white?"

"Red, and not too big."

She straightened up.

"Here, take it," she said, but immediately pulled back her outstretched hand and, biting her lip, glanced at the entrance to the arbor, then pricked up her ears.

"What is it?" asked Bazarov. "Nikolai Petrovich?"

"No . . . he went out to the fields . . . and I'm not afraid of him . . . but Pavel Petrovich . . . I thought that . . ."

"What?"

"I thought I saw *him* there. No . . . it's no one. Here, take it." Fenechka gave Bazarov the rose.

"Why're you afraid of Pavel Petrovich?"

"He always frightens me. It's not what he says, but the way he looks at me. Besides, you don't like him either. Remember how you used to argue with him all the time? I don't even know what your quarrels were about, but I saw how you twisted him around your little finger . . ."

Fenechka demonstrated with her own hands how, in her opinion, Bazarov twisted Pavel Petrovich around his little finger.

Bazarov smiled.

"And if he started to gain the upper hand," he asked, "would you stand up for me?"

"How could I stand up for you? No one can gain the upper hand over you."

"You think? I know one hand that could knock me over with a finger, if it wanted to."

"Whose hand is that?"

"You really don't know? Smell how sweet this rose is, the one you just gave me."

Fenechka stretched out her little neck and brought her face close to the flower . . . The kerchief slipped from her head onto her shoulders, revealing a mass of soft, dark, shining, slightly disheveled hair.

"Wait a moment, I want to smell it with you," Bazarov said. Leaning over he planted a kiss firmly on her parted lips.

She shuddered, pushed him away with both her hands against his chest, but she pushed so weakly that he was able to renew and prolong his kiss.

A dry cough was heard behind the lilacs. Fenechka instantly retreated to the other end of the bench. Pavel Petrovich appeared, made a slight bow, and said with malicious despondence, "So you're here," and then withdrew. Fenechka immediately gathered all her roses and left the arbor. "That was wrong, Evgeny Vasilevich," she whispered as she went out. Her voice contained a note of genuine reproach.

Bazarov recalled another recent scene and felt both guilty and contemptuously annoyed. But he shook his head at once, ironically congratulating himself on his "formal admission into the ranks of womanizing Céladons"[6] and then returned to his own room.

Meanwhile Pavel Petrovich left the garden; walking slowly, he made his way to the woods. He remained there for rather a long time; when he came back to breakfast, Nikolai Petrovich inquired solicitously after his health because his face looked so dark.

"You know, I sometimes suffer from an excess of bile," Pavel Petrovich replied serenely.

XXIV

Two hours later he knocked at Bazarov's door.

"I must apologize for disturbing you during your scientific work," he began, sitting down on the chair near the window and resting both hands on his beautiful walking stick with an ivory handle (he usually took walks without a stick). "But I'm compelled to ask you to spare me five minutes of your time . . . no more."

"All my time is at your disposal," replied Bazarov, whose face rapidly changed expression as soon as Pavel Petrovich had crossed his threshold.

"Five minutes is all I need. I've come to put a question to you."

"A question? What about?"

"Be so good as to hear me out. At the beginning of your stay here in my brother's house, when I still afforded myself the pleasure of con-

6. Céladon is the womanizing hero of *L'Astrée* (pub. 1607–10) by the French pastoral novelist Honoré d'Urfé (1567–1625).

versing with you, I had the occasion to hear your opinions on many matters; but, as far as I can recall, neither between us nor in my presence was the subject of a duel ever discussed, that is, dueling in general. Allow me to inquire what opinion you hold on that subject."

Bazarov, who'd stood up to meet Pavel Petrovich, sat back down on the edge of the table and crossed his arms.

"Here's my opinion," he said. "From a theoretical standpoint, dueling is ridiculous; but, from a practical standpoint, well, that's a different matter."

"That is, you mean to say, if I've understood you correctly, no matter what your theoretical view of dueling, in practice you wouldn't allow yourself to be insulted without demanding satisfaction."

"You've divined my meaning entirely."

"Very good, sir. I'm very glad to hear you say that. Your words have removed any uncertainty . . ."

"Any indecision, you mean."

"It's all the same, sir; I express myself so I'll be understood; I'm no . . . seminary rat. Your words relieve me of a certain unpleasant obligation. I've decided to fight a duel with you."

Bazarov opened his eyes very wide.

"With me?"

"With you, absolutely."

"What on earth for?"

"I could explain the reason to you," Pavel Petrovich replied. "But I prefer to keep silent on that score. To my way of thinking, you're superfluous here; I can't stand you, I despise you, and if that's not enough . . ."

Pavel Petrovich's eyes were gleaming . . . Bazarov's eyes were also flashing.

"Very well, sir," he said. "Further explanations are unnecessary. You've taken it into your head to test your chivalric spirit on me. I could deny you that pleasure, but—so be it!"

"I'm sincerely grateful to you," replied Pavel Petrovich, "and now I hope you'll accept my challenge without forcing me to resort to violent measures."

"That is, leaving aside all allegory, without resorting to your walking stick?" Bazarov observed coolly. "That's entirely correct. There's absolutely no need for you to insult me. Nor would it be altogether safe for you to do so. You can remain a gentleman . . . I also accept your challenge as a gentleman."

"Splendid," replied Pavel Petrovich, placing the stick in the corner. "Now let's exchange a few words about the conditions of our duel; first I'd like to know if you consider it necessary to resort to the formality of a small quarrel to serve as a pretext for my challenge?"

"No, it's better to dispense with such formalities."

"That's what I think, too. I assume it would also be inappropriate to delve into the real reasons for our confrontation. We can't stand each other. What more is needed?"

"What more?" Bazarov repeated ironically.

"Concerning the actual conditions of our duel, since there won't be any seconds—after all, where would we find them?"

"Precisely, where would we?"

"Then I have the honor of proposing the following: we'll fight early tomorrow morning, let's say at six o'clock, beyond the grove, with pistols, at a distance of ten paces . . ."

"Ten paces? That's fine; we can despise each other at that distance."

"We could set it at eight paces," observed Pavel Petrovich.

"We could, why not?"

"We'll each fire twice; and, just in case, each of us will have a short note in his pocket blaming himself entirely for his own demise."

"I don't entirely agree with that," said Bazarov. "It sounds a bit like a French novel, somewhat unlikely."

"Perhaps. Still, you do agree it would be unpleasant to arouse any suspicion of murder?"

"I agree. But there's another way to avoid that grim outcome. We won't have seconds, but there could be a witness present."

"Who would that be, may I ask?"

"Why, Peter."

"What Peter?"

"Your brother's valet. He's a man who's attained the very summit of contemporary education and would fulfill the role with all the *comilfo*[7] required in such circumstances."

"You must be joking, my dear sir."

"Not at all. After considering my proposal, you'll see it's replete with common sense and simplicity. You can't hide a pig in a poke; I'll take it upon myself to prepare Peter in an appropriate manner and bring him along to the site of our bloody battle."

"You continue to jest," Pavel Petrovich said, getting up from his chair. "But after the generous acquiescence you've demonstrated, I've no right to complain . . . So, everything's been settled . . . By the way, you don't have any pistols, do you?"

"Where would I get pistols, Pavel Petrovich? I'm not a warrior."

"In that case, I can offer you my own. You may be sure I haven't fired them in the last five years."

"That's very comforting news."

Pavel Petrovich took his walking stick.

"Then, my good sir, all that remains is for me to thank you and allow you to return to your work. I have the honor of taking my leave."

7. *Comme il faut*: "appropriateness" (French).

"Until our next pleasant meeting, my dear sir," said Bazarov, seeing his guest out.

Pavel Petrovich left; Bazarov remained standing in front of the door and suddenly exclaimed: "Damn it all! So elegant and so stupid! What a farce we've just acted! That's how trained dogs dance on their hind legs. But it was impossible to refuse; he'd have thrashed me, and then . . . [Bazarov grew pale at the very thought of it, all his pride suddenly rearing up.] Then I'd have had to strangle him like a little kitten." He returned to his microscope, but his heart was pounding; the serenity required for scientific observation had disappeared. "He must've seen us today," he thought. "But can he really be intervening on his brother's behalf? What's so important about a kiss? There must be more to it. Bah! Could he be in love with her himself? Of course, he is; it's as clear as day. What a mess, just think! . . . Bad!" he concluded finally. "It's bad from whatever side you look at it. In the first place, I'll have to risk getting shot and I'll have to leave; then there's Arkady . . . and gentle old Nikolai Petrovich. It's bad, very bad."

That day was particularly quiet and uneventful. Fenechka was nowhere to be seen; she stayed in her little room, like a mouse in its hole. Nikolai Petrovich had a worried look. He was informed that some rust had appeared on his wheat, the crop on which he'd placed such great hope. Pavel Petrovich oppressed everyone, even Prokofich, with his frigid courtesy. Bazarov began writing a letter to his father, but tore it up and threw it under the table. "If I die," he thought, "they'll find out; but I won't die. No, I'll stick around for a while yet." He told Peter to report to him the next day at dawn for some important business; Peter thought he planned to take him along to Petersburg. Bazarov went to bed late and was tormented by disordered dreams all night . . . Odintsova whirled in front of him; she was his mother and was being followed by a little kitten who had black whiskers, and this kitten was Fenechka; Pavel Petrovich appeared to him as a large forest with which he'd still have to fight a duel. Peter woke him at four o'clock; he got dressed at once and left with him.

The morning was lovely, the air, fresh; small, dappled clouds stood like fleecy lambs in a clear, pale blue sky; light dew scattered on leaves and grass glistened like silver on spider webs; the damp, dark earth seemed to retain traces of the rosy dawn; the sky was filled with the songs of larks. Bazarov arrived at the grove, sat down in the shade at the edge, and only then explained to Peter what was expected of him. The educated valet was scared to death; Bazarov calmed him with the assurance that all he had to do was stand at a distance and watch. He wouldn't have to accept any responsibility. "Meanwhile," he added, "just think how important your role will be!" Peter wrung his hands in despair and hung his head; turning green, he leaned against a birch tree.

The road from Marino circled the little grove; it was covered with a light layer of dust, undisturbed since the day before by wheels or feet. Bazarov glanced down the road carelessly, tore off and chewed some blades of grass, and kept repeating to himself, "What stupidity!" The morning chill caused him to shudder once or twice . . . Peter regarded him gloomily, but Bazarov merely grinned: he was no coward.

The sound of horses' hooves rang out along the road . . . A peasant appeared from behind some trees. He was driving two horses harnessed together; going past Bazarov, he gave him a strange look without raising his cap, which, apparently, troubled Peter, striking him as a bad omen. "Looks like he got up early, too," thought Bazarov, "but at least he's going to work, while here we . . ."

"I think he's coming," Peter whispered all of a sudden.

Bazarov raised his head and saw Pavel Petrovich. Dressed in a light checked jacket with trousers as white as snow, he strode quickly along the road; under his arm he carried a box wrapped in green cloth.

"Excuse me, it seems I've made you wait," he said, nodding first to Bazarov, then to Peter, whom at this moment he treated a bit like a second. "I didn't want to wake my valet."

"Never mind, sir," replied Bazarov. "We just got here ourselves."

"Ah! All the better!" Pavel Petrovich said, glancing around. "No one in sight, no one to interfere . . . Shall we begin?"

"Indeed."

"I assume you don't require any further explanation?"

"Correct."

"Would you care to load?" asked Pavel Petrovich, removing the pistols from the box.

"No; you load while I measure off the distance. I have longer legs," added Bazarov with a grin. "One, two, three . . ."

"Evgeny Vasilich," muttered Peter with difficulty (shaking as if in a fever). "If you'll permit me, I'll move away."

"Four . . . five . . . Go on, brother, go on; you can even stand behind the tree and cover your ears, but don't close your eyes; and if anyone falls, come help him up. Six . . . seven . . . eight . . ." Bazarov stopped. "Enough?" he asked, turning to Pavel Petrovich, "or shall I add a few more?"

"As you wish," he replied, inserting a second bullet.

"Well, let's add a few more paces." Bazarov drew a line on the ground with the toe of his boot. "Here's the barrier. By the way: how many paces from the barrier will each of us stand? That's an important question as well. There was no discussion of this yesterday."

"I suggest ten," replied Pavel Petrovich, handing Bazarov both pistols. "Be so good as to choose."

"I will. You'll agree, Pavel Petrovich, our duel is so unusual as to be ridiculous? One need only look at the face of our second."

"You seek to make light of everything," replied Pavel Petrovich. "I don't deny the strange nature of our duel, but I consider it my duty to warn you that I intend to fight seriously. A *bon entendeur, salut!*"[8]

"Oh! I don't doubt we're determined to annihilate each other; but why not laugh and combine *utile* with *dulci*?[9] So, you speak to me in French, I reply in Latin."

"I intend to fight seriously," repeated Pavel Petrovich and went to take up his position. Bazarov, on his side, counted ten paces from the barrier and stopped.

"Ready?" asked Pavel Petrovich.

"Absolutely."

"We can begin."

Bazarov moved forward slowly, while Pavel Petrovich advanced toward him, his left hand in his pocket, the other gradually raising the barrel of the pistol . . . "He's aiming straight for my nose," thought Bazarov, "and he's squinting hard, the scoundrel! This is a most unpleasant sensation. I'll stare at his watch chain . . ." Something whizzed sharply past Bazarov's ear, and, at the same moment a shot rang out. "I heard it; that means I'm all right" flashed quickly through his mind. He took another step and without aiming squeezed the trigger.

Pavel Petrovich shuddered slightly and grabbed his thigh. A stream of blood trickled down his white trousers.

Bazarov tossed his pistol away and approached his opponent.

"Are you wounded?" he asked.

"You had the right to summon me to the barrier," Pavel Petrovich said. "The wound's not serious. According to our conditions, each of us still has one shot left."

"Well, forgive me, that can wait for another time," replied Bazarov, grabbing Pavel Petrovich, who'd begun to turn pale. "Now I'm no longer a duelist, but a doctor. First I must examine your wound. Peter! Come here. Peter! Where have you got to?"

"It's nothing at all . . . I don't need any assistance," Pavel Petrovich said haltingly," and . . . we must . . . once more . . ." He tried to give his mustache a tug, but his hand grew weak, his eyes rolled up, and he lost consciousness.

"What have we got here? A faint! What next?" Bazarov cried unwittingly, as he lowered Pavel Petrovich onto the grass. "Let's have a look!" He took out a handkerchief, wiped away the blood, and felt around the wound . . . "The bone's intact," he muttered through his teeth. "The bullet entered one muscle but not too far; the *vastus externus* has been hit. He'll be up and dancing in three weeks! . . . But fainting! Oh, these high-strung people are too much! Just look at his delicate skin!"

"Is he dead, sir?" Peter's quavering voice croaked from behind.

Bazarov looked around.

8. "Let he who has ears listen" (French).
9. "Sweet" and "useful" (Latin), from the famous treatise on poetic form *Ars Poetica* by Horace (65–8 B.C.).

"Go get some water, friend, as fast as you can; he'll outlive us both."

But the enlightened servant seemed not to understand these words and didn't budge. Pavel Petrovich opened his eyes slowly. "He's dying!" whispered Peter and began crossing himself.

"You're right . . . What a stupid face!" remarked the wounded gentleman with a forced smile.

"Get some water right away, you devil!" shouted Bazarov.

"There's no need . . . It was a momentary *vertige*[1] . . . Help me sit up . . . that's fine . . . This scratch only needs to be wrapped, and I'll make it home on foot, or else they can send the droshky[2] for me. Our duel, if you agree, need not be continued. You behaved honorably . . . today, note I said 'today.' "

"There's no need to dwell on the past," replied Bazarov. "As for the future, there's no point in worrying your head about that either, because I plan to leave here today. Now let me bind your leg; your wound isn't serious, but it's always better to stop the bleeding. First we must bring this creature back to his senses."

Bazarov shook Peter by the collar and sent him off for the droshky.

"Be sure not to scare my brother," Pavel Petrovich said to him. "Don't even think of telling him what's happened."

Peter ran off; while he went to fetch the droshky, the two opponents sat on the ground in silence. Pavel Petrovich tried not to look at Bazarov; he still didn't want to be reconciled with him; he was ashamed of his own arrogance and failure, ashamed of the whole business, even though he felt it couldn't have turned out better. "At least he won't be hanging around here any longer," he comforted himself. "Thank heaven for that." The silence persisted, painful and awkward. Both of them felt uncomfortable. Each was aware that the other understood him. Friends find that experience pleasant, but for enemies, it's extremely unpleasant, especially when they find it impossible either to reach any understanding or to go their separate ways.

"Did I tie the bandage too tight around your leg?" Bazarov asked finally.

"No, it's all right, it's fine," replied Pavel Petrovich. After a moment he added: "There's no fooling my brother. We'll have to tell him we quarreled over politics."

"Fine," said Bazarov. "You can tell him I insulted all Anglomaniacs."

"Splendid. What do you suppose that fellow's thinking about us now?" continued Pavel Petrovich, pointing to the same peasant who, a few minutes before the duel, had been driving his harnessed horses past Bazarov; now, going down the road, he "kowtowed" and doffed his cap at the sight of the "masters."

"Who knows?" replied Bazarov. "Most likely he's not thinking any-

1. "Dizzy spell" (French).
2. A low, open four-wheeled carriage in which passengers sit astride a narrow bench connecting the front and rear axles.

thing at all. The Russian peasant's just like the mysterious stranger that Mrs. Radcliffe[3] used to go on about at such length. Who can understand him? He doesn't even understand himself."

"Ah! So that's what you think!" Pavel Petrovich began and suddenly cried: "Look what that idiot Peter's gone and done! My brother's galloping toward us!"

Bazarov turned and saw the pale face of Nikolai Petrovich in the droshky. He jumped down before it had even stopped and rushed toward his brother.

"What's all this about?" he asked in an agitated voice. "Evgeny Vasilich, tell me, what's going on?"

"Nothing," replied Pavel Petrovich, "you've been disturbed for no reason. Mr. Bazarov and I had a little quarrel, and I've had to pay a small price for it."

"What was the cause of it, for God's sake?"

"How shall I put it? Mr. Bazarov referred disrespectfully to Sir Robert Peel.[4] I hasten to add, I'm completely to blame for everything, while Mr. Bazarov's behaved himself in an exemplary way. I challenged him."

"Good heavens, you're bleeding."

"Did you think I had water in my veins? But this bloodletting may even be good for me. Isn't that right, Doctor? Help me get into the droshky and don't give way to melancholy. I'll feel fine tomorrow. That's it; splendid. Drive on, coachman."

Nikolai Petrovich followed the droshky; Bazarov was going to remain behind . . .

"I must ask you to take care of my brother," Nikolai Petrovich said to him, "until another doctor can be summoned from town."

Bazarov nodded his head in silence.

An hour later Pavel Petrovich was already lying in bed with a proper bandage tied skillfully around his leg. The whole household was in a state of agitation; Fenechka didn't feel at all well. Nikolai Petrovich wrung his hands surreptitiously, while Pavel Petrovich laughed and made jokes, especially with Bazarov; he put on a fine white linen shirt, a fashionable morning jacket, and a fez; he didn't allow the curtains to be drawn and complained amusingly about the need to refrain from eating.

But toward evening he grew feverish and his head started to ache. The doctor arrived from town. (Nikolai Petrovich refused to listen to his brother, and Bazarov himself requested it. Bazarov spent the whole day in his own room, feeling bitter and angry, dropping in to see the patient for very brief visits; he happened to meet Fenechka a few times, but she scurried away from him in terror.) The new doctor prescribed cooling

---

3. Anne Radcliffe (1764–1823), a very popular writer of Gothic tales of mystery and intrigue.
4. English conservative statesman and prime minister (1788–1850) noted for his powerful oratory and persuasive character.

drinks, meanwhile confirming Bazarov's diagnosis that there was no danger of any kind. Nikolai Petrovich told him that his brother had accidentally wounded himself, to which the doctor replied, "Hmmm." But, when twenty-five rubles in silver were suddenly placed in the doctor's hand, he said: "You don't say! That sort of thing happens quite frequently, you know."

No one in the house got undressed or went to bed. Nikolai Petrovich kept tiptoeing in to look at his brother and left on tiptoe as well; Pavel would doze, moan a little, say to him, *"Couchez-vous,"*[5] and then ask for something to drink. Once Nikolai Petrovich had Fenechka bring him a glass of lemonade; Pavel Petrovich stared at her intently and emptied the glass. Toward morning the fever worsened a bit and he became slightly delirious. At first Pavel Petrovich uttered disconnected words; then he suddenly opened his eyes and, seeing his brother next to his bed, bending over him solicitously, he asked, "Nikolai, don't you think Fenechka has something in common with Nellie?"

"With what Nellie, Pasha?"

"How can you ask that? With Princess R.[6] Especially the upper part of her face. *C'est de la même famille.*"[7]

Nikolai Petrovich made no reply, but inwardly was amazed at the persistence of former passions in a man. "Just see when that's come to the surface," he thought.

"Ah, how I love that silly creature!" Pavel Petrovich moaned, sadly clasping his hands behind his head. "I won't let any insolent fellow touch her . . ." he muttered several moments later.

Nikolai Petrovich merely sighed; he didn't even suspect to whom these words might pertain.

Bazarov came in to see him around eight o'clock the next morning. He'd already managed to pack his belongings and free his frogs, insects, and birds.

"You've come to say good-bye to me?" Nikolai Petrovich asked, getting up to greet him.

"Exactly, sir."

"I understand and approve entirely. My poor brother's at fault, of course: he's been punished for it. He said he put you in an impossible position, leaving you no choice. I believe you found it impossible to avoid this duel, which . . . which, to a certain extent, can be explained by the persistent antagonism that exists between your respective views. [Nikolai Petrovich got a bit lost in his own words.] My brother's a man of the old school, hot-tempered and stubborn . . . Thank God it ended the way it did. I've taken all necessary precautions to prevent the news from spreading."

5. "Go to bed" (French).
6. See above, pp. 22–26.
7. "It's of the same stock" (French).

"I'll leave you my address in case of any consequences," Bazarov said in an offhanded manner.

"I trust there won't be any, Evgeny Vasilich . . . I'm very sorry your stay in my house had such . . . an ending. It's all the more upsetting that Arkady . . ."

"I'll most likely be seeing him," replied Bazarov; every sort of "explanation" and "declaration" always aroused impatience in him. "In case I don't, I ask that you give him my regards and beg him to accept my regrets."

When he learned of Bazarov's departure, Pavel Petrovich wished to see him and shake his hand. Even then Bazarov remained as cold as ice; he realized that Pavel Petrovich simply wanted to appear magnanimous. He didn't manage to say good-bye to Fenechka: he merely exchanged glances with her through the window. Her face looked sad to him. "Done for, no doubt!" he said to himself . . . "Well, she'll survive somehow!" On the other hand, Peter was so overcome he wept on his shoulder until Bazarov stifled his emotions by asking, "Do your eyes always drip water?" Dunyasha had to take refuge in the grove to hide her dismay. The party responsible for all this grief climbed into the cart, lit a cigar, and after some four versts, when, at a bend in the road, the Kirsanov estate, stretching in a long line with its new manor house, came into view for the last time, he merely spat, muttered: "Damned aristocrats!" and wrapped himself up in his overcoat.

Pavel Petrovich soon recovered, but had to stay in bed for almost a week. He endured his *captivity*, as he described it, rather well, except that he fussed a great deal over his toilette and insisted that everything be scented with eau de cologne. Nikolai Petrovich used to read to him from journals, Fenechka waited on him as before, bringing him bouillon, lemonade, soft-boiled eggs, and tea; but a secret terror would seize her each time she had to enter his room. Pavel Petrovich's unexpected action had frightened everyone in the house, her most of all; only Prokofich was undisturbed and described how in his day gentlemen used to fight duels, "but it was only noble gentlemen who fought between themselves, while upstarts like that one they'd have flogged in the stable for his insolence."

Fenechka's conscience hardly bothered her, but from time to time she was tormented by the real cause of the quarrel; besides, Pavel Petrovich would look at her in such a strange way . . . even when her back was turned toward him she still felt him staring at her. She grew thin from constant inner agitation and, as so often happens, became even more attractive.

Once—it was morning—Pavel Petrovich was feeling better and had been moved from his bed to the sofa; after inquiring about his health, Nikolai Petrovich set off for the barn. Fenechka brought him a cup of tea and, after placing it on the little table, was just about to leave. Pavel Petrovich detained her.

"Where are you off to, Fedosya Nikolaevna?" he began. "Do you really have things to do?"

"No, sir . . . yes, sir . . . I must go pour the tea."

"Dunyasha will do it if you're not there; sit here for a while with a sick man. Besides, I want to have a little chat with you."

Fenechka sat down in silence on the edge of the armchair.

"Listen," said Pavel Petrovich, tugging at his mustache. "I've been wanting to ask you something for a long time: why are you so frightened of me?"

"Me, sir?"

"Yes, you. You never look at me; it's as if your conscience wasn't clear."

Fenechka blushed, but glanced up at Pavel Petrovich. He seemed a bit strange and her heart began quivering softly.

"Your conscience is clear, isn't it?" he asked her.

"Why shouldn't it be?" she whispered.

"Any number of reasons! Besides, whom could you have wronged? Me? Unlikely. Other people here in the house? That's also hard to believe. My brother? But you love him, don't you?"

"I do."

"With all your heart and soul?"

"I love Nikolai Petrovich with all my heart."

"Really? Look at me, Fenechka [it was the first time he called her that . . .]. You know, it's a great sin to lie!"

"I'm not lying, Pavel Petrovich. If I didn't love Nikolai Petrovich there'd be nothing left for me to live for!"

"And you wouldn't trade him for anyone else?"

"Who would I trade him for?"

"Any number of people! Why, even for the gentleman who just left here."

Fenechka stood up.

"Good Lord, Pavel Petrovich, why are you tormenting me? What have I done to you? How can you say such a thing? . . ."

"Fenechka," said Pavel Petrovich in a somber voice, "I saw . . ."

"What did you see, sir?"

"There . . . in the arbor."

Fenechka turned red to her ears and the roots of her hair.

"How was I to blame for that?" she uttered with difficulty.

Pavel Petrovich raised himself up a little.

"You weren't to blame? No? Not at all?"

"Nikolai Petrovich is the only one in the world I love and ever will love!" Fenechka said with unexpected force, while sobs rose in her throat. "As to what you saw, I'll declare on Judgment Day that I'm not to blame and wasn't, and it'd be better for me to die right here and now than be suspected of doing such a thing to my benefactor Nikolai Petrovich . . ."

But at this point her voice failed her; at the same time she realized that Pavel Petrovich had seized her and was squeezing her hand . . . She looked at him and froze. He was even paler than before; his eyes were gleaming and, what was even more astonishing, a single, large tear was running down his cheek.

"Fenechka!" he said in a very strange whisper. "Love him, love my brother! He's such a good, kind man! Don't betray him for anyone in the world, don't listen to anyone else! Think what could be more terrible than not loving and not being loved! Never forsake my poor brother Nikolai!"

Fenechka was so astounded that her eyes dried and her terror disappeared. But imagine her surprise when Pavel Petrovich, Pavel Petrovich himself, brought her hand toward his lips and leaned over, without kissing it, merely emitting convulsive sighs from time to time . . .

"Good Lord!" she thought, "is he having some sort of attack? . . ."

At that very moment his whole desolate life was trembling inside him.

The staircase creaked under quick footsteps . . . He pushed her away and let his head drop back on the pillow. The door flung open—and a happy, fresh, ruddy Nikolai Petrovich appeared. Mitya, just as fresh and ruddy as his father, dressed only in a little shirt, was bouncing up and down on his father's chest, catching hold of the big buttons on his country coat with his bare little feet.

Fenechka simply threw herself at him, wound her arms around him and her son, and rested her head on his shoulder. Nikolai Petrovich was surprised: Fenechka, bashful and modest, never displayed any affection in the presence of a third party.

"What's the matter?" he asked. He glanced at his brother and handed Mitya to Fenechka. "You aren't feeling worse, are you?" he inquired, going up to Pavel Petrovich.

The latter buried his face in his cambric handkerchief.

"No . . . it's . . . nothing . . . On the contrary, I feel much better."

"You were in too great a hurry to move to the sofa. Where're you going?" added Nikolai Petrovich, turning to Fenechka; but she'd already slammed the door behind her. "I came to show you my little bogatyr;[8] he missed seeing his uncle. Why did she take him away? What's the matter with you? Something's happened in here, hasn't it?"

"Brother!" Pavel Petrovich announced solemnly.

Nikolai Petrovich shuddered. He felt terrified, but didn't understand why.

"Brother," Pavel Petrovich repeated. "Promise me you'll carry out one request of mine."

"What is it? Tell me."

"It's very important; in my opinion all the happiness of your life

8. A hero of legendary strength in Russian folklore.

depends on it. All along I've been thinking about what I want to say to you . . . Brother, fulfill your obligation, the obligation of an honest, generous man; end temptation and the bad example you're setting, you, the best of men."

"What do you mean, Pavel?"

"Marry Fenechka . . . She loves you; she's the mother of your son."

Nikolai Petrovich took a step back and flung his arms open wide.

"Is it you saying this, Pavel? You, whom I always considered the most implacable foe of such marriages? Is it you saying this? Surely you must know it was solely out of respect for you that I didn't fulfill what you justly describe as my obligation."

"You were wrong to respect me in this instance," Pavel Petrovich replied with a mournful smile. "I'm beginning to think that Bazarov was right when he accused me of aristocratism. No, dear brother, we've spent enough time putting on airs and worrying about what other people think: we've already become old and tranquil folk; it's time for us to put aside all vanity. Let's do our duty, precisely as you say, and let's see if we can achieve happiness in the bargain."

Nikolai Petrovich rushed to embrace his brother.

"You've opened my eyes once and for all!" he cried. "It's not for nothing I've always said you were the kindest, smartest man in the whole world; now I see you're as reasonable as you are magnanimous."

"Easy, easy," Pavel Petrovich said, interrupting him. "Don't hurt the leg of your reasonable brother, who, at age fifty, fought a duel like a young lieutenant. And so, it's all settled: Fenechka will be my . . . *belle-soeur.*"[9]

"My dear Pavel! But what will Arkady say?"

"Arkady? He'll be delighted, of course! Marriage isn't one of his principles; on the other hand, his sense of equality will be gratified. And, in fact, what do class distinctions matter *au dix-neuvième siècle*?"[1]

"Ah, Pavel, Pavel! Let me kiss you again. Don't worry, I'll be careful."

The brothers embraced.

"What do you think, shouldn't you tell her what you intend to do right away?" asked Pavel Petrovich.

"What's the rush?" Nikolai Petrovich replied. "You didn't mention it to her, did you?"

"Mention it? Me? *Quelle idée!*"[2]

"Well, that's splendid. First of all, you must get well. This won't run away from us; we must think about it, consider it . . ."

"But you've decided?"

"Of course I've decided, and I thank you from the bottom of my heart. I'll leave you now; you must get some rest. Any sort of excitement

9. "Sister-in-law" (French).
1. "In the nineteenth century" (French).
2. "What an idea!" (French).

can be harmful . . . We'll talk more about it. Go to sleep, my dear; God grant you good health."

"Why does he feel so grateful to me?" wondered Pavel Petrovich when left alone. "As if it didn't all depend on him! As soon as he gets married, I'll go somewhere far away, to Dresden or Florence and live there until I pass on."

Pavel Petrovich wiped his forehead with eau de cologne and closed his eyes. Lit by the bright daylight, his handsome, emaciated head resting on the white pillow looked like the head of a dead man . . . In effect, he was a dead man.

XXV

In the garden at Nikolskoe, Katya and Arkady were sitting on a turf seat in the shade of a tall ash tree; on the ground next to them lay Fifi, her long body forming that graceful curve sportsmen refer to as "a hare's lie." Both Arkady and Katya were silent; he held in his hands a half-open book, while she picked a few remaining crumbs of white bread from a basket and tossed them to a small family of sparrows that, with their characteristic timorous impudence, were hopping about and chirping at her feet. A faint breeze, rustling in the leaves of the ash, moved pale gold spots of light slowly back and forth across the dark path and Fifi's yellow back; Arkady and Katya were enveloped in deep shade; only occasionally did a bright streak gleam in her hair. They were both silent; but it was precisely the way they were silent, the way they sat there side by side, that made their trusting intimacy so apparent: each one seemed not to be thinking about the other, while secretly rejoicing in the other's proximity. Their faces had changed since last we saw them: Arkady appeared calmer, Katya, livelier and bolder.

"Don't you think," Arkady began, "that the *ash* tree[3] is very aptly named in Russian? No other tree is as light and translucent against the sky as it is."

Katya raised her eyes and said, "Yes," and Arkady thought: "She never reproaches me for using fine phrases."

"I don't like Heine,"[4] Katya said, indicating with her eyes the book Arkady was holding, "when he laughs or cries; I like him when he's pensive and sad."

"I like him when he laughs," remarked Arkady.

"Remnants of your satirical inclination showing through . . . ["Remnants!" thought Arkady. "If Bazarov could only hear that!"] Wait a bit, we'll remake you."

"Who'll remake me? You?"

---

3. The Russian word for the ash tree is *yasen'*, while the adjective *yasnyi* means "clear, bright."
4. Heinrich Heine (1797–1856), a German romantic poet and strong supporter of the ideals of the French Revolution.

"Who? My sister; Porfiry Platonovich, with whom you no longer quarrel; and Auntie, whom you escorted to church a few days ago."

"I couldn't refuse! And as far as Anna Sergeevna's concerned, you recall, she agreed with Bazarov about many things."

"My sister was under his influence at the time, just like you."

"Just like me! Have you decided that I've already freed myself from his influence?"

Katya was silent.

"I know," Arkady continued, "you never liked him."

"I can't pass judgment on him."

"You know something, Katerina Sergeevna? Every time I hear that, I don't believe it . . . There's no one about whom each of us can't pass judgment! It's merely an excuse."

"Well, then I'll say he . . . it's not exactly that I don't like him, but I feel he's totally different from me, and I'm different from him . . . and you're different from him, too."

"Why's that?"

"How can I explain it to you? . . . He's a predator, while you and I are domesticated."

"Am I domesticated?"

Katya nodded her head.

Arkady scratched behind his ear.

"Listen, Katerina Sergeevna: that's really an insult."

"Do you really want to be a predator?"

"No, not a predator, but strong and energetic."

"That doesn't come from wishing . . . Your friend didn't want to be like that, yet he has it in him."

"Hmmm! So you assume he exercised great influence on Anna Sergeevna?"

"Yes. But no one can keep the upper hand with her for very long," Katya added in a low voice.

"Why do you think that?"

"She's very proud . . . That's not what I wanted to say . . . she's very eager to maintain her own independence."

"Who isn't?" asked Arkady, while the question, "What use is it?" flashed through his head. "What use is it?" also flashed through Katya's head. When young people are together frequently and intimately, they constantly hit upon one and the same idea.

Arkady smiled; drawing slightly closer to Katya, he said in a whisper, "Admit it, you're just a little bit afraid of *her*."

"Of whom?"

"*Her*," Arkady repeated meaningfully.

"What about you?" Katya asked in turn.

"Me, too; notice I said *too*."

Katya threatened him with her finger.

"That surprises me," she began. "My sister's never been so favorably disposed toward you as she is now, much more so than on your first visit here."

"Is that so?"

"You haven't noticed? Doesn't it make you happy?"

Arkady became thoughtful.

"What have I done to deserve Anna Sergeevna's goodwill? Was it perhaps that I came bearing letters from your mother?"

"For that and for some other reasons I won't list."

"Why not?"

"I just won't."

"Oh! I know why: you're very stubborn."

"That's right."

"And observant."

Katya gave Arkady a sidelong glance.

"Does that make you angry, perhaps? What're you thinking about?"

"I'm wondering where you acquired those powers of observation you genuinely possess. You're so timid and distrustful, so removed from everyone . . ."

"I've lived alone for a long time: that forces you to become reflective. But am I really so removed from everyone?"

Arkady cast a grateful glance at Katya.

"That's all well and good," he continued, "but people in your position, that is, with your income, rarely have that gift; it's as hard for the truth to reach them, as it is for it to reach the tsar."

"But I'm not rich."

Arkady was amazed and didn't understand Katya immediately. "Why, of course," the thought suddenly occurred to him, "the estate belongs entirely to her sister!" That idea was not altogether unpleasant to him.

"You said that so well."

"What?"

"You said it well: simply, without embarrassment, without posturing. By the way, I imagine there must be something special, a particular kind of vanity in the feeling of a person who knows and says he's poor."

"I've never experienced anything of that sort, thanks to my sister; I mentioned my income simply because it seemed appropriate at the time."

"I see; but you must admit, you too possess a bit of that vanity we were just talking about."

"For instance?"

"For instance, you—forgive my question—you wouldn't marry a wealthy man, would you?"

"If I loved him very much . . . No, I think even then I wouldn't do it."

"Ah! You see!" cried Arkady. After waiting a little while, he added, "Why wouldn't you?"

"Because even our folk songs warn about unequal matches."

"Perhaps you want to dominate or . . ."

"Oh, no! Why? On the contrary, I'm ready to submit, but inequality is difficult to accept. However, to respect oneself and submit—that I understand, that's happiness. But a subservient existence . . . No, I've had enough of that."

"Enough of that," Arkady repeated after Katya. "Yes, yes," he continued, "it's not for nothing you're related to Anna Sergeevna; you're just as independent as she is, but you're more discreet. I'm sure you wouldn't ever be the first to express your feelings, no matter how strong or sacred they were . . ."

"How else could it be?"

"You're just as clever as she is; and you have just as much character as she does, if not more . . ."

"Don't compare me to my sister, please," Katya interrupted him hurriedly. "It's not at all to my advantage. You seem to have forgotten my sister is both beautiful and clever, and . . . you in particular, Arkady Nikolaevich, shouldn't say such things, especially with such a serious expression."

"Why me in particular? And why do you think I'm joking?"

"Of course, you're joking."

"You think so? What if I'm convinced about what I'm saying? What if I feel I've yet to express myself forcefully enough?"

"I don't understand you."

"Really? Well, now I see I've overestimated your powers of observation."

"How?"

Arkady made no reply and turned away, while Katya looked in her basket for a few more crumbs and began tossing them to the sparrows; but the swing of her hand was too strong, and the birds flew away before they could peck at the food.

"Katerina Sergeevna!" Arkady began suddenly. "It's probably all the same to you, but you should know that not only wouldn't I trade you for your sister, I wouldn't trade you for anyone else in the world."

He stood up and quickly walked away, as if frightened by the words that had just escaped his lips.

Katya dropped both hands and the basket into her lap; she lowered her head, her eyes following Arkady for a long time. Gradually a crimson flush covered her cheeks; but her lips didn't form a smile and her dark eyes expressed confusion and some other, still unnamed feeling.

"Are you alone?" Anna Sergeevna's voice rang out near her. "I thought you came out into the garden with Arkady?"

Katya slowly raised her eyes to her sister (elegantly, even exquisitely dressed, she was standing on the path and scratching Fifi's ears with the tip of her closed parasol), and said slowly, "I'm alone."

"I see that," her sister replied with a laugh. "Has he gone back to his room?"

"Yes."

"Were you reading together?"

"Yes."

Anna Sergeevna took hold of Katya's chin and raised her face.

"You didn't quarrel, I hope?"

"No," said Katya, gently removing her sister's hand.

"How solemnly you reply! I thought I'd find him here and propose he take a walk with me. He's always asking me. They've brought you some shoes from town; go try them on. Yesterday I noticed your old ones had worn out. In general you don't pay enough attention to such things, and you have such nice little feet! And your hands are so pretty . . . though a bit large, so you must make the most of your little feet. But you're certainly no coquette."

Anna Sergeevna continued farther down the path, her beautiful dress rustling lightly. Katya stood up from the bench; picking up her Heine, she also walked away—but not to try on the shoes.

"Charming little feet," she thought, slowly and lightly climbing the stone steps of the terrace baked by the sun. "Charming little feet, you say . . . Well, soon he'll be lying at these feet, won't he?"

But she immediately felt ashamed and quickly ran up the stairs.

Arkady was walking along the corridor toward his own room; the butler caught up with him and announced that Mr. Bazarov was sitting there waiting for him.

"Evgeny!" muttered Arkady, almost in fear. "Has he been here long?"

"He's just arrived and asked that he not be announced to Anna Sergeevna, but be shown right up to your room."

"Has something bad happened at home?" Arkady wondered, and hurriedly ran up the stairs and opened the door at once. Bazarov's appearance reassured him immediately, although a more experienced eye might have discerned in the still energetic, but haggard figure of his unexpected guest signs of internal agitation. With a dusty coat over his shoulders, a cap on his head, he was perched on the windowsill; he didn't stand even when Arkady flung himself on his neck with noisy exclamations.

"What a surprise! How on earth did you get here?" he said, bustling about the room like a man who imagines himself delighted and wishes to show that he is. "Is everything all right at home? Everyone's well, I hope."

"Everything's fine at home, though not everyone's well," Bazarov replied. "But stop your jabbering; have them bring me some kvass,[5] sit

<hr>

5. A traditional Russian beverage, slightly alcoholic, usually made from flour or dark rye bread soaked in water and malt.

down, and listen to what I have to say in a few, but I hope rather telling, phrases."

Arkady quieted down and Bazarov told him about his duel with Pavel Petrovich. Arkady was very surprised, even saddened; but he didn't think it necessary to say that; he merely asked whether his uncle's wound was serious or not. The wound was very interesting, indeed, but not from any medical point of view. He was forced to smile, even though he felt sick at heart and somehow ashamed. Bazarov seemed to understand him.

"Yes, friend," he said, "that's what it means to live with feudal types. You become one yourself and take part in chivalric tournaments. Well, sir, I've decided to head home 'to the fathers,' "[6] Bazarov concluded, "and along the way I stopped by here . . . to tell you all this, I would've said, if I didn't believe a useless lie was stupid. No, I stopped by here —the devil knows why. You see, it's sometimes useful for a man to take himself by the scruff of the neck and pull himself up like a radish from a row in the vegetable garden; I did that several days ago . . . I wanted to have one more look at what I was leaving behind, at the row in which I'd been planted."

"I hope these words don't refer to me," Arkady objected with some annoyance. "I hope you're not planning to leave *me* behind."

Bazarov stared at him intently, almost piercingly.

"Would that really upset you so much? It seems to me it's *you* who've left me behind. You're so fresh and pure . . . Your affair with Anna Sergeevna must be proceeding well."

"What affair with Anna Sergeevna?"

"Wasn't it because of her you came here from town, my little fledgling? By the way, how are the Sunday schools[7] getting on? Aren't you in love with her? Or have you already decided to be discreet about it?"

"Evgeny, you know I've always been honest with you; I can assure you, I can swear to you, you're mistaken."

"Hmmm! A new word," Bazarov observed in a low voice. "But you've got no reason to get excited; it doesn't matter to me. A romantic would say, 'I feel our paths are beginning to diverge'; while I merely say, we're fed up with each other."

"Evgeny . . ."

"My dear boy, it's no disaster. The world's full of things to get fed up with! Now I think it's time for us to say farewell. Since my arrival, I've felt really rotten, as if I'd been reading Gogol's letter to the wife of the governor of Kaluga.[8] Incidentally, I told them not to unhitch my horses."

"Good heavens, that's impossible!"

"Why so?"

---

6. A sarcastic and ominous reference to "*ad patres*"; see above, p. 91, n. 1.
7. See above, p. 109, n. 4.
8. A letter by the Russian writer Nikolai Gogol (1809–52) to A. O. Smirnova originally included in his conservative and sententious work *Selected Passages from Correspondence with Friends* (1847), but forbidden by the censor and not published until 1857.

"I'm not even thinking about myself: it'd be the height of rudeness to Anna Sergeevna, who'd certainly want to see you."

"Well, you're wrong about that."

"On the contrary, I'm sure I'm right," Arkady retorted. "And why're you pretending? It it's come to that, didn't you really stop here to see her?"

"That may be, but you're still wrong."

Arkady was right. Anna Sergeevna did want to see Bazarov and sent him an invitation through the butler. Bazarov changed his clothes before he went to see her: as it turned out, he'd packed a change of outfit so he could get to it easily.

Odintsova didn't receive him in the room where he'd abruptly confessed his love for her, but in the drawing room. She politely extended the tips of her fingers, but her face expressed unintended tension.

"Anna Sergeevna," Bazarov hastened to say, "first of all, let me set your mind at ease. Before you stands a mortal who's long since come to his senses and hopes that others have also forgotten his indiscretions. I'm going away for a long time; as you'll agree, I'm no tender creature, but I'd prefer not to carry away with me the thought that you'll remember me with repugnance."

Anna Sergeevna sighed deeply like a person who's just climbed to the top of a hill, and her face was enlivened with a smile. She extended her hand to Bazarov once again and responded to his handshake.

"Let's let bygones by bygones," she said, "all the more so since, in all honesty, I was at fault then, if not for flirting, then for something else. In a word: let's be friends just as we were before. That was only a dream, wasn't it? And who remembers dreams?"

"Who remembers them? Besides, love is . . . such a spurious feeling."

"Really? I'm so glad to hear that."

Thus Anna Sergeevna expressed herself, and thus Bazarov expressed himself; they both thought they were telling the truth. Was the truth, the whole truth, contained in their words? They didn't know, and the author knows even less. But a conversation ensued between them as if they believed one another completely.

Anna Sergeevna asked, among other things, what he'd been doing at the Kirsanovs. He was just about to tell her about his duel with Pavel Petrovich, but hesitated at the thought that she might think he was trying to appear interesting; he told her he'd spent all his time there working.

"And I," said Anna Sergeevna, "I was depressed at first, God knows why, and even thought about going abroad, just imagine! . . . But then it passed; your friend Arkady arrived and once again I returned to my old routine, resumed my usual role."

"What role is that, if I may ask?"

"The role of aunt, guardian, mother, whatever you want to call it. Incidentally, you know that formerly I never really appreciated your close friendship with Arkady Nikolaevich; I considered him rather insignificant. But now I've come to know him better and am convinced he's clever . . . The main thing is, he's young, so young . . . not like you and me, Evgeny Vasilich."

"Is he still so timid in your presence?" Bazarov asked.

"Was he ever?" Anna Sergeevna began, but after pausing a little, added: "Now he's more confident and talks to me. Before he used to avoid me. But I didn't seek out his company either. He's become good friends with Katya."

Bazarov was annoyed. "A woman can't help dissembling," he thought.

"You say he was avoiding you," he said with a cold grin, "but surely it's probably no secret to you that he was in love with you?"

"What? He, too?" burst forth from Anna Sergeevna's lips.

"He, too," repeated Bazarov with a humble bow. "Did you really not know that? Have I told you something new?"

Anna Sergeevna lowered her eyes.

"You're mistaken, Evgeny Vasilich."

"I don't think so. But perhaps I shouldn't have mentioned it." He added to himself, "And as for you, no more dissembling from now on."

"Why not mention it? But I suggest that here again you're attributing too much importance to a passing fancy. I'm beginning to suspect you're inclined to exaggerate."

"Let's not talk about it any more, Anna Sergeevna."

"Why not?" she replied, but then directed the conversation in a different direction. She still felt awkward with Bazarov, even though she'd told him, and she herself believed, that everything had been forgotten. Exchanging the simplest words with him, even joking, she experienced a slight sense of apprehension. Just as people on a steamship at sea chat and laugh in a carefree manner, as though they were on dry land, but if only the slightest interruption occurs, the least indication of something out of the ordinary, each and every face immediately assumes an expression of special alarm, testifying to the constant awareness of constant danger.

Anna Sergeevna's conversation with Bazarov didn't last very long. She became distracted, replied in an absentminded manner, and finally suggested they move into the main hall, where they found the princess and Katya. "Where's Arkady Nikolaevich?" the hostess inquired; after learning that he'd not been seen for more than an hour, she sent for him. He was not to be found right away: he'd made his way to the very depths of the garden and, resting his chin on clasped hands, sat there, lost in thought. They were deep and important, these thoughts of his, but not sad. He knew that Anna Sergeevna was alone with Bazarov, but felt none of his previous jealousy; on the contrary, his face was brightening slowly; he seemed to be surprised at something, delighted by it, and had made up his mind about it.

XXVI

The late Odintsov didn't care for innovations, but he tolerated "a certain play of ennobled taste"; consequently, in his garden, between the greenhouse and the pond, he built himself a structure resembling a Greek portico made of Russian bricks. In the rear blind wall of this portico or gallery, there were six niches for statues, which Odintsov had planned to order from abroad. These were supposed to represent: Solitude, Silence, Meditation, Melancholy, Modesty, and Sensitivity. Only one of them, the goddess of Silence, with her finger on her lips, had actually been delivered and set in place; but that same day some boys from the estate had broken the statue's nose, and even though a local plasterer had managed to provide her with a new one, "twice as good as the previous nose," Odintsov had ordered her removed. The statue turned up in a corner of the threshing barn, where it stood for many years, arousing superstitious horror among the peasant women. The front part of the portico had long since become overgrown with thick bushes; only the capitals of the columns could be seen above the abundant greenery. Inside the portico it was cool, even at midday. Anna Sergeevna didn't like visiting the place ever since she'd seen a grass snake there; but Katya came often to sit on a large stone bench under one of the niches. Surrounded by fresh scents and shade, she used to read, work, or surrender herself to absolute silence, a feeling probably familiar to everyone, the charm of which consists in a scarcely conscious, quiet attentiveness to the broad wave of life constantly flowing in and around us.

The day after Bazarov's arrival, Katya was sitting on her favorite bench and Arkady was once again sitting next to her. He'd asked her to accompany him to the portico.

There was about an hour left before breakfast; the dewy morning had already been replaced by the hot day. Arkady's face retained its expression of the previous day; Katya had a worried look. Her sister, right after tea, had summoned her to the study and, after some preliminary compliments, which always frightened Katya a bit, advised her to be more careful in her behavior with Arkady and particularly to avoid private conversations with him, which had apparently been noticed by Auntie and others in the household. In addition, Anna Sergeevna hadn't been in a very good mood the previous evening; even Katya felt some consternation, as if she were to blame for something. In acceding to Arkady's request, she told herself it would be the last time.

"Katerina Sergeevna," he began in a somewhat bashful, free-and-easy manner. "Since I've had the good fortune to reside in the same house with you, we've discussed many things, but there's still one very important . . . question . . . for me at least, which I haven't touched on. Yesterday you noted that I've been remade during my time here," he added, both catching and avoiding the inquisitive glance Katya was directing at him. "As a matter of fact, I have changed a great deal; you yourself know that better than anyone else—you, to whom I essentially owe this change."

"I? . . . To me? . . ." replied Katya.

"I'm no longer the haughty little boy I was when I came here," continued Arkady. "I've not reached the age of twenty-three for nothing; I still wish to be useful as I did before, to devote all my strength to the truth; but I'm no longer searching for ideals where I did previously; they're appearing to me . . . much closer at hand. Up to now I didn't understand myself; I set myself tasks beyond my powers . . . My eyes have recently been opened thanks to one feeling . . . I'm not expressing myself altogether clearly, but I hope you'll understand me."

Katya said nothing in reply, but stopped looking at Arkady.

"I suppose," he began again, but in a more excited tone of voice, while a chaffinch in the birch foliage above him burst into carefree song, "I suppose it's the obligation of every honest man to be entirely candid with those . . . those people who . . . in a word, those he's closest to; therefore I . . . I intend . . ."

But here Arkady's eloquence failed him; he lost his train of thought, stumbled, and was forced to fall silent for a moment; Katya still didn't raise her eyes. She seemed not to understand where all this was leading and kept waiting for something more.

"I foresee that I may surprise you," Arkady began, after mustering his strength again, "all the more so since this feeling relates in a certain way . . . in a certain way—mind you—to you. Yesterday, you may recall, you reproached me for a lack of seriousness," continued Arkady, looking like a man who's entered a swamp and feels as if he's sinking deeper and deeper with every step, but who still goes on in the hope he might soon get to the end of it. "This same reproach is often directed at . . . falls upon . . . young men, even when they no longer deserve it; and if I had more self-confidence . . . ["Help me, please help me!" Arkady thought in desperation, but Katya still wouldn't turn her head.] If I could hope for . . ."

"If only I could be sure of what you're saying," Anna Sergeevna's clear voice rang out at that very moment.

Arkady immediately fell silent and Katya grew pale. A little path ran right past the bushes that concealed the portico. Anna Sergeevna was walking along it, accompanied by Bazarov. Katya and Arkady couldn't see them, but heard their every word, the rustle of her dress, their breathing. They took several steps and stopped right in front of the portico, as if deliberately.

"Don't you see?" Anna Sergeevna continued. "You and I were mistaken; we're not all that young anymore, especially me; we've lived our lives, we're tired out; we're both—why pretend it's not so?—clever peo-

ple: at first we interested each other, our curiosity was aroused . . . but
then . . ."

"Then it fizzled," Bazarov inserted.

"You know that wasn't the cause of our separation. But whatever
happened, the main thing was we didn't need each other; there was too
much—how can I put it?—too much alike in us. We didn't understand
that at first. On the other hand, Arkady . . ."

"Do you need him?" asked Bazarov.

"Enough of that, Evgeny Vasilich. You say he's not indifferent to
me, and it's always seemed to me that he liked me. I know I could pass
for his aunt; but I don't want to hide from you the fact that I've begun
thinking about him more often. There's a kind of charm in that young,
fresh feeling . . ."

"The word *fascination* is more applicable in such circumstances,"
Bazarov said, interrupting her; a note of seething vexation could be
heard in his calm but hollow voice. "Arkady was very secretive with me
yesterday and didn't say anything about you or your sister . . . That's a
serious symptom."

"He's just like a brother to Katya," Anna Sergeevna said, "and I like
that about him, although perhaps I shouldn't permit such intimacy
between them."

"Are you saying that as . . . a sister?" Bazarov said, dragging out his
words.

"Naturally . . . But why are we standing here? Let's move on. This
is a strange conversation for us to have, isn't it? I'd never have expected
I'd be able to talk to you like this. You know I'm afraid of you . . . yet
at the same time I trust you because you're really a very kind person."

"In the first place, I'm not kind at all; in the second, I've lost all
importance for you, and you tell me I'm a kind person . . . That's just
like placing a wreath of flowers on a corpse's head."

"Evgeny Vasilich, we don't have the power to . . ." Anna Sergeevna
started to say, but the wind came up, rustled the leaves, and carried her
voice away.

"But you're free to . . ." Bazarov said after a short pause.

It was impossible to make out any other words; the footsteps died away
and everything became quiet.

Arkady turned to Katya. She was sitting in the same position, but her
head was hanging even lower.

"Katerina Sergeevna," he began, his voice trembling, his hands
clasped tightly together. "I love you irrevocably, forever and ever; I love
no one else but you. I wanted to tell you, find out your opinion, and
ask for your hand, because I'm not a wealthy man and feel I'm ready
to make any sacrifice . . . You're not answering? You don't believe me?
You don't think I'm serious? Just consider these last few days! Surely
you must be convinced by now that everything—understand what I

say—everything else has long since disappeared without trace. Look at me, say one word . . . I love . . . I love you . . . please believe me!"

Katya gave Arkady a bright and serious look and, after a long pause for thought, with scarcely a smile, said, "Yes."

Arkady jumped up from the bench.

"Yes! Katerina Sergeevna, you said, 'Yes'! What does that mean? That I love you, that you believe me? . . . Or . . . or . . . I dare not go on . . ."

"Yes," Katya repeated, and this time he understood her. He took hold of her lovely large hands; sighing with ecstasy, he pressed them to his heart. He was hardly able to stand and merely repeated, "Katya, Katya . . ." while she wept innocently, laughing softly at her own tears. He who's never seen such tears in the eyes of a beloved has yet to experience the degree to which, totally consumed by gratitude and shame, a man can be happy on earth.

The next day, early in the morning, Anna Sergeevna summoned Bazarov to her study and with forced laughter showed him a folded piece of writing paper. It was a letter from Arkady: he was asking for her sister's hand in marriage.

Bazarov read through the letter quickly and made an effort not to display the malicious feeling welling up immediately inside him.

"So that's how it is," he said. "And it seems that as recently as yesterday, you supposed he loved Katya like a brother. What do you intend to do now?"

"What do *you* advise me to do?" Anna Sergeevna asked, continuing to laugh.

"Well, I suppose," replied Bazarov also with a laugh, even though he didn't feel at all cheerful and didn't want to laugh any more than she did, "I suppose you should give the young couple your blessing. The match is a fine one in all respects; Kirsanov has a considerable income, he's his father's only son, and the father's a good fellow who won't object."

Odintsova paced around the room. Her color alternated between pink and pale.

"You think so?" she asked. "Well then? I don't see any obstacles . . . I'm happy for Katya . . . and for Arkady Nikolaich. Naturally I'll wait for his father's reply. I'll send word to him myself. But it turns out I was right yesterday when I said we were both too old . . . How is it I didn't foresee this? That surprises me!"

Anna Sergeevna began laughing once again and immediately turned away.

"Young people today have become awfully sly," Bazarov observed and also started laughing. "Good-bye," he said after a brief pause. "I hope this matter's concluded in the best possible way; I'll enjoy it from afar."

Odintsova quickly turned to face him.

"Are you really leaving? Why shouldn't you stay *now*? Do stay . . . it's nice talking to you . . . like walking along the edge of an abyss. At first you're timid, but then you feel more courageous. Do stay."

"Thanks for the offer, Anna Sergeevna, and for the flattering opinion of my conversational skills. But I find I've already spent too much time in spheres alien to my nature. Flying fish can survive in the air only for a short while; soon they've got to flop down into the water. Allow me to return to my own element."

Odintsova looked at Bazarov. A bitter smile was tugging at his pale face. "This man used to love me!" she thought; she felt sorry for him and extended her hand with sympathy.

But he understood her, too.

"No!" he said, taking a step back. "I may be a poor man, but up to now I've never accepted charity. Good-bye, madame; I wish you good health."

"I'm sure we'll be seeing each other again," Anna Sergeevna said with an unintentional movement.

"Anything can happen!" replied Bazarov; he bowed and left.

"So, you've decided to make a nest for yourself?" he said to Arkady that same day, squatting as he packed his suitcase. "Well, it's a fine thing to do. But there was no reason to be so underhanded about it. I expected things to take a completely different direction. Perhaps you yourself were taken aback by it?"

"I really didn't expect anything like this when we separated," replied Arkady. "But why are you being so underhanded now when you say, 'It's a fine thing you do'—as if I didn't know your views on marriage?"

"Hey, my dear friend!" Bazarov said. "The things you say! You see what I'm doing: it turns out there's empty space in my suitcase and I'm stuffing hay into it. That's just how it is in the suitcase of our lives; it doesn't matter what you stuff in, as long as there's no empty space. Please, don't be offended: you probably recall my former opinion of Katerina Sergeevna. Other young ladies pass for being clever merely because they can sigh cleverly; but your young lady can stand up for herself, so much so she'll have you under her thumb—well, that's as it should be." He slammed the top of the case shut and stood up from the floor. "Now I say once again in farewell . . . because there's no reason to deceive ourselves: we're saying good-bye forever, and you know that too . . . You've behaved sensibly; you're not made for our bitter, tart, lonely existence. There's no arrogance in you, no malice; there's only youthful audacity and youthful fervor; that's not commensurate to our task. You aristocrats can never get any further than noble submission or noble indignation, and all that's nonsense. You, for instance, you won't fight—yet you think you're a fine fellow—but we want to fight.

What of it? The dust we raise will blind your eyes, our mud will splatter you, but you haven't reached our level; you admire yourself unconsciously, take pleasure in abusing yourself; but we find all this boring —give us someone else! We've got to smash someone else! You're a fine fellow, but you're still a soft, liberal gentleman—*eh vollatoo*,[9] as my father would say."

"Are you saying good-bye forever, Evgeny?" asked Arkady sadly. "Have you nothing else to say to me?"

Bazarov scratched the back of his head.

"I do, Arkady, I do have something else to say to you, but I won't say it because it's romanticism—that is, getting sugary. You just go and get married as soon as you can; fix up your nest and have lots and lots of children. They'll be smart enough to be born at a better time than you and me. Hey! I see the horses are ready. It's time! I've said good-bye to everyone . . . Well, then, shall we embrace?"

Arkady threw himself on the neck of his former mentor and friend, and tears literally gushed from his eyes.

"That's what it means to be young!" Bazarov said serenely. "But I'm relying on Katerina Sergeevna. Just wait and see how she'll comfort you!"

"Farewell, brother!" he said to Arkady, after climbing into the cart; pointing to a pair of jackdaws sitting side by side on the stable roof, he added, "There you are! Study that example!"

"What does that mean?" asked Arkady.

"What? Are you really that weak in natural history or have you forgotten that the jackdaw's the most respectable family bird? Let that be an example to you! . . . Farewell, signor!"

Bazarov was telling the truth. While talking with Katya that evening, Arkady forgot all about his mentor. He'd already begun to submit to her; Katya felt this and wasn't at all surprised. The next day he was supposed to leave for Marino to see Nikolai Petrovich. Anna Sergeevna didn't want to get in the young couple's way, and it was only out of a sense of propriety that she didn't leave them alone for too long. She magnanimously kept the princess away from them; the old woman had been reduced to a fit of tears by news of the impending marriage. At first Anna Sergeevna was afraid that the sight of their happiness might be too difficult for her to bear; but it turned out to be the complete opposite: it not only failed to oppress her, but even interested her, mellowed her at long last. Anna Sergeevna was both gladdened and saddened by this fact. "Apparently Bazarov was right," she thought, "it was curiosity, mere curiosity, love of serenity, and egoism . . ."

"Children!" she said aloud to herself. "Tell me, is love an imaginary feeling?"

---

9. *Et voilà tout*: "and that's all" (French).

But neither Katya nor Arkady even understood her. They avoided her; the conversation they'd overheard accidentally wouldn't leave their minds. But Anna Sergeevna soon calmed them down; that wasn't too hard for her to do: she herself calmed down.

XXVII

Bazarov's old parents were all the more delighted with their son's sudden arrival since it was so unexpected. Arina Vlasevna was so flustered and scurried around the house so much that Vasily Ivanovich compared her to a "partridge": the cropped tail of her short jacket actually did make her look a bit like a bird. Meanwhile he himself mumbled and chewed the amber mouthpiece of his pipe; clutching his neck with his fingers, he twisted his head as if checking to see that it was attached properly and suddenly opened his broad mouth and laughed without ever emitting a sound.

"I've come to stay with you for six whole weeks, old man," Bazarov said to him. "I want to work, so please don't disturb me."

"You'll even forget what I look like, that's how much I'll disturb you!" replied Vasily Ivanovich.

He kept his promise. After installing his son in his study again, not only did he keep himself hidden away, but he also kept his wife from making any unnecessary demonstrations of affection. "You and I, my dear woman," he said to her, "pestered Enyusha too much on his first visit here: now we have to be smarter." Arina Vlasevna agreed with her husband, but gained very little from it because she saw her son only at the table and was absolutely afraid to talk to him. "Enyushenka!" she'd start to say, and before he'd even time to turn around, she was already fingering the laces of her handbag and would mutter: "Never mind, it's nothing, I was only . . ." Then she'd go off to find Vasily Ivanovich and, resting her cheek on her hand, would say to him, "My dear, how can I find out what Enyusha would like for dinner today, cabbage soup or borsch?"[1] "Why didn't you ask him yourself?" "I'd be pestering him!" But Bazarov soon stopped locking himself in: the fever to work had *deserted* him and been replaced by dreary boredom and vague restlessness. A strange lethargy could be detected in all his movements; even his step, usually forceful and decisively bold, was different. He stopped taking walks alone and began seeking company; he took tea in the living room, wandered around the garden with Vasily Ivanovich, and smoked his pipe with him "in peace and quiet"; he even inquired once about Father Aleksei. At first Vasily Ivanovich was overjoyed by this change, but his joy was short-lived. "Enyusha's breaking my heart," he complained to his wife in secret. "It's not that he's dissatisfied or angry; that wouldn't mean a thing. He's embittered and gloomy—that's what's so terrible. He's always silent—it'd be better if he'd berate us; he's growing

1. Traditional Russian soup made with beets, cabbage, and potatoes, among other ingredients.

thin and his color is poor." "Good Lord!" whispered the old woman, "I'd like to put an amulet around his neck, but he wouldn't let me." Several times Vasily Ivanovich tried in a most careful manner to question Bazarov about his work, his health, Arkady . . . But Bazarov replied unwillingly and carelessly; once, noticing that his father's conversation seemed to be slowly leading up to something, he said to him in annoyance: "Why are you always tiptoeing around me? That's even worse than what you were doing before." "Well, well, well, I didn't mean anything!" poor Vasily Ivanovich hastened to reply. His political allusions were just as unproductive. Once, having mentioned progress in connection with the impending emancipation of the serfs, he hoped to arouse his son's sympathy: "Yesterday I was coming past the fence and overheard our local peasant lads: instead of singing a folk song, they were bawling out some romance:[2] 'The true time has come, my heart is full of love . . .' That's progress for you."

Sometimes Bazarov would set off for the village and, in his usual mocking manner, enter into conversation with some peasant. "Well, brother," he'd say to him, "expound your views on life to me: after all, they say you have all the strength, the future of Russia is yours, the new epoch in history will begin with you—you'll give us real language and laws." The peasant would either say nothing at all or utter a few phrases such as, "Well, we're like . . . also, because, that is . . . it's how it is, about, the bounds." "Tell me what the peasant *mir*[3] is all about?" Bazarov would ask, interrupting him. "Is it the same *mir* that rests on three fishes?"

"It's the earth that rests on three fishes, sir," the peasant would explain reassuringly, in a patriarchal-magnanimous singsong voice, "but against ours, that is, the *mir*, as everyone knows, it's the landowner's will; because you're our fathers. And the stricter the master, the better for the peasant."

On one occasion, after listening to this kind of thing, Bazarov shrugged his shoulders contemptuously and turned away, while the peasant returned to his house.

"What was he wanting?" asked another peasant, middle-aged and sullen, from a distance, standing on the threshold of his hut, who'd overheard the conversation with Bazarov. "Was it the arrears, or what?"

"Not the arrears, my friend!" the first peasant replied, and his voice no longer had any trace of that patriarchal singsong quality; on the contrary, it contained a note of offhand severity. "He was just blabbing, felt like wagging his tongue. He's a gentleman, you know; you think he understands anything?"

"How could he?" replied the other peasant. Shoving back their caps

2. The spread of nineteenth-century "popular culture" among the people threatened to replace authentic folk culture.
3. The Russian village commune—see above, p. 42, n. 5; the word also means "world" and thus gives rise to the confusion Bazarov exploits. The peasant assures him that it's the world, not the commune, that rests on three fishes (as Russian folk tradition had it).

and tugging their belts, they both began talking about their own needs and wants. Alas! Bazarov, who'd shrugged his shoulders contemptuously, who thought he knew how to talk to peasants (so he'd boasted in that argument with Pavel Petrovich), that same self-confident Bazarov didn't even suspect that in their eyes he was still something of a laughing-stock . . .

However, he finally found something to do. Once in his presence Vasily Ivanovich was bandaging a peasant's wounded leg, but the old man's hands were trembling and he was unable to deal with the strips of cloth; his son helped him and from that time on began assisting him in his practice, even though he never stopped making fun of the treatments he advocated and of his father, who'd immediately administer them. But Bazarov's ridicule didn't upset Vasily Ivanovich in the least; it even comforted him. Holding his greasy dressing gown across his stomach with two fingers and smoking his pipe, he listened to Bazarov with pleasure; the more malicious his son's quips, the more good-naturedly did he laugh, displaying every last one of his blackened teeth. He even quoted these sometimes stupid or meaningless remarks; for example, in the course of several days, for no good reason, he'd keep repeating, "Well, that's the last straw!" merely because his son, after hearing that he was going off to a morning liturgy, had used that expression. "Thank heavens! He's no longer so depressed!" he whispered to his spouse. "You should've seen how he abused me today!" On the other hand, the fact that he had such an assistant made him ecstatic and filled him with pride. "Yes, yes," he'd say to some peasant woman in a man's coat and horn-shaped headdress,[4] as he handed her a bottle of Goulard's extract[5] or a jar of white ointment, "my dear, you should thank God every minute of the day that my son's visiting us: now you're being treated with the most scientific, most up-to-date methods, do you understand that? Even Napoleon, emperor of the French, doesn't have a better doctor." But the peasant woman, who'd come to complain that she felt "hoisted by the gripes" (the meaning of which words, however, even she was unable to explain), merely bowed and reached into her bosom, where she'd stashed four eggs wrapped in the end of a towel.[6]

Bazarov once even pulled a tooth for a passing peddler selling cloth; even though the tooth was really quite ordinary, Vasily Ivanovich preserved it as a rare specimen. Showing it to Father Aleksei, he constantly repeated, "Just look at those roots! What strength that Evgeny has! The peddler almost jumped up straight in the air . . . I think if it's been an oak tree instead of a tooth, he'd have pulled that out, too!"

"Most praiseworthy!" said Father Aleksei at last, not knowing what to reply or how to escape the rapturous old man.

4. The *kichka* was the headdress worn by married peasant women.
5. A remedy (*Aqua vegetomineralis Goulardi*) named for the French physician Thomas Goulard (1720–90), who invented it.
6. I.e., as a payment for the doctor's services.

On one occasion a peasant from the neighboring village brought his brother, who was sick with typhus, to see Vasily Ivanovich. Lying face-down on a straw litter, the unfortunate man was dying; dark spots already covered his body and he'd long since lost consciousness. Vasily Ivanovich expressed his regret that no one had thought of seeking medical assistance sooner and declared that there was no hope of saving him. In fact the peasant was unable even to get his brother back home: he died in the cart along the way.

Some three days later Bazarov entered his father's room and asked if he had any strong caustic.

"I do; what for?"

"I have to . . . cauterize a cut."

"Whose?"

"Mine."

"What do you mean, yours? How so? What cut? Where?"

"Right here on my finger. Today I went to the village—you know, the one from which they brought that man with typhus. For some reason they wanted to have an autopsy performed, and I hadn't done one in a long time."

"Well?"

"Well, I asked the local doctor if I could; and, well, I cut myself."

Vasily Ivanovich suddenly turned completely pale; without saying a word, he rushed to the cupboard and returned at once with a piece of strong caustic in his hands. Bazarov wanted to take it and leave.

"For God's sake," said Vasily Ivanovich, "let me do that myself."

Bazarov grinned.

"Never miss a chance to practice your trade!"

"Please don't joke. Show me your finger. The cut's not too big. Is this painful?"

"Press harder; don't be afraid."

Vasily Ivanovich finished.

"What do you think, Evgeny, wouldn't it be better to burn it with a hot iron?"

"That should've been done sooner; now, as a matter of fact, even the caustic's of no use. If I'm infected, it's already too late."

"What do you mean . . . too late?" Vasily Ivanovich could hardly utter the words.

"I'll say it is! It's already more than four hours since it happened."

Vasily Ivanovich cauterized the cut a little longer.

"Didn't the local doctor have any caustic?"

"No."

"My God, how can that be? A doctor—and he doesn't have such an essential thing!"

"You should've seen his lancets," said Bazarov and left the room.

Throughout that evening and during the course of the whole next day, Vasily Ivanovich resorted to any possible pretext for entering his son's room; although he never mentioned the wound and even tried talking about peripheral matters, he still stared so intently into his son's eyes and scrutinized him so anxiously that Bazarov lost all patience and threatened to leave. Vasily Ivanovich gave him his word not to disturb him, all the more so since Arina Vlasevna, from whom he'd naturally concealed everything, had begun to pester him, wanting to know why he couldn't sleep and what was wrong with him. He held out for a few days, although his son's appearance, which he continued to monitor on the sly, wasn't much to his liking . . . but on the third day at dinner he couldn't endure it. Bazarov sat there looking down at his plate, not touching any of his food.

"Why aren't you eating, Evgeny?" he asked, his face assuming a most casual expression. "The food's well prepared, isn't it?"

"I don't feel like it, so I'm not eating."

"Don't you have any appetite? What about your head?" he added in a timid voice. "Does it ache?"

"Yes. Why shouldn't it ache?"

Arina Vlasevna sat up straight and pricked up her ears.

"Please don't be angry, Evgeny," continued Vasily Ivanovich, "won't you let me check your pulse?"

Bazarov stood up.

"Without even checking my pulse, I can tell you I have a fever."

"And shivers?"

"And shivers. I'm going to lie down; you send me some lime flower tea. I must've caught a cold."

"That's why I heard you coughing last night," said Arina Vlasevna.

"I caught a cold," repeated Bazarov and moved away.

Arina Vlasevna set about preparing the tea from lime flowers, while Vasily Ivanovich went into the next room and tore his hair in silence.

Bazarov didn't get up at all that day and spent the whole night in a heavy, semiconscious torpor. Around one o'clock in the morning, he made an effort to open his eyes and saw before him in the lamplight his father's pale face and ordered him to go away; he obeyed, but immediately crept back in on tiptoe and, half-hidden by the cupboard doors, stared relentlessly at his son. Arina Vlasevna didn't go to bed either; leaving the door to the study slightly open, she kept going in to see "how Enyusha was breathing" and to have a look at Vasily Ivanovich. All she could see was his motionless, hunched-over back, but even that afforded her some relief. In the morning Bazarov tried to get up; his head started spinning and his nose began bleeding; he lay down again. Vasily Ivanovich attended him in silence; Arina Vlasevna came in to ask him how he was feeling. He replied, "Better," and turned toward the wall. Vasily Ivanovich motioned his wife away with both hands; she bit her lip to keep from crying and left the room. Everything in the house suddenly seemed to grow darker; everyone's face fell and a strange silence prevailed; a boisterous rooster was carried away from the yard to the village, unable to understand for the longest time why he was so mistreated. Bazarov continued lying there, facing the wall. Vasily Ivanovich put several questions to him, but these queries exhausted Bazarov, and the old man fell silent in his armchair, only occasionally cracking his knuckles. He went out into the garden for a few moments, stood there like a statue as if overwhelmed by some inexplicable consternation (a look of consternation never left his face the whole time), and returned to his son once again, trying to avoid his wife's inquiries. At last she grabbed him by the hand and feverishly, almost threateningly, demanded, "What's wrong with him?" Then he came to his senses and forced himself to smile at her in reply; but, to his own horror, instead of a smile, he emitted a strange laugh. That morning he sent for a doctor. He thought it necessary to inform his son so he wouldn't get angry.

Bazarov suddenly turned around on the sofa, stared at his father slowly and intently, and asked for something to drink.

Vasily Ivanovich gave him some water and managed to feel his forehead. It was burning with fever.

"Old man," began Bazarov in a hoarse and deliberate voice, "things don't look very good. I'm infected and in a few days you'll be burying me."

"Evgeny!" he whispered, "what're you saying? Good Lord! You've caught a cold . . ."

"Enough of that!" Evgeny said, interrupting him without hurrying. "A doctor isn't allowed to talk like that. You know I've got all the symptoms of infection."

"What symptoms . . . of infection, Evgeny? . . . Mercy!"

"Then what's this?" Bazarov said, and raising the sleeve of his shirt, he showed his father the ominous red blotches appearing on his arm.

Vasily Ivanovich shuddered and froze with fear.

"Let's assume," he said at last, "let's assume . . . if . . . even if it's some kind of . . . infection . . ."

"*Pyaemia*,"[7] his son prompted him.

"Well, yes . . . something like . . . an epidemic . . ."

"*Pyaemia*," Bazarov repeated sternly and distinctly. "Or have you already forgotten your textbooks?"

"Well, yes, yes, whatever you say . . . Still, we're going to cure you!"

"Not on your life! But that's not the point. I never expected to die so soon; to tell you the truth, it's a most unpleasant circumstance. You and Mother must now make the most of your strong faith; here's a chance to put it to the test." He drank down a little more water. "I want to ask you one thing . . . while my head's still working. You know

---

7. An infection caused by the presence of pus-producing microorganisms in the bloodstream.

tomorrow or the day after my brain will tender its resignation. Even now I'm not too sure I'm expressing myself clearly. When I was lying there before, I seemed to see red dogs running all around me and you pointing at me as if I were a woodcock. Just like I was drunk. Can you understand me well?"

"Good heavens, Evgeny, you're speaking just as you should."

"All the better; you told me you sent for a doctor . . . You did that to comfort yourself . . . now comfort me: send someone to fetch . . ."

"Arkady Nikolaevich?" the old man interrupted.

"Who's Arkady Nikolaevich?" asked Bazarov, as if lost in thought. "Oh, yes! That fledgling! No, don't bother him; he's become a jackdaw. Don't be surprised, it's not delirium just yet. Send someone to fetch Odintsova, Anna Sergeevna; she's a landowner who lives nearby . . . Do you know her? [Vasily Ivanovich nodded his head.] Tell her that Evgeny Bazarov sends his greetings and wants her to know he's dying. Will you do that?"

"Yes, I will . . . But is it really possible you're going to die, Evgeny? . . . Judge for yourself! Where will justice be found afterward?"

"I don't know; but send someone to fetch her."

"I will right away, and I'll write to her myself."

"No, why? Tell her I send greetings, nothing else's needed. Now I'm going to return to my dogs. It's odd! I want to focus on death, but nothing comes of it. I see some sort of spot . . . and nothing else."

He turned back clumsily to the wall; Vasily Ivanovich left the study and when he reached his wife's bedroom, threw himself down on his knees in front of the icons.

"Pray, Arina, pray!" he moaned. "Our son's dying."

The doctor, the same country doctor who lacked the caustic, arrived and after examining the patient, advised them to continue waiting it out and then added a few words about the possibility of recovery.

"Have you ever seen people in my condition *not* set off for the Elysian fields?"[8] asked Bazarov; suddenly grabbing the leg of a heavy table that stood next to the sofa, he shook it and pushed it away. "Strength," he said, "what strength I still possess, yet I have to die! . . . At least an old man has time to get used to the idea of leaving life behind. It renounces you, and that's all there is to it! Who's weeping over there?" he added, after a little while. "Mother? Poor dear! Who'll she feed her wonderful borsch to now? And you, Vasily Ivanovich, are you sniveling, too? Well, if Christianity doesn't help you, be a philosopher, a stoic, or something! You boasted you were a philosopher, didn't you?"

"What kind of philosopher am I?" wailed Vasily Ivanovich, tears streaming down his cheeks.

Bazarov grew worse with every passing hour; his illness took a rapid

---

8. In Greek mythology, the happy otherworld for heroes favored by the gods.

course, as is usually the case with surgical poisonings. He hadn't yet lost his memory and could still understand what people were saying to him; he was still fighting. "I don't want to become delirious," he whispered, clenching his fists, "what nonsense that is!" Then he'd say, "Well, eight take away ten, what's left?" Vasily Ivanovich went around like a man possessed, suggesting first one remedy then another; the only thing he actually did was cover his son's legs. "Wrap him up in cold sheets . . . give him an emetic . . . mustard plasters on the stomach . . . bleeding," he kept saying anxiously. The doctor, whom he implored to stay, would nod his head in agreement, give the patient lemonade to drink, and asked first for a pipe for himself, then for something "fortifying and warming," that is, vodka. Arina Vlasevna sat on a small low stool near the door and from time to time went out to say a prayer; a few days ago a small mirror from her dressing table slipped out of her hands and broke, something she'd always considered a bad omen. Even Anfisushka couldn't say anything to her. Timofeich had set off to fetch Odintsova.

The night wasn't a very good one for Bazarov . . . He was cruelly tormented by fever. Toward morning he felt a bit better. He asked Arina Vlasevna to comb his hair, kissed her hand, and drank a few mouthfuls of tea. Vasily Ivanovich cheered up a little.

"Thank God!" he declared. "The crisis has come . . . the crisis has gone."

"Just imagine!" muttered Bazarov. "What a word can mean! He finds one and says it, 'crisis,' and now he feels relieved. It's an astonishing thing how a man can still believe in words. For instance, if you call him a fool, but don't give him a beating, he gets depressed; if you call him a clever fellow, but don't give him any money, he feels terrific."

This short speech of Bazarov, reminiscent of his previous "sallies," evoked great tenderness in Vasily Ivanovich.

"Bravo! Well said, very well said!" he exclaimed, pretending to applaud.

Bazarov smiled wanly.

"So then, what do you think?" he asked. "Has the crisis come or gone?"

"You're better, that's what I see, that makes me happy," replied Vasily Ivanovich.

"Well, splendid; it's always good to be happy. Did you remember to send someone for her?"

"Of course I did."

This change for the better didn't last long. The illness resumed its attacks. Vasily Ivanovich sat next to Bazarov. Some kind of unusual anguish seemed to be tormenting the old man. Several times he was about to say something—but couldn't.

"Evgeny!" he said at last. "My son, my dear, kind son!"

This special form of address had an impact on Bazarov . . . He turned his head a little; obviously trying to free himself from the burden of oppressive oblivion, he uttered, "What is it, Father?"

"Evgeny," continued Vasily Ivanovich, going down on his knees in front of Bazarov, even though his son hadn't opened his eyes and couldn't see him. "Evgeny, you're better now; God willing, you'll recover; but make use of this time, console your mother and me, do your duty as a Christian! It's terrible for me to have to say this to you; but it's even more terrible to . . . it's forever, Evgeny . . . just think what that would be like . . ."

The old man's voice broke off; but on his son's face, even though he continued lying there with his eyes closed, he could see a strange look.

"I won't refuse, if it would provide you some consolation," he said at last. "But I think there's no need to hurry. You yourself say I'm better."

"Better, Evgeny, better; but who knows, it's all in God's hands, while doing your duty . . ."

"No, I want to wait a bit," Bazarov said, interrupting him. "I agree that the crisis has come. And if we're wrong, so what? They administer the sacrament to people who've lost consciousness, don't they?"

"Evgeny, for heaven's sake . . ."

"I'll wait. Now I want to sleep. Don't bother me."

He turned his head back to its previous position.

The old man got up and then sat down in the armchair; grabbing hold of his chin, he began gnawing on his own fingers . . .

The sound of carriage springs, particularly noticeable in the depths of the countryside, suddenly reached his ears. The light wheels came closer and closer; now he could even hear horses snorting . . . Vasily Ivanovich jumped up and rushed to the small window. A twin-seated carriage drawn by four horses was entering the courtyard of his little house. Without even stopping to consider what all this might mean, in a burst of nonsensical joy, he ran out onto the steps . . . A footman in livery opened the carriage door; a lady wearing a black veil and black mantilla was emerging . . .

"I'm Odintsova," she said. "Is Evgeny Vasilevich still alive? Are you his father? I've brought a doctor with me."

"Benefactress!" cried Vasily Ivanovich; grabbing her hand, he pressed it feverishly to his lips, while the doctor who accompanied Anna Sergeevna, a small man with a German face, wearing glasses, climbed out of the carriage in a deliberate manner. "He's still alive, my Evgeny's still alive, and now he'll be saved! Wife! Wife! . . . An angel's been sent to us from heaven . . ."

"Good Lord, what is it?" muttered the old woman as she came running from the living room. Without understanding anything, right there in the hall, she threw herself at Anna Sergeevna's feet and began kissing her dress like a madwoman.

"What's this? What're you doing?" Anna Sergeevna objected; but Arina Vlasevna didn't hear her, and Vasily Ivanovich merely repeated: "Angel! Angel!"

"*Wo ist der Kranke*? Where is the patient?" the doctor said at last, not without a certain indignation.

Vasily Ivanovich came to his senses. "Here, here, please come with me, *werthester Gerr Kollega*,"[9] he added, recalling a phrase from memory.

"Eh!" replied the doctor, smiling sourly.

Vasily Ivanovich led him into the study.

"It's a doctor from Anna Sergeevna Odintsova," he said, bending over to his son's ear. "And she's come as well."

Bazarov suddenly opened his eyes. "What did you say?"

"I said Anna Sergeevna Odintsova's here and has brought a gentleman with her, a doctor."

Bazarov looked around the room.

"She's here . . . I want to see her."

"You'll see her, Evgeny; but first we must have a little chat with the doctor. I'll tell him the history of your illness since Sidor Sidorych has gone [that was the name of the local doctor], and we'll have a short consultation."

Bazarov looked at the German. "Well, confer quickly, but not in Latin; after all, I know the meaning of '*jam moritur.*' "[1]

"*Der Herr scheint des Deutschen mächtig zu sein*,"[2] began this latest follower of Aesculapius,[3] addressing Vasily Ivanovich.

"*Ikh . . . gabe . . .* [4] We'd better speak Russian," said the old man.

"*Ach*, so! Zat iss how it iss . . . Pleeze . . ."

And the consultation began.

Half an hour later Anna Sergeevna entered the study accompanied by Vasily Ivanovich. The doctor managed to whisper to her that there was no point in even thinking about the patient's recovery.

She glanced at Bazarov . . . and stopped at the door, so astounded was she by the sight of the inflamed and at the same time deathly countenance, its dim eyes directed at her. She was simply seized by a cold, enervating terror; the thought that she wouldn't have felt like that if she'd really loved him momentarily flashed through her mind.

"Thank you," he said with effort, "I didn't expect this. It's a good deed. So, we meet again, as you promised."

"Anna Sergeevna was so kind . . ." Vasily Ivanovich began.

"Leave us, Father. You'll allow it, Anna Sergeevna, won't you? It seems that now . . ."

9. *Würdigster Herr Kollege*: "most worthy colleague" (German).
1. "He's already dying" (Latin).
2. "Apparently the gentleman has a good command of German" (German).
3. Legendary Greek physician and god of medicine.
4. *Ich habe*: "I have" (German).

With a nod of his head, he indicated his outstretched, enfeebled body. Vasily Ivanovich left the room.

"Well, thank you," Bazarov repeated. "It's a regal gesture. They say that tsars also visit the dying."

"Evgeny Vasilich, I hope that . . ."

"Hey, Anna Sergeevna, let's speak the truth. It's all over for me. I've fallen beneath the wheel. It now seems there was no reason at all to think about the future. Death's an old story, but new for each person. Up to this point I haven't been afraid . . . unconsciousness will come and then, that's that! [He waved his hand weakly.] Well, what do I have to tell you? . . . I did love you! It didn't mean anything then and it means even less now. Love's just a form, and my own form's going to pieces already. I'd rather say how lovely you are! And now you stand here looking so beautiful . . ."

Anna Sergeevna gave an involuntary shudder.

"Never mind, don't be alarmed . . . sit down . . . Don't come near me: my illness is contagious."

Anna Sergeevna crossed the room quickly and sat down on an armchair next to the sofa where Bazarov was lying.

"Oh, magnanimous one!" he whispered. "Oh, how near, how young, fresh, pure . . . in this nasty room! . . . Well, farewell! Live a long life, that's best of all, enjoy it while there's still time. You see what an ugly spectacle I am: a worm half-crushed, but still writhing. I used to think: I'll do so much, I won't die, not me! There're tasks to perform, and, after all, I'm a giant! Now the giant's only task is to die in a decent manner, even though no one really cares about that either . . . All the same, I'm not going to start wagging my tail."

Bazarov fell silent and began reaching for his glass. Anna Sergeevna gave him a drink without removing her glove, drawing her breath apprehensively.

"You'll forget me," he began again. "The dead make no companions for the living. My father'll tell you what a great man Russia's losing . . . That's nonsense, but don't try to argue with the old man. Don't deny the child anything that comforts him . . . you know what I mean. And be kind to my mother. After all, you won't find people like them anywhere in the world, even if you search by daylight with a candle . . . I'm needed by Russia . . . No, obviously I'm not needed. Who is needed? The shoemaker's needed, the tailor's needed, the butcher . . . sells meat . . . the butcher . . . wait a minute, I'm getting all confused . . . There's a forest here . . ."

Bazarov put his hand on his forehead.

Anna Sergeevna bent over to him.

"Evgeny Vasilich, I'm here . . ."

He took her hand at once and lifted himself up.

"Farewell," he said with unexpected strength, his eyes gleaming with their last light. "Farewell . . . Listen . . . you know, I didn't kiss you then . . . Blow on the dying lamp and let it go out . . ."

She pressed her lips to his forehead.

"That's enough!" he said, sinking back into his pillow. "Now . . . darkness . . ."

Anna Sergeevna left quietly.

"Well?" asked Vasily Ivanovich in a whisper.

"He's asleep," she replied, barely audible.

Bazarov wasn't fated to awaken again. Toward evening he sank into complete unconsciousness and died the next day. Father Aleksei performed religious rites over him. When they were administering extreme unction, just as the holy oil touched his breast, one of his eyes opened and, at the sight of the priest in his vestments, the smoking censer, the candle in front of the icon, something resembling a shudder of horror seemed to pass momentarily across his deathly countenance. When he finally drew his last breath and the sound of universal lamentation filled the house, Vasily Ivanovich was overcome with sudden frenzy. "I said I'd rebel," he cried hoarsely, his face inflamed and contorted, brandishing his fist in the air as if threatening someone, "and I do rebel, I do!" But Arina Vlasevna, all in tears, put her arms around his neck and they both dropped to their knees. "That's how it was," Anfisushka used to relate afterward in the servants' quarters, "side by side, their little heads drooping, just like lambs at midday . . ."

But the heat of midday passes, evening comes, then night, and the return to a quiet refuge where sweet sleep awaits all who are tired and tormented . . .

XXVIII

Six months passed. White winter had arrived with its cruel stillness of cloudless frosts, thick, squeaky snow, pink hoarfrost on trees, pale emerald green sky, caps of smoke above chimneys, clouds of steam from doors opened hurriedly, people's fresh faces nipped by the cold, and the brisk trot of shivering horses. The January day was already nearing its end; evening cold was tightening its grip on the motionless air, and the bloodred sunset was quickly fading. Lights burned in the windows of the house at Marino; Prokofich, in a black frockcoat and white gloves, was setting the table for seven with special solemnity. A week before in the small parish church, two weddings had taken place, quietly and almost without witnesses: Arkady to Katya and Nikolai to Fenechka; on this very day, Nikolai Petrovich was giving a farewell dinner for his brother, who was leaving to go to Moscow on business. Anna Sergeevna had also repaired there right after the wedding, having gifted the young couple handsomely.

At precisely three o'clock everyone gathered at the table. Mitya was seated there as well; he'd already been provided with a nanny who wore a brocade peasant headdress. Pavel Petrovich took his place between Katya and Fenechka; the "husbands" were seated next to their wives. Our friends had changed of late; they all seemed to have grown stronger and better looking. Only Pavel Petrovich was thinner, which, however, lent his expressive features even more elegance and made him look even more like a *grand seigneur* . . . Fenechka had also changed. In a new silk dress, with a broad velvet band in her hair, a gold chain around her neck, she sat in respectful stillness, respectful of herself and her surroundings, and smiling as if she wanted to say, "You must forgive me, I'm not to blame." And she wasn't the only one—all the others were also smiling and seemed to be asking forgiveness; everyone was feeling a little awkward, a little melancholy, and, in reality, very happy. Each one attended to the other's needs with amusing solicitude, as if everyone had agreed to play a role in some good-natured comedy. Katya was the calmest of all: she looked around confidently; it was apparent that Nikolai Petrovich had already managed to fall dotingly in love with her. Before the end of dinner, he stood up; glass in hand, he turned to Pavel Petrovich.

"You're leaving us . . . dear brother, you're leaving us," he began. "Of course, not for long; but I can't help expressing what I . . . what we . . . how much I . . . how much we . . . The trouble is, I really don't know how to make speeches! Arkady, you say something."

"No, Papa, I haven't prepared anything."

"As if I've made extensive preparations! Brother, let me simply embrace you and wish you all the best; come back to us as soon as you can!"

Pavel Petrovich exchanged kisses with everyone, including even little Mitya, of course; what's more, in Fenechka's case, he kissed her hand, which she didn't know how to offer properly; drinking a second glass, he said with a deep sigh, "Be happy, my friends! Farewell!" This last word uttered in English went almost unnoticed, but everyone was touched.

"To the memory of Bazarov," Katya whispered into her husband's ear, clinking glasses with him. Arkady squeezed her hand firmly in reply, but decided not to propose that toast aloud.

That would seem to be the end. But perhaps some of our readers would like to know what each of our characters is doing now, at this very moment.[5] We're prepared to satisfy their curiosity.

Odintsova recently married, not for love, but out of conviction, one of Russia's future statesmen, a very clever man, a lawyer, with good practical sense, a strong will, and a remarkable talent with words—still young, kind, and cold as ice. They live together in great harmony, and

5. I.e., *after* the emancipation of the serfs, which occurred in February 1861.

perhaps will live long enough to find happiness . . . perhaps even love. Princess Kh. passed away, forgotten the day she died. The Kirsanovs, father and son, have settled at Marino. Their affairs have begun to improve. Arkady has become a zealous proprietor and the "farm" is already bringing in a fairly substantial income. Nikolai Petrovich has become an arbitrator[6] and works at it with all his might; he's constantly traveling throughout the district; he delivers long speeches (being of the opinion that peasants must be "made to understand," that is, driven to exhaustion by frequent repetition of one and the same thing); but, to tell the truth, he fails to satisfy fully either the educated nobles who talk with *chic* or melancholy about the *mancipation* (pronouncing the French nasal *an*) or the uneducated nobles, who swear unceremoniously at that "damned *muncipation*." He's seen as far too generous by both sides. Katerina Sergeevna gave birth to a son, Kolya, while Mitya's already running around and talking spiritedly. After her husband and child, Fenechka, Fedosya Nikolaevna, adores no one as much as her daughter-in-law, and whenever Katya sits down at the piano, she's happy to spend the whole day there with her. We must also say a word or two about Peter. He's become perfectly numb from stupidity and self-importance and now pronounces every "e" as "u"—but he also married and received a considerable dowry with his bride, the daughter of the town vegetable-gardener, who turned down offers from two fine suitors because neither of them owned a watch, whereas Peter owned not only a watch but also a pair of patent leather boots.

In Dresden, on the Brühl Terrace, between two and four in the afternoon, the most fashionable time for strolling, you can meet a man aged about fifty, already quite gray, seeming to suffer from gout, but still handsome, elegantly dressed, with the special air conferred only on those who've spent considerable time mixing with high society. This is Pavel Petrovich. He left Moscow to go abroad to improve his health and took up residence in Dresden, where he associates mostly with the English and with visiting Russians. With the English he behaves simply, almost modestly, but not without dignity; they find him a bit of a bore, but respect him for being "a perfect gentleman," as they say. With Russians he's more casual, gives vent to his spleen, makes fun of himself and them; but this is all accomplished in a very nice, easy, decent manner. He holds Slavophile views: it's well known that in high society this is considered *très distingué*.[7] He doesn't read anything in Russian, but keeps a silver ashtray in the shape of a peasant's bast sandal[8] on his writing desk. He's much sought after by our tourists. Matvei Ilich Kolyazin, finding himself a member of the "temporary opposition,"[9] gra-

---

6. After the emancipation, an official appointed to serve as mediator between landowners and peasants.
7. "Very distinguished" (French).
8. Shoes or sandals woven from bast (tree) fibers were worn by peasants.
9. A group of reactionaries opposed to the reforms carried out by Alexander II.

ciously paid him a visit on his way to take the waters in Bohemia;
meanwhile, the locals, with whom he has very little to do, practically
grovel before him. No one can obtain a ticket to the court chapel, the
theater, etc., as quickly and easily as *der Herr Baron von Kirsanoff*. He
still does as much good as he can and continues to make something of
an impression: it's not for nothing he was once a social lion. But life's
become a burden for him . . . more than he suspects . . . One need
only catch a glimpse of him in the Russian church, where, leaning
against the wall on one side, he sinks deep into thought and remains
motionless for some time, his teeth clenched in bitterness, then suddenly
comes to his senses and begins crossing himself almost imperceptibly . . .

Kukshina also wound up living abroad. She's now in Heidelberg,
studying not natural science, but architecture, where, in her own words,
she's discovered some new laws. As before she still hobnobs with students, especially young Russians studying physics and chemistry, with
whom Heidelberg's filled to the brim, and who, astonishing their naive
German professors at first with their sober view of things, subsequently
astonish those same professors with their total inactivity and absolute
idleness. With two or three chemistry students who can't distinguish
oxygen from nitrogen, but who're filled with self-importance and a
penchant for negation, and with the great Elisevich,[1] too, Sitnikov,
who's also preparing himself for greatness, wanders around Petersburg
and, according to his own assurances, is carrying on Bazarov's "work."
They say he was given a beating not too long ago, but wasn't kept down
for long: in an obscure little article, hidden in an obscure little journal,
he implied that the fellow who beat him was a coward. He calls this
irony. His father orders him about as before, and his wife considers him
a perfect fool . . . and a man of letters.

There's a little village graveyard in one remote corner of Russia. Like
almost all our graveyards, it's a sorry sight: ditches surrounding it have
long since been overgrown; gray wooden crosses have fallen over and
lie rotting beneath their once-painted little roofs; headstones have been
displaced as if someone had pushed them aside from below; two or three
pitiful trees barely provide any shade; some sheep graze unchecked
around the graves . . . Among them there's one grave untouched by
people, untrampled by animals: only birds perch on it and sing in the
heat. An iron railing surrounds it; two young pine trees have been planted
there, one on each side: Evgeny Bazarov lies buried in this grave. Two
feeble old people come frequently from the nearby village to visit it—
a man and his wife. They walk with a heavy step, supporting each other;
when they approach the railing, they fall on their knees and remain
there for a long time, weeping bitterly, gazing attentively at the headstone

1. See above, p. 52, n. 6.

under which their son lies buried: they exchange a few words, brush the dust off the stone, move a branch of the pine tree, and pray once again; they can't forsake this place where they seem to feel closer to their son, to their memories of him . . . Can it really be that their prayers and tears are futile? Can it really be that love, sacred, devoted love is not all-powerful? Oh, no! However passionate, sinful, rebellious the heart buried in this grave, the flowers growing on it look out at us serenely with their innocent eyes: they tell us not only of that eternal peace, that great peace of "indifferent" nature; they tell us also of eternal reconciliation and life everlasting . . .

THE AUTHOR ON
THE NOVEL

IVAN TURGENEV

Apropos of *Fathers and Sons*†

I was sea-bathing in Ventnor, a small town on the Isle of Wight—it was in August of 1860—when I first thought of *Fathers and Sons*, that tale thanks to which I lost—and apparently forever—the younger Russian generation's friendly disposition toward me. I have frequently heard and read in critical articles that in my works I "started with an idea"; some praised me for it, others, on the contrary, blamed me; for my part I must confess that I never attempted "to create a figure" unless I had a living character rather than an idea, to whom appropriate elements were gradually added and mixed in. Since I do not possess a great deal of free invention, I always needed solid ground on which I could step firmly. That is precisely what occurred with *Fathers and Sons*. At the basis of the main character, Bazarov, there lay the figure of a young provincial doctor that had struck me. (He died shortly before 1860.) This remarkable man embodied in my view that barely nascent still fermenting principle that was later called nihilism. The impression that man made on me was very strong and at the time not entirely clear: at first, I could not myself make him out clearly, and I intently listened and examined everything around me as though I wanted to verify the justness of my own feelings. I was disturbed by the following fact: I did not even find a hint in any work of our literature of what I seemed to see everywhere; against my will I was beset by doubts: was I not chasing a phantom? I remember that on the Isle of Wight there lived at the same time a certain Russian gifted with extremely fine tastes and a remarkable sensitivity to what the late Apollon Grigoriev called the "Waft" of the era. I communicated to him the thoughts that occupied me and with speechless amazement heard the following remark: "But haven't you already presented a similar type in Rudin?"[1] I remained silent: what could I say? Rudin and Bazarov—one and the same type!

Those words had such an effect on me that during the course of several weeks I avoided any consideration of the work I had conceived; however, after I returned to Paris I again took it up—the *plot* gradually took shape in my mind: I wrote the first chapters during the course of the winter, but finished the tale in Russia, in the countryside, in the month of July. In the autumn I read it to several friends, corrected a few things, elaborated others, and in March 1862 *Fathers and Sons* appeared in *The Russian Herald*.

† From "Literary and Autobiographical Reminiscences," I. S. Turgenev, *Polnoe sobranie sochinenij*, vol. xiv (Moscow, 1967) 97–109. Translated by Ralph E. Matlaw. First published in 1869. Reprinted by permission.
1. The hero of Turgenev's first novel, *Rudin* (1856) [*Editor*].

I will not expatiate on the impression made by that tale; I will only say that when I returned to St. Petersburg, the very day of the notorious fires in the Apraksin Palace, the word "nihilist" had already been taken up by thousands of voices, and the first exclamation that burst from the lips of the first acquaintance I encountered on the Nevsky was "See what *your* nihilists are doing! They are burning Petersburg!" My impressions at that time though of various sorts were all similarly oppressive. I noted the coldness, practically indignation, of many people close and sympathetic to me; I was congratulated, almost embraced by people belonging to a camp repugnant to me, by enemies. I was troubled, and embittered and grieved by that, but my conscience was clear: I knew very well that my attitude toward the character I had introduced was not only honorable and free of prejudice but even sympathetic,[2] for I valued the calling of an artist, of a literary man too highly to be hypocritical in such a matter. The word "valued" is even not quite appropriate here: I simply could not and cannot work differently; and in the final analysis there was no reason for me to do so. My critics called my tale a "broadside pamphlet," mentioned "exasperated," "wounded" egoism; but why would I write a pamphlet on Dobrolyubov, whom I had hardly met, but whom I esteemed highly as a man and as a talented writer? Whatever modest opinion I might have of my talent, I would nevertheless have considered and do consider the writing of a pamphlet, a "pasquil" beneath it and unworthy of it. As for "wounded" egoism, I will only note that Dobrolyubov's article about my last work before *Fathers and Sons*—about *On the Eve* (and he properly considered himself the spokesman of public opinion)—that the article, which appeared in 1861, is full of the warmest praise, which, in all conscience, it does not merit. But the critics found it necessary to present me as a humiliated pamphleteer: *"leur siège était fait"*[3]—and even this year I could read the following lines in Appendix #1 to *The Cosmos* (p. 96): "Finally everyone knows that the pedestal on which Mr. Turgenev stood was destroyed chiefly by Dobrolyubov . . ." and later (p. 98) my "bitterness" is mentioned, which the critic, however, understands—and "perhaps even forgives."

Critics in general do not quite correctly conceive what goes on in an author's soul, what precisely causes his joys and sorrows, his stirrings, his successes and failures. For example, they do not even suspect the existence of that pleasure that Gogol mentions and which consists in chastising oneself and one's shortcomings in depicted characters one has created. They are completely convinced that all an author does is to

---

2. I permit myself to cite the following excerpt from my diary: "July 30, Sunday. An hour and a half ago I finally finished my novel . . . I do not know whether it will be successful. *The Contemporary* will probably treat me with contempt because of Bazarov and will not believe that during the whole time I was writing I was involuntarily attracted to him." [*The Contemporary* was a leading periodical, in which the ideas repeated by Bazarov appeared—*Editor.*]

3. "They have taken their stand" [*Editor*].

"convey his ideas"; they do not wish to believe that to reproduce the truth, the reality of life accurately and powerfully, is the literary man's highest joy, even if that truth does not correspond to his own sympathies. I will permit myself to cite a small example. I am an inveterate and incorrigible Westerner[4] and I have never in any way concealed it, nor do I do so now; nevertheless despite that, I derived particular satisfaction in depicting in Panshin (in A *Nest of Noblemen*) all the comical and vulgar aspects of Westernism; I made the Slavophile Lavretsky "destroy him at every point." Why did I do that—I, who consider Slavophile doctrine false and barren? Because *in this instance, as I saw it that was precisely* how life turned out and above all I wanted to be honest and truthful. In drawing the character of Bazarov I excluded everything artistic from his sympathies, I endowed him with harshness and an unceremonious tone—not out of a blind desire to insult the younger generation (!!!),[5] but simply as a result of observing my acquaintance Dr. D. and people like him. "That is how that *life* turned out,"—experience again told me—perhaps mistakenly, but, I repeat, scrupulously; there was no reason for hair-splitting, and I had to depict him precisely *that way*. My personal inclinations meant nothing here; but no doubt many of my readers would be amazed if I told them that I share almost all of Bazarov's convictions with the exception of those on art. Yet I am assured that I was on the side of the "fathers" . . . I, who in the character of Pavel Kirsanov even erred against artistic truth and overdid it, practically turned his faults into caricature, made him comic![6]

The whole reason for the misunderstandings, the whole "fault" so to speak consisted in that the Bazarov type created by me was not able to pass through gradual stages, as other literary types ordinarily do. It was not his lot—as it was Onegin's or Pechorin's[7]—to experience a period of idealization, of sympathetic exaltation. At the moment of the *new* man's—Bazarov's—appearance, the author treated him critically . . .

---

4. The two opposing camps in Russia were the Westerners, who thought that Russians should emulate European civilization, and the Slavophiles, who wanted to depend on native traditions [*Editor*].

5. Among many proofs of my "spite against youth" one critic even brought forth the fact that I made Bazarov lose at cards to Father Alexey. "He just doesn't know how to wound and humiliate enough! He doesn't even know how to play cards!" There is absolutely no doubt that if I had made Bazarov win, the same critic would triumphantly exclaim: "Isn't it clear? The author wants to suggest that Bazarov is a cheat!"

6. Foreigners simply cannot understand the merciless reproaches directed at me for Bazarov. *Fathers and Sons* was translated into German several times. This is what one critic writes, reviewing the latest translation that appeared in Riga ([?] *Zeitung*, Thursday, June 10, Supplement 2, page 3): "The unprejudiced reader will be completely puzzled how the radical Russian younger generation could become so frenzied about a representative of its convictions and strivings as Turgenev depicted Bazarov that it subjected Turgenev to formal disgrace and covered him with abuse. One might rather have thought that every young radical would rather have recognized with a feeling of joyous satisfaction his own portrait and the portrait of his partisans in so proud an image, gifted with such a strength of character, such total independence from everything petty, vulgar, slothful, and false." [Turgenev quotes the German original before translating into Russian—*Editor*.]

7. In Pushkin's *Eugene Onegin* and Lermontov's *Hero of Our Time* [*Editor*].

objectively. That led many astray and, who knows, perhaps that was, if not a mistake, at least unfair. The Bazarov type was at least entitled to as much idealization as his predecessors. I just said that the author's relation to his created character led the reader astray: the reader is always uneasy, doubts, even vexation seizes him if an author treats an invented character like a living human being, that is, he sees and presents his bad and good traits, and most of all, if he doesn't show a clear sympathy or antipathy toward his own offspring. The reader is ready to take offense: he has to clear his own path rather than follow an established one. "Why should I trouble myself?" the reader involuntarily begins to think— "books exist for distraction not for breaking one's head; and what would it have cost the author to say how I should think about a particular figure—what he himself thinks of him!" And if the author's relation to that figure is of even vaguer character, if the author doesn't know himself whether he loves the created character or not (as happened to me in regard to Bazarov, since that "involuntary attraction" which I mention in my diary is not love)—then things are altogether bad. The reader is ready to attribute fictitious sympathies or fictitious antipathies to the author, only in order to escape from unpleasant "vagueness."

"*Neither Fathers nor Sons*," a witty lady said to me after reading my book, "that is the real title of your book—and you are a nihilist yourself." A similar opinion was expressed even more forcefully after the publication of *Smoke*. I won't undertake a refutation; perhaps the lady even told the truth. In the work of composition (to judge by myself) each does not what he wishes but what he can—and in so far as it succeeds I suppose that works of *belles-lettres* must be judged *en gros* and while demanding strict conscientiousness from the author, other aspects of his activity should be considered I won't say unconcernedly but calmly. But much as I would like to oblige my critics, I cannot consider myself guilty of a lack of conscientiousness.

I have gathered a rather curious collection of letters and other documents relating to *Fathers and Sons*. Comparing them is not without some interest. While some accuse me of insulting the younger generation, of being out of touch, of obscurantism, inform me that "they burn my photographs with contemptuous laughter"—others, on the other hand, indignantly reproach me with grovelling before that same younger generation. "You are crawling at Bazarov's feet," one correspondent exclaims. "You only pretend to condemn him; in reality you ingratiate yourself with him, and await a single careless smile of his as a favor!" I remember that one critic, in forceful and eloquent expressions addressed directly at me, presented me and Mr. Katkov[8] as two conspirators who devised their despicable plot, their calumny against

8. See n. 2, p. 168.

younger Russian forces in the quiet of an isolated study. It was an effective picture! In fact, this is how that "conspiracy" took place. When Mr. Katkov received from me the manuscript of *Fathers and Sons*, of whose contents he had not even an inkling, he felt bewildered.[9] The type of Bazarov seemed to him "practically an apotheosis of *The Contemporary*," and I would not have been surprised if he had refused to publish my tale in his journal. *"Et voilà comme on écrit l'histoire!"*[1] one might exclaim. But can such minor matters really be inflated by so sonorous a name?

On the other hand, I understand the reasons for the anger my book aroused in a certain faction. They are not groundless, and I accept— without false humility—part of the reproaches made to me. The term "nihilist," which I launched, was at that time used by many who only sought an incident, an excuse, to stop a movement that had taken possession of Russian society. The term was not used by me as a reproach nor with the intent to insult; but as an exact and appropriate expression of a fact that had materialized, a historical fact; it was turned into a weapon of denunciation, of irrevocable condemnation,—almost as a brand of shame. Several unfortunate events that took place at that time further nurtured suspicions that were arising and seemed to confirm the apprehensions that were spreading, justifying the efforts and fussing of our "saviors of the Fatherland" . . . since "saviors of the Fatherland" appeared among us as in Rus[2] at that time. The tide of public opinion, still so vague with us, turned . . . but a shadow was cast on my name. I do not deceive myself, I know that that shadow will not disappear from my name. But other people, before whom I all too deeply feel my insignificance, might utter the great words *"Perissent nos noms, pourvu que la chose publique soit sauvée!"*[3] Imitating them I too could console myself with the notion that my book was of some use. That compensates me for the unpleasantness of undeserved reproaches. And really what does it signify? Twenty or thirty years from now who will remember all these storms in a teacup and my name, with or without a shadow cast upon it?

9. I hope Mr. Katkov will not complain to me for citing several places from a letter he wrote to me at the time. "Even if Bazarov isn't raised to an apotheosis," he wrote, "one must still admit that somehow he accidentally landed on a very high pedestal. He really crushes everything around him. Everything before him is either tinsel, or feeble and immature. Was that the impression one would have wished? One feels in the tale that the author wanted to characterize a principle he was little sympathetic to, but he seemed to waiver in his tone and unconsciously came under its sway. Some sort of constraint is felt in the author's relationship to the tale's hero, some sort of uneasiness and stiffness. The author somehow loses his head before him, he doesn't like him, but he is even more afraid of him!" Further, Mr. Katkov regrets that I didn't make Odintsov treat Bazarov ironically, etc.—all in the same tone! It is clear that one of the "conspirators" was not entirely satisfied with the work of the other.
1. "And that's how history is written!" [*Editor*].
2. The term for Ancient Russia [*Editor*].
3. That is, "Let our names perish as long as our common cause is saved."

But enough about me—and it is time to stop these sporadic reminiscences which, I fear, will hardly satisfy readers. I only wish, before signing off, to say a few words to my young contemporaries, my colleagues who embark on the slippery field of literature. I have already stated and am ready to repeat that I am not blinded so far as my own position is concerned. My twenty-five years' "service of the muses" ended in the gradual disenchantment of the reading public and I do not foresee any reason why it should reverse its view. New times have come, new people are required; literary old timers are like the army's—almost always cripples—and blessed are those that retire in time! Without a hortatory tone, to which, actually, I have no right, I intend to pronounce my parting words in the tones of an old friend who is listened to with half-condescending, half-impatient attention, if only he does not become excessively long-winded. I shall try to avoid that.

And so, my young colleagues, I address myself to you.

> *Greift nur hinein in's volle Menschenleben!—*

I would say to you in the words of our common teacher, Goethe,—

> *Ein jeder lebt's—nicht vielen ist's bekannt,*
> *Und wo ihr's packt—da ist's interessant!*[4]

Only talent gives one the power for that "apprehension," that "catching" of life, and one cannot grant oneself talent; but mere talent is in itself insufficient. Constant communion with the sphere you undertake to reproduce is required, honesty, implacable honesty toward one's own feelings is required, and, finally, education is required, knowledge is required! "Aha! We understand! We see what you're driving at!" many will perhaps exclaim here. "Potugin's ideas—Ci-vi-li-za-tion, *prenez mon ours!*"[5] Such exclamations do not surprise me; but neither will they make me renounce one iota of what I said. Learning is not only light, according to the Russian proverb—it is freedom as well. Nothing liberates man as much as learning, and nowhere is freedom as necessary as in art, in poetry: not for nothing are the arts called "liberal," free, even in bureaucratic language. Can a man "seize," "catch" what surrounds him if he is tied up inside? Pushkin felt that deeply; not for nothing did he write in his immortal sonnet, that sonnet that every beginning writer should memorize and remember like a commandment;

> . . . Go by a *free* road,
> Where your *free* mind draws you.

---

4. That is, "Put your hand right in (I cannot translate it any better) into the depths of human life! Everyone lives by it, few know it and wherever you grab it, there it will be interesting."
5. "The same old story!" Potugin is Turgenev's spokesman in the novel *Smoke* (1866) [*Editor*].

The lack of such freedom, incidentally, also explains why not one of the Slavophiles, despite their undoubted talent,[6] ever created anything that is alive; not one of them was able to remove his rose-tinted glasses even for a minute. But the saddest example of the lack of true freedom stemming from the lack of true knowledge is seen in Count L. N. Tolstoy's latest work (*War and Peace*), which at the same time through its creative, poetic gifts most likely stands at the head of everything produced in European literature since 1840. No! Without veracity, without education, without freedom in the broadest sense—toward one's self, toward one's preconceived ideas and systems, even toward one's people, one's history—a true artist is inconceivable; without that air you cannot breathe.

So far as a final result, a final appraisal of a so-called literary career is concerned, here too one must remember Goethe's words

Sind's Rosen—nun sie werden blühen.[7]

There are no unacknowledged geniuses just as there are no services that lie beyond their alloted time. "Sooner or later everyone finds his niche," the late Belinsky used to say. One can be grateful if one has contributed all one's mite in one's time and place. Only the chosen ones are in a position to convey to posterity not only the content but also the *form* of their thoughts and views, their personality which, generally speaking, doesn't concern the public. Ordinary individuals are condemned to disappear in the whole, to be swallowed up in its stream; but they augmented its force, broadened and deepened its course—what more could they want?

I put down my pen . . . One more bit of advice to young writers and one last request. My friends, never justify yourself no matter how you may be slandered; don't try to clear up misunderstandings, don't try either to say "the final word" or to listen to it. Do your work—everything will sort itself out later. In any case, first let a long period of time pass—and then look at all the rubbish of the past from the historical point of view, as I have tried to do now. Let the following example serve to guide you. Only once in the course of my literary career did I try to "establish the facts." Namely, when the editors of *The Contemporary* started to assure its subscribers in print that they had dispensed with me for my wretched convictions (while in fact I would not publish there— despite their pleas—for which I have documentary proof), I could not keep up my character, and publicly proclaimed what was involved, and of course, suffered a complete fiasco! The younger generation became even more indignant with me . . . "How dared I raise my hand against

6. One cannot, of course, reproach the Slavophiles with ignorance, with inadequate education; but for achieving an artistic result one needs—to use the latest terminology—the interaction of many *factors*. The factor Slavophiles lack is freedom; others lack education, still others talent, etc.
7. "If they are roses—they will bloom."

its idol! What does it matter that I was right! I should have kept quiet!" That lesson was useful to me; I hope that it will be useful to you as well.

And my request consists of the following: guard our language, our splendid Russian language, transmitted to us by our predecessors, at whose head Pushkin again shines! Treat that powerful weapon respectfully; in able hands it can achieve marvels! Even those who don't care for "philosophical abstractions" and "poetic tenderness," practical people for whom language is only a means for expressing a thought, like a simple lever,—even to them I say: at least respect the laws of mechanics, extract the maximum use of everything. Or else, scanning some pale, confused, feebly long-winded verbiage, a reader involuntarily will think that you have exchanged a *lever* for some primitive props, that you are returning to the infancy of mechanics itself . . .

But enough, otherwise I too will become verbose.

1868–1869
Baden-Baden

From Turgenev's Letters†

P. V. Annenkov to Turgenev[1]

September 26 (October 9), 1861.

* * * In Moscow I took your novel from Katkov[2] and read it carefully. In my opinion it is a masterful thing in exposition and finish, surpassing in its external form everything written by its author till now. That is the general consensus rather than my own or somebody's in particular, and therefore you may rest secure on that score. Bazarov is something else. There are different opinions about him as a result of a single cause: the author himself is somewhat constrained about him and doesn't know what to consider him—a productive force in the future or a stinking

---

† From I. S. Turgenev, *Pis'ma v 13—i tomakh*, vols. 4, 7, and 8 (Moscow, 1961–66) and I. S. Turgenev, *Sobranie sochineniy*, vol. XI (letters of 1874–82; Moscow, 1949). Translated by Ralph E. Matlaw. Reprinted by permission.

   All dates are given in both old and new style. The first is the Julian calendar used in Russia until 1917, the second the Gregorian used in the West. In the nineteenth century the Julian calendar was 12 days behind the Gregorian, and in the twentieth it was 13 days behind. The liberation of the serfs, February 19, 1861, thus took place on March 3 in our calendar, and the October Revolution is annually commemorated in the Soviet Union on November 7. Almost all Turgenev's letters bear the double date.

1. This important letter, to which Turgenev frequently alludes, was published only recently in *Russkaya Literatura*, 1958, No. 1, pp. 147–49. P. V. Annenkov (1813–87) was a critic of the mid-century and friend to many leading writers, including Turgenev. His reminiscences of that period are his most important and lasting work [*Editor*].

2. M. N. Katkov (1818–87), publisher of *The Russian Herald*, where *Fathers and Sons* appeared. Katkov became increasingly conservative and by the 1860's the journal was already considered reactionary [*Editor*].

abscess of an empty culture, of which one should rid oneself quickly. Bazarov cannot be both things at the same time, yet the author's indecisiveness sways the reader's thought too from one pole to the other. In the form that he (that is, Bazarov) appears now, he is able at one and the same time to flatter pleasantly all negators of Tryapichkin's ilk, creating for them an honored ideal, at which they will gaze very willingly, and, on the other hand, he is capable of arousing the loathing of people who work, have faith in science and in history. He is two-faced, like Janus, and each party will see only that facet which comforts it most or which it is most capable of understanding. That's precisely what I have already seen in practice. Katkov is horrified by that force, power, superiority to the crowd, and ability to subjugate people which he noted in Bazarov; he says it is *The Contemporary* raised to an apotheosis, and despairs for thought and science when people like the author of the tale instead of fighting with the corrupting tendency, strike the colors before it, yield before it, give up, venerate in thought its empty, phosphorescent, and deceptive lustre. Another person, Katkov's direct opposite, daring to do battle with him on that score, am I. In clear conscience, that gentleman, on the contrary, sees in Bazarov the same Mongol, Genghis Khan, etc., that the real ones were; his animal brute force is not only not attractive, but increases one's repulsion toward him and is tainted with sterility. The whole type *in toto* is a condemnation of the savage society wherein he could be born, and if that type becomes known to foreigners, it will be used by them as proof of that coarse, nomadic, brutal condition in which our state finds itself, though it has a gloss of books from the Leipzig Fair. That's the kind of nonsense and disagreement Bazarov already produces now.

And you, friend, are responsible for it just the same.

Let us assume that Katkov's eyes start in fear and that I, on the contrary, am completely correct, which I do not doubt for a minute, but you really did cast a Plutarchian aura over Bazarov, because you did not even give him that "burning, diseased egotism" that distinguishes the entire generation of nihilists. An inveterate romantic may still be without "egotism" among us, but is this possible for the latest negator? That is a real trait, after all, and its absence will have the effect of making people doubt that Bazarov belongs to this world, relating him to a heroic cycle, to kinship with Ossian turned inside out, etc. In order to show the other side of the character, that splendid scene with Arkady on the haystack is not enough; occasionally or at least at some time, the Sitnikov in Bazarov must creep out too. Only through venomous egotism can Bazarov be tied to reality—that artery from the real world to his navel—and there is no reason for cutting it off. For that matter it's easy to alleviate the situation if, while maintaining all his contempt for Sitnikov, he at some time mentions to Arkady that one must preserve the Sitnikovs on the basis of the rules promulgated by Prince Vorontsov, who replied to complaints about the abominations of a certain police inspector, "I know that he is a scoundrel but he has one important merit—he is genuinely devoted to me." Finally, in one of the conversations between Bazarov and Pavel Petrovich, one of them mentions Cavour, directly citing a passage in *The Contemporary*. I think that has to be changed: one must not approach such a special phenomenon of life so directly and indiscriminately. The tale reflects the guiding idea of life but not its actual statement, expression, mannerisms. Speaking entirely in the Hegel manner, that's *schlechte Realität*. [3] But having said all that, at the same time I figuratively kiss your brow for creating that type, which discloses your usual feeling for social phenomena and which is destined to teach, to sober, to make our era pensive, though, of course, our era will undergo all these with a certain amount of stubbornness.

My second remark concerns the splendid Anna Sergeyevna. That type is drawn so delicately by you that its future judges will hardly be able to understand it completely. Only in one place does it become obscure, namely in chapter XXV, where in a conversation with Bazarov a new inclination toward Arkady on A. S.'s part is expressed. The traits are so minute here that strong mental magnifying glasses are needed for understanding them, and not everyone is obliged to have them. I think one ought to hint at her new psychological state with some sort of striking turn, otherwise it'll turn out something like a Japanese snuffbox, which contains miniature trees with fruit, ponds, and boats; and that's the more annoying since the general tone of the tale is sharp, in relief, and its progress completely solid. And so far as the scene with Bazarov after receiving Arkady's request for permission to marry Katya is concerned, it is simply unbearable. It's something like Prince Kuchumov or current Russian dramatic literature in general where there is talk for talk's sake and where a kind of repellent, tepid, and fetid psychology reigns. Change that scene any way you like, let it be the mutual gaiety of the conversants, one of whom laughs out of malice and the other out of despair, but change it without fail if you value my respect.

And having said that, I congratulate you on an excellent tale, which proves that its author is still in full possession of his creative power, and that's what was most important of all for me to discover. It will create a great stir—you can expect that. It will not raise the question of talent and artistic merit but rather whether its author is the historian or ring-leader of the party. Serious writers have always given birth to such questions among their contemporaries and that sort of argument around a well-known name always proves the importance and significance of that name. There is no point in speaking of the many splendid details in that tale, and it is so absorbing that while reading it you think the first line stands next to the last one—the middle is swallowed up so

3. "Bad actuality" [*Editor*].

quickly! I have heard that Countess Lambert[4] is dissatisfied with the novel: don't believe it. The world into which you led her is so terrible that she has confused its hideousness with the hideousness of the creative work—that's how I explain her judgment to myself. So, it seems, I have conscientiously fulfilled the task placed before me, and would like to know to what extent you yourself share my opinions, which, for that matter, are far from incontrovertible. * * *

To P. V. Annenkov

Paris, October 1 (13), 1861

Dear Pavel Vasil'evich:

Please accept my sincere thanks for your letter in which you express your frank opinion of my tale. It made me very glad, the more so as my confidence in my own work was badly shaken. I agree completely with all your observations (the more so since V. P. Botkin[5] also finds them just), and tomorrow I will begin work on corrections and revisions, which apparently will be of considerable scope, and I have already written Katkov to that effect. I still have a great deal of time at my disposal. Botkin, who is apparently getting better, also made several apt suggestions to me and differs with you in only one thing: he does not like Anna Sergeyevna much. But I think that I know how to bring that whole business into proper balance. When I finish my work I will send it to you, and you pass it on to Katkov. But enough about that and once again my sincere and warm thanks. * * *

To M. N. Katkov

Paris, October 1 (13), 1861

Dear Mikhail Nikiforovich:

Forgive me for bombarding you with letters, but I wanted to forewarn you that as a result of letters I received from Annenkov and the remarks of Botkin to whom I read my tale here, the revisions of *Fathers and Sons* will be more extensive than I had anticipated, and will occupy me approximately two weeks, during which time you will receive a careful list of all omissions and additions. And therefore I repeat my request *not to publish an excerpt* and also to hold on to the manuscript, that is, not to let others read it. I hope that as a result of my corrections the figure of Bazarov will become clear to you and will not create in you the impression of an apotheosis, which was not my idea at all. Other figures will gain, too, I think. In short, I consider my piece not completely finished, and since I have expended a great deal of work on it I would like to issue it in the best possible form. * * *

4. A close friend of Turgenev's (died 1883). He valued her literary opinions [*Editor*].
5. Literary critic, author, member of liberal sets Turgenev frequented, and a lifelong friend (1810–69) [*Editor*].

To M. N. Katkov

Paris, October 27 (*November* 8), 1861

Dear Mikhail Nikoforovich:

On the advice of friends and on my own conviction, which probably coincides with yours, I think that under the current circumstances[6] the publication of *Fathers and Sons* should be put off for some time, the more so since the censorship may create difficulties now. And therefore I ask you to delay publication, which, however, does not prevent me from sending you the substantial changes and corrections I have made. In any case, rest assured that *Fathers and Sons* will appear—if at all— nowhere other than in *The Russian Herald*. Drop me a note so that I will know that you have received this letter. I also repeat my request to hold on to the manuscript and not let others read it. * * *

To M. N. Katkov

Paris, October 30 (*November* 11), 1861

Dear Mikhail Nikoforovich:

I recently wrote you, but after your letter which I received yesterday I consider it necessary to write a couple of words in reply. I agree with your comments, with almost all of them, particularly about *Pavel Petrovich* and Bazarov himself. So far as Odintsov is concerned, the unclear impression produced by that character indicates to me that here, too, I have to take more pains. (Incidentally, the *argument* between Pavel Petrovich and Bazarov has been completely revised and shortened.)

* * * I cannot agree with one thing: Odintsov ought not to be ironic with Bazarov, nor should the peasant stand higher than he, though Bazarov himself is empty and barren. Perhaps my view of Russia is more misanthropic than you suppose: in my mind he is the real hero of our time. A fine hero and a fine time you'll say. But that's how it is.

I repeat my request to keep my product hidden. * * *

To F. M. Dostoevsky

Paris, March 18 (30), 1862

Dear Fedor Mikhailovich:

I cannot tell you to what extent your opinion of *Fathers and Sons* has made me happy. It isn't a question of satisfying one's pride but in the assurance that you haven't made a mistake and haven't missed the mark, and that labor hasn't been wasted. That was the more important for me since people whom I trust very much (I am not talking about Kolbasin) seriously advised me to throw my work into the fire—and only

---

6. Turgenev refers to student demonstrations in the fall of 1861 and the arrests that followed. The censors would be far more strict and would strike anything that mentioned or implied the disorders or radical thought among students [*Editor*].

recently (but this is confidential) Pisemsky[7] wrote me that Bazarov is a complete failure. How can one then not doubt oneself and be led astray? It is hard for an author to feel *immediately* to what extent his idea has come to life, and whether it is true, and whether he has mastered it, etc. In his own work he is lost in the woods.

You have probably experienced this more than once yourself. And therefore thank you again. You have so completely and subtly grasped what I wanted to express through Bazarov that I simply throw my hands up in amazement—and in pleasure. It's as if you had entered my soul and felt even what I didn't consider necessary to express. God grant that this indicates not only the keen penetration of a master but also the simple comprehension of a reader—that is, God grant that everyone realize at least a part of what you have seen! Now I am at ease about the destiny of my tale: it has done its work and I have nothing to repent for.

Here is another proof of the extent to which you familiarized yourself with that character: in the meeting between Arkady and Bazarov, at that place where, according to you, something was missing, Bazarov made fun of *knights* and Arkady listened to him with secret horror, etc. I struck it out and now I regret it:[8] in general I rescribbled and revised a great deal under the influence of unfavorable comments, and the sluggishness you noticed may, perhaps, have come from that.

I have received a pleasant letter from Maykov and will answer him. I shall be roundly cursed—but that has to be waited out, like a summer rain. * * *

To A. N. Maykov[9]

Paris, March 18 (30), 1862

Dear Apollon Nikolaevich:

I'll tell you straight out, like a peasant, "God grant you health for your kind and good letter!" You've comforted me greatly. I have not lacked confidence in a single one of my things as strongly as in that very one. The remarks and judgments of people whom I am accustomed to believe were extremely unfavorable. But for Katkov's persistent demands *Fathers and Sons* would never have appeared. Now I can say to myself that I couldn't have written complete nonsense if people like you and Dostoevsky stroke my head and say "Good, little man, we'll give you a 'B'." The image of a student who has solidly passed an examination is much more accurate than your image of the triumphant man, and let

---

7. A. F. Pisemsky (1820–81), an outstanding novelist and playwright [*Editor*].
8. The passage was in chapter XXV and was later reintroduced. It reads, "he became terrified and somehow ashamed. Bazarov seemed to understand him. 'Yes, friend,' he said 'that's what it is to live with feudal people. You become feudal yourself and start participating in jousting tournaments. Well, sir . . .' [*Editor*].
9. A. N. Maykov (1821–97), a poet and friend of Turgenev's [*Editor*].

me tell you that your comparing yourself to a pigmy is worthless. No, you are a fellow artist, extending your hand in brotherly gesture to your friend. And I reply to your embrace with mine, to your greeting with a warm greeting and with gratitude. You have really set me at ease. Not in vain did Schiller say

> Wer für die Besten seiner Zeit gelebt—
> Der hat gelebt für alle Zeiten.[1]

* * *

To A. A. Fet[2]

Paris, March 19 (31), 1862

* * * I have not yet received a copy of my tale, but three letters have already arrived about the thing from Pisemsky, Dostoevsky, and Maykov. The first abuses the main character, the other two enthusiastically praise everything. That made me rejoice, because I was full of doubts. I think I wrote you that people whom I trust advised me to burn my work. But I tell you without flattery that I await your opinion in order to ascertain definitely what I should think. I argue with you at every step, but I firmly believe in your esthetic sense and in your taste. * * *

To A. A. Fet

Paris, April 6 (18), 1862

First of all, dear Afanasy Afanas'evich, thank you for your letter— and my thanks would be greater if you didn't consider it necessary to put on kid gloves. Believe me, I have borne and am able to bear the harshest truth from my friends. And so, despite your euphemisms, you don't like *Fathers and Sons*. I bow my head, since there is nothing to be done about it, but I want to say a few words in my defense, though I know how unseemly and pointless it is. You ascribe the whole trouble to *tendentiousness reflection*, in short, to reason. But in reality, you had only to say that the craft was inadequate. It seems that I am more naïve than you assume. Tendentiousness! But let me ask you, what kind of tendentiousness in *Fathers and Sons*? Did I want to abuse Bazarov or to extol him? *I do not know that myself*, since I don't know whether I love him or hate him! There you have tendentiousness! Katkov took me to task for making Bazarov into an apotheosis. You also mention *parallelism*. But where is it, permit me to ask you, and where are these *pairs*, believers and nonbelievers? Does Pavel Petrovich believe or not?

---

1. "He who has lived for the best men of his time / Has lived for all time." The quotation is not accurate [*Editor*].
2. A. A. Fet (1820–92), one of Russia's most sensitive and delicate lyric poets, who was also a hard-fisted, reactionary landowner [*Editor*].

I wouldn't know since I simply wanted to portray in him the type of the Stolypins, the Rossets, and other Russian ex-lions. It is a strange thing: you blame me for parallelism, but others write me "Why isn't Anna Sergeyevna a lofty person, to contrast her more fully with Bazarov? Why aren't Bazarov's old people completely patriarchical? Why is Arkady banal, and wouldn't it be better to portray him as an upright young man who is carried away for a moment? What purpose does Fenichka serve, and what conclusions can be drawn from her?" I'll tell you one thing, I drew all those characters as I would draw mushrooms, leaves, and trees. They were an eyesore to me and so I started to sketch them. But it would be strange and amusing to dismiss my own impressions simply because they resemble tendentiousness. I don't want you to draw the conclusion from that that I am a courageous fellow. On the contrary: what can be concluded from my words is even more injurious to me: it's not that I have been too shrewd, but that I was not capable enough. But truth above all. But actually—*omnia vanitas*. * * *

To K. K. Sluchevsky[3]

Paris, April 14 (26), 1862

I hasten to answer your letter, for which I am very grateful to you, dear Sluchevsky. One must value the opinion of youth. In any case I very much want there to be no misunderstandings about my intentions. I'll answer point by point.

1) The first reproach is reminiscent of the accusation made against Gogol and others, why they did not introduce *good* people among the others. Bazarov crushes all the other characters in the novel just the same (Katkov thought I presented an apotheosis of *The Contemporary* in him). The qualities given to him are not accidental. I wanted to make a tragic figure out of him—there was no place for tenderness here. He is honest, upright, and a democrat to his fingertips—and you fail to find *good* sides in him? He recommends *Stoff and Kraft* precisely as a *popular* book, that is, an empty one; the duel with Pavel Petrovich is introduced precisely as graphic proof of the emptiness of elegantly noble knighthood, presented almost in an exaggeratedly comic way. And how could he decline it? After all, Pavel Petrovich would have hit him. I think Bazarov constantly beats Pavel Petrovich and not the other way around. And if he is called a "nihilist" that word must be read as "revolutionary."

2) What you said about Arkady, the rehabilitation of the fathers, etc., only proves—alas!—that I was not understood. *My entire tale is directed against the nobility as the leading class.* Look at Nikolai Petrovich, Pavel Petrovich, and Arkady. Weakness and languor, or limitations. Esthetic

3. K. K. Sluchevsky (1837–1904) was voicing the objections of Russian students studying in Heidelberg. He was already then known as a poet. [*Editor*].

feelings made me choose precisely *good* representatives of the nobility, in order to prove my theme the more surely: if the cream is bad what will the milk be like? It would be coarse, *le point aux ânes*[4]—and untrue to take functionaries, generals, exploiters, etc. All the real *negators* I have known, without exception (Belinsky, Bakunin, Herzen, Dobrolyubov, Speshnev, etc.), came from comparatively good and honest parents. A great idea is contained therein: it removes from the *men of action*, the negators, every suspicion of *personal* dissatisfaction, personal irritation. They go their way only because they are more sensitive to the demands of national life. Countess Sal'yas[5] is wrong when she says that characters like Nikolai Petrovich and Pavel Petrovich are our grandfathers: I am Nikolai Petrovich, as are Ogarev and thousands of others; Stolypin, Esakov, Rosset, our contemporaries too—are Pavel Petrovich. They are the best of the nobility and were chosen by me for precisely that reason, in order to prove their bankruptcy. To present grafters on the one hand and ideal youth on the other—let others draw that picture. I wanted something larger. In one place (I struck it because of the censorship), Bazarov says to Arkady, that very Arkady in whom your Heidelberg friends see *a more successful type:* "Your father is an honest fellow. But even if he were the worst grafter you wouldn't go any farther than noble resignation or flaring up because you're a little nobleman."

3) My God! You consider Kukshin, that caricature, *most successful* of all! One should not even answer that. Odintsov *falls in love* as little with Arkady as with *Bazarov*—how can you fail to see that? She, too, is the representative of our idle, dreaming, curious and cold epicurean young ladies, our female nobility. Countess Sal'yas understood *that* character completely clearly. At first she would like to stroke the wolf's fur (Bazarov's), so long as he doesn't bite, then stroke the little boy's curls—and continue to recline, all clean, on velvet.

4) Bazarov's death (which Countess Sal'yas calls *heroic* and therefore criticizes) should, I think, have added the last stroke to his tragic figure. And our young people find it, too, accidental! I close with the following remark: if the reader does not come to love Bazarov with all his coarseness, heartlessness, pitiless dryness and sharpness—if he does not come to love him, I repeat—I am at fault and have not attained my aim. But I did not want to "sugar-coat" him, to use his own words, though through that I would have had the young on my side immediately. I did not want to purchase popularity through those kinds of concessions. Better to lose the battle (and apparently I have lost it) than to win it through a trick. I dreamt of a figure that was grim, wild, huge, half grown out of the ground, powerful, sardonic, honest—and doomed to destruction nevertheless—since it nevertheless still stands only at the threshold of

4. "Trite" [*Editor*].
5. Countess Sal'yas (1810–81) wrote novels, criticism, and children's stories under the pseudonym Evgeniya Tur [*Editor*].

the future—I dreamt of some sort of strange *pendant* to Pugachev,[6] etc.—and my young contemporaries tell me, shaking their heads: "You, friend, have made a mistake and have even insulted us: your Arkady has turned out better, you should have taken greater pains with him." I can only "Take off my hat and bow low" as in the gypsy song. Up to now only two people, Dostoevsky and Botkin, have understood Bazarov completely, that is, understood my intentions. I shall try to send you a copy of my tale. But now *basta* about that. * * *

A. I. Herzen to Turgenev[7]

London, April 9 (21), 1862

* * * You grew very angry at Bazarov, out of vexation lampooned him, made him say various stupidities, wanted to finish him off "with lead"—finished him off with typhus, but nevertheless he crushed that empty man with the fragrant mustache and that watery gruel of a father and that blancmange Arkady. Behind Bazarov the characters of the doctor and his wife are sketched masterfully—they are completely alive and live not in order to support your polemic but because they were born. Those are real people. It seems to me that, like an amiable rowdy, you took offense at the insolent, airy, bilious exterior, at the plebeian-bourgeois turn, and taking that as an insult, went further. But where is the explanation for his young soul's turning callous on the outside, stiff, irritable? What turned away everything tender, expansive in him? Was it Büchner's book?

In general it seems to me that you are unfair toward serious, realistic experienced opinion and confound it with some sort of coarse, bragging materialism. Yet that isn't the fault of materialism but of those "Neuvazhay-Korytos"[8] who understand it in a brutish way. Their idealism is repulsive too.

The Requiem at the end, with the further moving toward the immortality of the soul is good, but dangerous: you'll slip into mysticism that way.

There for the moment are some of the impressions I've gathered on the wing. I do not think that the great strength of your talent lies in *Tendenzschriften*.[9] In addition, if you had forgotten about all the Chernyshevskys in the world while you were writing it would have been better for Bazarov. * * *

---

6. *Pendant*—"counterpart, offshoot." Pugachev was the Cossack leader of a major uprising against Catherine II in 1773, finally crushed in a battle with Russia's most brilliant general, Suvorov [*Editor*].
7. A. I. Herzen (1812–70), a leading Russian writer, philosopher, and journalist in revolutionary causes, spent the last twenty years of his life in exile in London, publishing the most influential Russian newspaper (*The Bell*) of the time. He was a close friend of Turgenev's [*Editor*].
8. "Disrespect-pigtrough." A comical name that figures on a list of peasants in Gogol's novel *Dead Souls* (1842). He "was run over by a careless cart as he lay sleeping in the middle of the road" [*Editor*].
9. "Polemics" [*Editor*].

To A. I. Herzen

Paris, April 16 (28), 1862

My dear Alexander Ivanovich:

I reply to your letter immediately—not in order to defend myself, but to thank you, and at the same time to declare that in creating Bazarov I was not only not angry with him, but felt "an attraction, a sort of disease"[1] toward him, so that Katkov was at first horrified and saw in him the apotheosis of *The Contemporary* and as a result convinced me to delete not a few traits that would have mellowed him, which I now regret. Of course he crushes "the man with the fragrant mustache" and others! That is the triumph of democracy over the aristocracy. With hand on heart I feel no guilt toward Bazarov and could not give him an unnecessary sweetness. If he is disliked as he is, with all his ugliness, it means that *I* am at fault and was not able to cope with the figure I chose. It wouldn't take much to present him as an ideal; but to make him a wolf and justify him just the same—that was difficult. And in that I probably did not succeed; but I only want to fend off the reproach that I was exasperated with him. It seems to me, on the contrary, that the feeling opposite to exasperation appears in everything, in his death, etc. But *basta così*—we'll talk more when we see each other.

I haven't become addicted to mysticism and will not be; in my relations to God I share Faust's opinion:

> Wer darf ihn nennen,
> Und wer bekennen:
> Ich glaub' ihn!
> Wer empfinden
> Und sich unterwinden
> Zu sagen: Ich glaub' ihn nicht![2]

Moreover, that feeling in me has never been a secret to you. * * *

To Ludwig Pietsch[3]

Karlsruhe, January 22 (*February* 3), 1869
[Original in German]

Dear Friend:

Your letter evoked in my heart a mixed feeling of pity, gratefulness, and adoration! Quite seriously! A man as busy as you, to whom time is so valuable, to occupy himself with the painstaking, nerve-irritating

1. A quotation from Griboedov's play *Woe from Wit* (1825), act 4, scene 4 [*Editor*].
2. Why may name him / And who confess / "I believe in him!" / Who can feel / And dare / To say "I don't believe in him!" [*Editor*].
3. Ludwig Pietsch (1824–1911), a German journalist and writer, who helped popularize Turgenev in Germany [*Editor*].

work of revision [of the translation of *Fathers and Sons* into German]!
That is a great proof of friendship!

So far as the translation is concerned you naturally have complete
carte blanche! If you wish, you can have Bazarov marry Odintsov; I
won't protest! On the contrary!

Bazarov has the habit of expressing himself contemptuously: he calls
his old coat *"une loque,"* *"ein Fetzen,"*[4]—use whatever word you
like. * * *

To Ludwig Pietsch

Baden-Baden, May 22 *(June* 3), 1869
[Original in German]

* * * You write that you have to do reviews of *Fathers and Sons.*
Splendid! Do one of them that is cool and strict toward it, but do express
in it your incomprehension and amazement that the young generation
in Russia took the portrait of Bazarov as an insulting caricature and a
slanderous satire. Show instead that I portrait the fellow entirely too
heroically—idealistically (which is *true*) and that Russian youth has
entirely too sensitive a skin. Precisely through Bazarov I was (and still
am) bespattered with mud and filth. So much abuse and invective, so
many curses have been heaped on my head that was consigned to all
the spirits of Hell (Vidocq, Judas bought for money, fool, ass, adder,
spittoon—that was the *least* that I was called) that it would be a satisfaction for me to show that other nations see the matter in a different
light. I dare ask you for such publicity because it corresponds completely
to the truth and, of course, in no way contradicts your convictions.
Otherwise I would not have troubled you. If you wish to fulfill my
request, do so quickly, so that I could add a translation of the most
important parts of the review to my literary reminiscences, which are
to appear soon.[5] * * *

To P. V. Annenkov

Baden-Baden, December 20, 1869 *(January* 1, 1870)

* * * I have reread my article "Apropos of *Fathers and Sons*" and,
just think, I feel that every word seems to have poured out of my soul.
It seems that one must either not speak the truth or—what is more
likely—that no author understands completely what he is doing. There
is a kind of contradiction here which one cannot resolve oneself no
matter how one approaches it. It is clearer for an outsider. * * *

4. "A rag, a tatter" [*Editor*].
5. The request was fulfilled. See Turgenev's "Apropos of *Fathers and Sons*" [*Editor*].

To Ya. P. Polonsky[6]

Baden-Baden, December 24, 1869 *(January* 5, 1870)
* * * It seems that everyone is dissatisfied with my little article "Apropos of *Fathers and Sons.*" From this I gather that one shouldn't always speak the truth; since each word in that article is the truth itself, so far as I am concerned, of course. * * *

To I. P. Borisov

Baden-Baden, December 24, 1869 *(January* 5, 1870)
* * * It seems that my little article on *Fathers and Sons* has satisfied no one. Just think I will disown my fame, like Rostopchin did the burning of Moscow. Annenkov has even scolded me roundly. And yet every word in it is the sacred truth, at least in my judgment. It seems that an author doesn't always know himself what he is creating. My feelings toward Bazarov—my own personal feelings—were of a confused nature (God only knows whether I loved him or hated him), nevertheless the figure came out so specific that it immediately entered life and started acting by itself, in its own manner. In the final analysis what does it matter what the author himself thinks about his work. He is one thing and the work is another; but I repeat, my article was as sincere as a confession. * * *

To A. F. Onegin

Baden-Baden, December 27, 1869 *(January* 8, 1870)
* * * You don't like my little article "Apropos of *Fathers and Sons.*" In Russia they abuse it terribly: they see in it something like apostasy on my part from my own service in approaching the "nihilists" and so forth. But why don't you like it? I hope you will not doubt that every word in it, every letter, is true. Consequently you, as a positive man, must look upon it as a fact—bluntly, to look down upon it: that's how a man jumps in a given instance, that's how he could grapple, that's what he expressed—what can you not like about it? * * *

To A. P. Filosofov

Bougival, August 18 (30), 1874
* * * You write that in Bazarov I wanted to present a caricature of current youth. You repeat that—forgive the blunt expression—silly reproach. Bazarov is my favorite child, for whom I quarreled with Katkov, on whom I expended all the colors at my disposal, Bazarov, that bright man, that hero—a caricature? But apparently it cannot be helped. As Louis Blanc, despite all his protestations, is still constantly accused of

6. Ya. P. Polonsky (1819–98), an important Russian poet [*Editor*].

bringing about the national workshops (*ateliers nationaux*), so they ascribed to me the desire to offend youth by a caricature. For a long time now I have reacted to that accusation with contempt. I did not expect that I would have to renew that feeling in reading your letter. * * *

To A. P. Filosofov

Bougival, September 11 (23), 1874

* * * You began with Bazarov: I, too, shall start with him. You seek him in real life, but you won't find him. I shall tell you why. Times have changed. Bazarovs are not necessary now. For current social activity neither special talents nor even special intelligence is needed—nothing great, outstanding, too individualistic. Assiduity and patience are necessary. One must know how to sacrifice oneself without any ado; one must know how to humble oneself and not to abhor petty and obscure, even lowly work—I choose the word "lowly" in the sense of simple, straightforward, *terra à terre*. What, for example, could be more lowly than to teach a peasant to read, to help him, to found hospitals, etc.? What does talent and even erudition have to do with that? Only the heart is necessary, the ability to sacrifice one's egoism—one cannot even speak of a calling here (not to mention Mr. V. D.'s decoration). A feeling of duty, the glorious feeling of patriotism in the true sense of that word—that's all that's necessary.

And yet Bazarov is still a figure, a prophet, a huge figure endowed with a certain charm, not devoid of a certain aureole: all that is out of place now, and it is silly to speak of *heroes* or *artists* of work. . . . Yet your search for Bazarov—"the real one"—nevertheless expresses, unconsciously perhaps, the thirst for beauty, of a special kind, of course. All these dreams must be given up. * * *

To M. E. Saltykov[7]

Paris, January 3 (15), 1876

* * * Well, now I'll say a couple of words about *Fathers and Sons* too, since you mentioned it. Do you really suppose that I have not thought of everything you have reproached me with? That's why I did not want to disappear from the face of the earth without having finished my large novel, [*Virgin Soil*], which, so far as I can judge, would clarify many misunderstandings and would place me in the position where I really should be put. I don't wonder, incidentally, that Bazarov has remained an enigma for many people. I can hardly figure out how I wrote him. There was a *fatum* [fate] there—please don't laugh—something stronger than the author himself, something independent of him.

7. M. E. Saltykov-Schedrin (1826–89), Russia's leading satirist of that era and a major novelist [*Editor*].

I know one thing: there was no preconceived idea, no tendentiousness in me then. I wrote naïvely, as if I was struck myself by what came out. You refer to the disciple's teacher.[8] But it was precisely after *Fathers and Sons* that I became estranged from that circle, where, strictly speaking, I was never a member, and would have considered it stupid and shameful to write or to work for it. Tell me honestly, can a comparison to Bazarov be insulting to anyone? Do you not yourself notice that he is the most sympathetic of my characters? "A certain delicate fragrance" is added by readers. But I am ready to confess (and already did so in print in my *Reminiscences*) that I had no right to give our reactionary rabble the chance to pick up a catchword, a name. The writer in me should have sacrificed that to the citizen, and therefore I consider fair both the alienation of youth from me and all sorts of reproaches heaped on me. The problem rising then was more important than artistic truth, and I should have known it in advance. * * *

To A. V. *Toporov*

Paris, November 26 (*December* 8), 1882

* * * Incidentally, I forgot one important thing: under the heading *Fathers and Sons*, you must *without fail* put in brackets:

Dedicated to the memory of Vissarion Grigor'evich Belinsky. Don't forget. * * *

---

8. Bazarov's "teacher" is Chernyshevsky or Dobrolyubov, and the circle is that of the journal *The Contemporary* [Editor].

THE CONTEMPORARY
REACTION

DMITRY I. PISAREV

Bazarov†

Turgenev's new novel affords us all those pleasures which we have learned to expect from his works. The artistic finish is irreproachably good: the characters and situations, the episodes and scenes are rendered so graphically and yet so unobtrusively, that the most arrant repudiator of art will feel on reading the novel a kind of incomprehensible delight which can be explained neither by the inherent interest of the narrated events, nor by the striking truth of the fundamental idea. The fact is that the events are not particularly entertaining and that the idea is not startlingly true. The novel has neither plot nor denouement, nor a particularly well-considered structure; it has types and characters, it has episodes and scenes, and above all through the fabric of the narration we see the personal, deeply felt involvement of the author with the phenomena he has portrayed. And these phenomena are very close to us, so close that our whole younger generation with its aspirations and ideas can recognize itself in the characters of this novel. By this I do not mean to say that in Turgenev's novel the ideas and aspirations of the younger generation are depicted just as the younger generation itself understands them: Turgenev regards these ideas and aspirations from his own point of view, and age and youth almost never share the same convictions and sympathies. But if you go up to a mirror which while reflecting objects also changes their color a little bit, then you recognize your own physiognomy in spite of the distortions of the mirror. We see in Turgenev's novel contemporary types and at the same time we are aware of the changes which the phenomena of reality have undergone while passing through the consciousness of the artist. It is interesting to observe the effects on a man like Turgenev of the ideas and aspirations stirring in our younger generation and manifesting themselves, as do all living things, in the most diverse forms, seldom attractive, often original, sometimes misshapen.

Such an investigation may have profound significance. Turgenev is one of the best men of the last generation; to determine how he looks at us and why he looks at us thus and not otherwise is to find the reason for that conflict which is apparent everywhere in our private family life; this same conflict which so often leads to the destruction of young lives

---

† "Bazarov," D. I. Pisarev, in *Sochineniya* 2 (Moscow, 1955) 7–50. Translated by Lydia Hooke. Pisarev (1840–68), the most radical critic of the 1860's, published his review of *Fathers and Sons* within a month of the novel's appearance, and was in part responsible for the controversy that arose over the work. This essay is somewhat atypical of his work, where he usually sacrificed his genuine critical insight to further "The Destruction of Aesthetics," as he entitled one of his essays.

and which causes the continual moaning and groaning of our old men and women, who have not been able to fit the deeds and ideas of their sons and daughters to their own mold. As you can see, this is a task of vital importance, substantial and complex; I probably will not be able to cope with it but I am willing to try.

Turgenev's novel, in addition to its artistic beauty, is remarkable for the fact that it stirs the mind, leads to reflection, although, it does not solve a single problem itself and clearly illuminates not so much the phenomena depicted by the author as his own attitudes toward these phenomena. It leads to reflection precisely because everything is permeated with the most complete and most touching sincerity. Every last line in Turgenev's latest novel is deeply felt; this feeling breaks through against the will and realization of the author himself and suffuses the objective narration, instead of merely expressing itself in lyric digressions. The author himself is not clearly aware of his feelings; he does not subject them to analysis, nor does he assume a critical attitude toward them. This circumstance gives us the opportunity to see these feelings in all their unspoiled spontaneity. We see what shines through and not just what the author wants to show us or prove. Turgenev's opinions and judgments do not change our view of the younger generation or the ideas of our time by one iota; we do not even take them into consideration, we will not even argue with them; these opinions, judgments, and feelings, expressed in inimitably lifelike images, merely afford us material for a characterization of the older generation, in the person of one of its best representatives. I shall endeavor to organize this material and, if I succeed, I shall explain why our old people will not come to terms with us, why they shake their heads and, depending on the individual and the mood, are angry, bewildered, or quietly melancholy on account of our deeds and ideas.

II

The action of the novel takes place in the summer of 1859. A young university graduate, Arkady Nikolaevich Kirsanov, comes to the country to visit his father, accompanied by his friend, Evgeny Vassilyich Bazarov, who, evidently, exerts a strong influence on his young comrade's mode of thought. This Bazarov, a man of strong mind and character, occupies the center of the novel. He is the representative of our young generation; he possesses those personality traits which are distributed among the masses in small quantities; and the image of this man clearly and distinctly stands out in the reader's imagination.

Bazarov is the son of a poor district doctor; Turgenev says nothing about his life as a student, but it must be surmised that this life was poor, laborious, and difficult; Bazarov's father says of his son that he never in his life took an extra kopeck from them; to tell the truth, it would have been impossible to take very much even if he had wanted to; consequently, if the elder Bazarov says this in praise of his son, it means that Evgeny Vassilyich supported himself at the university by his own labor, eking out a living by giving cheap lessons and at the same time finding it possible to prepare himself ably for his future occupation. Bazarov emerged from this school of labor and deprivation a strong and stern man; the course of studies in natural and medical sciences which he pursued developed his innate intelligence and taught him never to accept any idea and conviction whatsoever on faith; he became a pure empiricist; experience became for him the sole source of knowledge, his own sensations—the sole and ultimate proof. "I maintain a negative attitude," he says, "by virtue of my sensations; I like to deny—my brain's made on that plan, and that's all! Why do I like chemistry? Why do you like apples?—also by virtue of our sensations. It's all the same thing. Men will never penetrate deeper than that. Not everyone will tell you that, and, in fact, I won't tell you so another time." As an empiricist, Bazarov acknowledges only what can be felt with the hands, seen with the eyes, tasted by the tongue, in a word, only what can be examined with one of the five senses. All other human feelings he reduces to the activity of the nervous system; consequently, the enjoyment of the beauty of nature, of music, painting, poetry, the love of a woman do not seem to him to be any loftier or purer than the enjoyment of a copious dinner or a bottle of good wine. What rapturous youths call an ideal does not exist for Bazarov; he calls all this "romanticism," and sometimes instead of the word "romanticism" he uses the word "nonsense." In spite of all this, Bazarov does not steal other people's handkerchiefs, he does not extract money from his parents, he works assiduously and is even not unwilling to do something useful in life. I have a presentiment that many of my readers will ask themselves: what restrains Bazarov from foul deeds and what motivates him to do anything useful? This question leads to the following doubt: is not Bazarov pretending to himself and to others? Is he not showing off? Perhaps in the depths of his soul he acknowledges much of what he repudiates aloud, and perhaps it is precisely what he thus acknowledges which secretly saves him from moral degradation and moral worthlessness. Although Bazarov is nothing to me, although I, perhaps, feel no sympathy for him, for the sake of abstract justice, I shall endeavor to answer this question and refute this silly doubt.

You can be as indignant as you please with people like Bazarov, but you absolutely must acknowledge their sincerity. These people can be honorable or dishonorable, civic stalwarts or inveterate swindlers, depending on circumstances and their personal tastes. Nothing but personal taste prevents them from killing or stealing and nothing but personal taste motivates such people to make discoveries in the realms of science and social life. Bazarov would not steal a handkerchief for the same reason that he would not eat a piece of putrid beef. If Bazarov were starving to death, then he probably would do both. The agonizing feeling of an unsatisfied physical need would conquer his aversion to the smell of rotting meat and to the secret encroachment on other people's property. In addition to direct inclination, Bazarov has one other guiding principle in life—calculation. When he is sick, he takes medicine, although he feels no direct inclination to swallow castor oil or assafetida. He acts thus through calculation: he pays the price of a minor unpleasantness in order to secure greater comfort in the future or deliverance from a greater unpleasantness. In a word, he chooses the lesser of two evils, although he feels no attraction even to the lesser evil. This sort of calculation generally proves useless to average people; they are calculatingly cunning and mean, they steal, become entangled and wind up being made fools of anyway. Very clever people act differently; they understand that being honorable is very advantageous and that every crime, from a simple lie to murder, is dangerous and consequently inconvenient. Thus very clever people can be honorable through calculation and act openly where limited people would equivocate and lay snares. By working tirelessly, Bazarov is following his direct inclination and taste, and, furthermore, acts according to the truest calculation. If he had sought patronage, bowed and scraped, acted meanly instead of working and conducting himself proudly and independently, he would have been acting against his best interests. Careers forged through one's own work are always more secure and broader than a career built with low bows or the intercession of an important uncle. By the two latter means, it is possible to wind up as a provincial or even a metropolitan bigwig, but since the world began, no one has ever succeeded in becoming a Washington, Copernicus, Garibaldi, or Heinrich Heine through such means. Even Herostratus built his career by his own efforts and did not find his way into history through patronage. As for Bazarov, he does not aspire to become a provincial bigwig: if his imagination sometimes pictures the future, then this future is somehow indefinitely broad; he works without a goal, in order to earn his crust of bread or from love of the process of work, but, nevertheless, he vaguely feels that given the caliber of his mind his work will not pass without a trace and will lead to something. Bazarov is exceedingly full of self-esteem, but this self-esteem is unnoticeable as a direct consequence of his vastness. He is not interested in the trifles of which commonplace human relationships are composed; it would be impossible to insult him with obvious disdain or to make him happy with signs of respect; he is so full of himself and stands so unshakably high in his own eyes that he is almost completely indifferent to other people's opinions. Kirsanov's uncle, who closely resembles Bazarov in his cast of mind and character, calls his self-esteem "satanic pride." This expression is well-chosen and characterizes our hero perfectly. In truth, it would take nothing short of a whole eternity of constantly expanding activity and constantly increasing pleasures to satisfy Bazarov, but to his misfortune, Bazarov does not believe in the eternal existence of the human personality. "You said, for instance," he says to his friend Arkady, "to-day as we passed our bailiff Philip's cottage—it's the one that's so nice and clean—well, you said Russia will attain perfection when the poorest peasant has a hut like that, and every one of us ought to work to bring it about. . . . And I felt such a hatred for this poorest peasant, this Philip or Sidor, for whom I'm to be ready to jump out of my skin, and who won't even thank me for it . . . and what do I need his thanks for? Why, suppose he does live in a clean hut, while I am pushing up daisies,—well, what comes after that?"

Thus Bazarov, everywhere and in everything, does only what he wishes or what seems to him to be advantageous or convenient. He is ruled only by his whims or his personal calculations. Neither over himself, nor outside himself, nor within himself does he recognize a moderator, a moral law or principle; ahead—no exalted goal; in his mind —no high design, and yet he has such great capacities.—But this is an immoral man! A villain, a monster!—I hear the exclamations of indignant readers on all sides. Well, all right, a villain and a monster; abuse him further; abuse him more, persecute him with satire and epigrams, indignant lyricism and aroused public opinion, the fires of the Inquisition and the executioners' axes—and you will neither rout him out nor kill this monster, nor preserve him in alcohol for the edification of the respectable public. If Bazarovism is a disease, then it is a disease of our time, and must be endured to the end, no matter what palliatives and amputations are employed. Treat Bazarovism however you please—that is your business; but you will not be able to put a stop to it; it is just the same as cholera.

III

The disease of an age first infects the people who by virtue of their mental powers stand higher than the common level. Bazarov, who is possessed by this disease, is distinguished by his remarkable mind and consequently produces a strong impression on people who come into contact with him. "A real man," he says, "is one whom it's no use thinking about, whom one must either obey or hate." This definition of a real man precisely fits Bazarov himself: he continually seizes the attention of the people surrounding him at once; some he frightens and antagonizes; others he conquers, not so much with arguments as with the direct force, simplicity, and integrity of his ideas. As a remarkably intelligent man, he has never yet met his equal. " 'When I meet a man who can hold his own beside me,' he said, dwelling on every syllable, 'then I'll change my opinion of myself.' "

He looks down on people and rarely even takes the trouble to conceal his half-disdainful, half-patronizing attitude toward those who hate him and those who obey him. He loves no one; although he does not break existing ties and relationships, he does not move a muscle to renew or maintain these relationships, nor does he soften one note in his harsh voice or sacrifice one cutting joke or witty remark.

He acts thus not in the name of a principle, not in order to be completely frank at every moment, but simply because he considers it completely unnecessary to lay any restraint whatsoever on himself; for the same motive from which Americans throw their legs over the backs of chairs and spit tobacco juice on the parquet floors of elegant hotels. Bazarov needs no one, fears no one, loves no one and consequently spares no one. Like Diogenes he is almost ready to live in a barrel and because of this grants himself the right to tell people to their faces the harsh truth, simply because it pleases him to do so. We can distinguish two sides to Bazarov's cynicism—an internal and an external one; a cynicism of thought and feeling and a cynicism of manner and expression. An ironic attitude toward emotion of any sort, toward dreaminess, lyrical transports and effusions, is the essence of the internal cynicism. The rude expression of this irony, and a causeless and purposeless harshness in the treatment of others relates to external cynicism. The first depends on the cast of mind and general world view; the second is conditioned by purely external conditions of development; the traits of the society in which the subject under consideration lived. Bazarov's derisive attitude toward the softhearted Kirsanov follows from the basic characteristic of the general Bazarov type. His rude clashes with Kirsanov and his uncle arise from his individual traits. Bazarov is not only an empiricist, he is also an uncouth rowdy, who has known no life other than the homeless, laborious, sometimes wildly dissipated life of the poor student. In the ranks of Bazarov's admirers there will undoubtedly be those who will be enraptured by his coarse manners, the vestiges of student life, who will imitate these manners, which are, in any case, a shortcoming and not a virtue, who will perhaps even exaggerate his harshness, gracelessness, and abruptness. In the ranks of Bazarov's enemies there will undoubtedly be those who will pay particular attention to these ugly features of his personality and will use them to reproach the general type. Both of these groups would be mistaken and would only be displaying their profound incomprehension of the real matter. We may remind them of Pushkin's lines:

> One may be a man of sense
> Yet consider the beauty of his fingernails.

It is possible to be an extreme materialist, a complete empiricist and at the same time look after your toilet, treat your acquaintances politely, be amiable in conversation and a perfect gentleman. I say this for the

benefit of those readers who attribute great significance to refined manners, who look with aversion on Bazarov, as on a man who is *mal élevé*[1]
and *mauvais ton.*[2] He really is *mal élevé* and *mauvais ton,* but this really
has no relevance to the essence of the type and speaks neither against
it nor in its favor. Turgenev decided to choose as a representative of the
Bazarov type an uncouth man; of course as he delineated his hero, he
did not conceal or try to gloss over his awkwardness. Turgenev's choice
can be explained by two motives: first, the character's personality, the
tendency to deny ruthlessly and with complete conviction everything
which others consider exalted and beautiful, is most often engendered
by the drab conditions of a life of labor; from hard labor the hands
coarsen, so do the manners and emotions; the man grows stronger and
banishes youthful dreaminess, rids himself of lachrymose sensitivity; it
is not possible to daydream at work, the attention is directed on the
business at hand, and after work one must rest and really satisfy one's
physical needs and one has no time for dreams. This man has become
used to looking on dreams as on a whim, peculiar to idleness and
aristocratic pampering; he has begun to consider moral sufferings to be
products of daydreams; moral aspirations and actions as imagined and
ridiculous. For him, the laboring man, there exists only one, eternally
recurring care: today he must think about how not to starve tomorrow.
This simple care, terrible in its simplicity, overshadows everything else
for him, secondary anxieties, the petty troubles and cares of life; in
comparison with this care the artificial products of various unsolved
problems, unresolved doubts, indefinite relations which poison the lives
of secure, idle people seem to him to be trivial and insignificant.

Thus the proletarian laborer, by the very process of his life, independently of the process of reflection, arrives at practical realism; from lack
of leisure he forgets how to dream, to pursue an ideal, to aspire to an
unattainably lofty goal. By developing the laborer's energy, labor teaches
him to unite thought and deed, an act of will with an act of the mind.
The man who has learned to rely on himself and on his own capacities,
who has become used to accomplishing today what he conceived yesterday, begins to look with more or less obvious disdain on people who
dream of love, of useful activity, of the happiness of the whole human
race, and yet are not capable of lifting a finger to improve even a little
whether he be doctor, artisan, pedagogue, or even a writer (it is possible
to be a writer and at the same time a man of action), feels a natural,
indefinable aversion to phrase making, to waste of words, to sweet
thoughts, to sentimental aspirations, and in general to all pretensions
not based on real tangible forces. This aversion to everything estranged
from life and everything that has turned into empty phrases is the fundamental characteristic of the Bazarov type. This fundamental charac-

1. "Badly brought up" [*Editor*].
2. "Ill-bred" [*Editor*].

teristic is engendered in precisely those various workshops where man, sharpening his mind and straining his muscles, struggles with nature for the right to live in the wide world. On these grounds, Turgenev had the right to take his hero from one of these workshops and to bring him into the society of cavaliers and ladies, in a work apron, with dirty hands, and a gloomy and preoccupied gaze. But justice forces me to put forward the proposition that the author of *Fathers and Sons* acted thus not without an insidious intention. This insidious intention is the second motive to which I referred earlier. The fact is that Turgenev, evidently, looks with no great favor on his hero. His soft, loving nature, striving for faith and sympathy, is jarred by corrosive realism; his delicate esthetic sensibility, not devoid of a large dose of aristocratism, takes offense at the faintest glimmer of cynicism; he is too weak and sensitive to bear dismal repudiations; he must become reconciled with existence, if not in the realm of life, at least in the realm of thought, or, more precisely, dreams. Like a nervous woman or the plant "touch-me not," Turgenev shrinks from the slightest contact with the bouquet of Bazarovism.

This feeling, an involuntary antipathy toward this tenor of thought, he presented to the reading public in a specimen as ungraceful as possible. He knows very well that there are very many fashionable readers in our public and, counting on the refinement of their aristocratic tastes, he did not spare the coarse details, with the evident desire of debasing and vulgarizing not only his hero but the cast of ideas which form the defining characteristic of the type. He knows very well that the majority of his readers will say of Bazarov that he is badly brought up and that it would be impossible to have him in a respectable drawing room; they will go no further or deeper; but speaking with such people, a talented artist and honorable man must be extremely careful out of respect for himself and the idea which he is upholding or refuting. Here one must hold one's personal antipathy in check since under some conditions it can turn into the involuntary slander of people who do not have the opportunity to defend themselves with the same weapons. * * *

* * * Arkady's uncle, Pavel Petrovich, might be called a small-scale Pechorin; he sowed some wild oats in his time and played the fool but finally began to tire of it all; he never succeeded in settling down, it just was not in his character; when he reached the time of life when, as Turgenev puts it, regrets resemble hopes and hopes resemble regrets, the former lion moved in with his brother in the country, surrounded himself with elegant comfort and turned his life into a peaceful vegetation. The outstanding memory of Pavel Petrovich's noisy and brilliant life was his strong feeling for a woman of high society, a feeling which had afforded him much pleasure, and afterward, as is almost always the case, much suffering. When Pavel Petrovich's relations with this woman were severed, his life became perfectly empty.

"He wandered from place to place like a man possessed;" Turgenev writes, "he still went into society; he still retained the habits of a man of the world; he could boast of two or three fresh conquests; but he no longer expected anything special of himself or of others, and he undertook nothing. He aged and his hair turned grey; to spend his evenings at the club in jaded boredom, and to argue in bachelor society became a necessity for him—a bad sign as we all know. He did not even think of marriage, of course. Ten years passed in this way. They passed by colorless and fruitless—and quickly, fearfully quickly. Nowhere does time fly past as in Russia; in prison they say it flies even faster."

An acrimonious and passionate man, endowed with a versatile mind and a strong will, Pavel Petrovich is sharply distinguished from his brother and from his nephew. He does not succumb to the influence of other people; he himself dominates the people around him and he hates those people from whom he suffers a rebuff. He has no convictions, truth to tell, but he has habits by which he sets great store. From habit he speaks of the rights and duties of the aristocracy, and from habit proves in arguments the necessity for *principles*. He is used to the ideas which are held by society and he stands up for these ideas, just as he stands up for his comfort. He cannot bear it when someone refutes his ideas, although, at bottom, he has no heartfelt attachment to them. He argues with Bazarov much more energetically than does his brother, and yet Nikolai Petrovich suffers much more from his merciless repudiations. In the depths of his soul, Pavel Petrovich is just as much of a skeptic and empiricist as Bazarov himself; in practical life he always acted and acts as he sees fit, but in the realm of thought he is not able to admit this to himself and thus he adheres in words to doctrines which his actions continually contradict. It would be well if uncle and nephew were to exchange convictions, since the first mistakenly ascribes to himself a belief in *principes* and the second just as mistakenly imagines himself to be an extreme skeptic and a daring rationalist. Pavel Petrovich begins to feel a strong antipathy toward Bazarov from their first meeting. Bazarov's plebeian manners rouse the indignation of the outdated dandy; his self-confidence and unceremoniousness irritate Pavel Petrovich as a lack of respect for his elegant person. Pavel Petrovich sees that Bazarov does not allow him to predominate over himself and this arouses in him a feeling of vexation on which he seizes as a diversion amidst the profound boredom of country life. Hating Bazarov himself, Pavel Petrovich is outraged by all his opinions, he carps at him, forces him into arguments, and argues with the zealous enthusiasm which is displayed by people who are idle and easily bored.

And what does Bazarov do amidst these three personalities? First of all, he endeavors to pay them as little attention as possible and spends the greater part of his time at work; he roams about the neighborhood, collects plants and insects, dissects frogs, and occupies himself with his microscope; he regards Arkady as a child, Nikolai Petrovich as a good-natured old man or, as he puts it, an old romantic. His feeling toward Pavel Petrovich is not exactly amicable; he is annoyed by the element of haughtiness in him, but he involuntarily tries to conceal his irritation under the guise of disdainful indifference. He does not want to admit to himself that he can be angered by a "provincial aristocrat," yet his passionate nature outs, frequently he replies vehemently to Pavel Petrovich's tirades and does not immediately succeed in gaining control over himself and once more shutting himself up in his derisive coldness. Bazarov does not like to argue or, in general, to express his opinions and only Pavel Petrovich is sometimes able to draw him into a significant discussion. These two strong characters react with hostility to each other; seeing these two men face to face it is easy to be reminded of the struggle between two successive generations. Nikolai Petrovich, of course, is not capable of being an oppressor: Arkady Nikolaevich, of course, is incapable of struggling against familial despotism; but Pavel Petrovich and Bazarov could, under certain conditions, be clear representatives: the former of the congealing, hardening forces of the past, the latter of the liberating, destructive forces of the present.

On whose side are the artist's feelings? This vitally important question may be answered definitely: Turgenev does not fully sympathize with any of his characters; his analysis does not miss one weak or ridiculous trait; we see how Bazarov senselessly repudiates everything, how Arkady revels in his enlightenment, how Nikolai Petrovich is as timid as a fifteen-year-old boy, and how Pavel Petrovich shows off and is angry that he has not won the admiration of Bazarov, the only man whom he respects, despite his hatred of him.

Bazarov talks nonsense—this is unfortunately true. He bluntly repudiates things which he does not know or understand: poetry, in his opinion is rubbish; reading Pushkin is a waste of time; to be interested in music is ludicrous; to enjoy nature is absurd. It is very possible that he, a man stifled by a life of labor, lost or never had time to develop the capacity to enjoy the pleasant stimulation of the visual and auditory nerves, but it does not follow from this that he has a rational basis for repudiating or ridiculing this capacity in others. To cut other people down to fit your own measure is to fall into narrow-minded intellectual despotism. To deny completely arbitrarily one or another natural and real human need is to break with pure empiricism.

Bazarov's tendency to get carried away is very natural; it can be explained, first by the one-sidedness of his development, and secondly by the general character of the time in which we live. Bazarov knows natural and medical sciences thoroughly: with their assistance he has rid himself of all prejudices; however, he has remained an extremely uneducated man; he has heard something or other about poetry, something or other about art, and not troubling to think, he passed abrupt sentence on these subjects which were unknown to him. This arrogance is generally a characteristic of ours; it has its good sides such as intellectual courage, but on the other hand, of course, it leads at times to flagrant errors. The general character of the time is practicality: we all want to live by the rule that fine words butter no parsnips. Very energetic people often exaggerate the prevailing tendency; on these grounds, Bazarov's overly indiscriminate repudiations and the very one-sidedness of his development are tied directly to the prevailing striving for tangible benefits. We have become tired of the phrases of the Hegelians, our heads have begun to spin from soaring around in the clouds, and many of us, having sobered up and come down to earth, have gone to the other extreme and while banishing dreaminess have started to persecute simple feelings and even purely physical sensations, like the enjoyment of music. There is no great harm in this extremity, but it will not hurt to point it out; and to call it ludicrous does not mean to join the ranks of the obscurantists and old romantics. Many of our realists are up in arms against Turgenev because he does not sympathize with Bazarov and does not conceal his hero's blunders from the reader; many express the desire that Bazarov had been presented as an irreproachable man, a knight of thought without fear and reproach, and that thereby the superiority of realism to all other schools of thought would thus have been proved to the reading public. In my opinion, realism is indeed a fine thing; but let us not, in the name of this very realism, idealize either ourselves or our movement. We coldly and soberly regard all that surrounds us; let us regard ourselves just as coldly and soberly; all around us is nonsense and backwardness, but, God knows, we are far from perfect. What we repudiate is ridiculous but the repudiators have also been known, at times, to commit colossal follies; all the same, they stand higher than what they repudiate, but this is no great honor; to stand higher than flagrant absurdity does not yet mean to become a great thinker. But we, the speaking and writing realists, are now too carried away by the mental struggle of the moment, by this fiery skirmish with backward idealists, with whom it is not even worthwhile to argue; we, in my view, have gotten too carried away to maintain a skeptical attitude toward ourselves and to submit to rigorous analysis the possibility that we might have fallen into the dust of the dialectic battles which go on in journalistic pamphlets and in everyday life. Our children will regard us skeptically, or, perhaps, we ourselves will learn our real value and will begin to look *à vol d'oiseau*[3] on our present beloved ideas. Then we will regard the past from the height of the present; Turgenev is now regarding the present from the height of the past. He does not follow us, but tranquilly gazes after us and describes our gait, telling us how we quicken our pace, how we jump across ditches, how now and then we stumble over rough places in the road. There is no irritation in the tone of his description; he has simply

3. "As the crow flies," that is, "straight." Pisarev seems to think it means to have a "bird's eye view" [*Editor*].

grown tired of moving on; the development of his own world view has come to an end, but his capacity to observe the movement of another person's thought process, to understand and reproduce all its windings, has remained in all its fullness and freshness. Turgenev himself will never be a Bazarov, but he has pondered this type and gained an understanding of it so true that not one of our young realists has yet achieved it. There is no apotheosis of the past in Turgenev's novel. The author of *Rudin* and "Asya," who laid bare the weaknesses of his generation and who revealed in *A Hunter's Sketches* a whole world of wonders which had been taking place right in front of the eyes of this very generation, has remained true to himself and has not acted against his conscience in his latest work. The representatives of the past, the "fathers," are depicted with ruthless fidelity; they are good people, but Russia will not regret these good people; there is not one element in them which would be worth saving from the grave and oblivion, but still there are moments when one can sympathize more fully with these fathers than with Bazarov himself. When Nikolai Petrovich admires the evening landscape he appears more human than Bazarov who groundlessly denies the beauty of nature to every unprejudiced reader.

> "And is nature nonsense?" said Arkady, looking pensively at the bright-colored fields in the distance, in the beautiful soft light of the sun, which was no longer high in the sky.
> "Nature, too, is nonsense in the sense you understand it. Nature's not a temple, but a workshop, and man's the workman in it."

In these words, Bazarov's repudiation has turned into something artificial and has even ceased to be consistent. Nature is a workshop and man is a worker in it—with this idea I am ready to agree; but when I carry this idea further, I by no means arrive at the conclusion which Bazarov draws. A worker needs rest and rest does not only mean heavy sleep after exhausting labor. A man must refresh himself with pleasant sensations; life without pleasant sensations, even if all the vital needs are satisfied, turns into unbearable suffering. The consistent materialists, like Karl Vogt, Moleschotte, and Büchner do not deny a day-laborer his glass of vodka, nor the well-to-do classes the use of narcotics. They indulgently regard even the excessive use of such substances, although they acknowledge that such excesses are harmful to the health. If a worker found pleasure in spending his free time lying on his back and gazing at the walls and ceiling of his workshop, then every sensible man would say to him: gaze on, dear friend, stare as much as you please, it won't harm your health but don't you spend your working hours staring or you will make mistakes. Why then, if we permit the use of vodka and narcotics, should we not tolerate the enjoyment of beautiful scenery, mild air, fresh verdure, the gentle play of form and color? Bazarov, in his persecution of romanticism, with incredible suspiciousness seeks it in places where it never has existed. Taking arms against idealism and destroying its castles in the air, he himself, at times, becomes an idealist, that is, he begins to prescribe to man how he should enjoy himself and how he should regulate his own sensations. Telling a man not to enjoy nature is like telling him to mortify his flesh. The more harmless sources of pleasure there are, the easier it is to live in the world, and the whole task of our generation is precisely to decrease the sum of suffering and increase the strength and amount of pleasure. Many will retort that we live in such a difficult time that it is out of the question to think about pleasure; our job, they will say, is to work, to eradicate evil, disseminate good, to clear a site for the great building where our remote descendants will feast. All right, I agree that we are compelled to work for the future, since the fruit we have sown can ripen only after several centuries; let us suppose that our goal is very lofty, still this loftiness of goal affords very little comfort in everyday unpleasantnesses. It is doubtful whether an exhausted and worn-out man will become gay and contented from the thought that his great-great-grandson will enjoy his life. Comforting oneself in the hard moments of life with a lofty goal is, if you will, just the same as drinking unsweetened tea while gazing on a piece of sugar hung from the ceiling. For people without exceedingly vivid imaginations, these wistful upward looks do not make the tea any tastier. In precisely the same way, a life consisting exclusively of work is not to the taste and beyond the powers of contemporary man. Thus, with whatever viewpoint you regard life, you will still be brought up against the fact that pleasure is absolutely indispensable. Some regard pleasure as a final goal; others are compelled to acknowledge pleasure as a very important source of the strength necessary for work. This is the sole difference between the epicureans and stoics of our day.

Thus, Turgenev does not fully sympathize with anyone or anything in his novel. If you were to say to him: "Ivan Sergeevich, you do not like Bazarov, but what would you prefer?" he would not answer the question. He would not wish the younger generation to share their fathers' ideas and enthusiasms. Neither the fathers nor the sons satisfy him, and in this case, his repudiation is more profound and more serious than the repudiations of those people, who, having destroyed everything that existed before them, imagine that they are the salt of the earth and the purest expression of total humanity. These people are perhaps right in their destruction, but in their naïve self-adoration or in their adoration of the type which they consider that represents, lies their limitation and one-sidedness. The forms and types with which we can be contented and feel no need to look further have not yet been and perhaps never will be created by life. People who give up their intellectual independence and substitute servile worship for criticism, by giving themselves over completely to one or another prevailing theory, reveal that they are narrow, impotent, and often harmful people. Arkady is capable of acting in this way, but it would be completely impossible for Bazarov, and it is precisely this trait of mind and character which produces the captivating power of Turgenev's hero. The author understands and acknowledges this captivating power, despite the fact that neither in temperament nor in the conditions of his development does he resemble his nihilist. Furthermore, Turgenev's general attitudes toward the phenomena of life which make up his novel are so calm and disinterested, so devoid of slavish worship of one or another theory, that Bazarov himself would not have found anything timid or false in these attitudes. Turgenev does not like ruthless negations, but, nevertheless, the personality of the ruthless negator appears as a powerful one—and commands the involuntary respect of every reader. Turgenev has a propensity for idealism, but, nevertheless, not one of the idealists in his novel can be compared to Bazarov either in strength of mind or in strength of character. I am certain that many of our journalistic critics will want, at all costs, to find in Turgenev's novel a repressed urge to debase the younger generation and prove that the children are worse than their parents, but I am just as certain that the readers' spontaneous feelings, unfettered by the necessity of supporting a theory, will approve Turgenev and will find in his work not a dissertation on a particular theme, but a true, deeply felt picture of contemporary life drawn without the slightest attempt at concealment of anything. If a writer belonging to our younger generation and profoundly sympathizing with the "Bazarov school" had happened upon Turgenev's theme, then, of course, the picture would have been drawn otherwise and the colors would have been applied differently. Bazarov would not have been portrayed as an awkward student dominating the people around him through the natural strength of his healthy mind; he, perhaps, would have been turned into the embodiment of the ideas which make up the essence of this type; he, perhaps, would have manifested in his personality the clear expression of the author's tendencies, but it is doubtful whether he would have been Bazarov's equal in faithfulness to life and roundness of characterization. My young artist would have said to his contemporaries of his work: "This, my friends, is what a fully developed man must be like! This is the final goal of our efforts!" But Turgenev just says calmly and simply: "This is the sort of young people there are nowadays!" and does not even try to conceal the fact that such young people are not completely to his taste. "How can this be?" many of our contemporary journalists and publicists will cry. "This is obscurantism!" Gentlemen, we could answer, why should Turgenev's personal sensations concern you? Whether he likes such people or does not like them is a matter of taste; if, for instance, feeling no sympathy for the type, he were to slander it, then every honorable man would have the right to unmask him, but you will not find such slander in the novel: even Bazarov's awkwardnesses, to which I already alluded, are perfectly satisfactorily explained by the circumstances of his life and constitute, if not an essential requirement, at least a very frequently encountered trait of people of the Bazarov type. It would, of course, have been much more pleasant for us, the young people, if Turgenev had concealed and glossed over the graceless rough places in Bazarov, but I do not think that an artist who indulged our capricious desires could better capture the phenomena of reality. Both virtues and shortcomings are more clearly apparent when regarded from a detached point of view, and, for this reason, a detached, severely critical view of Bazarov proves, at present, to be much more fruitful than indiscriminate admiration or slavish worship. By regarding Bazarov detachedly as is possible only for a man who is "behind the times" and not involved in the contemporary movement of ideas; by examining him with the cold, probing gaze which is only engendered by long experience of life, Turgenev has justified his hero and valued him at his true worth. Bazarov has emerged from this examination as a pure and a strong man. Turgenev did not find one essential indictment against this type, and thus his voice, the voice of a man who finds himself in a camp which is inconsistent with his age and his views of life, has an especially important and decisive meaning. Turgenev did not grow fond of Bazarov, but he acknowledged his strength and his superiority and offered him a full tribute of respect.

This is more than sufficient to absolve Turgenev's novel from the powerful charge of being behind the times; it is even sufficient to compel us to acknowledge his novel as practically useful for the present age.

VI

Bazarov's relations with his comrade throw a bright streak of light on his character: Bazarov has no friends, since he has not yet met a man "who could hold his own" with him; Bazarov stands alone at the cold heights of sober thought and he is not oppressed by his isolation, he is completely engrossed in himself and in his work; observations and experiments on living nature, observations and experiments on living people fill for him the emptiness of his life and insure him against boredom. He does not feel the need to look for sympathy and understanding in another person; when some thought occurs to him, he simply expresses it, paying no attention whether his listeners agree with his opinion, or whether his ideas please them. Most frequently he does not even feel the need to express himself; he thinks to himself and, from time to time, lets drop a cursory remark, which is usually seized upon with respectful eagerness by his proselytes and pupils like Arkady. Bazarov's personality is self-contained and reserved, since it finds practically no kindred elements either outside or around itself. This reserve of Bazarov's has a dampening effect on the people who would like to see tenderness and communicativeness from him, but there is nothing artificial or pre-

meditated in this reserve. The people who surround Bazarov are insignificant intellectually and can in no way move him, thus he is either
silent or speaks in abrupt aphorisms, or breaks off an argument he has
begun because he recognizes its ludicrous uselessness. If you put an
adult in the same room with a dozen children, you will probably feel
no surprise if the adult does not begin to converse with his roommates
about his humanistic, social, and scientific convictions. Bazarov does
not put on airs before other people, he does not consider himself a man
of genius misunderstood by his contemporaries; he is merely obliged to
regard his acquaintances from above because these acquaintances only
come up to his knees; what else can he do? Is he to sit on the floor so
that he will be the same height as they? He cannot pretend to be a child
just so that the children will share their immature ideas with him. He
involuntarily remains in isolation, and this isolation does not oppress
him because he is young and strong and occupied with the seething
activity of his own thoughts. The process of these thoughts remains in
the shadows; I doubt whether Turgenev was in a position to render the
description of this process: in order to portray it, he would have had to
live through it in his own head, he would have had to himself become
Bazarov, but we can be sure that this did not happen to Turgenev,
because anyone who had even once, even for a few minutes, looked at
things through Bazarov's eyes would have remained a nihilist for the
rest of his life. In Turgenev, we see only the results at which Bazarov
arrived, we see the external side of the phenomena; that is, we hear
what Bazarov says and we know how he acts in life, how he treats various
people. But we do not find a psychological analysis or a coherent com-
pendium of Bazarov's thoughts; we can only guess what he thought and
how he formulated his convictions to himself. By not initiating the reader
into the secret of Bazarov's intellectual life, Turgenev may cause bewilderment among the segment of the public which is not used to filling
in through their own mental efforts what is not stated or written in the
works of a writer. The inattentive reader may come to the conclusion
that Bazarov has no internal substance and that his entire nihilism
consists of an interweaving of daring phrases snatched from the air and
not created by independent thought. It is possible to say positively that
Turgenev himself does not fully understand his hero, and does not trace
the gradual development and maturation of his ideas only because he
cannot and does not want to render Bazarov's thoughts as they would
have arisen in his hero's mind. Bazarov's thoughts are expressed in his
deeds, in his treatment of people; they shine through and it is not difficult
to make them out, if only the reader carefully organizes the facts and
is aware of their causes.

Two episodes fill in the details of this remarkable personality: first,
his treatment of the woman who attracts him; secondly, his death.

I will consider both of these, but first I consider it not out of place to turn my attention to other, secondary details.

Bazarov's treatment of his parents will predispose some readers against the character, and others against the author. The former, becoming carried away by sentimental feelings, will reproach Bazarov for callousness; the latter, becoming carried away by their attachment to the Bazarov type, will reproach Turgenev for injustice to his hero and for a desire to show him in a disadvantageous light. Both sides, in my opinion, would be completely wrong. Bazarov really does not afford his parents the pleasures which the good old people were expecting from his visit to them, but between him and his parents there is not one thing in common. * * *

In town, at the governor's ball, Arkady becomes acquainted with a young widow, Anna Sergeyevna Odintsov; while dancing the mazurka with her, he happens to mention his friend Bazarov and excites her interest with his rapturous description of his friend's daring intellect and decisive character. She invites him to visit her and asks him to bring Bazarov. Bazarov, who had noticed her the instant she appeared at the ball, speaks to Arkady about her, involuntarily intensifying the usual cynicism of his tone, partially in order to conceal both from himself and from Arkady the impression that this woman has made on him. He willingly agrees to visit Odintsov with Arkady and explains his pleasure to himself and to Arkady by his hope of beginning a pleasant intrigue. Arkady, who has not failed to succumb to Odintsov's charms, takes offense at Bazarov's jocular tone, but, of course, Bazarov pays not the slightest attention and keeps on talking about Odintsov's beautiful shoulders, he asks Arkady whether this lady is really "ooh la la!", he says that still waters run deep and that a cold woman is just like ice cream. As he approaches Odintsov's apartments Bazarov feels a certain agitation and, wanting to overcome it, at the beginning of the visit behaves unnaturally informally and, according to Turgenev, sprawls in his chair just like Sitnikov. Odintsov notices Bazarov's agitation and, partially guessing its cause, calms our hero down with the gentle affability of her manner, and the young people's unhurried, diverse, and lively conversation continues for three hours. Bazarov treats her with special respect; it is evident that he is not indifferent to what she thinks of him, to the impression he is making; contrary to his usual habit, he speaks quite a lot, tries to interest his listener, does not make cutting remarks and even, carefully avoiding topics of general concern, discusses botany, medicine, and other subjects he is well-versed in. As the young men take their leave, Odintsov invites them to visit her in the country. Bazarov bows silently to indicate his acceptance and flushes. Arkady notices all this and is astonished by it. After this first meeting with Odintsov, Bazarov endeavors to speak of her in his former jocular tone, but the very cynicism of his expressions belies an involuntary, repressed respect. It is evident that he admires this woman and wishes to come into friendship with her; he jokes about her because he does not want to speak seriously with Arkady, either about this woman or about the new sensations which he notices in himself. Bazarov could not fall in love with Odintsov at first sight or after their first meeting; such things only happen to very shallow people in very bad novels. He was simply taken by her beautiful, or as he himself puts it, splendid body; her conversation did not destroy the general harmony of impressions, and this was enough at first to reinforce his desire to know her better. Bazarov has not yet formulated a theory about love. His student years, about which Turgenev does not say a word, probably did not pass without some affair of the heart; Bazarov, as we shall see later on, proves to be an experienced man, but, in all probability, he has had to do with women who were completely un-educated and far from refined and, consequently, incapable of strongly interesting his intellect or stirring his nerves; when he meets Odintsov he sees that it is possible to speak to her as an equal and senses that she possesses the versatile mind and firm character which he is conscious of and likes in himself. When Bazarov and Odintsov speak to each other they are able, intellectually speaking, to look each other in the eye over the fledgling Arkady's head and this instinctive mutual understanding affords them both pleasant sensations. Bazarov sees an elegant figure and involuntarily admires it; beyond this figure he discerns innate strength and unconsciously begins to respect this strength. As a pure empiricist, he enjoys the pleasant sensation and gradually becomes so accustomed to it, that when the time comes to tear himself away, it is difficult and painful for him to do so. Bazarov does not subject love to an analysis because he feels no mistrust in himself. He goes to the country to see Odintsov, with curiosity and without the slightest fear, because he wants to have a closer look at this pretty woman, wants to be with her and to spend a few days pleasantly. In the country, fifteen days pass imperceptibly; Bazarov talks with Anna Sergeyevna a lot, argues with her, expresses himself fully, and finally begins to feel for her a kind of malicious, tormenting passion. Such passion is most frequently en-gendered in energetic men by women who are beautiful, intelligent, and cold. The beauty of the woman stirs the blood of her admirer; her mind allows her to understand and to subject to subtle psychological analysis the feelings which she does not share or even sympathize with; her coldness insures her against getting carried away, and by increasing the obstacles, increases the man's desire to overcome them. Looking at such a woman, a man involuntarily thinks: she is so beautiful, she speaks so well about emotion, at times she becomes so animated when she expresses her subtle psychological analysis or listens to my deeply felt speeches. Why are her feelings so obstinately silent? How can I touch her to the quick? Can it be that her whole being is concentrated in her brain? Can it be that she is only amusing herself with impressions and is not capable of becoming carried away by them? Time passes in strenuous efforts to puzzle out the vital enigma; the intellect labors alongside the passions; heavy, torturous sensations appear; the whole romance of the relationship between a man and a woman takes on the strange character of a struggle. Becoming acquainted with Odintsov, Bazarov thought to amuse himself with a pleasant intrigue; knowing her better, he felt respect for her but began to see that he had little hope of success; if he had not managed to become strongly attached to Odintsov, he simply would have dismissed her with a shrug and immediately have occupied himself with the practical observation that the world is very large and there are many women in it who are easier to handle; he tried to act in such a way but he did not have the strength to shrug off Odintsov. Common sense advised him to abandon the whole affair and go away so as not to torment himself in vain, but his craving for pleasure spoke more loudly than his common sense and Bazarov remained. He was angry and he was conscious of the fact that he was committing a folly but, nevertheless, went on committing it, because his desire to live for his pleasure was stronger than his desire to be consistent. This capacity consciously to behave stupidly is an enviable virtue of strong and intelligent people. A dispassionate and dried-up person always acts according to logical calculations; a timid and weak person tries to deceive himself with sophistry and assure himself of the rightness of his desires and actions; but Bazarov has no need for such trickery; he says to himself straightforwardly: this is stupid, but nevertheless, I will do what I want, and I do not want to torment myself over it. When it becomes necessary I will have the time and strength to do what I must. A wholehearted, strong nature is manifested in this capacity to become completely carried away: a healthy, incorruptible mind is expressed in this capability to recognize as folly the passion which has consumed the whole organism.

Bazarov's relationship with Odintsov is brought to an end by a strange scene which takes place between them. She draws him into a discussion about happiness and love; with the curiosity peculiar to cold and intelligent women she questions him about what is taking place within him, she extracts a confession of love from him, with a trace of involuntary tenderness she utters his name; then, when stunned by the sudden onslaught of sensation, and new hopes, he rushes to her and clasps her to his breast, she jumps away in fear to the other end of the room and assures him that he had misunderstood her, that he was mistaken.

Bazarov leaves the room and with this their relationship comes to an end. He leaves her house the day after this incident; afterward, he sees Anna Sergeyevna twice, even visits her in the company of Arkady, but for both of them past events prove to be irrevocably past, and they regard each other calmly and speak together in the tones of reasonable and sedate people. Nevertheless, it saddens Bazarov to look on his relationship with Odintsov as on an episode from his past; he loves her and, while he does not allow himself to complain, suffer, or play the rejected lover, he becomes irregular in his way of life, now throwing himself into his work, now falling into idleness, now merely becoming bored and grumbling at the people around him. He does not want to talk about it to anyone, he does not even acknowledge to himself that he feels something resembling anguish and yearning. He becomes angry and sour because of his failure, it annoys him to think that happiness beckoned to him but then passed on and it annoys him to feel that this event has made an impression on him. All this would have worked itself out in his organism, he would again have taken up his work and cursed in the most energetic manner damnable romanticism and the inaccessible lady who had led him by the nose, and would have lived as he had before, occupied with the dissection of frogs and the courting of less unconquerable beauties. But Turgenev did not bring Bazarov out of his gloomy mood. Bazarov suddenly dies, not from grief, of course, and the novel comes to an end, or, more precisely, sharply and unexpectedly breaks off. * * *

The description of Bazarov's death is one of the best passages in Turgenev's novel; indeed, I doubt whether anything more remarkable can be found in the whole body of his work. It would be impossible for me to quote an excerpt from this magnificent episode; it would destroy the integrity of the effect; I should really quote the whole ten pages, but I do not have the space; furthermore, I hope that all my readers have read or will read Turgenev's novel. Thus, without quoting a single line, I shall endeavor to trace and explicate Bazarov's mental state from the beginning to the end of his illness. Bazarov cuts his finger while dissecting a corpse and does not have the opportunity to cauterize the cut immediately with a caustic stone or iron. Only after four hours does Bazarov come to his father's room and cauterize the sore spot, without concealing either from himself or from Vassily Ivanovich that this measure is useless if the infected matter from the corpse has entered the blood. Vassily Ivanovich knows as a doctor how great the danger is, but he cannot bring himself to look it in the face and tries to deceive himself. Two days pass, Bazarov steels himself, he does not go to bed, but he has fever and chills, loses his appetite, and suffers from a severe headache. His father's sympathy and questions irritate him because he knows that all this will not help and that the old man is pampering himself and diverting himself with empty illusions. It vexes him to see a man, and a doctor besides, not daring to view the matter in its proper light. Bazarov spares Arina Vlasyevna; he tells her that he has caught cold; on the third day he goes to bed and asks for lime tea. On the fourth day he turns to his father and straightforwardly and seriously tells him that he will die soon, shows him the red spots on his body which are a sign of infection, gives him the medical term for his illness, and coldly refutes the timid objections of the broken old man. Nevertheless, he wants to live, he is sorry to give up his self-awareness, his thoughts, his strong personality, but this pain at parting with his young life and untried power expresses itself not in a gentle melancholy but in a bitter, ironic vexation, in his scornful attitude toward himself, an impotent being, and toward the crude, meaningless accident which has trampled and crushed him. The nihilist remains true to himself to the last moment.

As a doctor, he has seen that infected people always die and he does not doubt the immutability of this law, despite the fact that it condemns him to death. In precisely the same way, he does not replace his gloomy world view by another more comforting one in a crucial moment: neither as a doctor nor as a man does he comfort himself with mirages. * * *

The author sees that Bazarov loves no one, because around him all is petty, stupid, and flabby, while he himself is fresh, intelligent, and strong; the author sees this and, in his mind, relieves his hero of the last undeserved reproach. Turgenev has studied Bazarov's character, he has pondered its elements and the conditions of its development, and he has come to see that for him there can be neither occupation nor happiness. He lives as an isolated figure and dies an isolated figure, and a useless isolated figure besides, dies as a hero who has nowhere to turn, nothing to draw breath on, nothing to do with his mighty powers, no one to love with a powerful love. As there is no reason for him to live, we must observe how he dies. The whole interest, the whole meaning of the novel is contained in the death of Bazarov. If he had turned coward, if he had been untrue to himself, it would have shed a completely different light on his whole character; he would have appeared to have been an empty braggart from whom it would be impossible to expect fortitude or decisiveness in a time of need; the whole novel would have been turned into a slander on the younger generation, an undeserved reproach; with such a novel, Turgenev would have been saying: look here, young people, here is an example: even the best of you is no good. But Turgenev, as an honorable man and a true artist, could not have brought himself to tell such a grievous lie. Bazarov did not become abased, and the meaning of the novel emerged as follows: today's young people become carried away and go to extremes; but this very tendency to get carried away points to fresh strength and incorruptible intellect; this strength and this intellect, without any outside assistance or influence, will lead these young people on to the right road and will support them in life.

Whoever has found this splendid thought in Turgenev's novel could not help but express his deep and warm gratitude to this great artist and honorable citizen of Russia.

But all the same, the Bazarovs have a bad time of it in this life, although they make a point of humming and whistling. There is no occupation, no love—consequently, there is no pleasure either.

They do not know how to suffer, they will not complain, but at times they feel only that all is empty, boring, drab, and meaningless.

But what is to be done? Is it possible to infect ourselves on purpose just in order to have the satisfaction of dying beautifully and tranquilly? No! What is to be done? We must live while we are alive, eat dry bread if there is no roast beef, know many women if it is not possible to love a woman, and, in general, we must not dream about orange trees and palms, when under foot are snowdrifts and the cold tundra.

N. N. STRAKHOV

Fathers and Sons†

* * * In order to be completely consistent to the very end, Bazarov refrains from preaching, as another form of empty chatter. And in reality, preaching would be nothing other than the admission of the rights of thought and the force of ideas. Preaching would be that justification which, as we have seen, was superfluous for Bazarov. To attach importance to preaching would mean to admit intellectual activity, to admit that men are ruled not by the senses and need, but also by thought and the words in which it is vested. To start preaching would mean to start going into abstractions, would mean calling logic and history to one's aid, would mean to concern oneself with those things already admitted to be trifles in their very essence. That is why Bazarov is not fond of arguments, disputation, and does not attach great value to them. He sees that one cannot gain much by logic; he tries instead to act through his personal example, and is sure that Bazarovs will spring up by themselves in abundance, as certain plants spring up where their seeds are. Pisarev understands that position very well. He says, for example: "Indignation at stupidity and baseness in general is understandable, though it is for that matter as fruitful as indignation at autumn dampness or winter cold." He judges Bazarov's tendency in the same way: "If Bazarovism is a disease, then it is a disease of our time, and must be endured to the end, no matter what palliatives and amputations are employed. Treat Bazarovism however you please—that is your business; but you will not be able to put a stop to it; it is just the same as Cholera."

Therefore it is clear that all the chatterer-Bazarovs, the preacher-Bazarovs, the Bazarovs occupied only with their Bazarovism rather than with deeds are on the wrong road, which will lead them to endless

† From N. Strakhov, *Kriticheskiya stat'i*, vol. 1 (Kiev, 1908) 1–39. Translated by Ralph E. Matlaw. Reprinted by permission. The article first appeared in Dostoevsky's periodical *Time* in April, 1862. Strakhov (1828–96) was a philosopher and literary critic, and a close friend of Tolstoy's and Dostoevsky's.

contradictions and stupidities, that they are far less consistent and stand much lower than Bazarov.

Such is the stern cast of mind, the solid store of thoughts Turgenev embodied in Bazarov. He clothed that mind with flesh and blood, and fulfilled that task with amazing mastery. Bazarov emerged as a simple man, free of all affectation, and at the same time firm and powerful in soul and body. Everything in him fits his strong character unusually well. It is quite noteworthy that he is *more Russian*, so to speak, than all the rest of the characters in the novel. His speech is distinguished by its simplicity, appropriateness, mockery, and completely Russian cast. In the same way he approaches the common people more easily than any other character in the novel and knows better than they how to behave with them.

Nothing could correspond so well as this to the simplicity and straightforwardness of the view Bazarov professes. A man who is profoundly imbued with certain convictions, who is their complete embodiment, must without fail also turn out natural and therefore close to his native traditions and at the same time a strong man. That is why Turgenev, who up to this point had created divided characters, so to speak, for example, the Hamlet of the Shchigry District, Rudin, and Lavretsky,[1] finally attained the type of an undivided personality in Bazarov. Bazarov is the first strong character, the first whole character, to appear in Russian literature from the sphere of so called educated society. Whoever fails to value that, whoever fails to understand the importance of that phenomenon, had best not judge our literature. Even Antonovich[2] noticed it, as one may see by the following strange sentence: "Apparently Turgenev wanted to portray in his hero what is called a *demonic or Byronic character, something on the order of Hamlet.*" Hamlet—a demonic character! That indicated a confused notion of Byron and Shakespeare. Yet actually *something of a demonic order* does emerge in Turgenev's work, that is, a figure rich in force, though that force is not pure.

In what does the action of the novel really consist?

Bazarov together with his friend Arkady Kirsanov arrives in the provinces from Petersburg. Both are students who have just completed their courses, one in the medical academy, the other at the university. Bazarov is no longer a man in his first youth; he has already acquired a certain reputation, has managed to present his mode of thought; while Arkady is still completely a youth. The entire action of the novel takes place during one vacation, perhaps for both the first vacation after completing their courses. For the most part the friends visit together, in the Kirsanov family, in the Bazarov family, in the provincial capital, in the village

---

1. Characters in the story by that name (1849), the novels *Rudin* (1856), and *Nest of Noblemen* (1859) [*Editor*].
2. Reviewer for *The Contemporary* [*Editor*].

of the widow Odintsov. They meet many people, whom they either meet for the first time or have not seen for many years. To be precise, Bazarov had not gone home in three years. Therefore there occurs a variegated collision of their new views, brought from Petersburg, with the views of the people they meet. The entire interest of the novel is contained in these collisions. There are very few events and little action in it. Toward the end of the vacation Bazarov dies, almost by accident, becoming infected from a decomposing body, and Kirsanov marries, having fallen in love with Odintsov's sister. With that the entire novel ends.

In this Bazarov appears completely the hero, despite the fact that there is apparently nothing brilliant or striking in him. The reader's attention is focused on him from the first, and all the other characters begin to turn about him as around the main center of gravity. He is least of all interested in other characters, but the others are all the more interested in him. He does not try to attach anyone to himself and does not force himself on them, and yet wherever he appears he arouses the greatest attention and becomes the main object of feelings and thoughts, love and hatred.

In setting off to spend time with his parents and with friends Bazarov had no particular aim in mind. He does not seek anything and does not expect anything from that trip. He simply wants to rest and travel. At the most he sometimes wants to *look at people*. But with that superiority he has over those around him and as a result of their all feeling his strength, these characters themselves seek closer relations with him and involve him in a drama he did not at all want and did not even anticipate.

He had hardly appeared in the Kirsanov family when he immediately arouses irritation and hatred in Pavel Petrovich, respect mixed with fear in Nikolai Petrovich, the friendly disposition of Fenichka, Dunyasha, the servants' children, even of the baby Mitya, and the contempt of Prokofich. Later on, things reach the stage that he is himself carried away for a moment and kisses Fenichka, and Pavel Petrovich challenges him to a duel. "What a piece of foolery!" Bazarov repeats, not at all having expected such *events*.

The trip to town, its purpose to *look at people*, also is not without consequences for him. Various characters begin to mill around him. Sitnikov and Kukshin, masterfully depicted characters of the false progressive and the false emancipated woman, begin to court him. Of course they do not disconcert him; he treats them with contempt and they only serve as a contrast, from which his mind and force, his total integrity emerge still more sharply and in greater relief. But here the stumbling block, Anna Sergeyevna Odintsov, is also met. Despite his coolness Bazarov begins to waver. To the great amazement of his worshipper Arkady he is even embarrassed once, and on another occasion blushes.

Without suspecting any danger, however, firmly confident of himself, Bazarov goes to visit Odintsov, at Nikolskoe. And he really does control himself splendidly. And Odintsov, like all the other characters, becomes interested in him, as she probably had not become interested in anyone else in her whole life. The matter ends badly, however. Too great a passion is aroused in Bazarov, while Odintsov's inclination does not rise to real love. Bazarov leaves almost completely rejected and again begins to be amazed at himself and to upbraid himself. "The devil knows what nonsense it is! Every man hangs on a thread, the abyss may open under his feet any minute, and yet he must go and invent all sorts of discomforts for himself, and spoil his life."

But despite these wise comments, Bazarov continues involuntarily to spoil his life just the same. Even after that lesson, even during his second visit to the Kirsanovs, he is carried away with Fenichka and is forced to fight a duel with Pavel Petrovich.

Apparently Bazarov does not at all desire and does not expect a love affair, but the love affair takes place against his iron will; life, which he had thought he would rule, catches him in its huge wave.

Near the end of the story, when Bazarov visits his father and mother, he apparently is somewhat bewildered after all the shocks he had undergone. He was not so bewildered that he could not be cured, that he would not rise again in full force after a short while. But nevertheless the shadow of sorrow which lay over that iron man even at the beginning becomes deeper toward the end. He loses the desire to work, loses weight, begins to make fun of the peasants no longer in a friendly way but rather sardonically. As a result, it turns out that this time he and the peasant fail to understand each other, while formerly mutual understanding was possible up to a point. Finally, Bazarov begins to improve and becomes interested in medical practice. The infection of which he dies nevertheless seems to testify to inadequate attention and agility, to a momentary diversion of his spiritual forces.

Death is the last test of life, the last accident that Bazarov did not expect. He dies, but to the very last moment he remains foreign to that life with which he came into conflict so strangely, which bothered him with such *trifles*, made him commit such *fooleries*, and finally killed him as result of such an *insignificant* cause.

Bazarov dies altogether the hero and his death creates a shattering impression. To the very end, to the last flash of conscience, he does not betray himself by a single word nor by a single sign of cowardice. He is broken, but not conquered.

Thus despite the short time of action in the novel and despite his quick death, Bazarov was able to express himself completely and completely show his force. Life did not destroy him—one cannot possibly draw that conclusion from the novel—but only gave him occasions to disclose his energy. In the readers' eyes Bazarov emerges the victor from his trials. Everyone will say that people like Bazarov can do much, and that with such strength one may expect much from them.

Strictly speaking, Bazarov is shown only in a narrow frame and not with all the sweep of human life. The author says practically nothing about his hero's development, how such a character could have been formed. In precisely the same way, the novel's rapid ending leaves the question "would Bazarov have remained the same Bazarov, or in general what development awaited him in the future" as a complete puzzle. And yet silence on the first as on the second question has, it seems to me, its reason in realistic basis. If the hero's gradual development is not shown, it is unquestionably because Bazarov did not become educated through the gradual accumulation of influences but, on the contrary, by a rapid, sharp break. Bazarov had not been home for three years. During that time he studied, and now suddenly he appears before us imbued with everything he has managed to learn. The morning after his arrival he already goes forth after frogs and in general he continues his *educational* life at every convenient opportunity. He is a man of theory, and theory created him, created him imperceptibly, without events, without anything that one might have related, created him with a single intellectual turnabout.

Bazarov soon dies. That was necessary to the artist in order to make the picture simple and clear. Bazarov could not long remain in his present tense mood. Sooner or later he would have to change and stop being Bazarov. We have no right to complain to the author that he did not choose a broader task and limited himself to the narrower one. He decided to stop at a single step in his hero's development. Nonetheless the *whole man*, not fragmentary traits, appears at that step of his development, as generally happens in development. In relation to the fullness of character the author's task is splendidly fulfilled.

A living, whole man is caught by the author in each of Bazarov's actions and movements. Here is the great merit of the novel, which contains its main idea, and which our hurried moralizers did not notice. Bazarov is a theoretician; he is a strange and sharply one-sided person; he preaches unusual things; he acts eccentrically; he is a schoolboy in whom the coarsest *affectation* is united with profound sincerity; as we said before, he is a man foreign to life; that is, he himself avoids life. But a warm stream of life courses beneath all these external forms. With all his sharpness and the artificiality of his actions Bazarov is a completely live person, not a phantom, not an invention but real flesh and blood. He rejects life yet at the same time lives profoundly and strongly.

After one of the most wonderful scenes in the novel, namely, after the conversation in which Pavel Kirsanov challenges Bazarov to a duel and the latter accepts the challenge and agrees on its terms, Bazarov, amazed by the unexpected turn of events and the strangeness of the conversation, exclaims: "Well, I'll be damned! How fine, and how foolish! A pretty farce we've been through! Like trained dogs dancing on their hind paws." It would be difficult to make a more caustic remark. And yet the reader feels that the conversation Bazarov so characterizes was in reality a completely live and serious conversation; that despite all the deformity and artificiality of its form, the conflict of two energetic characters has been accurately expressed in it.

The poet shows us the same thing with unusual clarity through the whole novel. It may constantly be seen that the characters and particularly Bazarov *put on a farce* and that like trained dogs they *dance on their hind legs*. Yet beneath this appearance, as beneath a transparent veil, the reader clearly discerns that the feelings and actions underlying it are not at all canine but purely and profoundly human.

That is the point of view from which the action and events of the novel may best be evaluated. Beneath the rough, deformed, artificial, and affected forms, the profound vitality of all the phenomena and characters brought to the scene is heard. If Bazarov, for example, possesses the reader's attention and sympathy, he does so because in reality all these words and actions flow out of a living soul, not because each of his words is sacred and each action fair. Apparently Bazarov is a proud man, terribly egoistic and offending others by his egoism. But the reader makes his peace with that pride because simultaneously Bazarov lacks all smugness and self-satisfaction; pride brings him no joy. Bazarov treats his parents carelessly and curtly. But no one could suspect him, in that instance, of pleasure in the feeling of his personal superiority or the feeling of his power over them. Still less can he be reproached for abusing that superiority and that power. He simply refuses tender relationship with his parent and refuses it incompletely. Something strange emerges: he is uncommunicative with his father, laughs at him, sharply accuses him either of ignorance or tenderness. And yet the father is not only not offended but rather happy and satisfied. "Bazarov's jeers did not in the least perturb Vassily Ivanovich; they were positively a comfort to him. Holding his greasy dressing-gown across his stomach with two fingers, and smoking his pipe, he used to listen with enjoyment to Bazarov; and the more malicious his sallies, the more good-naturedly did his delighted father chuckle, showing every one of his black teeth." Such are the wonders of love. Soft and good-natured Arkady could never *delight* his father as Bazarov does his. Bazarov himself, of course, feels and understands that very well. Why should he be tender with his father and betray his inexorable consistency!

Bazarov is not at all so dry a man as his external actions and the cast of his thoughts might lead one to believe. In life, in his relations to people, Bazarov is not consistent (with himself); but in that very thing his vitality is disclosed. He likes people. "Man is a strange being," he says, noticing the presence of that liking in himself, "he wants to be with people, just to curse them, so long as he can be with them." Bazarov is not an abstract theoretician who solves all problems and is completely calmed by that solution. In such a case he would be a monstrous phenomenon, a caricature, not a man. That is why Bazarov is easily excited, why everything vexes him, everything has an effect on him, despite all his firmness and consistency in words and actions. This excitement does not betray his view and his intentions at all; for the most part it only arouses his bile and vexes him. Once he says the following to his friend Arkady: "You said, for instance, to-day as we passed our bailiff Philip's cottage—it's the one that's so nice and clean—well, you said Russia will attain perfection when the poorest peasant has a house like that, and every one of us ought to work to bring it about. And I felt such a hatred for this poorest peasant, this Philip or Sidor, for whom I'm to be ready to jump out of my skin, and * * * what do I need his thanks for? Why, suppose he does live in a clean hut, while the nettles are growing out of me,—well, what comes after that?" What a terrible, shocking speech, isn't it?

A few minutes later Bazarov does still worse: he discloses a longing to choke his tender friend Arkady, to choke him for no particular reason and in the guise of a pleasant trial already spreads wide his long and hard fingers.

Why does all this not arm the reader against Bazarov? What could be worse than that? And yet the impression created by these incidents does not serve to harm Bazarov. So much so that even Antonovich (striking proof!) who with extreme diligence explains everything in Bazarov on the bad side in order to prove Turgenev's sly intention to blacken Bazarov—completely left that incident out!

What does this mean? Apparently Bazarov, who so easily meets people, takes such lively interest in them, and so easily begins to feel rancor toward them, suffers more from that rancor than those for whom it is destined. That rancor is not the expression of destroyed egoism or insulted self-esteem, it is the expression of suffering, and oppression created by the absence of love. Despite all his views, Bazarov eagerly seeks love for people. If that desire appears as rancor, that rancor only represents the reverse of love. Bazarov cannot be a cold, abstract man. His heart demands fullness and demands feeling. And so he rages at others but feels that he should really rage at himself more than at them.

From all this it at least becomes apparent what a difficult task Turgenev undertook in his latest novel and how successfully in our view he carried it out. He depicted life under the deadening influence of theory; he gave us a living being, though that man apparently embodied himself in an abstract formula without leaving a remnant behind. Through this, if one were to judge the novel superficially, it is not very comprehensible, presents little that is appealing, and seems to consist entirely of an obscure logical construction. But in reality, it is actually marvelously clear, unusually attractive, and throbs with warm life.

There is practically no need to explain why Bazarov turned out and had to turn out a theoretician. Everyone knows that our *real* representatives, that the "carriers of thought" in our generation, have long ago renounced being *practical*, that active participation in the life around them had long ago become impossible. From that point of view Bazarov is a direct and immediate imitator of Onegin, Pechorin, Rudin, and Lavretsky. Exactly like them he lives in the mental sphere for the time being and spends his spiritual forces on it. But the thirst for activity has reached the final, extreme point in him. His entire theory consists in the direct demand for action. His mood is such that he inevitably would come to grips with that action at the first convenient possibility.

The characters surrounding Bazarov unconsciously feel the living man in him. That is why so many attachments turn upon him, far more than on any other character in the novel. Not only do his father and mother remember him and pray for him with infinite and inexpressible tenderness; in other characters too the memory of Bazarov is accompanied by love; in a moment of happiness Katya and Arkady drink "to Bazarov's memory."

Such is Bazarov's image for us, too. He is not a hateful being who repels through his shortcomings; on the contrary, his gloomy figure is grandiose and attractive.

"What then is the idea of the novel?" Lovers of bare and exact conclusions will ask. Does Bazarov present a subject for imitation according to you? Or should his failure and roughness on the contrary teach the Bazarovs not to fall into the errors and extremes of the real Bazarov? In short, is the novel written *for* the young generation or *against* it? Is it progressive or reactionary?

If the question so insistently concerns the author's intentions, what he wanted to teach and what he wanted to have unlearned, then it seems these questions would have to be answered as follows: Turgenev does in fact want to be instructive, but he chooses tasks far higher and more difficult than you suppose. It is not a difficult thing to write a novel with a progressive or reactionary tendency. But Turgenev had the pretension and daring to create a novel that had *all possible* tendencies. The worshipper of eternal truth and eternal beauty, he had the proud aim of showing the eternal in the temporary and to write a novel neither progressive nor reactionary but, so to speak, *constant*. In this instance he may be compared to a mathematician who tries to find some important theorem. Let us assume that he has finally found that theorem. Would he not be terribly amazed and disconcerted if he were suddenly approached with the question whether his theorem was progressive or reactionary? Does it conform to the *modern* spirit or does it obey the *old*?

He could only answer such questions thus: your questions make no sense and have no bearing on my findings: my theorem is an *eternal truth*.

> Alas! In life's furrows
> By Providence's secret will
> Generations are the fleeting harvest
> They rise, ripen and fall;
> Others come in their wake . . .

The change of generations is the outward theme of the novel. If Turgenev did not depict all fathers and sons, or not *those* fathers and sons who would like to be different, he splendidly described fathers *in general* and children *in general* and the relationship between those two generations. Perhaps the difference between generations has never been as great as it is at the present, and therefore their relationship too appears to be particularly acute. However that may be, in order to measure the difference between objects the same measure must be used for both; in order to draw a picture all objects must be described from a point of view common to all of them.

That single measure, that general point of view for Turgenev is *human life* in its broadest and fullest meaning. The reader of his novel feels that behind the mirage of external actions and scenes there flows such a profound, such an inexhaustible current of life, that all these actions and scenes, all the characters and events are insignificant in comparison to that current.

If we understand Turgenev's novel that way, then, perhaps the moral we are seeking will also be disclosed to us more clearly. There is a moral, even a very important one, for truth and poetry are very instructive.

If we look at the picture presented by the novel more calmly and at some distance, we note easily that though Bazarov stands head and shoulders above all the other characters, though he majestically passes over the scene, triumphant, bowed down to, respected, loved, and lamented, there is nevertheless something that taken as a whole stands above Bazarov. What is that? If we examine it attentively, we will find that that higher something is not a character but that *life* which inspires them. Above Bazarov stands that fear, that love, those tears he inspires. Above Bazarov is that scene he passes through. The enchantment of nature, the charm of art, feminine love, family love, parents' love, *even* religion, all that—living, full, powerful—is the background against which Bazarov is drawn. That background is so clear and sparkling that Bazarov's huge figure stands out clearly but at the same time gloomily against it. Those who think that for sake of a supposed condemnation of Bazarov the author contrasts to him one of his characters, say Pavel Petrovich, or Arkady, or Odintsov, are terribly wrong. All these characters are insignificant in comparison to Bazarov. And yet their life, the human element in their feelings is not insignificant.

We will not discuss here the description of nature, of Russian nature, which is so difficult to describe and in describing which Turgenev is such a master. It is the same in this as in previous novels. The sky, air, fields, trees, even horses, even chicks—everything is caught graphically and exactly.

Let's simply take people. What could be weaker or more insignificant than Bazarov's young friend Arkady? He apparently submits to every passing influence; he is the most ordinary of mortals. And yet he is extremely nice. The magnanimous agitation of his young feelings, his nobility and purity are emphasized by the author with great finesse and are clearly depicted. Nikolai Petrovich, as is proper, is the real father of his son. There is not a single clear trait in him and the only good thing is that he is a man, though a very simple man. Further, what could be emptier than Fenichka? The author writes "The expression of her eyes was charming, particularly when she seemed to gaze up from beneath her brow and smiled kindly and a little stupidly." Pavel Petrovich himself calls her an *empty creature*. And yet that silly Fenichka attracts almost more adorers than the clever Odintsov. Not only does Nikolai Petrovich love her, but in part Pavel Petrovich falls in love with her as does Bazarov himself. And yet that love and falling in love are real and valuable human feelings. Finally, what is Pavel Petrovich—a dandy, a fop with gray hair, completely taken up with his concern for his toilette? But even in him, despite the apparent distortion there are living and even energetic vibrations of the heartstrings.

The farther we go in the novel, the nearer to the end of the drama, the more gloomy and tense does Bazarov's figure become, while the background becomes clearer and clearer. The creation of such figures as Bazarov's mother and father is a real triumph of talent. Apparently nothing could be less significant and useless than these people who have lived out their time and who become decrepit and disfigured in the new life with all their prejudices of old. And yet what richness of *simple* human feeling! What depth and breadth of spiritual life among the most ordinary life that does not rise a jot above the lowest level.

When Bazarov becomes ill, when he rots alive and inexorably undergoes the cruel battle with illness, life around him becomes more tense and clear in proportion to his becoming gloomier. Odintsov comes to say farewell to Bazarov! She had probably done nothing generous in her life and will not do so again all her life. So far as the father and mother are concerned, it would be difficult to find anything more touching. Their love bursts forth like some sort of lightning, for a moment striking the reader. From their simple hearts there seem to be torn infinitely sad hymns, some sort of limitlessly deep and tender outcries that irresistibly touch the soul.

Bazarov dies amidst that light and that warmth. For a moment a storm flares up in his father's soul. It is harder to imagine anything more fearful. But it soon dies down and everything again becomes bright. Bazarov's very grave is illuminated by light and peace. Birds sing over it and tears are poured on it.

So there it is, there is that secret moral which Turgenev put in his work. Bazarov turns away from nature; Turgenev does not reproach him for it; he only depicts nature in all its beauty. Bazarov does not value friendship and rejects romantic love; the author does not reproach him for it; he only describes Arkady's friendship toward Bazarov and his happy love for Katya. Bazarov denies close bonds between parents and children; the author does not reproach him for it; he only develops a picture of parental love before us. Bazarov shuns life; the author does not present him as a villain for it; he only shows us life in all its beauty. Bazarov repudiates poetry; Turgenev does not make him a fool for it; he only depicts him with all the fullness and penetration of poetry.

In short, Turgenev stands for the eternal principles of human life; for those fundamental elements which can endlessly change their forms but actually always remain unchangeable. But what have we said? It turns out that Turgenev stands for those things all poets stand for, that every real poet must stand for. And, consequently, in this case Turgenev put himself above any reproach for ulterior motives; whatever the particular circumstances he chose for his work may be, he examines them from the most general and highest point of view.

All his attention is concentrated on the general forces of life. He has shown us how these forces are embodied in Bazarov, in that same Bazarov who denies them. He has shown us if not a more powerful then a more apparent, clearer embodiment of those forces in those simple people who surround Bazarov. Bazarov is a titan, rising against mother earth; no matter how great his force it only testifies to the greatness of the forces that begot him and fed him, but it does not come up to mother earth's force.

However it may be, Bazarov is defeated all the same. He is not defeated by the characters and occurrences of life but by the very idea of that life. Such an ideal victory over him is only possible if he is done all justice, if he is exalted to his appropriate grandeur. Otherwise the victory would have no force or meaning.

In his *Government Inspector* Gogol said there was a single honorable character in the play—laughter. One might say similarly about *Fathers and Sons* that it contains one character who stands higher than the others and even higher than Bazarov—*life*. That life that rises above Bazarov would apparently be smaller and lower to the extent that the main hero of the novel, Bazarov, would be portrayed smaller and lower.

APOLLON GRIGOREV

[Nihilists]†

* * * Now the matter has become clear once and for all. It is not a question of Pushkin's "rattlings" or the "vulgarity" of certain of his poems (like "The Hero," for example)—it is not at all a question of the "kingdom of darkness," supposedly described only satirically by Ostrovsky,[1] —now the matter consists of matter, that is, in that:

1. *Art* is nonsense, useful only to arouse dormant human energy to something more substantial and important, and swept away as soon as any kind of positive results are attained.

2. *Nationality*—that is, certain national organisms—is also nonsense, which must disappear during the amalgamation the result of which will be a world where the moon is joined to the earth.

3. *History* (this had been said two years ago completely clearly) is nonsense, a senseless canvas of inept errors, shameful blindness and the most amusing enthusiasms.

4. *Science*—except for its exact and positive sides, expressed in the branches of mathematics and natural science—is the greatest nonsense, the ravings of fruitlessly stultifying human heads.

5. *Thought* is a completely senseless process, useless and quite conveniently replaced by the good teachings of the five—excuse me!—six clever little books.

But any person who is accustomed to the noxious process of thinking will involuntarily repeat Galileo's words "And yet it does turn!" Since even these results, that in the final analysis deny thought any meaning, are in themselves the results of thought—whatever it may be, it is thinking nevertheless and not the digestive process. ("And perhaps the digestive process too?" You will ask me again to note.)

Certain "generalizations" so reluctantly used by the adepts of our nihilism, which they flee and fear as the devil fears holy water, were nevertheless present at the conception of their theories. In order to say "I dissect frogs," or "I make soap" [as in Ustryalov's parody of *Fathers and Sons*], certain generalizations, albeit negative ones, are necessary —to wit, to elevate disbelief in any other knowledge than particular knowledge into a principle. These very words are insincere in Bazarov and childishly vulgar in his parody. On Bazarov's lips they simply cover

† From A. A. Grigorev, *Sochineniya*, edited by N. N. Strakhov (St. Petersburg, 1876) 626–27. Translated by Ralph E. Matlaw. Reprinted by permission. This is a section of an article, "Paradoxes of Organic Criticism," that appeared in Dostoevsky's *The Epoch* in 1864. Grigorev (1822–64) was a brilliant though eccentric critic extolling traditional Russian life, and a good poet.

1. A. N. Ostrovsky (1823–86), leading Russian dramatist. His early plays, dealing with the merchant world, were "analyzed" by Dobrolyubov in a long article entitled "The Kingdom of Darkness" (1859) [*Editor*].

a certain intellectual despair, a despair of conscience that has been scalded several times and consequently fears cold water, conscience that had been stopped short by several insubstantial systems that tried grandiosely though not completely successfully to contain all of universal life in a single principle. Such a completely comprehensible moment of consciousness, considered ideal by Bazarov and ideal by nihilism too, has a completely legitimate place in the general process of human consciousness,—and therefore though I laugh wholeheartedly at the facts, that is, at one foolish representative or another of so-called nihilism, I do not permit myself to laugh at the general stream, at the general spirit christened with that name—whether successfully or not —and am still less capable of denying the organic-historical necessity of that eructation of materialism in new forms. But that this organic-historical eructation is no more than a passing moment—no dreams about white blackamoors will dissuade me of that.

Thought, science, art, nationality, history are not at all steps in some sort of progress, a husk swept away by the human spirit as soon as it has attained some positive results, but the eternal, organic work of eternal forces inherent in him as an organism. It seems to be a very simple and clear thing, and yet that's just what one has to explain in our day, as if it were something completely new . . . and yet it would seem, it is completely simple and clear, so simple and clear that the most organic view that emerges immediately from it is nothing other than a simple, untheoretical view of life and its manifestations or expression in science, art, and the history of nations. * * *

ALEXANDER HERZEN

Bazarov Once Again†

First Letter

Instead of a letter, dear friend, I am sending you a dissertation, and an unfinished one at that. After our conversation I reread Pisarev's article on Bazarov, which I had completely forgotten, and I am very glad of it; that is, not that I had forgotten it, but that I reread it.

This article confirms my own viewpoint. In its one-sidedness it is truer and more remarkable than its adversaries thought.

Whether Pisarev understood Turgenev's Bazarov correctly does not concern me. What is important is that he recognized *himself* and *others*

† From Alexander Herzen, *Sobranie sochineniy*, vol. XX (Moscow, 1954–61) 335–40. Translated by Lydia Hooke. In this essay of 1868 Herzen undertook to show other forms of civic action than those the nihilists proclaimed. In particular he emphasized the "fathers'" activity in publishing, at home and abroad, and their salutary effect on social development in Russia.

like him in Bazarov and supplied what was lacking in the book. The less Pisarev kept to the mold in which the angry parent sought to fit the refractory son, the more freely does he project his own ideal on him.

"But why should Pisarev's ideal interest us? Pisarev is an incisive critic, he wrote much, he wrote about everything, sometimes on subjects he knew, but all this does not give his ideal the right to claim general consideration."

But the point is that this is not just his personal ideal, but the ideal that was cherished by the young generation *before* Turgenev's Bazarov and *after him* and which was embodied, not only by various characters in stories and novels, but also by real people who endeavored to base their actions and words on Bazarovism. I have heard and seen a dozen times what Pisarev is talking about; he has artlessly given away the heartfelt idea of a whole group; he has focused diffuse rays on one point and with them illuminated the original Bazarov.

Bazarov is more than an outsider to Turgenev, but to Pisarev he is more than a brother; for heuristic purposes, of course, we should choose the viewpoint which regards Bazarov as its *desideratum.*

Pisarev's adversaries were frightened by his imprudence; they repudiated Turgenev's Bazarov as a caricature and even more vehemently rejected his transfigured double; they were displeased that Pisarev had made a fool of himself, but this does not mean that he had misunderstood Bazarov.

Pisarev knows the heart of his Bazarov to the core. He even confesses for him: "Perhaps," he says, "in the depths of his soul Bazarov acknowledges much of what he repudiates aloud and perhaps it is precisely what he thus acknowledges which secretly saves him from moral degradation and moral worthlessness." We consider this immodesty, peering so deeply into the soul of another, to be very significant.

Pisarev further characterizes his hero as follows: "Bazarov is exceedingly full of self-esteem, but this self-esteem is unnoticeable [it is clear that this is not Turgenev's Bazarov] as a direct consequence of his vastness." Bazarov could be satisfied only by "a *whole eternity of constantly expanding activity and constantly increasing pleasures.*"[1]

> Bazarov, everywhere and in everything, does what he pleases or what seems to him to be advantageous or convenient. He is ruled only by his whims or his personal calculations. Neither over himself, nor outside himself, nor within himself does he recognize a moderator . . . ahead—no exalted goal; in his mind—no high design, and yet he has such great capacities. . . . If Bazarovism is a *disease*, then it is the disease of our time, and must be endured to the end no matter what palliatives and amputations are employed.

1. Youth likes to express itself in various extravagant conceits and to strike the imagination with infinitely large images. The last sentence reminds me of Karl Moor, Ferdinand, and Don Carlos [in Schiller's plays].

[Bazarov] looks down on people and rarely even takes the trouble to conceal *his half disdainful, half patronizing attitude* toward those who hate him and those who obey him. He loves no one. . . . he considers it completely unnecessary to lay any restraint whatsoever on himself . . .

His cynicism has two aspects, an internal and an external one, a cynicism of thought and feeling and a cynicism of manner and expression. An ironic attitude toward emotion of any sort, toward dreaminess, lyrical transports and effusions, is the essence of the internal cynicism. The rude expression of this irony, and a causeless and purposeless harshness in the treatment of others relates to external cynicism. . . . Bazarov is not only an empiricist, he is also an uncouth rowdy . . . In the ranks of Bazarov's admirers there will undoubtedly be those who will be enraptured by his coarse manners, . . . which are, in any case, a shortcoming and not a virtue.[2]

. . . [Such people are] most often engendered by the drab conditions of a life of labor; from hard labor the hands coarsen, so do the manners and emotions; the man grows stronger and banishes youthful dreaminess, rids himself of lachrymose sensitivity; it is not possible to daydream at work . . . This man has become used to looking on dreams as on a whim, peculiar to idleness and aristocratic pampering; . . . moral aspirations and actions as imagined and ridiculous. . . . [He feels an] aversion to phrase making.

Then Pisarev introduces Bazarov's family tree: the Onegins and the Pechorins begat the Rudins and Bel'tovs.[3] The Rudins and Bel'tovs begat Bazarov. (Whether the Decembrists were omitted purposely or not, I do not know.)[4]

Weary, bored people are replaced by people yearning for action, life rejects them both as unfit and incomplete. "At times they will have to suffer, but they will never succeed in accomplishing deeds. Society is deaf and implacable toward them. They are not capable of accommodating themselves to its conditions, not one of them ever attained the rank of *head of a department*. Some console themselves by becoming

2. This prediction came true. This mutual interaction of people and books is a strange thing. A book takes its whole shape from the society that spawns it, then generalizes the material, renders it clearer and sharper, and as a consequence reality is transformed. The originals become caricatures of their own sharply drawn portraits and real people take on the character of their literary shadows. At the end of the last century all German men were a little like Werther, all German women like Charlotte; at the beginning of this century, the university Werthers began to turn into "robbers," Schiller's, not real ones. Young Russians were almost all out of [Chernyshevsky's] *What's to be done?* after 1862, with the addition of a few of Bazarov's traits.
3. Leading character of Herzen's novel *Whose Fault?* [*Editor*].
4. The four characters named are the protagonists of novels by Pushkin, Lermontov, Turgenev, and Herzen. They formed a historic series of the "superfluous man" in Dobrolyubov's interpretation. The Decembrists were real, the participants in the abortive revolt of December, 1825 [*Editor*].

professors and working for the future generation." There is no doubt of the negative service they perform. They increase the number of people *incapable* of practical action, consequently, this practical action itself or, more precisely, the forms which it usually takes at present, slowly but surely are lowered in the opinion of society.

It seemed (after the Crimean campaign) that Rudinism was coming to an end, that the epoch of fruitless dreaming and yearning was to be followed by an epoch of tireless and useful activity. But the mirage was dispelled. The Rudins did not become practical men, from them came a new generation, which regards its predecessors with *reproach and mockery*. 'What are you complaining about, what are you seeking, what do you ask of life? No doubt, you want happiness? That's not much, is it? Happiness must be won. If you have the power, take it. If not—*be silent*, things are bad enough without you.' A gloomy, intense energy is manifested in the younger generation's *unfriendly* attitude toward its mentors. In its concepts of good and evil this generation was like the best people of the preceding generation, their sympathies and antipathies were the same, they *desired one and the same thing*, but the people of the past *fussed and bustled about*. The people of the present do not fuss, they seek nothing, they submit to no compromises and they *place their hopes on nothing*. They are just as impotent as the Rudins, but they have acknowledged their impotence.

'I cannot act now,' thinks each of these new people, 'I will not even try, *I disdain everything around me* and I will not conceal my disdain. I shall enter the battle against evil only when I feel myself to be strong.' Since they cannot act, these people begin to think and analyze . . . superstitions and authorities are shattered and their world view becomes completely devoid of various illusory notions. They are not concerned with whether society is following them; they are full of themselves, of their inner life. In a word, the Pechorins have *the will but not the knowledge*, the Rudins have *the knowledge but not the will*, the Bazarovs have *both the knowledge and the will*. Thought and deed merge in one stable whole.

Everything is here, if there are no errors, both characterization and classification—all is concise and clear, the sum is tallied, the account is rendered, and from the point of view from which the author approached the problem everything is perfectly correct.

But we do not accept this account, we protest against it from our premature and unready graves. We are not Karl V and do not wish to be buried alive.[5]

The fates of the *fathers and sons* are strange! Clearly Turgenev did

5. Charles V, Emperor of the Holy Roman Empire, abdicated in 1555 and retired to a monastery [*Editor*].

not introduce Bazarov to pat him on the head; it is also clear that he had wanted to do something for the benefit of the fathers. But, juxtaposed to such pitiful and insignificant fathers as the Kirsanovs, the stern Bazarov captivated Turgenev and, instead of spanking the son, he flogged the fathers.

This is why it happened that a portion of the younger generation recognized itself in Bazarov. But we do not recognize ourselves at all in the Kirsanovs; just as we do not recognize ourselves in the Manilovs and Sobakeviches,[6] although the Manilovs and Sobakeviches existed right up to the time of our youth and exist today.

There is no lack of moral abortions living at the same time in different strata of society, and in its different tendencies; without doubt, they represent more or less general types, but they do not present the sharpest and most characteristic aspects of their generation—the aspects which most express its intensiveness. Pisarev's Bazarov, in one sense, is to some degree the extreme type of what Turgenev called the sons, while the Kirsanovs are the most insignificant and vulgar representatives of the fathers.

Turgenev was more of an artist in his novel than people think and because of this he lost his way, and, in my view, this is very fortunate —he was going into one room, stumbled into another, but into a better one.

What good would it have done to send Bazarov to London? The despicable Pisemsky did not stint on travel funds for his agitated monsters.[7] We, perhaps, would have proved to him, on the banks of the Thames, that it is possible, without attaining the rank of *head of a department*, to be of just as much use as any *head of a department*, that society is not always deaf and implacable when a protest strikes the right note, that the job sometimes does get done, that the Rudins and Bel'tovs sometimes do have the will and steadfastness and that, recognizing the impossibility of the action for which they were yearning, they gave up *much*, went to a strange land and "without fussing or bustling around" started to print Russian books and disseminate Russian propaganda.

The influence of the Russian press in London from 1856 to the end of 1863—is not only a practical fact, but a historical one as well. It is impossible to erase it, it must be accepted.

In London, Bazarov would have seen that only from a distance does it seem as if we are waving our hands in the air, and that, actually, we are working with them. Perhaps he would have replaced his anger with favor and would have ceased to regard us "with reproach and mockery."

I openly admit that this throwing of stones at one's predecessors is repugnant to me. . . . I repeat what I have said before. (*My Past and*

---

6. Characters in Gogol's *Dead Souls* [*Editor*].
7. In Pisemsky's anti-nihilist novel *The Agitated Sea* (1863) "nihilists" come to London to confront Russian political emigrants with their ostensible failure to do something worthwhile [*Editor*].

Thoughts, volume IV): "I would like to save the younger generation from historical ingratitude and even from historical errors. It is time that father Saturn refrained from making a snack of his children, but it is also time that the children stop following the example of the Kamchadals who kill their old men."

CRITICISM

EDMUND WILSON

[On Translating Turgenev]†

The work of Turgenev has, of course, no scope that is comparable to
Tolstoy's or Dostoevsky's, but the ten volumes collected by him for his
edition of 1883 (he omitted his early poems) represent a literary achievement of the concentratedly "artistic" kind that has few equals in
nineteenth-century fiction. There are moments, to be sure, in Turgenev
novels—*On the Eve* and *Virgin Soil*—when they become a little thin
or unreal, but none can be called a failure, and one cannot find a single
weak piece, unless one becomes impatient with *Enough*, in the whole
four volumes of stories. No fiction writer can be read through with a
steadier admiration. Greater novelists are more uneven: they betray our
belief with extravagances; they bore or they fall into bathos; they combine
poetic vision with rubbish. But Turgenev hardly even skirts these failings,
and he is never mediocre; his texture is as distinguished as his temperament.

This texture barely survives in translation. Turgenev is a master of
language; he is interested in words in a way that the other great
nineteenth-century Russian novelists—with the exception of Gogol—
are not. His writing is dense and substantial, yet it never marks time,
always moves. The translations of Constance Garnett are full of omissions and errors; the translations of Isabel Hapgood do not omit, but are
also full of errors and often extremely clumsy. Neither lady seems ever
to have thought of taking the indispensable precaution of reading her
version to a Russian holding the Russian text, who would at once have
spotted the dropped-out negatives and the cases of one word mistaken
for another. The translations of Turgenev into French—though some
are by Mérimée and Turgenev himself—have a tendency to strip him
down to something much barer and poorer. The task of translating this
writer does present some impossible problems. "What an amazing language!" wrote Chekhov on rereading the story called *The Dog*. But this
language will not reach the foreigner. How to render the tight little work
of art that Turgenev has made of *The Dog*, narrated by an ex-hussar,
with his colloquialisms, his pungent sayings, his terseness and his droll
turns? And the problems of translating Turgenev are to some extent the
problems of translating poetry. There is a passage in *The Torrents of
Spring*—a tour de force of onomatopoeia—that imitates in a single
sentence the whispering of leaves, the buzzing of bees and the droning

† Excerpt from "Turgenev and the Life-Giving Drop" from *Turgenev's Literary Reminiscences*
by Edmund Wilson. Copyright © 1957 by Edmund Wilson. Reprinted by permission of Farrar,
Straus & Giroux, Inc.

of a solitary dove. This is probably a conscious attempt to rival the well-known passage in Virgil's First Eclogue and Tennyson's imitation of it:

> *The moan of doves in immemorial elms,*
> *And murmuring of innumerable bees.*

But it would take another master to reproduce Turgenev's effects, just as it took a Tennyson to reproduce those of Virgil, and a Turgenev to compete with these.

*   *   *

SIR ISAIAH BERLIN

Fathers and Children: Turgenev and the Liberal Predicament†

*   *   *

Young Man to Middle-Aged Man: 'You had content but no force.'
Middle-Aged Man to Young Man: 'And you have force but no content.'
From a contemporary conversation[1]

This is the topic of Turgenev's most famous, and politically most interesting, novel *Fathers and Children*. It was an attempt to give flesh and substance to his image of the new men, whose mysterious, implacable presence, he declared, he felt about him everywhere, and who inspired in him feelings that he found difficult to analyse. 'There was', he wrote many years later to a friend, '—please don't laugh—some sort of *fatum*, something stronger than the author himself, something independent of him. I know one thing: I started with no preconceived idea, no "tendency"; I wrote naïvely, as if myself astonished at what was emerging.'[2] He said that the central figure of the novel, Bazarov, was mainly modelled on a Russian doctor whom he met in a train in Russia. But Bazarov has some of the characteristics of Belinsky too. Like him, he is the son of a poor army doctor, and he possesses some of Belinsky's brusqueness, his directness, his intolerance, his liability to explode at any sign of hypocrisy, of solemnity, of pompous conservative, or evasive liberal, cant. And there is, despite Turgenev's denials, something of the ferocious, militant, anti-aestheticism of Dobrolyubov too. The central

† Copyright © Isaiah Berlin 1972, first published by Oxford University Press. Reproduced by permission of Curtis Brown Ltd, London, on behalf of the copyright owner. Footnotes curtailed.

1. The original epigraph to *Fathers and Children* which Turgenev later discarded. See A. Mazon, *Manuscrits parisiens d'Ivan Tourguénev*, Paris, 1930, pp. 64–5.
2. From a letter to Saltykov-Shchedrin, 15 January 1876.

topic of the novel is the confrontation of the old and the young, of liberals and radicals, traditional civilization and the new, harsh positivism which has no use for anything except what is needed by a rational man. Bazarov, a young medical researcher, is invited by his fellow student and disciple, Arkady Kirsanov, to stay at his father's house in the country. Nicolai Kirsanov, the father, is a gentle, kindly, modest country gentleman, who adores poetry and nature, and greets his son's brilliant friend with touching courtesy. Also in the house is Nicolai Kirsanov's brother, Paul, a retired army officer, a carefully dressed, vain, pompous, old-fashioned dandy, who had once been a minor lion in the *salons* of the capital, and is now living out his life in elegant and irritated boredom. Bazarov scents an enemy, and takes deliberate pleasure in describing himself and his allies as 'nihilists', by which he means no more than that he, and those who think like him, reject everything that cannot be established by the rational methods of natural science. Truth alone matters: what cannot be established by observation and experiment is useless or harmful ballast—'romantic rubbish'—which an intelligent man will ruthlessly eliminate. In this heap of irrational nonsense Bazarov includes all that is impalpable, that cannot be reduced to quantitative measurement—literature and philosophy, the beauty of art and the beauty of nature, tradition and authority, religion and intuition, the uncriticized assumptions of conservatives and liberals, of populists and socialists, of landowners and serfs. He believes in strength, will-power, energy, utility, work, in ruthless criticism of all that exists. He wishes to tear off masks, blow up all revered principles and norms. Only irrefutable facts, only useful knowledge, matter. He clashes almost immediately with the touchy, conventional Paul Kirsanov: 'At present', he tells him, 'the most useful thing is to deny. So we deny.' 'Everything?' asks Paul Kirsanov. 'Everything.' 'What? Not only art, poetry . . . but even . . . too horrible to utter . . .' 'Everything.' 'So you destroy everything . . . but surely one must build, too?' 'That's not our business . . . First one must clear the ground.'

The fiery revolutionary agitator Bakunin, who had just then escaped from Siberia to London, was saying something of this kind: the entire rotten structure, the corrupt old world, must be razed to the ground, before something new can be built upon it; what this is to be is not for us to say; we are revolutionaries, our business is to demolish. The new men, purified from the infection of the world of idlers and exploiters and its bogus values—these men will know what to do. The French anarchist Georges Sorel once quoted Marx as saying 'Anyone who makes plans for after the revolution is a reactionary.'[3]

3. Sorel declares that this passage occurs in a letter which, according to the economist Lujo Brentano, Marx wrote to one of his English friends, Professor Beesly (*Réfléxions sur la violence*, 7th edn, Paris, 1930, p. 199, n. 2). I have not found it in any published collection of Marx's letters.

This went beyond the position of Turgenev's radical critics of the *Contemporary Review*; they did have a programme of sorts: they were democratic populists. But faith in the people seems just as irrational to Bazarov as the rest of the 'romantic rubbish.' 'Peasants?' he says, 'They are prepared to rob themselves in order to drink themselves blind at the inn.' A man's first duty is to develop his own powers, to be strong and rational, to create a society in which other rational men can breathe and live and learn. His mild disciple Arkady suggests to him that it would be ideal if all peasants lived in a pleasant, whitewashed hut, like the head man of their village. 'I have conceived a loathing for this . . . peasant,' Bazarov says, 'I have to work the skin off my hands for him, and he won't so much as thank me for it; anyway, what do I need his thanks for? He'll go on living in his whitewashed hut, while weeds grow out of me.' Arkady is shocked by such talk; but it is the voice of the new, hard-boiled, unashamed materialism. Nevertheless Bazarov is at his ease with peasants, they are not self-conscious with him even if they think him an odd sort of member of the gentry. Bazarov spends his afternoon in dissecting frogs. 'A decent chemist', he tells his shaken host, 'is twenty times more use than any poet.' Arkady, after consulting Bazarov, gently draws a volume of Pushkin out of his father's hands, and slips into them Büchner's *Kraft und Stoff*,[4] the latest popular exposition of materialism. Turgenev describes the older Kirsanov walking in his garden: 'Nikolai Petrovich dropped his head, and passed his hand over his face. "But to reject poetry," he thought again, "not to have a feeling for art, for nature . . ." and he cast about him, as if trying to understand how it was possible not to have a feeling for nature.' All principles, Bazarov declares, are reducible to mere sensations. Arkady asks whether, in that case, honesty is only a sensation. 'You find this hard to swallow?' says Bazarov. 'No, friend, if you have decided to knock everything down, you must knock yourself down, too! . . .' This is the voice of Bakunin and Dobrolyubov: 'one must clear the ground.' The new culture must be founded on real, that is materialist, scientific values: socialism is just as unreal and abstract as any other of the 'isms' imported from abroad. As for the old aesthetic, literary culture, it will crumble before the realists, the new, tough-minded men who can look the brutal truth in the face. 'Aristocracy, liberalism, progress, principles . . . what a lot of foreign . . . and useless words. A Russian would not want them as a gift.' Paul Kirsanov rejects this contemptuously; but his nephew Arkady cannot, in the end, accept it either. 'You aren't made for our harsh, bitter, solitary kind of life,' Bazarov tells him, 'you aren't insolent, you aren't nasty, all you have is the audacity, the impulsiveness of youth, and that is of no use in our business. Your type, the gentry, cannot get beyond noble humility, noble indignation, and that is nonsense. You

---

4. Turgenev calls it *Stoff und Kraft*.

won't, for instance, fight, and yet you think yourselves terrific. We want to fight . . . Our dust will eat out your eyes, our dirt will spoil your clothes, you haven't risen to our level yet, you still can't help admiring yourselves, you like castigating yourselves, and that bores us. Hand us others—it is them we want to break. You are a good fellow, but, all the same, you are nothing but a soft, beautifully bred, liberal boy . . .'

Bazarov, someone once said, is the first Bolshevik; even though he is not a socialist, there is some truth in this. He wants a radical change and does not shrink from brute force. The old dandy, Paul Kirsanov, protests against this: 'Force? There is force in savage Kalmucks and Mongols, too . . . What do we want it for? . . . Civilization, its fruits, are dear to us. And don't tell me they are worthless. The most miserable dauber . . . the pianist who taps on the keys in a restaurant . . . they are more useful than you are, because they represent civilization and not brute Mongol force. You imagine that you are progressive; you should be sitting in a Kalmuck wagon!' In the end, Bazarov, against all his principles, falls in love with a cold, clever, well-born society beauty, is rejected by her, suffers deeply, and not long after dies as a result of an infection caught while dissecting a corpse in a village autopsy. He dies stoically, wondering whether his country had any real need of him and men like him; and his death is bitterly lamented by his old, humble, loving parents. Bazarov falls because he is broken by fate, not through failure of will or intellect. 'I conceived him', Turgenev later wrote to a young student, 'as a sombre figure, wild, huge, half-grown out of the soil, powerful, nasty, honest, but doomed to destruction because he still stands only in the gateway to the future . . .'[5] This brutal, fanatical, dedicated figure, with his unused powers, is represented as an avenger for insulted human reason; yet, in the end, he is crushed by heartless nature, by what the author calls the cold-eyed goddess Isis who does not care for good or evil, or art or beauty, still less for man, the creature of an hour; he struggles to assert himself; but she is indifferent; she obeys her own inexorable laws.

Fathers and Children was published in the spring of 1862 and caused the greatest storm among its Russian readers of any novel before or, indeed, since. What was Bazarov? How was he to be taken? Was he a positive or a negative figure? A hero or a devil? He is young, bold, intelligent, strong, he has thrown off the burden of the past, the melancholy impotence of the 'superfluous men' beating vainly against the bars of the prison house of Russian society. The critic Strakhov in his review spoke of him as a character conceived on a heroic scale. Many years later Lunacharsky described him as the first 'positive' hero in Russian literature. Does he then symbolize progress? Freedom? Yet his hatred of art and culture, of the entire world of liberal values, his cynical

5. Letter to Sluchevsky, 26 April 1862.

asides—does the author mean to hold these up for admiration? Even before the novel was published his editor, Mikhail Katkov, protested to Turgenev. This glorification of nihilism, he complained, was nothing but grovelling at the feet of the young radicals. 'Turgenev', he said to the novelist's friend Annenkov, 'should be ashamed of lowering the flag before a radical, or saluting him as an honourable soldier.' Katkov declared that he was not deceived by the author's apparent objectivity: 'There is concealed approval lurking here . . . this fellow, Bazarov, definitely dominates the others and does not encounter proper resistance,' and he concluded that what Turgenev had done was politically dangerous. Strakhov was more sympathetic. He wrote that Turgenev, with his devotion to timeless truth and beauty, only wanted to describe reality, not to judge it. He too, however, spoke of Bazarov as towering over the other characters, and declared that Turgenev might claim to be drawn to him by an irresistible attraction, but it would be truer to say that he feared him. Katkov echoes this: 'One gets the impression of a kind of embarrassment in the author's attitude of the hero of his story . . . It is as if the author didn't like him, felt lost before him, and, more than this, was terrified of him!'

The attack from the Left was a good deal more virulent. Dobrolyubov's successor, Antonovich, accused Turgenev in the *Contemporary* of perpetrating a hideous and disgusting caricature of the young. Bazarov was a brutish, cynical sensualist, hankering after wine and women, unconcerned with the fate of the people; his creator, whatever his views in the past, had evidently crossed over to the blackest reactionaries and oppressors. And, indeed, there were conservatives who congratulated Turgenev for exposing the horrors of the new, destructive nihilism, and thereby rendering a public service for which all men of decent feeling must be grateful. But it was the attack from the Left that hurt Turgenev most. Seven years later he wrote to a friend that 'mud and filth' had been flung at him by the young. He had been called fool, donkey, reptile, Judas, police agent. And again, 'While some accused me of . . . backwardness, black obscurantism, and informed me that "my photographs were being burnt amid contemptuous laughter", yet others indignantly reproached me with kowtowing to the . . . young. "You are crawling at Bazarov's feet!" cried one of my correspondents. "You are only pretending to condemn him. Actually you scrape and bow to him, you wait obsequiously for the favor of a casual smile." . . . A shadow has fallen upon my name.'

At least one of his liberal friends who had read the manuscript of *Fathers and Children* told him to burn it, since it would compromise him for ever with the progressives. Hostile caricatures appeared in the left-wing press, in which Turgenev was represented as pandering to the fathers, with Bazarov as a leering Mephistopheles, mocking his disciple Arkady's love for his father. At best, the author was drawn as a bewildered figure simultaneously attacked by frantic democrats from the Left and threatened by armed fathers from the Right, as he stood helplessly between them. But the Left was not unanimous. The radical critic Pisarev came to Turgenev's aid. He boldly identified himself with Bazarov and his position. Turgenev, Pisarev wrote, might be too soft or tired to accompany us, the men of the future; but he knows that true progress is to be found not in men tied to tradition, but in active, self-emancipated, independent men, like Bazarov, free from fantasies, from romantic or religious nonsense. The author does not bully us, he does not tell us to accept the values of the 'fathers'. Bazarov is in revolt; he is the prisoner of no theory; that is his attractive strength; that is what makes for progress and freedom. Turgenev may wish to tell us that we are on a false path, but in fact he is a kind of Balaam: he has become deeply attached to the hero of his novel through the very process of creation, and pins all his hopes to him. 'Nature is a workshop, not a temple' and we are workers in it; not melancholy daydreams, but will, strength, intelligence, realism—these, Pisarev declares, speaking through Bazarov, these will find the road. Bazarov, he adds, is what parents today see emerging in their sons and daughters, sisters in their brothers. They may be frightened by it, they may be puzzled, but that is where the road to the future lies.

Turgenev's familiar friend, Annenkov, to whom he submitted all his novels for criticism before he published them, saw Bazarov as a Mongol, a Genghiz Khan, a wild beast symptomatic of the savage condition of Russia, only 'thinly concealed by books from the Leipzig Fair'. Was Turgenev aiming to become the leader of a political movement? 'The author himself . . . does not know how to take him,' he wrote, 'as a fruitful force for the future, or as a disgusting boil on the body of a hollow civilization, to be removed as rapidly as possible.' Yet he cannot be both, 'he is a Janus with two faces, each party will see only what it wants to see or can understand.' Katkov, in an unsigned review in his own journal (in which the novel had appeared), went a good deal further. After mocking the confusion on the Left as a result of being unexpectedly faced with its own image in nihilism, which pleased some and horrified others, he reproaches the author for being altogether too anxious not to be unjust to Bazarov, and consequently of representing him always in the best possible light. There is such a thing, he says, as being too fair; this leads to its own brand of distortion of the truth. As for the hero, he is represented as being brutally candid: that is good, very good; he believes in telling the whole truth, however upsetting to the poor, gentle Kirsanovs, father and son, with no respect for persons or circumstances: most admirable; he attacks art, riches, luxurious living, yes, but in the name of what? Of science and knowledge? But, Katkov declares, this is simply not true. Bazarov's purpose is not the discovery of scientific truth, else he would not peddle cheap popular tracts—Büchner and the rest

—which are not science at all, but journalism, materialist propaganda. Bazarov (he goes on to say) is not a scientist; this species scarcely exists in Russia in our time. Bazarov and his fellow nihilists are merely preachers: they denounce phrases, rhetoric, inflated language—Bazarov tells Arkady not to talk so 'beautifully'—but only in order to substitute for this their own political propaganda; they offer not hard scientific facts, in which they are not interested, with which, indeed they are not acquainted, but slogans, diatribes, radical cant. Bazarov's dissection of frogs is not genuine pursuit of the truth, it is only an occasion for rejecting civilized and traditional values which Paul Kirsanov, who in a better-ordered society—say England—would have done useful work, rightly defends. Bazarov and his friends will discover nothing; they are not researchers; they are mere ranters, men who declaim in the name of a science which they do not trouble to master; in the end they are no better than the ignorant, benighted Russian priesthood from whose ranks they mostly spring, and far more dangerous.

Herzen, as always, was both penetrating and amusing. 'Turgenev was more of an artist in his novel than people think, and for this reason lost his way, and, in my opinion, did very well. He wanted to go to one room, but ended up in another and a better one.' The author clearly started by wanting to do something for the fathers, but they turned out to be such nonentities that he 'became carried away by Bazarov's very extremism; with the result that instead of flogging the son, he whipped the fathers.' Nature sometimes follows art: Bazarov affected the young as Werther, in the previous century, influenced them, like Schiller's *The Robbers*, like Byron's Laras and Giaours and Childe Harolds in their day. Yet these new men, Herzen added in a later essay, are so dogmatic, doctrinaire, jargon-ridden, as to exhibit the least attractive aspect of the Russian character, the policeman's—the martinet's—side of it, the brutal bureaucratic jackboot; they want to break the yoke of the old despotism, but only in order to replace it with one of their own. The 'generation of the forties', his own and Turgenev's, may have been fatuous and weak, but does it follow that their successors—the brutally rude, loveless, cynical, philistine young men of the sixties, who sneer and mock and push and jostle and don't apologize—are necessarily superior beings? What new principles, what new constructive answers have they provided? Destruction is destruction. It is not creation.

In the violent babel of voices aroused by the novel, at least five attitudes can be distinguished. There was the angry right wing which thought that Bazarov represented the apotheosis of the new nihilists, and sprang from Turgenev's unworthy desire to flatter and be accepted by the young. There were those who congratulated him on successfully exposing barbarism and subversion. There were those who denounced him for his wicked travesty of the radicals, for providing reactionaries with ammunition and playing into the hands of the police; by them he was called renegade and traitor. Still others, like Dimitri Pisarev, proudly nailed Bazarov's colors to their mast and expressed gratitude to Turgenev for his honesty and sympathy with all that was most living and fearless in the growing party of the future. Finally there were some who detected that the author himself was not wholly sure of what he wanted to do, that his attitude was genuinely ambivalent, that he was an artist and not a pamphleteer, that he told the truth as he saw it, without a clear partisan purpose.

This controversy continued in full strength after Turgenev's death. It says something for the vitality of his creation that the debate did not die even in the following century, neither before nor after the Russian Revolution. Indeed, as lately as ten years ago the battle was still raging amongst Soviet critics. Was Turgenev for us or against us? Was he a Hamlet blinded by the pessimism of his declining class, or did he, like Balzac or Tolstoy, see beyond it? Is Bazarov a forerunner of the politically committed, militant Soviet intellectual, or a malicious caricature of the fathers of Russian communism? The debate is not over yet.[6]

Turgenev was upset and bewildered by the reception of his book. Before sending it to the printer, he had taken his usual precaution of seeking endless advice. He read the manuscript to friends in Paris, he altered, he modified, he tried to please everyone. The figure of Bazarov suffered several transformations in successive drafts, up and down the moral scale as this or that friend or consultant reported his impressions. The attack from the Left inflicted wounds which festered for the rest of his life. Years later he wrote 'I am told that I am on the side of the "fathers"—I, who in the person of Paul Kirsanov, actually sinned against artistic truth, went too far, exaggerated his defects to the point of travesty, and made him ridiculous!' As for Bazarov, he was 'honest, truthful, a democrat to his fingertips'. Many years later, Turgenev told the anarchist Kropotkin that he loved Bazarov 'very, very much . . . I will show you my diaries—you will see how I wept when I ended the book with Bazarov's death.' 'Tell me honestly,' he wrote to one of his most caustic critics, the satirist Saltykov (who complained that the word 'nihilist' was used by reactionaries to damn anyone they did not like), 'how could anybody be offended by being compared to Bazarov? Do you not yourself realize that he is the most sympathetic of all my characters?' As for 'nihilism', that, perhaps, was a mistake. 'I am ready to admit . . . that

6. The literature, mostly polemical, is very extensive, [and] represents the continuing controversy, in which Lenin's scathing reference to the similarity of Turgenev's views to those of German right-wing social democrats is constantly quoted both for and against the conception of Bazarov as a prototype of Bolshevik activists. There is an even more extensive mass of writing on the question of whether, and how far, Katkov managed to persuade Turgenev to amend his text in a 'moderate' direction by darkening Bazarov's image. That Turgenev did alter his text as a result of Katkov's pleading is certain; he may, however, have restored some, at any rate, of the original language when the novel was published as a book. His relations with Katkov deteriorated rapidly; Turgenev came to look on him as a vicious reactionary and refused his proffered hand at a banquet in honour of Pushkin in 1880; one of his favorite habits was to refer to the arthritis which tormented him as Katkovitis (*Katkovka*).

I had no right to give our reactionary scum the opportunity to seize on a name, a catchword; the writer in me should have brought the sacrifice to the citizen—I admit the justice of my rejection by the young and of all the gibes hurled at me . . . The issue was more important than artistic truth, and I ought to have foreseen this.' He claimed that he shared almost all Bazarov's views, all save those on art. A lady of his acquaintance had told him that he was neither for the fathers, nor for the children, but was a nihilist himself; he thought she might be right. Herzen had said that there had been something of Bazarov in them all, in himself, in Belinsky, in Bakunin, in all those who in the forties denounced the Russian kingdom of darkness in the name of the West and science and civilization. Turgenev did not deny this either. He did, no doubt, adopt a different tone in writing to different correspondents. When radical Russian students in Heidelberg demanded clarification of his own position, he told them that 'if the reader does not love Bazarov, as he is—coarse, heartless, ruthlessly dry and brusque . . . the fault is mine; I have not succeeded in my task. But to "melt him in syrup" (to use his own expression)—that I was not prepared to do . . . I did not wish to buy popularity by this sort of concession. Better lose a battle (and I think I have lost this one), than win it by a trick.' Yet to his friend the poet Fet, a conservative landowner, he wrote that he did not himself know if he loved Bazarov or hated him. Did he mean to praise or denigrate him? He did not not know. And this is echoed eight years later: 'My personal feelings [towards Bazarov] were confused (God only knows whether I loved him or hated him!).' To the liberal Madame Filosofova he wrote, 'Bazarov is my beloved child; on his account I quarrelled with Katkov . . . Bazarov, that intelligent, heroic man—a caricature?!' And he added that this was 'a senseless charge'. He found the scorn of the young unjust beyond endurance. He wrote that in the summer of 1862 'despicable generals praised me, the young insulted me.' The socialist leader Lavrov reports that he bitterly complained to him of the injustice of the radicals' change of attitude towards him. He returns to this in one of his late *Poems in Prose*: 'Honest souls turned away from him. Honest faces grew red with indignation at the mere mention of his name.' This was not mere wounded *amour propre*. He suffered from a genuine sense of having got himself into a politically false position. All his life he wished to march with the progressives, with the party of liberty and protest. But, in the end, he could not bring himself to accept their brutal contempt for art, civilized behavior, for everything that he held dear in European culture. He hated their dogmatism, their arrogance, their destructiveness, their appalling ignorance of life. He went abroad, lived in Germany and France, and returned to Russia only on flying visits. In the West he was universally praised and admired. But in the end it was to Russians that he wished to speak. Although his popularity with the Russian public in the sixties, and at all times, was very great, it was the radicals he most of all wanted to please. They were hostile or unresponsive.

* * *

RALPH E. MATLAW

Fathers and Sons†

Perhaps the most suggestive insight ever made into *Fathers and Sons* was V. E. Meyerhold's attempt to cast the poet Vladimir Mayakovsky in the role of Bazarov for a film version contemplated in 1929. Among those who remember the young Mayakovsky's early appearances in films, Yuri Olesha described his face as "sad, passionate, evoking infinite pity, the face of a strong and suffering man." It is a little hard to imagine Mayakovsky with side-whiskers (Bazarov, after all, presumably wears these to resemble more closely his intellectual prototype, the studious and sickly N. A. Dobrolyubov), but apart from that one could not conceive of a better reincarnation of Bazarov than Mayakovsky. For Mayakovsky, in his flamboyant and tragic life, and frequently in his verse, was or would have been if Bazarov had not already staked out a claim to that title, the arch example of the phenomenon we now call "the angry young man."

The term, with due allowance for the changes of a century and of cultures, points to two fundamental aspects of Bazarov that underlie both his attractive and repulsive traits for most readers—his immaturity and his position as an outsider in "a world he never made." And these, in turn, point to the psychological and social verities that secure so high place for *Fathers and Sons* in modern literature. The second of these has a specifical historical context and prototype, V. G. Belinsky, to whom the novel is dedicated. Bazarov's portrait, like Belinsky's career, is associated with and typifies two important notions in Russian intellectual history. The first is the rise of the "intelligentsia," a term, apparently of Russian invention, that designates intellectuals of all persuasions dedicated in one form or another to the improvement of life in Russia, and so carries far greater ethical implications than the mere word "intellectual." The second is that of the *raznochintsy*, literally "persons of various classes," a term applied to those members of classes other than the gentry, usually the clergy or the minor and provincial professional and bureaucratic classes, who sought to pursue a career other than the one their background would normally indicate. Fre-

† From Ralph E. Matlaw, "Turgenev's Novels," *Harvard Slavic Studies* IV (1957). Reprinted by permission of the President and Fellows of Harvard College.

quently they became members of the intelligentsia, usually after considerable privation. Unlike members of the gentry like Herzen or Turgenev, who could always turn to other sources if necessary, they were entirely dependent upon their intellectual labors, whether as tutors, journalists, writers, or in other pursuits, and from their difficult position derived no small part of their exaltation and indefatigability. While there were factions and enmities within the intelligentsia, all its members were in principle agreed on one point: opposition to the conditions of life around them. Clearly connected with these conditions is the intrusion of the *raznochintsy* into literature, until 1830 or so the exclusive purview of the gentry, who were all too eager to avoid the imputation of professionalism. In style and in tone a sharp shift may be observed, and no one better exemplifies this change in real life than Belinsky or in literature than Bazarov.

Intellectual equality, unfortunately, offered no social prerogatives. Beyond his intellectual circles and his normal habitat, the major cities, even in the rapidly changing society of the mid-nineteenth century, the *raznochinets* was an outsider, if not an upstart. Bazarov, with his enormous sensitivity and vanity, feels out of place at the Governor's Ball and at Odintsov's estate (the wording of his request for vodka amazes the butler). He frequently and deliberately emphasizes his plebeian origin, as in the ironic reference to his similarity to the great Speransky, his sharp reaction to his father's apologies, his feelings about Pavel Kirsanov, and in numerous turns of speech that the English translation cannot convey completely. As for Pavel Kirsanov, we need only think of Prince André's disdain for Speransky in *War and Peace* to judge the gulf that in Pavel's mind separates Bazarov from him. To the aristocrat who has cultivated and refined his privileged position, the democratic virtue of being a self-made man does not appear so laudable. And from this point of view Bazarov's contempt for Pavel Petrovich, "snobism in reverse," to adapt Bazarov's witticism, is another manifestation of his discomfort when out of his class. Still, as Bazarov makes clear, his prospects are very meager, and it leads to great bitterness. Outside the "establishment," which he cannot tolerate, there is no opposition party, not even a real hierarchy, and the consciousness of insuperable obstacles leads to Bazarov's great "anger." As Turgenev chose to present the matter it appears more as a social than political theme, but its motive force is just as operative. The point may profitably be compared to a similar one in *The Red and The Black* where, in Stendhal's happier imagination, Julien Sorel rises to the top, only to insist perversely at his trial on his peasant origin and to accuse his jury of seeking "to punish in me and to discourage forever that class of young men who, born in an inferior station and in a sense burdened with poverty, have the good fortune to secure a sound education, and the audacity to mingle with what the pride of rich people calls society."

The second component is more directly implied in the novel's title as the conflict between generations, apparently an inherent problem in human nature, though manifesting itself in different forms and in different degrees. *Fathers and Sons* presents it in particularly sharp form. Nikolai Kirsanov tells his brother of the remark he made to his mother, "Of course you can't understand me. We belong to different generations," and is now resigned to his turn having come to "swallow the pill." Bazarov's father similarly remembers how he scoffed at the earlier generation, accepts Bazarov's ridiculing his outdated notions, but as a matter of course indicates that in twenty years Bazarov's idols too will be replaced. The intensity of rejection, however, does differ and is a sign of the times. For Bazarov replies "For your consolation I will tell you that nowadays we laugh at medicine altogether, and don't bow down to anyone," which his father simply cannot comprehend. Normally, the problem of generations is resolved by time: the sons gradually move toward their permanent positions, give over being "angry young men," and become husbands and fathers, angry or not. It is perhaps the hardest subject of all to handle, as the reaction to the end of *War and Peace* with its assertion of domestic permanence, and, in *Fathers and Sons*, the quick taming of Arkady Kirsanov prove: the world of struggle and aspiration is more interesting to contemplate than that of fixity and acceptance. The "angry young man" cannot remain so, and is something of an anomaly if not of outright ridicule, when he maintains that view as paterfamilias. Bazarov denies the values of normal human behavior, but when his theory is put to a single test it collapses. Bazarov falls in love and can no longer return to his former mode. Turgenev permits him to maintain his character by shifting the problem of generations to its ultimate form, that of death. This condition, at least, Bazarov must accept: "An old man at least has time to be weaned from life, but I . . . Well, go and try to disprove death. Death will disprove you, and that's all!" And in his illness Bazarov compresses into a brief period that acceptance of traditional values—family, love, life itself—that otherwise would accrue slowly and undramatically, in the process to some extent attenuating the strident expression of his former views.

But this only occurs at the end. Throughout the novel the high-mindedness, dedication, and energy that make Bazarov tower over the other characters are occasionally expressed with an immaturity bordering on adolescent revolt. The ideas themselves thus in part express the temperament of the "sons." Superficially the state may seem to apply more readily to Arkady, but it is far more ingrained in Bazarov. There are such remarks as "Bazarov drew himself up haughtily. 'I don't share anyone's ideas: I have my own,' " and "When I meet a man who can hold his own beside me, then I'll change my opinion of myself," his deliberately offensive manners, his sponging on and abuse of Kukshin and Sitnikov, his trifling with Fenichka and his jejune declaration to

Odintsov. In short, the attempt to impose his own image on the world and to reshape the world accordingly. It is a point Turgenev made quite explicit in his draft for *Virgin Soil*:

> There are *Romantics of Realism* * * * They long for a reality and strive toward it, as former Romantics did toward the ideal. In reality they seek not poetry—that is ludicrous for them—but something grand and meaningful; and that's nonsense: real life is prosaic and should be so. They are unhappy, distorted, and torment themselves with this very distortion as something completely inappropriate to their work. Moreover, their appearance—possibly only in Russia, always with a *sermonizing* or educational aspect—is necessary and useful: they are preachers and prophets in their own way, but complete prophets, contained and defined in themselves. Preaching is an illness, a hunger, a desire; a healthy person cannot be a prophet or even a preacher. Therefore I put something of *that* romanticism in Bazarov too, but only Pisarev noticed it.[1]

The two problems of youth and anger, or maturity and acceptance, come to a head in Bazarov's involvement with Odintsov, the central episode in the novel, which also serves as a kind of structural dividing line between the political (or social) and the psychological. The discussions of nihilism and contemporary politics, that phase of the battle between the generations dominates the opening of the novel but is practically concluded when Bazarov and Arkady leave Odintsov in Chapter Nineteen. From this point on an opposite movement assumes primary importance: Bazarov's and Arkady's liberation from involvement with theories and the turn toward life itself, that is, toward those people and things in the characters' immediate existence. It entails a shift from scenes and formulations essentially intellectual to others that are more ruminative, inwardly speculative, communicating psychological states and feelings rather than ideas. With it, Bazarov's views and behavior assume a different cast, far more personal, more indicative of his real needs and dissatisfactions. His speeches about necessary reforms now turn into expressions of personal desire ("I felt such a hatred for this poorest peasant, this Philip or Sidor, for whom I'm to be ready to jump out of my skin, and who won't even thank me for it"), his rigorous materialism into the purely Pascalian speech on man's insignificance as a point in time and space. His brusqueness and former contempt for decorum now are so tempered that he accepts a challenge to a duel, has a frock coat easily accessible as he returns to Odintsov, and practices elaborate politeness as she visits him on his deathbed. The end with Bazarov's disquisition on strength, life, and necessity strike the reader as rather mawkish and hollow, for the words now have if not a false, at

1. André Mazon, "L'élaboration d'un roman de Turgenev: *Terres vierges.*" *Revue des études slaves*, V (1925), 87–88.

least a commonplace ring. Indeed, the great effect of the ending is achieved not through Bazarov's speeches but by communicating the despair of his parents.

In the final analysis Turgenev could neither condemn nor yet wholly redeem Bazarov without falsifying or diminishing the portrait. On the last page of the novel he instead implies the reconciliation of the character with a larger, permanent order of things, expressed in terms of the touchstone and overriding image of the novel—nature. The concluding words "[the flowers] tell us, too, of eternal reconciliation and of life without end" do not at all tend toward mysticism, as Herzen claimed and Turgenev denied, but affirm that "the passionate, sinning,[2] and rebellious heart" buried beneath the ground has finally come to terms with permanent reality. The passage is secular rather than religious: life is "without end" not "eternal"; it is life on earth, not in the hereafter.

IRVING HOWE

The Politics of Hesitation†

* * *

If Rudin has partly been created in Turgenev's own image, Bazarov, the hero of *Fathers and Sons*, is a figure in opposition to that image. The one rambles idealistic poetry, the other grumbles his faith in the dissection of frogs; the one is all too obviously weak, the other seems spectacularly strong. Yet between the two there is a parallel of social position. Both stand outside the manor-house that is Russia, peering in through a window; Rudin makes speeches and Bazarov would like to throw stones but no one pays attention, no one is disturbed. The two together might, like Dostoevsky's Shatov and Kirillov, come to a whole man; but they are not together, they alternate in Russian life, as in Russian literature, each testifying to the social impotence that has made the other possible.

Like all of Turgenev's superfluous men, Bazarov is essentially good. Among our more cultivated critics, those who insist that the heroes of novels be as high-minded as themselves, it has been fashionable to look with contempt upon Bazarov's nihilism, to see him as a specimen of Russian boorishness. Such a reading is not merely imperceptive, it is humorless. Would it really be better if Bazarov, instead of devoting

2. Perhaps "erring" conveys the spirit rather than the letter of the word better than "sinning" does.

† Reprinted by permission from *The Hudson Review* VIII, no. 4 (Winter 1956). Copyright © 1956 by The Hudson Review, Inc.

himself to frogs and viscera, were to proclaim about Poetry and the Soul? Would it be better if he were a metaphysician juggling the shells of Matter and Mind instead of a coarse materialist talking nonsense about the irrelevance of Pushkin?

For all that Bazarov's nihilism accurately reflects a phase of Russian and European history, it must be taken more as a symptom of political desperation than as a formal intellectual system. Bazarov is a man ready for life, and cannot find it. Bazarov is a man of the most intense emotions, but without confidence in his capacity to realize them. Bazarov is a revolutionary personality, but without revolutionary ideas or commitments. He is all potentiality and no possibility. The more his ideas seem outmoded, the more does he himself seem our contemporary.

No wonder Bazarov feels so desperate a need to be rude. There are times when society is so impervious to the kicks of criticism, when intellectual life softens so completely into the blur of gentility, that the rebellious man, who can tolerate everything but not being taken seriously, has no alternative to rudeness. How else is Bazarov to pierce the elegant composure of Pavel Petrovich, a typically "enlightened" member of the previous generation who combines the manners of a Parisian litterateur with an income derived from the labor of serfs. Bazarov does not really succeed, for Pavel Petrovich forces him to a duel, a romantic ceremony that is the very opposite of everything in which Bazarov believes. During the course of the duel, it is true, Pavel Petrovich must yield to Bazarov, but the mere fact that it takes place is a triumph for the old, not the new. Bazarov may regard Pavel Petrovich as an "archaic phenomenon," but the "archaic phenomenon" retains social power.

The formal components of Bazarov's nihilism are neither unfamiliar nor remarkable: 19th century scientism, utilitarianism, a crude materialism, a rejection of the esthetic, a belief in the powers of the free individual, a straining for tough-mindedness and a deliberate provocative rudeness. These ideas and attitudes can gain point only if Bazarov brings them to political coherence, and the book charts Bazarov's journey, as an uprooted plebeian, in search of a means of expression, a task, an obligation. On the face of it, Bazarov's ideas have little to do with politics, yet he is acute enough to think of them in political terms; he recognizes that they are functions of his frustrated political passion. "Your sort," he says to his mild young friend Arkady, "can never get beyond refined submission or refined indignation, and that's no good. You won't fight—and yet you fancy yourselves gallant chaps—but we mean to fight . . . We want to smash other people! You're a capital fellow; but you're a sugary liberal snob for all that . . ." This is the language of politics; it might almost be Lenin talking to a liberal parliamentarian. But even as Bazarov wants to "smash other people" he senses his own helplessness: he has no weapons for smashing anything. "A harmless person," he calls himself, and a little later, "A tame cat."

In the society of his day, as Turgenev fills it in with a few quick strokes, Bazarov is as superfluous as Rudin. His young disciple Arkady cannot keep pace with him; Arkady will marry, have a houseful of children and remember to be decent to his peasants. The older generation does not understand Bazarov and for that very reason fears him: Arkady's father, a soft slothful landowner, is acute enough, however, to remark that Bazarov is different: he has "fewer traces of the slaveowner." Bazarov's brief meeting with the radicals is a fine bit of horseplay, their emptyheaded chatter being matched only by his declaration, as preposterous as it is pathetic: "I don't adopt anyone's ideas; I have my own." At which one of them, in a transport of defiance, shouts: "Down with all authorities!" and Bazarov realizes that among a pack of fools it is hard not to play the fool. He is tempted, finally, by Madame Odintzov, the country-house Delilah; suddenly he finds his awkward callow tongue, admitting to her his inability to speak freely of everything in his heart. But again he is rejected, and humiliated too, almost like a servant who has been used by his mistress and then sent packing. Nothing remains but to go home, to his good sweet uncomprehending mother and father, those remnants of old Russia; and to die.

Turgenev himself saw Bazarov in his political aspect:

> If he [Bazarov] calls himself a nihilist, one ought to read—a revolutionary . . . I dreamed of a figure that should be gloomy, wild, great, growing one half of him out of the soil, strong, angry, honorable, and yet doomed to destruction—because as yet he still stands on the threshold of the future. I dreamed of a strange parallel to Pugatchev. And my young contemporaries shake their heads and tell me, "You have insulted us . . . It's a pity you haven't worked him out a little more." There is nothing left for me but, in the words of the gipsy song, "to take off my hat with a very low bow."

Seldom has a writer given a better cue to the meaning of his work, and most of all in the comparison between Bazarov and Pugatchev, the leader of an 18th century peasant rebellion who was hanged by a Tzar. Pugatchev, however, had his peasant followers, while Bazarov . . . what is Bazarov but a Pugatchev without the peasants?

It is at the end of *Fathers and Sons* that Turgenev reaches his highest point as an artist. The last twenty-five pages are of an incomparable elevation and intensity, worthy of Tolstoy and Dostoevsky, and in some respects, particularly in their blend of tragic power and a mute underlying sweetness, superior to them. When Bazarov, writhing in delirium, cries out, "Take ten from eight, what's left over?" we are close to the lucidity of Lear in the night. It is the lucidity of final self-confrontation, Bazarov's lament over his lost, his unused powers: "I was needed by Russia . . . No, it's clear, I wasn't needed . . ." And: "I said I should rebel . . . I rebel, I rebel!"

This ending too has failed to satisfy many critics, even one so perceptive as Prince Mirsky, who complains that there is something arbitrary in Bazarov's death. But given Russia, given Bazarov, how else *could* the novel end? Too strong to survive in Russia, what else is possible to Bazarov but death? The accident of fate that kills him comes only after he has been defeated in every possible social and personal encounter: it is the summation of those encounters. "I rebel, I rebel," he croaks on his death-bed, lying lonely and ignored in a corner of Russia, this man who was to change and destroy everything; and is not the whole meaning of the book, political and not political, that for his final cry of defiance he cannot find an object to go with the subject and the verb?

* * *

RICHARD FREEBORN

Turgenev and Revolution†

No one will pretend that Turgenev was a revolutionary. On many occasions he professed his political liberalism and gradualism and his abhorrence of revolution. But, with the exception of his friend Herzen, he was the only great Russian nineteenth-century writer to have direct experience of revolution. Unlike Herzen, he was the first to give fictional lineaments to the revolutionary type in Russian literature. It is this legacy and its meaning for Turgenev's reputation that I wish to examine.

There is, I believe, a fairly general consensus among those who have studied Turgenev that he was a writer who took a remarkably objective, fair-minded view of the political scene while always seeking to hold the middle ground. Government, the establishment, the die-hards, meaning in terms of his fiction the Pavel Kirsanovs, the Ratmirovs, the Sipyagins, could be said to be given a fair measure of verisimilitude and integrity as characterizations, just as the younger generation received perceptive, appreciative and critically just appraisals in such representative heroes as Litvinov and Nezhdanov or in such heroines as Yelena and Marianna. The balance of attitudes in Turgenev's picture of Russian society is what strikes one as so remarkable in an age when literature in its Russian context presupposed commitment to one set of ideas rather than another and was therefore a literature riven by polemic. It was a balance involving ' "the body and pressure of time" and that rapidly changing physiognomy

† This article, originally read at the Turgenev Symposium organized by Professor Robert L. Jackson at Yale University in April 1983, is intended as a tribute to I. S. Turgenev on the centenary of his death. Reprinted by permission of the Editors of *The Slavonic and East European Review* 61, no. 4 (October 1983) 518–27.

of Russians of the cultured stratum',[1] which he described as being preeminently the object of his observation as a novelist; it was therefore 'realistic' in its devotion to the realities of Russian life and topical in its concern with chronicling the history of the Russian intelligentsia. Where, though, in the final analysis, does a Turgenevan ideal emerge? Is it an ideal simply through being balanced in an unbalanced age? Where can one discern the impulse which makes his greatest work acquire a degree of transcendence beyond impartiality, conscientious objectivity and the rigorous topicality which is inseparable from realism?

That Turgenev strove to transcend the real and the supposed verities of reality is what his career demonstrates from *Steno* to *Klara Milich* and the *Poems in Prose*. Deliberately setting aside the consolations of religious faiths, his was a realistic view of life which attempted from first to last to peer beyond the veil, or to cross the threshold separating reality from eternity. Contemplating that divide, Steno thinks:

> Before me I see a threshold—
> It divides life from eternity
> And I stand before it. In vain my eyes
> Peer beyond it. Everything
> That awaits us there is covered in mist . . .
> Oh, if only I could guess the meaning of its secret,
> I would give up all I know to have that knowledge.[2]

Forty years later, in his famous 'Poem in Prose' entitled *Porog* (On the Threshold), which for Prince Peter Kropotkin was an expression of Turgenev's 'admiration of those women who gave their lives for the revolutionary movement',[3] he celebrated the self-sacrifice of the Russian girl who stands on the threshold of a life devoted to revolutionary endeavour, faces the consequences and yet decides to cross the threshold:

> The girl crossed the threshold and the heavy veil dropt behind her.
> 'Idiot!' someone behind her spat out.
> 'Saint!' came an answering cry from somewhere.[4]

The ideal of a life sacrificed in some great cause is one that Turgenev examined in so many of his works that it hardly needs emphasizing. It is better to stress the difference between the world-weariness of the Byronic Steno and the youthfulness of the Russian girl standing on the threshold. Here the religious note in Turgenev's picture of the young girl's sacrifice calls to mind at once his first extended essay in this kind

1. I. S. Turgenev, *Polnoye sobraniye sochineniy i pisem v dvadtsati vos'mi tomakh*, Moscow-Leningrad, 1960–68 (*Sochineniya*, 15 vols; *Pis'ma*, 13 vols, hereafter referred to as *Soch.* and *Pis'ma* respectively), *Soch.*, vol. 12, 1966, p. 303. All translations in the text are mine.
2. *Soch.*, vol. 1, 1960, p. 417.
3. P. A. Kropotkin, *Russian Literature: Ideals and Realities*, London, 1916, p. 114.
4. *Soch.*, vol. 13, 1967, p. 169. The story of the complications surrounding the publication of this 'Poem in Prose', which was originally written in 1878, it seems, in response to Vera Zasulich's attempt on the life of General Trepov, is given on pp. 650–55.

of portraiture, the figure of Yelena in his third novel, *On the Eve*. Sainthood and revolutionary dedication first emerged as prominent ideals in Turgenev's work with this novel. Principally, though, it was the youth of the heroine that lent poignancy to the characterization. Turgenev achieved his greatest fame, I believe, not as a champion of the serfs, but as a celebrant of youth's moral courage and self-sacrifice in the cause of freedom. Perhaps, in so doing, he may have contributed unwittingly to the fostering of that 'spiritual pedocracy', as Sergey Bulgakov called it, which became 'the greatest evil of our society as well as a symptom of intelligentsia heroism.'[5] The symptom came to be reflected in literature not only in Turgenev's own later writing, notoriously, for example, in his last novel *Virgin Soil* (*Nov'*), but in a more overtly revolutionary sense in the work of Stepniak-Kravchinsky. His novel, *The Career of a Nihilist*, paid more than lip service to Turgenev's celebration of the youthfulness of the revolutionary vocation; it gave overt expression to the religious aspect of it or, as Stepniak described his aim in his preface: 'I wanted to show in the full light of fiction the inmost heart and soul of those humanitarian enthusiasts, with whom devotion to a cause has attained the fervour of a religion, without being a religion.'[6] The literary model for the image of the revolutionary hero in Stepniak's novel can be traced to Turgenev in several ways, as Stepniak was quite ready to admit.[7]

The romanticism associated with the image of the youthful revolutionary, and the pedocracy to which it probably gave rise, had something inherently spurious and silly about it. There are grounds for arguing that Turgenev was doing no more than pandering to the younger generation when he chose to portray them as devoted to the cause of revolutionary freedom or national liberation. Dostoyevsky thought so. The figure of Karmazinov, that wickedly vicious caricature of Turgenev in *Besy* (*The Possessed*), expressed all Dostoyevsky's hostility and scorn:

> The great author trembled sickeningly before the latest revolutionary youth and, imagining out of ignorance that the key to Russia's future was in their hands, pandered ignominiously to them, chiefly because they paid him no attention whatever.[8]

In these words Dostoyevsky obviously referred to Turgenev and made the point even clearer in the chapter describing Pyotr Stepanovich Ver-

5. S. N. Bulgakov, 'Geroizm i podvizhnichestvo', *Vekhi*, 2nd edn, Moscow, 1909, p. 43.
6. Stepniak, *The Career of a Nihilist*, Walter Scott, London, 1889; 2nd edn with preface, London, n.d., p. ix. Stepniak was the pseudonym of S. M. Kravchinsky (1851–95).
7. Stepniak wrote a preface, for example, to Constance Garnett's translation of Turgenev's *Rudin* (1894), in which he described the type of Rudin as 'the living ferment which alone can leaven the unformed masses' (p. xi), and he also planned to write a study of Turgenev. For details, see M. I. Perper, 'Iz nezavershonnoy knigi S. M. Stepnyaka-Kravchinskogo o Turgeneve', in *Literaturnoye nasledstvo*, vol. 76, Moscow, 1967, pp. 255–76.
8. F. M. Dostoyevsky, *Polnoye sobraniye sochineniy v tridtsati tomakh*, Leningrad, 1972– , vol. 10, 1974, p. 170.

khovensky's visit to the great writer. With his grand manner of offering his cheek to be kissed, his fussy concern for his manuscript 'Merci' and his self-proclaimed loyalty to everything German, Karmazinov emerged as an attitudinizing, self-important littérateur who set great store by his reputation as the confidant of youth. The exchanges between him and Pyotr Stepanovich about the forthcoming revolution are a delight:

> Pyotr Stepanovich picked up his hat and rose to his feet. Karmazinov stretched out to him both hands in farewell.
> 'What', he chirruped in a small honeyed voice and with a special intonation, still holding the other's hands in his own, 'what if what is supposed to happen . . . about which everyone's thinking . . . then when could it come about?'
> 'How do I know?' somewhat rudely answered Pyotr Stepanovich. They both looked fixedly in each other's eyes.
> 'Probably? Approximately?' Karmazinov chirruped still more sweetly.
> 'You'll have time to sell your estate and get out,' still more rudely muttered Pyotr Stepanovich. They looked at each other still more fixedly.
> A minute passed in silence.
> 'It'll start at the beginning of May and it'll be over by 1st October,' Pyotr said suddenly.
> 'My sincere thanks,' uttered Karmazinov, obviously touched and pressing the other's hands.[9]

It is, of course, the ideal revolution. You know when it will begin and when it will end and you have time to sell your estate. Dostoyevsky mocked it and mocked Turgenev's interest in it. Moreover, Turgenev on many occasions in his life dissociated himself from revolution, whether simply by denying that he had any interest in politics or by declaring his liberal, gradualist views. On the last occasion he made public avowal of his feelings in the matter, he insisted: 'I have always been and have remained to this day a "gradualist", an old-style liberal in the dynastic English sense, a man who expects reform *only from above* and hostile in principle to all revolutions. . . .'[1] This view of Turgenev as liberal and antirevolutionary has persisted by and large throughout the hundred years since his death. Dostoyevsky's satirical portrayal no doubt helped to establish the view. But Dostoyevsky never knew revolution; Turgenev did.

His direct experience of the Paris Revolution of 1848 was confined principally to the June days which saw the revolution's defeat. His description of the events of 15 May 1848[2]—strictly speaking the only first-hand evidence we have of his experience of revolution—is that of an

9. Ibid., pp. 288–89.
1. *Soch.*, vol. xv, 1968, p. 185.
2. See his letter to Pauline Viardot: *Pis'ma*, vol. 1, 1961, pp. 299–304.

eye-witness who observed carefully but of necessity could not evaluate the events. Yet they evidently left their mark on him. He judged that the Parisian working classes were simply biding their time. When that time came—tragically—during the June days, Turgenev apparently witnessed their short-lived triumph and their bloody defeat at first hand;[3] but his first reaction to the revolutionary events of that summer, as he summarized them in his letter to Pauline Viardot, took the form of a question: 'What is history? . . . Providence, accident, irony or fate? . . .'[4] Even violent historical change, then, in Turgenev's cool assessment of it, had no specific aim, though he recognized that in the last resort, if a man is to achieve anything at all in his life, he must make that ultimate commitment to his ideals which demands of him the fullest sacrifice. On 26 June 1848 the bloodstained streets of the Faubourg St Antoine were to be the place where the first revolutionary hero in Russian literature laid down his life in the name of his own and his generation's ideals.

In any attempt to assess Turgenev's attitude to revolution and the ideals of his own generation, it is impossible to overlook his relations with Herzen. The revolutionary events of 1848 in Paris seem to have brought the two of them together and their relationship, particularly a decade later at the time of the emancipation of the serfs, seems to have been a determining factor in making Turgenev 'revolutionize' the hero of his first novel. For Turgenev the spirit of revolutionary change discernible in the Russian younger generation after the Crimean War did not at first have specifically Russian characteristics. For him a contrast between Hamlet and Don Quixote had to provide a theoretical framework, owing its origins to his experience of the 1848 revolution,[5] while clearly anticipating his portrayal of Yelena and Insarov in *On the Eve*. The 'revolutionary' impulse motivating the Don Quixotes, the altruistic men of action of this world, is centred in their readiness to die for an ideal and to regard their lives as having value only to the extent that they embodied an ideal of creating truth and justice on earth.[6] Herzen, whose disillusionment as a result of 1848 was far greater than Turgenev's, spoke of Don Quixote in a different sense, as the embodiment of the crisis that had overtaken utopian idealism, as the failed idealist who went on repeating the old revolutionary slogans.[7] His pejorative use of the term 'Don Quixote of revolution' was repeated in the most important of his public utterances directed at Turgenev, his 'Ends and Beginnings' (1862–63), where he invited Turgenev to consider the type of Don

3. See 'Turgenev o revolyutsionnom Parizhe 1848 g.: iz dnevnikovykh zapisey P. A. Vasil'chikova, 1853–4', in *Literaturnoye nasledstvo*, vol. 76, pp. 342–58.
4. 'Qu'est-ce que c'est donc que l'histoire? . . . Providence, hasard, ironie ou fatalité? . . .': *Pis'ma*, vol. 1, p. 304.
5. See *Soch.*, vol. 8, 1964, p. 553.
6. Ibid., p. 173.
7. Ibid., p. 559.

Quixote of revolution as one suitable for a writer of his stature, one who would be, as he put it, 'the laureate of the funeral oration over this world.'[8] No doubt, as in so many other instances, Turgenev and Herzen had discussed the question of Don Quixote before—and disagreed. It is obvious that Turgenev's view of Don Quixote was far more positive and 'revolutionary' than Herzen's. If, during Turgenev's visit to England in 1860, at the close of his Ventnor holiday that August, when he and Annenkov had visited Herzen at Bournemouth, they had discussed— among other things—those who were to be the new leaders of opinion in Russia, it seems probable that it was not only the 'new men' of the sixties, not only the bilious ones, not only the nihilists like Bazarov who were mentioned, but also the superfluous men, the failed Quixotic idealists of Herzen's and Turgenev's generation, men perhaps like Bakunin; and if that conjecture is correct (for it has to be admitted that it is only conjecture), then it is probable that Turgenev may have decided to rehabilitate the reputation of his own generation of the intelligentsia by turning his failed idealist of a hero, Dmitry Rudin, into a revolutionary through the addition of the final short epilogue describing his death on a Paris barricade. In doing so, he may have spoiled the portrait for some readers; he most certainly appears to have violated the novel's internal chronology; but, chiefly, he underlined that the idealism of his own generation of Westernists involved an ultimate commitment to revolutionary change and that to deny the revolutionary ideal was a betrayal.

While in Ventnor, in August 1860, we know that Turgenev conceived his greatest hero, Bazarov. The possible association between Turgenev's creation of Bazarov, his project for primary education and the 'revolutionary' planning of Ogaryov makes it likely that the claim in the letter to Sluchevsky that if Bazarov 'is called a nihilist, then one ought to read: revolutionary', is not accidental, nor simply an instance of Turgenev pandering to youth.[9] It may be regarded as an explicit statement of Turgenev's aim in the most explicit of all the statements that he made about his intentions in writing *Fathers and Children*. No one can surely doubt that this was a novel directed against the landed gentry as the leading class, that it represented Bazarov as honest, truthful and a democrat down to his fingernails, that it projected in him the image of the new scientific man who would reject all laws or authorities save those sanctioned by the natural sciences and that, inseparable from the tragic concept of Bazarov, was Turgenev's dream, as he put it, 'of a sombre, wild, huge figure, half-grown from the earth, powerful, wicked and honest—and yet doomed to perish—because it still stands on the thresh-

8. A. I. Gertsen, *Sobraniye sochineniy v 30 tomakh*, Moscow, 1954–66, vol. 16, 1959, p. 149.
9. For a discussion of the possible influences to which Turgenev was subjected while he was in Ventnor, see my article 'Turgenev at Ventnor' (*Slavonic and East European Review*, vol. 51, no. 3, July 1973, pp. 387–412); also the detailed and informative examination of his stay in Ventnor in chs. 6 and 7 of Patrick Waddington's excellent *Turgenev and England*, London, 1980; *Pis'ma*, vol. 4, 1962, p. 380.

old of the future—I dreamed of some strange pendant to the Pugachovs. . . .'[1] The image of Bazarov, less as a revolutionary than as a practical reformer, a man more given to healing than to political action, is perhaps what endures, though the controversy over his political meaning sparked off by the discovery of Annenkov's letter in 1958[2] and Sir Isaiah Berlin's treatment of him as an example of a new Jacobinism[3] have served to keep alive the controversial aspects of his portrayal and are testimony to the inherent vividness and distinctiveness of the portrait.

In the year of the novel's publication controversy surrounded not only the portrait of Bazarov but also Turgenev himself, and it was a controversy ultimately about revolution. Herzen's attack on Turgenev after the latter's brief visit to London in May 1862 had as its central theme the notion that the peasantry were a revolutionary force. Turgenev disputed this. Both had stated their positions earlier in different ways, but the direct confrontation between them in 1862 had all the features of a quarrel. Herzen's disparagement of the educated class in Russia provoked Turgenev into an eloquent defence. He accused Herzen and Ogaryov of Slavophilism in their thinking about the supposed revolutionary potential of the peasantry. To Herzen he wrote:

> The role of the *educated* class in Russia—to be a transmitter of civilization to the people, so that it can decide for itself what it wants to accept or reject—is, in essence, a modest role, although Peter the Great and Lomonosov were active in pursuing it, although revolution brings it into effect—and this role in my view is not yet over. You gentlemen, to the contrary, by a German process of thinking (like the Slavophiles), abstracting from the scarcely known and comprehensible substance of the people those principles on which you suppose that it bases its life, are wandering about in a fog and—which is more important—are in effect *crying off from revolution (otrekayetes' ot revolyutsii)*, because the people before whom you bow down are conservatives par excellence . . .[4]

Herzen was crying off from revolution because he rejected Western civilization. In this he appeared to be betraying what for Turgenev was the spirit of Russian Westernism. 'Civilization', meaning the civilization of the West, was the one and only item in the plethora of left-wing and right-wing ideas which Turgenev was prepared to defend. His fifth novel *Smoke* (1867) makes this abundantly clear. To that ideal of civilization Turgenev remained true all his life. He also remained true, I believe, to the idea 'that revolution brings it into effect' (. . . *Yeyo privodit v*

1. Ibid., p. 381.
2. See V. Arkhipov, 'K tvorcheskoy istorii romana I. S. Turgeneva "Ottsy i deti" ' (*Russkaya literatura*, no. 1, Leningrad, 1958, pp. 132–62); the controversy was summarized in part by G. Fridlender in 'K sporam ob "Ottsakh i detyakh" ' (*Russkaya literatura*, no. 2, 1959, pp. 131–48).
3. Isaiah Berlin, *Fathers and Children*, Oxford, 1972.
4. *Pis'ma*, vol. 5, 1963, pp. 51–52.

deystviye revolyutsiya). He may have despaired of any change in Russia
in the 1860s but as the revolutionary tide began to rise he made open
acknowledgement in his fiction of the zeal and dedication which he
sensed in the youthful revolutionaries of Populism, in the representatives
of 'anonymous Russia', as he called them in *Virgin Soil*. Though he
could not sympathize with the aims of the revolutionaries, he could
sympathize with them as people. The result may not have given rise to
any memorable portrayals, but *Virgin Soil* was the only major novel of
the 1870s to offer a sober and generally balanced appraisal of the Populists
and their revolutionary aspirations. Through this work—indeed through
his work as a whole, so Lavrov would claim—Turgenev

> unconsciously paved the way for and participated in the growth of
> the Russian revolutionary movement. . . . The dead Turgenev,
> surrounded by the singing of Orthodox priests whom he hated and
> numerous delegations from groups in whose political solvency he
> did not believe, carried on unconsciously the cause of his whole
> life, the fulfilment of his 'Hannibal's oath'. Like his purely artistic
> types, so his grave covered with innumerable wreaths were stepping
> stones by which, implacably and irresistibly, the Russian Revolution
> marched towards its goal.[5]

We may regard Lavrov's words as so much obituary rhetoric. If so,
we should not overlook the fact that Turgenev actively supported Lavrov's
Vperyod in the mid-1870s by annual donations of 500 francs,[6] that he
was friendly with many young revolutionaries and, at the very end of
his life, was preparing, so Ralston testifies, to write a novel about a
Russian girl of nihilist persuasion who marries a young French socialist
and settles in Paris where she eventually 'recognizes to her horror that
the ends and aims, the aspirations and yearnings of the Russian revo-
lutionists are widely different from those of the French and German
socialists, and that a great abyss divides her, so far as thought and feeling
are concerned, from the husband with whom she used to fancy herself
entirely in accord.'[7] In short, from the Hannibal's oath against serfdom
at the beginning of his life to the work about revolutionaries planned at
the end of his life, Turgenev was concerned with the forces which would
change the life of Russia. He knew as well as anyone that in political
terms there was a great gulf fixed between the representatives of the
Russian empire and the representatives of the Russian exiles in Paris,
of whom Lavrov was a recognized leader. He knew that change could
only be achieved by pressure. The ultimate pressure was, of course,
revolution, but guided by the educated class in Russia in the name of

5. P. L. Lavrov, 'Iz stat'i "I. S. Turgenev i razvitiye russkogo obshchestva" ', in *I. S. Turgenev
v vospominaniyakh sovremennikov*, vol. 1, Moscow, 1969, pp. 424–25.
6. Ibid., p. 392.
7. W. R. S. Ralston, 'Ivan Serguévitch Tourguénieff (*The Athenaeum*, London, 15 Sept. 1883,
p. 338).

greater civilization. Against an obdurate, if chastened, autocracy a politically insolvent, nihilistic revolutionary movement could achieve little. Turgenev knew this and despaired of both, though he hoped the two might be reconciled. On the occasion of his funeral, as Ralston put it, 'these two representatives of two utterly opposed schools of thought were manifestly in accord on one point, morally linked for an instant by a common sorrow, by a very sincere and poignant grief at finally parting with a compatriot whom both alike could admire and esteem.'[8] Turgenev's place was therefore in a middle ground, politically speaking. Admired though he might have been by both sides at his death, he surely in his attitude to life always celebrated the triumph of something greater than violent political change. He celebrated the triumph, no matter how short-lived, of a revolutionary ecstasy that could transform human life and human relationships. No other Russian writer evoked this ecstasy so powerfully.

If I may put it this way, the kind of revolution which Turgenev celebrated in the greatest of his works was what might be called 'a revolution of the heart'. In the last of his works to deal extensively with the experience of first love in an obviously autobiographical sense, he wrote:

> First love is like revolution; the uniformly correct ordering of life is smashed and destroyed in an instant, youth takes to the barricades, its bright banner raised on high, and no matter what awaits it in the future—death or a new life—it sends to all things its ecstatic greeting.[9]

Such were the transcendent moments in the Turgenevan view of things. No promise of eternity, no consolations of faith, but a recognition that momentary happiness could occur like one of life's accidents, with the swiftness of revolution. There can be no doubt that Turgenev's experience of revolution as a momentary event in history—providential, perhaps, accidental, ironical or fateful, he was himself unsure which— matched and possibly reinforced his sense that life's ultimate joy was to be experienced in the momentary ecstasy of first love. He knew in his own life the public fact of revolution. When he came to write his *Literaturnyye i zhiteyskiye vospominaniya* (Literary Reminiscences), it was precisely to the events of 1848 that he turned as among the most memorable in his life, as 'Chelovek v seıykh ochkakh' (The Man in Grey Spectacles) and 'Nashi poslali!' (Our People Sent Us) touchingly demonstrate. No other major nineteenth-century Russian novelist could rival him in that. In the experience of the world as we know it through his writings he emphasized both the ephemeral ecstasy that can suddenly transform life completely and the poignancy of lives sacrificed in the

8. Ibid., p. 337
9. *Soch.*, vol. 11, 1966, p. 87.

name of a revolutionary ideal. Unless we recognize that the ecstasy is there in Turgenev's view of things as 'a revolution of the heart', we are in danger of doing a disservice to his memory and of misconstruing his Westernism and his advocacy of European civilization. These were not vague commitments to gradualist liberalism. They were in fact convictions that changed his life, ideals to which he harnessed his reputation; and they shine through the realism of his work like images of transcendence.

RICHARD STITES

Nihilism and Women†

Although cultural anthropologists might not agree, the concept of ethnicity need not be confined to national, regional, or linguistic groups but ought to be applied to any category of human beings that constitutes a more or less clearly defined cultural community visibly distinguishable from the surrounding society. Indeed, when applied to communities with a homogeneous culture—whether political, social, or religious— it can have far more meaning than when used to conceptualize such internally diverse categories as "Jews," "Southern Blacks," or "Irish Catholics." The term "nihilists" has long been employed by both sympathizers and critics to describe a large, diffuse group of Russians who made their appearance in the late 1850's and early 1860's and who formed the pool out of which radical movements emerged. There have been many attempts to define Russian nihilism, but I think Nikolai Strakhov came close to the truth when he said that "nihilism itself hardly exists, although there is no denying the fact that nihilists do."[1] Nihilism was not so much a corpus of formal beliefs and programs (like populism, liberalism, Marxism) as it was a cluster of attitudes and social values and a set of behavioral affects—manners, dress, friendship patterns. In short, it was an ethos.

The origin of the term *nigilistka* (female nihilist) is just as difficult to trace as that of the word *nigilist*. One thing is certain: it was a derivative of the masculine word and followed it into the language of popular usage. But just as nihilists existed before the word was popularized in Turgenev's *Fathers and Children* (1861), so the woman nihilist was on the scene before the birth of Kukshina, the caricature of her from the same novel. Although the word had been used previously in Russian thought,[2] it was in the 1860's that it assumed its familiar meaning. "In

† From Richard Stites, *The Women's Liberation Movement*, pp. 99–102. Copyright © 1987 by Princeton University Press. Reprinted by permission of Princeton University Press.
1. *Iz istorii literatornogo nigilizma*, 201.
2. Professor Bervi in 1858 used the word nihilist to mean skeptic: Dobrolyubov, *Soch.*, 2, 332.

those days of national renewal," wrote Elizaveta Vodovozova, a representative woman of the 1860's, "the young intelligentsia was moved by
ardent faith, not by sweeping negation."[3] For many young women of
the 1860's, embarrassed by the restrictions, real or imaginary, which
Russian society imposed upon them, and impatient with the pace of
feminism, the philosophic posture and the social attitudes of the people
who were called nihilists had an enormous attraction. Only they, it
seemed, were trying to put into practice the grandiose notions of equality
and social justice which the publicists of recent years had preached.

Lev Deutsch, the well-known revolutionary and pioneer of Russian
Marxism, made the following observation:

> By rejecting obsolete custom, by rising up against unreasonable
> opinions, concepts, and prejudices, and by rejecting authority and
> anything resembling it, nihilism set on its way the idea of the
> equality of all people without distinction. To nihilism, incidentally,
> Russia owes the well-known and remarkable fact that in our cul-
> turally deprived country, women began, earlier than in most civ-
> ilized states, their surge toward higher education and equal rights
> —a fact which already [as of 1926] has had enormous significance
> and which in the future will obviously play a great role in the fate
> of our country and even perhaps throughout the civilized world.

"The idea of the equality of all people without distinction" was the
magnet which drew so many young idealistic women into the "nihilist"
camp. When it became clear that nihilism was the only intellectual
movement which emphatically included women in its idea of emancipation, the way was opened for a coalition of the sexes.[4]

Nihilist women, whatever their age or costume, approached the problem of their rights as women with an outlook basically different from
that of the feminists. If the feminists wanted to change pieces of the
world, the nihilists wanted to change the world itself, though not necessarily through political action. Their display of will and energy was
more visible; and their attitude toward mere charity was similar to that
of Thoreau—that it was better to *be* good than to *do* good.[5] The feminists
wanted a moderate amelioration of the condition of women, especially
in education and employment opportunities, assuming that their role
in the family would improve as these expanded. The nihilists insisted
on total liberation from the yoke of the traditional family (both as daughters and as wives), freedom of mating, sexual equality—in short, personal
emancipation. Better education and jobs were simply the corollaries of

3. Vodovozova, *Na zare zhizni*, 3d ed., 2v. (Moscow, 1964) 2, 38.
4. Lev Deutsch (Deich), *Rol Evreev v russkom revolyutsionnom dvizhenii* (Moscow, Petrograd,
   1926), 17. See also Pisarev, "Realisty" in *Soch.*, 3, 7–138 (50–51).
5. The comparison to Thoreau was made by Yunge, "Iz moikh vospom.," 265. The reference
   is to Thoreau's critique of philanthropy at the end of the first chapter of *Walden*.

this. Though they thirsted after learning, nihilist women often preferred to seek it abroad than to join the slow struggle for higher education in Russia itself. Where the feminists may have seen complete liberation as a vague apparition, the nihilists saw it as an urgent and realizable task. This is one reason why the social and personal behavior of the *nigilistka* was more angular and more dramatic than that of the feminist.

The outlook of the woman-as-nihilist has been differentiated here from that of the woman-as-radical whom we shall encounter in the following chapter. This differentiation is only slightly artificial for, while it is true that many women nihilists of the 1860's were drawn to radical causes, political radicalism as such was not a necessary condition for choosing "nihilist" solutions to the woman question. The techniques employed by the nihilists did not in themselves imply a politico-revolutionary view of life. Indeed there were some nihilists of both sexes whose extreme individualism, though drawing them to socially and sexually radical attitudes, actually prevented them from embracing causes, ideologies, or political action. Like the individualist sexual rebels of early nineteenth-century Europe, many women nihilists avoided or-ganized movements, whether feminist or radical. Their "feel-yourself orientation" was at odds with the imperatives of underground activity.[6] "Inner rebellion" and personal identification were sufficient, and they avoided revolutionary circles out of fear, lack of awareness, or plain distaste. Sexually emancipated behavior in a woman—to say nothing of a man—has never been a necessary indication of her political "modernity."

Precisely when the people of St. Petersburg began using the word *nigilistka* to describe the progressive, advanced, or educated woman is difficult to say. We can only be sure that after the publication of *Fathers and Children*, the image of the "female nihilist" (Turgenev did not use the word) was firmly fixed in the public eye. Much has been written about Turgenev's attitude to his hero, Bazarov, and the nihilists he seemed to represent; but there was no doubt that Evdoksiya Kukshina was an unflattering caricature. She surpassed the ludicrous in her atti-tudes and behavior. Her cigarette smoking, her slipshod attire, and her brusque manner were affected gestures of modernity, accompanying her shallow passion for chemistry. When asked why she wanted to go to Heidelberg, her answer was the hilarious "How can you ask! Bunsen lives there!" She is beyond George Sand ("a backward woman, knows

6. Celestine Ware, *Woman Power: the Movement for Women's Liberation* (New York, 1970) 12, uses this term to describe the outlook of nonpolitical liberated women of the 1960's in America. In the early 1860's, some Moscow women classified *nigilistki* in the following way: those who worshipped progress and socialism (in the abstract) and who scoffed at religion, customs, and convention; those who busied themselves exclusively with studying the exact sciences; and political radicals. (Karnovich, *O. razvitii*, 109–11).

nothing about education or embryology") and correctly denounces Proudhon, but in the same breath praises Michelet's *L'amour!*[7]

Dostoevsky called Kukshina "that progressive louse which Turgenev combed out of Russian reality." Pisarev pointed out that her counterparts in real life were not nihilists, but "false nihilists" and "false *emancipées*." The radical critic, Antonovich, however, blasted the novel in *The Contemporary*, and berated the author for his unfair portrayal of contemporary women. Seeing that the cartoon figure of Kukshina would be used as a weapon of ridicule against all advanced women, he suggested that, however ridiculous the unripe, progressive female might appear, the traditional upper-class woman was even more ridiculous. "Better to flaunt a book than a petticoat," he said. "Better to coquette with science than with a dandy. Better to show off in a lecture hall than at a ball."[8]

The nihilist view of women was further crystallized in the following year by the discussion of a satirical anti-nihilist play, *Word and Deed*, by Ustryalov. Its hero is stern, unbending, thoroughly unromantic; his credo is "to believe what I know, acknowledge what I see, and respect what is useful." Like Bazarov, he scorns love, only to be swept off his feet by a conventional young damsel. This buffoonery prompted Andrei Gieroglifov, a member of Pisarev's circle, to face the issue squarely in an essay bearing the title "Love and Nihilism," written just as Chernyshevsky was completing his novel, and drawn largely from Schopenhauer's "Metaphysics of Love." Gieroglifov proposed a thoroughgoing anti-idealistic explanation of love as no more than the awakening of the reproductive instinct, however innocent it might appear. Going well beyond Chernyshevsky, he insisted that love was not to be seen as a purely personal and individual pleasure. In it "the will of each person becomes the agent of the race," and "there is no participation by the individual will of man." All mating and the feelings that accompany it were based on nature's need to continue the species. Can a nihilist love? Yes, answered Gieroglifov, "for reason does not negate feeling;" but the nihilist must recognize love's relationship to nature. What kind of woman can he love? Not a doll or a plaything, says Gieroglifov, but a woman of knowledge who rejects the archaic, the passive, and the impotent and embraces the new, the creative, and the forceful. "Then there will be a greater correspondence and harmony between the men

7. *Fathers and Children*, tr. R. Hare (New York, 1957) 75–79. The name "Kukshina," as well as that of her foolish friend, Sitnikov, was still used as a polemical term in 1905 by people as different as Milyukov and Plekhanov to designate brash and unripe radicals: Milyukov, *God borby: publitsisticheskaya khronika, 1905–1906* (SPB, 1907) 466–71.

8. Dostoevsky, *Winter Notes on Summer Impressions*, trans. R. Renfield (New York, 1955), p. 68; Pisarev, "Bazarov," *Soch.*, 2, 7–50 (33–36); M. Antonovich, "Asmodei nashego vremeni," *Sov.*, 92 (Mar. 1862) 65–114. Vodovozova (*Na zare zhizni*, 3d. ed. 2, 46–49) described an obnoxious woman of her circle, Mariya Sychova, who thought that a sloppy appearance and rude manners sufficed to make her "advanced." On this, see also P.G. Pustvoit, *Roman I.S. Turgeneva "Ottsy i dety" i ideinaya borba 60-kh godov XIX veka* (Moscow, 1964) 108.

and women of the new generation. Without this it is impossible to reach that mutual happiness which nature itself demands."[9]

One of the most interesting and widely remarked features of the *nigilistka* was her personal appearance. Discarding the "muslin, ribbons, feathers, parasols, and flowers" of the Russian lady, the archetypical girl of the nihilist persuasion in the 1860's wore a plain dark woolen dress, which fell straight and loose from the waist with white cuffs and collar as the only embellishments. The hair was cut short and worn straight, and the wearer frequently assumed dark glasses. This "revolt in the dress" was part of the *nigilistka's* repudiation of the image of the "bread-and-butter miss," that pampered, helpless creature who was prepared exclusively for attracting a desirable husband and who was trained at school to wear *décolletée* even before she had anything to reveal. These "ethereal young ladies" in tarlatan gowns and outlandish crinolines—the phrase is Kovalevskaya's—bedecked themselves with jewelry and swept their hair into "attractive" and "feminine" coiffures. Such a sartorial ethos, requiring long hours of grooming and primping, gracefully underlined the leisure values of the society, the lady's inability to work, and a sweet, sheltered femininity. The *nigilistka's* rejection of all this fit in with her desire to be functional and useful, and with her repugnance for the day-to-day existence of "the superfluous woman."[1]

But it was also a rejection of her exclusive role as a passive sexual object. Long luxuriant tresses and capacious crinolines, so obviously suggestive of fertility, were clearly parts of the feminine apparatus of erotic attraction. The traditional results were romance, courtship, and marriage, followed by years of disappointing boredom or domestic tyranny. The machinery of sexual attraction through outward appearance that led into slavery was discarded by the new woman whose nihilist creed taught her that she must make her way with knowledge and action rather than feminine wiles. Linked to the defeminization of appearance was the unconscious longing to resemble the man, for the distinctive garb of the nihilist girl—short hair, cigarettes, plain garments—were boyish affectations. These, together with intensity of interest in academic

9. G—fov, "Lyubov i nigilizm," *RS* (Jan. 1863) 25–44. The chapter on sexual love of Schopenhauer's *Die Welt als Wille und Vorstellung* (1818) appeared in the following year in Russian translation: Shopengofer, *Metafizika lyubvi* (SPB, 1864).
1. Quotation from Tolstoy's *Anna Karenin*, tr. R. Edmonds (Harmondsworth, Middlesex, 1954) 225. Of the myriad descriptions of such attire, see: Vodovozova, *Na zare zhizni*, 3d ed. 2, 40; Stasov, *Stasova*, 58; A. F. Koni, "Peterburg," in *Vospominaniya o pisatelyakh* (Leningrad, 1963) 65–66; N. V. Davydov, *Zhenshchina pered ugolovnym sudom* (Moscow, 1906) 6; Kovalevskaya, *Vospom.*, 82. The term "muslin miss" or "bread-and-butter miss" (*kiseinaya devushka*) was given greater currency at the time by Pomyalovsky's story *Meshchanskoe schaste* (1861) and Pisarev's review of it (*Soch.*, 3, 185–216). Stackenschneider recalls that the term *nigilistka* was held in high regard among women of the sixties, while *kiseinaya devushka* was a pejorative term (*Dnevnik*, 292). The Smolny costume is described and pictured in Stefanie Dogorouky [Dologorukaya], *La Russie avant la débâcle* (Paris, 1926) 86–87. Both Kotlyarevsky (*Kanun*, 443) and Koni ("Peterburg," 66) date the appearance of the new women in public at the beginning of the 1860's.

and "serious" matters, tended to reduce the visible contrasts between
the sexes and represented the outward form of her inner desire—to
diminish the sharp social and cultural difference between men and
women.

Beneath her new costume, the nihilist of the 1860's also assumed a
new personality and self-image. The sickly romanticism and sentimen-
tality are gone. She realized that true personal autonomy required psychological independence, though not separation, from men. To establish
her identity, she needed a cause or a "path," rather than just a man.
So, in rejecting chivalric or tender attention from men, she often seemed
blunt, for she deeply longed to be received as a human being, not simply
as a woman. This also explains why she cut or hid her pretty hair beneath
a cap and covered her eyes with smoked lenses. "Value us as comrades
and fellow workers in life," she seemed to be saying to men; "as your
equals with whom you can speak simply and plainly."[2]

The new attitude was vividly reflected in her social behavior. The
typical *nigilistka*, like her male comrade, rejected the conventional hypocrisy of interpersonal relations and tended to be direct to the point of
rudeness, unconcerned with the ordinary amenities, and often enough
unconcerned with cleanliness as well.[3] The insistence upon complete
equality of the sexes also induced men of the new generation to cast
overboard the ballast of chivalry and stylized gallantry. As one of Kropotkin's acquaintances observed, they would not stand up when a woman
entered the room, but they would often travel halfway across the city to
help a girl in her studies. The new woman was anxious to be respected
for her knowledge and not for the size of her bust or the plenitude of
her skirts.[4]

The costumes and customs of the new culture were assumed, sometimes temporarily, by so many faddists that it was often difficult to tell
the nihilist from the *poseur*. The term nihilist was flung about as indiscriminately then as it was in the 1870's and 1880's when it became
a synonym for assassin. Leskov, for instance, reported in 1863 that "short
haired young ladies who married at the first chance" were considered
nihilists.[5] Like many such terms, it was loosely applied and was fluid
enough to serve many purposes—most of them pejorative: A *nigilistka*
could be an auditor at the university, a girl with bobbed hair, a grown

2. Kotlyarevsky, "Zhenshchina," in *Sbornik: Filosofova*, 2, 79 (the description, as well as the
   imaginary quotation, is his).
3. Not only disarray, but downright dirtiness was often noted as a prominent feature of the nihilist,
   the woman even more than the man. This is not strange: scorners of the conventions in every
   generation (including our own) since the early nineteenth century, beginning with the "bo-
   hemians," have looked upon neatness and cleanliness as part of the mantle of bourgeois
   hypocrisy. For a typical Russian reaction to this, see the diary entry of Prince Odoevskii in
   Lit. nasled., 22–24 (1935) 211.
4. Kropotkin, *Memoirs*, 197. In Vera Pavlovna's fourth dream, the Beautiful Tsaritsa expounds
   at length about the need for equality, respect for the whole person, the unimportance of
   physical beauty, and the loathesomeness of hypocrisy (*Chto delat?* 391–411).
5. N. S. Leskov, *Sobranie sochinenii*, ed. B. G. Bazanov, 11 v. (Moscow, 1956–1958) 10, 21.

woman with "advanced" ideas (whether or not she understood them), or a volunteer in one of the feminist or philanthropic bodies, depending upon the point of view of the describer.

* * *

JANE COSTLOW

[Odintseva's Bath and Bazarov's Dogs]†

* * *

When Arkady and Bazarov travel from the Kirsanovs' household to Odintseva's manor, they move from a world immersed in change and the preparations for change, to a world of order and immobility. Odintseva's house, like her life, is a model of absolute order, established by the dead husband whose spirit still presides. This woman's kingdom participates in Turgenev's allegorical topography as a world submitted to an authority that is absolute even in absence of its central figure: a husband who was old enough to be Odintseva's father. ("Odintsev, a rich man of forty-six or so, an eccentric, a hypochondriac, pudgy, difficult and bitter, but still neither stupid nor mean"—VIII, 270 [p. 60].) Odintseva's psychic and sensual retreats will be governed by this allegiance to an order both psychological and social. "Order visibly reigned in the house: everything was clean, there was a kind of decorous scent everywhere, as in ministerial receiving rooms" (VIII, 274 [p. 62]). "Reigned" (*tsarstvoval*), decorous (*prilichnyi*), ministerial (*ministerskii*): Turgenev's description of Odintseva's home conflates politics and decorum in the novel's most extreme example of repression and constraint.

The order of Odintseva's house is not, of course, Nicholaevan, despite the references to royalty and bureaucracy. Even Bazarov can appreciate its benevolence, its gentle temporality:

> Time (as is well known) sometimes flies like a bird, at others creeps like a worm; but a man feels particularly fine when he doesn't even notice if it goes quickly or quietly. Arkady and Bazarov spent their fifteen days at Odintseva's in just such a manner. In part that was due to the order she maintained in both her house and her life. (VIII, 284 [p. 69])

Odintseva's justification of her insistence on routine is that, otherwise, one would perish of boredom: ". . . one mustn't live in a disorderly

† From Jane Costlow, *Worlds Within Worlds*, pp. 123–37. Copyright © 1990 by Princeton University Press. Reprinted by permission of Princeton University Press.
  Norton Critical Edition page numbers appear in brackets.

fashion in the country, boredom takes over" (VIII, 285 [p. 70]). But Odintseva's own sense of something foregone, of the price paid for relief from boredom, is hinted at in a passage that describes this woman whom the narrator calls a "rather strange being" (VIII, 282 [p. 68]).

This passage—which was a later addition to the initial manuscript of *Fathers and Children*[1]—describes Odintseva as a woman of paradox, for whom wealth and comfort have prevented knowledge of passion, whose mind is "at once ardent and indifferent." Turgenev's description of Odintseva—his narrative of her childhood, her father's dissipation and her own resolve not to sink, impoverished, into provincial banality—are interesting and important, because they give a sense of this woman who can say to Bazarov: "You know, you're the same as I am" (VIII, 292 [p. 75]).

Turgenev begins this description of Odintseva with an enumeration of her unresolved longings, her lack of passion; he ends with a description of her in a moment of solitude—bathing—that both in allusions and rhetoric defies the decorum that Odintseva so meticulously observes. Turgenev's narrator, voyeurlike, watches Odintseva in a moment of literal nakedness; the narrator's own transgression, however, is matched by Odintseva's. Odintseva and Turgenev's narrator manage, in this scene, both to observe propriety and to suggest its violation; both point to an erotic imagination that was, in Turgenev's day, far more heavily veiled than in ours.[2]

Odintseva, says the narrator, was carried by her imagination "even beyond the boundaries of what is considered acceptable by the laws of conventional morality" (VIII, 283 [p. 68]). The narrator goes on to say that, even at such moments, her blood remained quiet in her "charmingly slender and quiet body." The narrator then proceeds—in a rhetorical sequence that links his own imagination to Odintseva's—to imagine her stepping out of a "sweet-smelling bath, all warm and languorous" (VIII, 283 [p. 68]). It is at such moments, the narrator tells us, that Odintseva thinks of life's worthlessness and sorrow—but she is immediately checked in her thoughts by a cold draft from a half-open window. From Odintseva's own illicit imagination, via a reference to this woman's beautiful body, the narrator has come to a vision of her bathing. Both imagination and vision carry us beyond the "permitted"; Odintseva's thoughts are a hidden defiance of the decorous house in which she lives, an erotic transgression she has no will to sustain. The narrator's vision of her is also, however, a transgression—an unveiling of a woman whose body is so much admired by the novel's men. What is so striking about this passage is how nearly it suggests Turgenev's identity with his heroine: his willingness to allude to a transgression that remains hidden, his final resolve not to break with decorum in favor of

1. See the manuscript variants appended to the Academy edition.
2. The storm that greeted *On the Eve* is suggestive of this.

passion. Turgenev plays here with the boundaries of decorum, in a manner that both points to the seductive beyond, and holds to the compromises of convention. Odintseva's flirtation with the forbidden will be repeated dramatically in her encounter with Bazarov; the narrator's own ambiguous position—between decorum and erotic curiosity—is played out in an earlier dialogue between Arkady and Bazarov, when they first meet Odintseva.

The young men's dialogue takes place at the governor's ball, where Arkady has spent an hour in conversation with Odintseva. Arkady is both enchanted and aware that Odintseva is fairly oblivious of him; as she leaves him to go to dinner, they follow the conventions of polite society—she turns to give him one last glance, he bows slightly—but Turgenev modifies this ritual by telling us something else: what Arkady is really perceiving in that moment. The parenthetical exclamation— "How shapely her figure seemed to him, engulfed in the grey shimmer of black silk."—is a glimpse into what that ritual of parting masks. The gaze of the young man is directed at the woman's figure (*stan*), paradoxically disrobed by allusion to the black silk that cloaks it. The dialogue that follows this narrated gaze will in turn be an "unmasking" of Arkady, who attempts to hide from Bazarov the real nature of his admiration for Odintseva. Bazarov's role as "unmasker" is here jovial, masculine, insinuating—but it is a frivolous rehearsal of more serious destruction. By disclosing Arkady's true sentiments Bazarov destroys the masks of civility—he effects a drawing room attack on that "civilization" he so ardently denounced in polemic with Pavel.

Arkady's glance at Odintseva is parenthetical and hidden: Bazarov approaches his friend and, in the spirit of male gossip, attempts to give expression to the hidden glance; the words he uses are elemental, implicitly dismissive of attempts to "dress up" what such a glance means. Arkady's response to this comment, as to all that follows, is denial:

> —Some landowner just told me that this lady is—*oh ho ho!* Anyway, he seemed like a fool. But what do you think, is she, in fact—*oh ho ho!?*
> —I don't completely understand that designation—answered Arkady.
> —Well, well! What an innocent! (VIII, 268 [p. 58])

Arkady—feigning innocence—refuses to be drawn into Bazarov's discourse; he refuses to admit that his own admiration of Odintseva's figure is akin to Bazarov's *oh-ho-ho!*: he insists on a linguistic distinction that marks a barrier of civility. The conversation about Odintseva, however, is not merely a dialogue of chivalry and bravado; the entire exchange is an assault (on Bazarov's part) on a culture that dissembles, presenting elegant form as a mask for something "unseemly." Bazarov's response to Arkady is to insist on what is hidden, to insist that outer form dissolves to reveal something darker: his citation of a popular proverb ("Still waters . . . you know how it goes!") and his comparison of Odintseva to ice cream—what is cold and solid melts—both attack surface stability. The manner in which he delivers the proverb, ending in ellipses, attempts to implicate Arkady in his playful destructions: Arkady again refuses, professing not to understand. (This profession of incomprehension will be Odintseva's later defense as well, masking her attraction to Bazarov and her flirtation with him.)

The proverbial words that Bazarov omits, which Arkady refuses to acknowledge, are demonic: "Devils lurk in still waters [V tikhom omute, cherty vodiatsia]." In a conversation that plays throughout with what is said and left unspoken, with intention and dissimulation, these unspoken words have an unexpected resonance: the devils that popular wisdom ascribes to the still depths seem to lurk beneath all the dissembling masks of Bazarov and Arkady's exchange—within Odintseva, within Arkady himself. These two are the passage's dissemblers: it is Bazarov who liberates the unspoken by giving it indecorous names.

The men's dialogue ends with one final example of displacement: Arkady reproaches Bazarov "not quite for that which displeased him" (VIII, 268 [p. 58]). The point here is not that Arkady is not being wholly honest or "sincere"—which of course he isn't. The more crucial aspect of the entire exchange is its representation of culture as a mask, as forms that cloak the "unspeakable"—Arkady's glance and Bazarov's devils. Arkady's glance disrobes Odintseva—he sees her body beneath grey silk—but he will not admit to it, just as he finally will reproach Bazarov on a matter of "principle," rather than say what really bothers him. Arkady refuses Bazarov's dismantling of civility and principle, in a small encounter that anticipates the young Kirsanov's ultimate allegiances. The very oppositions upon which Bazarov insists—stillness and frenzy, form and dissolution—will finally be irrelevant to Arkady, whose future promises pastoral harmony with Katya. Arkady will soon become "domesticated," a fate Bazarov will not choose. The rhetoric of Bazarov's convictions—as of his teasing—is absolute, and will not admit the gentler resolutions.

When Bazarov enters Odintseva's household he comes to a structure of civility and decorum, a structure he will attempt to penetrate and dissolve in the person of Odintseva. Her house—emblematic here of the woman—is a barricade thrown up against nature, lacking in the pastoral simplicity of either the Kirsanov or Bazarov households. When Katya enters Odintseva's drawing room with a dog and laden with flowers, the contrast with her elder sister is pointed. Katya is at home with a nature that is, for her, gentle; for Odintseva, the natural world is an object of indifference—but also of fear. "Katya adored nature, and Arkady loved it, although he didn't dare admit it; Odintseva was fairly indifferent to nature, as was Bazarov" (VIII, 286 [p. 70]). Odintseva, as we later discover, will not frequent her garden portico after seeing a grass snake there (VIII, 374 [p. 136]); it is in this portico that Arkady proposes to Katya. That Odintseva fears, and shuns, an animal that is tame, is emblematic of her response to everything that lies beyond her manor walls. If the grass snake she fears seems almost too obviously phallic, it is well to remember that the snake is also the biblical emblem of sensuality, a sensuality with which Arkady and Katya—like all couples of pastoral innocence—seem to exist in happy equilibrium.

The encounters of Bazarov and Odintseva, however, depict neither pastoral nor equilibrium, but a play of sensuality which is tinged with predation. If pastoral represents a natural world that has been humanized (conventionalized), Bazarov and Odintseva allude, in their desire, to a human world made animalistic: they flirt with descent into the inhuman, the passional, the formless. The hunter, as conventional figure, is unknown to the traditions of pastoral, but it is hunting, predation, will—in all their etymological complexity—that haunt the scenes of Odintseva and Bazarov's encounter. ("Bazarov was a great lover of women [*velikii okhotnik do zhenshchin*]"; "[Odintseva] willingly [*okhotno*] remained alone with him and willingly conversed with him"; "I'm unhappy because I have neither the desire, nor the will to live [*okhoty zhit'*]"—VII, 286, 287, 292 [pp. 71, 71, 75]). The hunter is unknown to pastoral because he does violence to the natural world, claims a supremacy of cunning and technique that destroys for him nature's benevolence; nature becomes his object, an object of will and desire, rather than a companion in his simplicity. He destroys that equilibrium of force that Turgenev described in "Journey into the Woodland" as nature's secret. The pastoral shepherd is liberated in his poverty from "the slavery of desire",[3] the hunter—and it is in this sense that Turgenev seems to choose his words—is in paradoxical bondage.

It is in the central encounters of Odintseva and Bazarov that Turgenev brings into most elemental contact this novel's opposites: unrestrained nature and a culture of dissimulation and restraint. Bazarov enters Odintseva's chambers as a figure possessed, whose passion has driven him to the solace of violent midnight walks ("He would set out for the woods and walk through them with great strides, breaking branches in his way and cursing under his breath both her and himself"—VIII, 287 [p. 71]). Odintseva admits Bazarov "as though she wanted both to tempt him and to know herself" (VIII, 287 [p. 71]). The deeper motivations for Odintseva's flirtation are nonetheless obscure, veiled—like so much else about this woman. The final unveiling that occurs in these encounters

3. Poggioli, *The Oaten Flute*, p. 11. See also his discussion of the hunter: "[The shepherd] never confronts the true wild, and this is why he never becomes even a part-time hunter. Venatical attitudes consistently oppose the pastoral . . ." (p. 7).

is of Odintseva to herself—a revelation startling in its suggestion of her kinship with Bazarov, a revelation from which she will flee to her familiar structures of order and repression.

The central gesture of these scenes is one of violent opening; it is stuffy, and Odintseva asks Bazarov to open the window: "Open that window—it feels a bit stuffy to me" (VIII, 290 [p. 74]). When Bazarov does as she asks, the window flies with a crash: the warm, soft night air floods the room (*"temnaia miagkaia noch' glianula v komnatu"*) (VII, 291 [p. 74]). Odintseva tells Bazarov to lower the curtain—literally to cover with cloth the opening she has requested—and then embarks on a conversation with Bazarov that flirts with revelation. Their dialogue is interrupted by a description of the warm, sweet-smelling night that fills the room, of the "night freshness" that presses against the lowered curtain: "The lamp burned dimly in the darkened, fragrant, solitary room; through the occasionally swaying shades there flowed in the keen freshness of night, whose mysterious whispering was audible (VIII, 292 [p. 75]). Throughout, Odintseva watches this veiled window—a window that stands as emblem of herself, of natural longing problematically hidden; the epithets of the room—fragrant (*blagovonnaia*), solitary (*uedinennaia*)—are also Odintseva's, echoing the earlier description of her emerging from the bath and the etymology of her own name. Odintseva watches this window as she will later watch her own face in the mirror—irresolute, apparently, unsure whether to welcome in her own person a similar gesture of opening and release. The woman who receives Bazarov is a study in nakedness and enclosure; as elsewhere, Turgenev's domestic details allude to a room's inhabitant. Like the narrative of Odintseva bathing and Arkady's glance, Turgenev's description disrobes the woman by alluding to what her clothes cover. "Odintseva threw her head back against the back of the chair and crossed her bare forearms on her breast. She seemed pale by the light of the single lamp, shaded in gauze of cutout paper. She was entirely covered in the soft folds of a full white dress; the very ends of her feet, also crossed, were barely visible" (VIII, 289 [p. 73]).

Odintseva here flirts not only with Bazarov, but also with her own sensuality, a passional existence that her conventions so exquisitely cloak. She asks Bazarov to open the window—but it seems her real desire is that he open *her*, that he disrobe her (both literally and figuratively), that he forcefully cast off her chill restraint. When Bazarov leaves Odintseva on the first night, the narrator describes her as she sits in solitude: "Her plaited hair came unwound and fell like a dark snake on her shoulder" (VIII, 295 [p. 77]). The dark serpent of Odintseva's hair is a figure for that sensuality she fears—the connection with the grass snake in the portico seems clear. What has happened here, though, is that the grass snake is no longer outside the manor—in a garden portico—

but has come inside, has in fact become a part of Odintseva herself. Turgenev's intent is not, I think, purely conventional; he is not merely depicting another Cleopatra of the Steppes.[4] His introduction of motifs associated with a literary type serves his central problematic: the relationship of men and women to their own passional nature. Odintseva's fear of nature, of sexuality, will extend to Bazarov ("I'm afraid of that man"—VIII, 301 [p. 81]); it is her fear that erects all the barriers of her life.

Odintseva's encounters with Bazarov bring what is most feared into most intimate proximity: not only Bazarov's embrace, but Odintseva's vision of her own face in the mirror, transform the domestic and familiar into something alien, unknown. The narrator's description of Odintseva after Bazarov's second evening visit closes with another revelation of her sensuality—only this time, Odintseva sees *herself*; it is not merely the narrator (and we) who see her: "(Or?)—she spoke suddenly, then stopped and shook back her hair. . . . She caught sight of herself in the mirror; her head, thrust back and with a mysterious smile on half-closed, half-opened eyes and lips, seemed to speak to her in that moment of something at which she herself grew confused" (VIII, 300 [p. 80]). Odintseva has accomplished what she intended: she has come to know herself. Like all elemental knowledge—both biblical and Freudian—her knowledge is sexual. Odintseva's vision of herself is also a final commentary on her remark to Bazarov—"You know, you're the same as I am" (VIII, 292 [p. 75]). The contextual motivation for that remark had to do with curiosity and the capacity for enthusiasm (*uvlekat'sia*); in Odintseva's final glance into the mirror, however, the identity is more elemental. Before looking into the mirror, she recalls Bazarov's "animal-like face" (*zverskoe litso*); it is that memory that precedes the vision of her *own* face—transformed into a face of brutal passion.

Odintseva's response to Bazarov's embrace is similar to Arkady's repulsion of his friend's masculine intimacies: she claims misunderstanding. "You didn't understand me. . . . I didn't understand you—and you didn't understand me" (VIII, 299 [p. 80]). Rather than admit identity, the sudden collapse of barriers, Odintseva insists that communication failed—an insistence that is itself an exemplary "civil" resolution. Her disclaimers reerect the boundaries that had fallen, and trade customary dissimulation for darker revelations. Still, after Bazarov leaves, Odintseva hovers about the emblems of her self-revelation, emblems of

4. Turgenev's most extensive use of the conventions associated with this figure is in *Spring Torrents*—where Marya Nikolaevna is depicted as Dido, the seductress of Aeneas (11, 147–48). His first essay to depict such a woman is in his unfinished play, "The Temptation of Saint Anthony" (1842), which is an explicit imitation of Merimée's *La Femme est un Diable*. Turgenev thus makes his own contributions to what Mario Praz discusses as the tradition of La Belle Dame sans Merci; see *The Romantic Agony* (Oxford, 1970), pp. 197–282. E. Kagan-Kans discusses Turgenev's use of the type in *Hamlet and Don-Quixote: Turgenev's Ambivalent Vision* (The Hague, 1975), pp. 41–56.

what she has repressed: the window and the mirror. "She kept walking back and forth across her room . . . stopping occasionally, either in front of the window or the mirror" (VIII, 299 [p. 80]). Emblems of flirtation with desire, they also mark the point Odintseva will not transgress: the point beyond which she sees "emptiness . . . or formlessness" (VIII, 300 [p. 81]).

Odintseva withdraws from an encounter she obscurely desires, but fears; it is a retreat Turgenev clearly endorses—a retreat that may in fact stand as emblematic of his own narrative distance from Bazarov, an alien hero who he became intimate with, but expelled.[5] The characters of this novel to whom Turgenev stands closest are, in fact, those who enter most consciously into conflict with Bazarov: Pavel and Odintseva. It is these figures of order and elegant culture whose insight and distance are closest to the author's: for all the affection with which he draws Russia's pastoral figures, Turgenev's eye is alien, "superfluous" to that world, as is Pavel's in his visit to Fenichka's room. The authorial consciousness, that overarching mind that gives the narrative its form, is touched by a knowledge more bitter than that possessed by either Kirsanov or the elder Bazarov: the vision of "emptiness . . . or formlessness" beyond the barriers of decorum does not belong to them. It is this distinction that Bazarov articulates in his Pascalian nostalgia for simplicity: "They're there—my parents, that is—occupied and unconcerned at their own insignificance, there's no stink of nothingness for them . . . while I . . . I feel only boredom and malice" (VIII, 323 [p. 98]).[6]

Turgenev ends his novel by returning us to the world of pastoral, to the figures of Baucis and Philemon from Ovid's *Metamorphoses*. When Bazarov's parents kneel at their son's graveside—in an enclosed plot where two trees stand—they evoke the harmonic resolution of the Latin poet, whose couple end their days as guardians of the temple, transformed finally into an oak and a linden: "An iron fence surrounds [the grave]; two young fir trees have been planted at each end: Evgeny Bazarov is buried in this grave" (VIII, 401 [p. 156]).

Turgenev's novel ends by an evocation of transformation that draws on the Latin lyricist and the traditions of pastoral, a transformation that implies harmony, resolution, and endurance. Ovid's work, however, is as filled with stories of violent metamorphoses as it is with tales of the peaceful permutations of suffering: Turgenev's novel alludes to one of the *Metamorphoses*' more violent tales in its rendering of Bazarov's death. Bazarov's transgression of culture and his painful death echo Ovid's rendering of the story of Actaeon, a hero whose transformation images

5. Turgenev kept a diary in Bazarov's name that he subsequently destroyed. Cf. "On *Fathers and Children*": "During the whole period of writing I felt an involuntary attraction to him" (14, 99).
6. A. I. Batiuto points to the Pascalian subtexts of this speech; Bazarov is echoing Pascal's "man without faith" from the *Pensées*. *Turgenev-romanist* (Leningrad, 1972), pp. 60–65.

destruction rather than reward. Actaeon's death—he was devoured by his own hounds—will also be Bazarov's.

In the scene that describes Bazarov's death, Turgenev's hero falls into delirium, and is possessed by a vision of dogs; he describes this vision to his father:

> Even now I'm not quite sure I'm expressing myself clearly. As I was lying here, it seemed to me that red dogs were running around me, and you were pointing over me, like you do over a black grouse.

> And now it's back to my dogs once more. Strange! I want to keep my thoughts on death, and nothing comes of it. I see some kind of spot . . . and nothing more. (VIII, 390 [p. 148])

These passages—like the whole account of Bazarov's death—are startling in their elemental power; they are also puzzling: Turgenev uses the hero's delirium to represent his dying, in images that both arrest and confound the reader. Bazarov, in this passage, sees himself amidst red dogs: but in a position radically different from his earlier stature as hunter (*okhotnik*). If Bazarov's father stands above him, pointing, as a dog does in pursuit of prey, then Bazarov *is* the prey, and the dogs have come to devour him.

This passage is arresting not merely because Turgenev uses delirium in a manner similar to that in *On the Eve* (both "positive heroes," Insarov and Bazarov, succumb to a language that will not cohere to their much-vaunted realms, the political and the scientific). It strikes us further because it returns us to the language of metamorphosis in which Turgenev first conceived of his hero ("I dreamt of a gloomy figure, wild and large, grown half out of the soil"), and because it returns us to the concerns of pastoral, equilibrium, and destruction that are central to *Fathers and Children*.

The hunter who is hounded by his own dogs is, in classic mythology, Actaeon, whose death is willed by Diana after he has seen her in a forest bathing. Diana, chagrined that Actaeon has seen her naked, transforms the hunter into a stag, who is then devoured by his own dogs. Actaeon is destroyed for an involuntary transgression: to see Diana naked is, apparently, to enter a realm of taboo in which volition is irrelevant.[7]

The scene of Bazarov's death, and the allusion to Actaeon, return us to the central theme of the novel: Bazarov's encounter with Odintseva, his entry into her household, his passionate embrace. It is, of course, the narrator—and not Bazarov—who has seen Odintseva naked; Turgenev reallots the mythic roles, and makes his Actaeon a willful—not innocent—transgressor. Turgenev nonetheless retains the act of sexual

---

7. Ovid, *The Metamorphoses*, bk. III; trans. R. Humphries (Bloomington, Ind., 1955), pp. 61–64.

violence that lies at the archaic center of the Ovidian story,[8] and makes that act emblematic of political transgressions. If Bazarov's throwing open of Odintseva's window is a metaphor for his desire to rape her, it is also a metaphor for his political desires: his longing to break into the kingdom of order, that paternal realm over which Odintseva presides. What Turgenev conflates, at his novel's center, are two acts of elemental transgression, acts of violence against body and *polis*: rape and revolution. It is symptomatic of Turgenev's aesthetic, both that he will veil those elemental acts, and that his narrative will work to reestablish the violated order. Turgenev's plot submits Bazarov to the forms of culture he has spurned—to those forms that contain eros and aggression: Bazarov's flirtation with Fenichka is a ritual of pastoral, filled with the *topoi* of sublimated eroticism;[9] his duel with Pavel sublimates violence in a highly conventionalized ritual.

Ovid veils, as does Turgenev, the act of rape to which the Actaeon story alludes. The metamorphosis of Actaeon into a stag is, however, present in all versions of the story—a transformation that, if we interpret the tale as being about man's urge to violate woman, seems to be less the consequence of Diana's curse than of Actaeon's own desire. His desire is in itself brutal; the change of outer form follows an inner metamorphosis. That Turgenev retains the "psychology of metamorphosis,"[1] the notion of a regression from the human to the animal, is suggested in his description of Bazarov's embrace and Odintseva's response: Bazarov's face is "bestial," while Odintseva's own face is transformed by desire. Both Bazarov and Odintseva experience the metamorphosis of passion.

That passion is destructive is both a psychological and political truth for Turgenev: violation of the taboo—for both Actaeon and Bazarov—leads to their being literally consumed by the animal world. We will understand the importance of this novel's ending, and of the pastoral for Turgenev, only if we accept the essential identity of his sexual and social insights. Turgenev does indeed resolve his novel with a celebration of form and order—but an order that is open, not repressive. Turgenev's pastoral resolutions evoke the possibility of an existence that does not

8. The version of the Actaeon story told by Hyginus reads the encounter more explicitly than does Ovid: "Actaeon, son of Aristaeus and Autonoe, a shepherd, saw Diana bathing and desired to ravish her. Angry at this, Diana made horns grow on his head, and he was devoured by his own dogs." The translation is by Mary Grant, *Myths of Hyginus* (Kansas University, 1960), p. 139. For a discussion of the representation and significance of rape throughout the *Metamorphoses* see Leo C. Curran, "Rape and Rape Victims in *The Metamorphoses*" in J. Peradotto and J. P. Sullivan, eds., *Women in the Ancient World: The Arethusa Papers* (Albany, N.Y., 1984), pp. 263–86.
9. Fenichka sits in the arbor with a pile of dew-laden roses: Bazarov's flirtation with her uses the classic vocabulary of pastoral seduction, where the rose stands for the innocent beauty the lover desires. Ronsard's poems on this topic are perhaps the most famous; Turgenev himself wrote a poem based on these conventions as a young man, "The Blossom" ("*Tsvetok*") (1, 29).
1. The phrase is Mary Grant's, *Myths of Hyginus*.

violate society's most fundamental boundaries: the epilogue's double weddings are comedy's convention for the restoration of order. What is restored in *Fathers and Children* is not, however, merely the past: Nikolay Kirsanov marries Fenichka (at Pavel's insistence)—the plebeian does after all enter the manor, but in an act that is legitimate, not transgressive.

Pavel's orchestration of the novel's ending is perhaps one final "wink" at a figure who stands so close to the author—for Turgenev's own consciousness is closest to Pavel's in his irrevocable knowledge of the "almost meaningless" that lurks both within and without the human form. The imagined social form of the novel's resolution is not, however, the structure associated with either Pavel or Odintseva. The gestural and social ideal of the novel will remain Arkady's: the throwing off of the heavy coat, the opening to his father and to nature, which was narrated at the novel's beginning. Turgenev imagines a world that can dispense with severe repression—both sexual and political—a world that is blessed by openness and equilibrium.

The novel is representative of its time in perhaps just this sense: that such imagination was still possible. In 1909, writing at a moment beyond such possibility, the symbolist writer Dmitry Merezhkovsky turned with regret and chagrin to Turgenev, now eclipsed by writers of very different imaginations: "Didn't our revolution fail because there was too much in it of Russian extremity, too little of European measure; too much of L. Tolstoy and Dostoevsky, too little Turgenev."[2] What is manifest in *Fathers and Children* is Turgenev's knowledge of what lay immanent in Bazarov the revolutionary. Kukshina—Turgenev's parody of a nihilist—lives in a house that burns down every five years. Turgenev's novel makes here its own image of universal conflagration: Kukshina's fires, however, unlike Bazarov's dogs, will consume not the transgressor, but culture itself. Turgenev does not depict this conflagration—though he alludes to it—for the same reason that he does not depict the meaningless (*bessmyslie*) or the formless (*bezobrazie*): his novel is itself an icon of that culture he defends—restraint, order, form. Beyond that lies "emptiness": *nihil*.

---

2. Merezhkovskii, "Turgenev," p. 58.

ELIZABETH CHERESH ALLEN

[Time in the Novel]†

* * *

Nowhere does Turgenev portray the psychological and moral struggles and ambiguities created by the consciousness of time more vividly or movingly than in his most famous novel, *Fathers and Sons*. To be sure, this narrative has often been discussed in terms of temporality—that is, the work is considered timely in its representation of the emergence of a new generation of intellectual rebels in mid-nineteenth-century Russia, or timeless in its depiction of the eternal conflict between different generations. Although both interpretations have validity, neither takes into account the extent to which these themes are overshadowed by the fact that *Fathers and Sons* is very much a novel about time itself. References to time begin and end *Fathers and Sons*; the nature of time is a subject of discussion within the narrative; the central protagonists define their identities in connection with different temporal phases; recurrent changes of tense provide reminders of temporal relativity. Time provides not merely a backdrop but a central focus of this masterpiece.

The inception of the novel marks a precise moment in time, a date: "May 20, 1859" (7: 7 [p. 3]), thereby suggesting that the events to be narrated are circumscribed by measurable historical time. But the final words of the text, "eternal reconciliation and life everlasting" (7: 188 [p. 157]), convey the opposite message; they take the novel beyond the confines of time itself. Turgenev thus frames his narrative with diametrically opposed conceptions of time, one concrete and limited, the other highly abstract and limitless. This dialectical frame makes possible the inclusion of an entire range of temporal visions within it—and just such a range appears, even as that range too is segmented and confined.

Several narrative digressions in the novel openly address variations in individual perceptions of time. For instance, after describing how "frighteningly quickly" ten years had passed for Pavel Petrovich after an ill-fated love affair, the narrator then remarks, "In no other country does time fly as fast as in Russia; in prison, they say, it flies faster still" (7: 32 [p. 24]). This assertion (adumbrating the sanitorium atmosphere of Thomas Mann's *The Magic Mountain*, where time is said to pass most quickly for those who are intellectually and emotionally disengaged from their surroundings, and to slow down for those psychologically engaged with theirs) stresses the subjectivity and relativity of temporal

† Reprinted from *Beyond Realism: Turgenev's Poetics of Secular Salvation* by Elizabeth Cheresh Allen with the permission of the publishers, Stanford University Press. © 1992 by the Board of Trustees of the Leland Stanford Junior University.
Norton Critical Edition page numbers appear in brackets.

awareness. A second assertion expands on the subject: "Time (it is a well-known fact) sometimes flies like a bird, sometimes crawls like a worm; but it is especially good when a person does not even notice whether it is passing quickly or quietly" (7: 85 [p. 69]). Here the narrator unequivocally attributes moral worth to ignorance of time's passage, since such ignorance constitutes a psychic escape from the press of time's chronological progression. Yet whether individuals can truly control their awareness of time and benefit morally as a result remains a subject unaddressed by the narrator.

This question is explored instead through the characterizations of the three main protagonists, Pavel Petrovich, Anna Sergeevna, and Bazarov, for each makes an effort to avoid acknowledging the chronological progression of time, and each finds a moral justification for doing so. Moreover, each does so in the same way, by psychologically entrenching a sense of self in a single temporal stage: one in the past, one in the present, and one in the future. Pavel Petrovich identifies himself wholly with the past. Prizing the values of honor, valor, and civility that he associates with the upper classes of society as organized by earlier generations, he affects the dress, manners, and views of a bygone era. The present and future hold no charms for him; it is with the past that he associates the particular psychological satisfaction of love, albeit unrequited love, and the general exaltation of aristocratic traditions. Hence he does not try to find grounds on which to communicate with the disrespectful and dismissive nihilist Bazarov, who has no use for the past, even after Bazarov's decency during a duel they fight earns Pavel Petrovich's grudging respect. But so invested is Pavel Petrovich in his conviction of the superiority of the past, and so ingrained is his psychic affiliation with past time alone, that he cannot extend himself to someone who does not share that conviction or affiliation. He remains at once defined and isolated by his fixed adherence to the past.

Anna Sergeevna, by contrast, adheres to the present. She evinces no sentimental attachment to the past, when she had to struggle to provide a secure home for herself and her younger sister after their parents' deaths. Having married a wealthy man who left her his estate and fortune upon his demise, Anna Sergeevna is wholly dedicated to the preservation of the status quo. She has no intention of tolerating any divergence from the course of life she currently conducts. Indeed, the prospect of an affair with Bazarov, who for her embodies all that is unknown and unstable ahead, although mildly tempting, mostly fills Anna Sergeevna with horror. She has struggled too hard to mold her immediate circumstances to suit her sense of responsibility to her sister and to satisfy her own need for psychic stability. Despite the relative solitude of her existence, she cannot and will not risk her own present well-being and that of her dependent sister by giving herself over to future uncertainty and upheaval, even if other gratifications come as well.

Finally, Bazarov gives his moral allegiance and psychological energy to the future. As a nihilist, he considers the past filled with outmoded and unconstructive conventions which must be abandoned, and as an idealist—which nihilists so often are—he regards the present as nothing but a workshop in which to labor toward future achievements. This investment in the future makes relationships in the present difficult for Bazarov, since emotional intimacy entails a diversion of strength that could otherwise be devoted to the scientific research that will provide knowledge for the welfare of generations to come. Thus his friendship with Arkadii breaks down, and his romantic desire for Anna Sergeevna is never fulfilled. Only on his deathbed does Bazarov concede having been psychologically and morally misguided; his rigid subscription to his ideas and his fixation on their future realization have deprived him of the satisfactions he might have found in the present.

These three characters are all tragic, therefore, in that none can partake of any intimate relationship with an individual psychically rooted in a phase of time other than the one with which their identity is entwined. And they have ethically valid reasons for this. The cause of self-preservation requires them to resist the incursions into their carefully constructed psychic integrity that such intimacy would inevitably permit: both Pavel Petrovich and Anna Sergeevna are sincerely threatened by Bazarov's obsessive orientation toward the future; Bazarov is rightly ambivalent about Anna Sergeevna's conservative bonds to her present life, and is understandably dismissive of Pavel Petrovich's idealized past. Yet they all pay a high price for their allegiance to their private cause. For they become frozen in time, psychologically removed from the warmth of close human contact, as the novel's complex conclusion demonstrates.

That conclusion shifts to a kind of perpetual present tense, allegedly to satisfy the reader's curiosity about what each character "is doing now, right now" (7: 185 [p. 154]). Its effect, though, is to lock Pavel Petrovich into an eternal past, Anna Sergeevna into an eternal present, and Bazarov into an eternal future. Pavel Petrovich returns to the Europe where he had once found happiness: "In Dresden . . . between two and four, at the most fashionable time for strolling, you can meet a man of about fifty, already completely grey and possibly suffering from gout, but still handsome, elegantly dressed, and with that special air which is given only to a person who has spent a long time amidst the highest strata of society. This is Pavel Petrovich" (7: 186 [p. 155]). He finally establishes himself in an environment where he can live out the traditional forms of the aristocratic life he so treasures. Nonetheless, tied to a mode of existence characteristic of the past, Pavel Petrovich finds life "hard" (7: 187 [p. 156]). He is respected, but not loved by his acquaintances, and he is forced to seek consolation from further past, in the ancient forms of religion: he is often observed to "fall into thought and remain motionless for a long time, bitterly clenching his teeth, then he suddenly recollects himself and begins almost imperceptibly to cross himself."

Anna Sergeevna, the reader is informed, was married "not long ago, not out of love but out of conviction" to "a man still young, good, and cold as ice" (7: 185 [p. 154]). Her "conviction," that she requires a husband who will continue to provide the security she insists on, weds her to a loveless marriage of convenience and an endlessly tranquil but probably unfulfilling existence. And Bazarov is consigned to the infinite future of life after death, as suggested by the flowers growing on his grave, which, the narrator concludes, "speak of eternal reconciliation and life everlasting" (7: 188 [p. 157]). Thus Bazarov, confined forever to solitary silence, is committed in death as he was in life to the hope of satisfactions of the world to come.

Turgenev brilliantly uses these characters' psychological connections to time in *Fathers and Sons* as a means of illuminating the costly sacrifices that may be required by subscription to his moral program. Pavel Petrovich, Anna Sergeevna, and Bazarov, however forceful their personalities, are sufficiently psychologically fragile to require the support provided by identification with a single temporal phase. Thus they must forgo pleasures that stronger selves can enjoy. The less prominent character Nikolai Kirsanov, for instance, has the constant strength of personality to create for himself an enduring familial circle that surrounds yet does not confine him. He can compose an identity and a way of life that unites past, present, and future. The others, by contrast, do not dare extend their psyches that far, lest they break under the strain.

* * *

MICHAEL R. KATZ

Fathers and Sons (and Daughters)†

In Chapter XXI of Turgenev's *Fathers and Sons*, Bazarov and Arkady are lying in the shade of a small haystack on the modest estate that belongs to Bazarov's parents. It is midday and the sun is burning hot. Bazarov begins reminiscing about his childhood and then moves on to a comparison between his parents' busy life and his own self-indulgent indolence:

> . . . here I lie under a haystack. . . . The tiny space I occupy is so small in comparison to the rest of space, where I am not and where things have nothing to do with me; and the amount of time in which I get to live my life is so insignificant compared to eternity,

---

† Prepared especially for this Norton Critical Edition.

where I've never been and won't ever be. . . . Yet in this atom, this mathematical point, blood circulates, a brain functions and desires something as well. . . . How absurd! What nonsense![1]

This passage has always struck me as intriguing: on the one hand, it provides evidence of the systematic investigation of time and space introduced by the new empirical and experimental science of the nineteenth century of which Bazarov is a staunch advocate; on the other hand, it sounds very modern—an inkling of Einsteinian relativity in the middle of a classical Russian novel. Bazarov attempts to locate himself existentially in the space/time continuum and manages to perceive his own insignificance compared not only to his parents', but to the infinity of space and the eternity of time.

But however intriguing this passage may be, I don't want to talk about it or about any of the male characters in the novel. Instead I plan to address the subject of Turgenev's women. English and American translators for the most part have been content to stick with the title of *Fathers and Sons*, rather than change to the more accurate, but less euphonic *Fathers and Children*. Nevertheless, it is important to recall that some of Turgenev's *deti* are most definitely of the female persuasion. And it is these *daughters* in general and their *temporality* in particular that I wish to consider.

In an important essay entitled "Women's Time" Julia Kristeva describes three concepts of temporality, the first two of which, she argues, are related to female subjectivity.[2] One she calls *cyclical* time; it involves repetition, gestation, and the eternal recurrence of biological rhythms conforming to nature. The second she calls *monumental* time; it is linked to eternity, all-encompassing and infinite, "like imaginary space." It is these two types of temporality which, Kristeva says, have traditionally been linked to female subjectivity, even though they are not fundamentally incompatible with masculine values. Finally, there is *linear* time; time as project, teleology, departure, progression, and arrival; time as history. Linear time also pertains to language understood as the enunciation of a sequence of words. Kristeva maintains that this last type of temporality has traditionally been associated with masculine subjectivity and is alien to other attempts to conceptualize time from the perspective of motherhood and reproduction.

When Bazarov lies in the shade of the haystack and contemplates the universe, it seems to me that he is temporarily forsaking the "masculine" conception of *linear* time as history, and instead is confronting the "feminine" concept of *monumental* time linked temporally to eternity and spatially to infinity. Up to this point in the novel Bazarov's "project"

1. I. S. Turgenev, *Polnoe sobranie sochinenii*, Moscow-Leningrad: Nauka, 1964, 8, 323 (my translation). Henceforth *PSS*.
2. Julia Kristeva, "Women's Time," in *The Kristeva Reader*, ed. by Toril Moi, New York: Columbia University Press, 1986, 187–213.

has been to make an impact on his contemporaries, to influence history, to arrest its progress and force it to proceed in a new direction: "And as regards the age [*vremya*]—why should I depend on it? Let it depend on me."[3] He may not know in *what* new direction, but he knows that the old one is unsatisfactory and must be changed. But suddenly his "project" is jeopardized by a traumatic encounter with an attractive young woman and by his subsequent discovery of the "romantic abyss" which lies deep within himself. It won't be long before Bazarov undertakes a second round of visits to the Kirsanov estate at Marino and Odintsova's manor house at Nikolskoe, and then returns home in despair, to join his father in his "palliative measures," in which pursuit the hero ultimately loses (sacrifices?) his own life.

Still, for one brief moment Bazarov forsakes *linear* time and encounters *monumental* time; yet neither of these two temporalities is ever valorized in Turgenev's narrative. In fact, *cyclical* time is the only mode that the author credits—and it is the women in the novel who make this point most emphatically and provide the clear model for the men to imitate—if only they are able to perceive it.

Turgenev's first two women are depicted only posthumously: they were beloved by the two Kirsanov brothers, Nikolai and Pavel. By the time the action of the novel begins, both women are deceased. Turgenev provides brief descriptions of the two, and they are clearly to be seen as contrasting types of femininity. Nikolai's great love, Marya (née Prepolovenskaya), in whose honor the estate at Marino is named, was the daughter of a low-ranking civil servant.[4] He made her acquaintance accidentally; she was very timid and shy, and their courtship consisted of half-words and half-smiles.

Marya was both an attractive and a *progressive* young woman (an unusual combination, as we shall see), who soon entered into a loving marriage with Nikolai. The young couple spent a great deal of time together: they read, played piano, and sang duets; when Nikolai used to go hunting, Marya would stay at home gardening. The couple had only one child, Arkady, whom they both adored. But, after a very short spell of such marital bliss, Marya suddenly died.

While there is only a limited amount of evidence to go on, it seems clear to me that Marya participates in what Kristeva calls *cyclical* time: she is connected to themes of nature through her garden and to gestation through the birth of her child. She feels at home everywhere: in a simple cottage, a town house, and on their country estate. Her marriage to Nikolai is described in no less than idyllic terms; had she lived longer, one presumes she would have produced more children and provided them with a loving and secure childhood.

3. *PSS*, 226.
4. In other words Nikolai married "beneath" his class, much to the chagrin of his parents. Note that his second marriage to the peasant girl Fenechka is even more "radical."

In stark contrast to this idyllic marriage, there is Pavel's extraordinary love affair with the enigmatic Princess R., an eccentric aristocrat. We're told that she's already been paired with a well-educated and decent, but foolish husband. In spite of that, she leads a strange life consisting primarily of mysterious departures and returns. By day she plays the role of society-lady and frivolous coquette; but at night she closets herself up for bouts of hysterical weeping and praying. She's reputed either to possess some secret or inaccessible mystery, or else to be in the power of an enigmatic force.

If Nikolai's Marya is tied to *cyclical* time, Pavel's Princess R. is closely connected to *monumental* time. Her life consists of departures and returns, all seemingly to some purpose, though we never find out what it is; and the enigma of the sphinx—with its suggestion of eternity—whose riddle is only "solved" after her death when the ring is returned to Pavel with a pair of crossed lines drawn over it, implying, perhaps, that "death" itself is the answer to the great riddle. In fact, it is Princess R.'s enigmatic nature primarily that attracts Pavel to her, and her desire to participate in the modality of *monumental* time that sets her so far apart from other women.

The most detailed portrait of a woman who actually participates in *cyclical* time is that of Katya; she enters the world of the novel carrying a basket full of fresh flowers, followed by a beautiful borzoi. With her young, dark, pleasant face, and her sweet, timid manner, she is a breath of fresh air, a fugitive from the natural world. When Arkady courts her, nature is one of the most important elements in their growing relationship. The ash tree, the dog, and the sparrows serve as background for the poetry and fine phrases that constitute their shared language.

During the course of the novel Arkady learns to appreciate Katya's qualities; although initially dazzled by Odintsova, he turns to Katya first for consolation when her older sister rebuffs him in favor of Bazarov; but later Arkady comes to love Katya and submit to her mode of temporality. In fact Bazarov even warns Arkady: "She'll have you under her thumb—well, that's how it should be."[5] He urges his friend to get married, fix up his nest, and have lots of children. Katya senses the dominant role she'll come to play: "Charming little feet" [she thinks to herself, repeating Arkady's compliment] . . . "well, he'll soon be lying at these feet, won't he?"[6] And sure enough, after Bazarov's departure, Arkady forgets all about his friend and the narrator informs us that he "had already begun submitting to Katya."[7]

At the end of the novel, when the most important surviving characters are gathered together for one last time, Katya is in complete control. In fact, *everyone* is in love with her: Arkady, of course; but also her father-

5. *PSS*, 380.
6. *PSS*, 369.
7. *PSS*, 381.

in-law Nikolai, since she shares so many of the values of his beloved first wife Marya, and has even named her first-born Kolya, after him; even Fenechka (who will be discussed below) is very fond of Katya, and for good reason.

The most fully portrayed female character in the novel and the one most responsible for Bazarov's "downfall" from his ideological heights into the "abyss" of romanticism, Anna Odintsova, seems to be the odd one out with respect to Kristeva's scheme of temporality. It can be argued that one of the characteristics of great literature is that not everything can be made to fit any theoretical grid. This attempt at mapping Turgenev's female characters simply cannot explain away Odintsova's complex character or her entire role in the novel.

On the other hand, Odintsova's "speaking name" indicates from the outset that she stands alone, isolated and alienated from the other characters and the world of the novel. She is presented as the epitome of elegance, taste, and style: aristocratic, wealthy, serene, dignified—but also "cold and severe" (in Arkady's words), even "frigid" (in Bazarov's). She is also very much her father's daughter—in fact, she is really the only woman in the novel who seems ever to have had a father. He was a dashing speculator and an inveterate gambler who lost everything and died early, leaving his two daughters to cope as best they could. Odintsova summoned an elderly aunt to live with them and reconciled herself to a wasted life. But she was rescued from such a sterile fate by a wealthy, eccentric hypochondriac who falls in love with and marries her, only to die not long after, leaving her considerable property.

When Bazarov accepts Odintsova's invitation to visit her estate and when their relationship reaches an emotional climax with his abrupt declaration of love, at first she yields to his embrace, but after a few moments, she withdraws and declares that he has totally misunderstood her:

> Under the influence of various vague emotions, an awareness of life passing by, a desire for novelty, she'd forced herself to reach a certain point, to look beyond it—and there she glimpsed not even an abyss, but emptiness . . . or formlessness.[8]

This literal "formlessness" (*bezobrazie*) is more than even she can deal with.

True to her name, Odintsova is also temporally isolated from all the other characters. It seems to me that she participates in none of Kristeva's modalities: neither cyclical, monumental, nor linear. She appears to be in some sort of a time warp, cut off from nature's biological rhythm, from eternity and infinity, as well as from history and teleology. Bazarov's appearance on the scene offers her a chance to escape from this temporal stagnation; after all, he is the quintessential man of history who sees

8. *PSS*, 300.

time as his project. But she is terrified at that prospect and opts to remain within the serene confines of her comfortable warp.[9]

In the end Odintsova remarries, but she does so without abandoning her icy composure. Her husband is said to be one of Russia's future statesmen, a lawyer who is clever, willful, kind, and "cold as ice." "They live together in great harmony—perhaps to find happiness, perhaps even love."[1] Rather than forsake that time warp, Odintsova finds an appropriate mate and invites him to join her there.

Even more than Odintsova's sister Katya, Fenechka is a genuine participant in *cyclical* time. Her room, which is described through Pavel's eyes, contains jars of "guzbery" jam, lots of fresh flowers, and a songbird in a cage. Like Katya, Fenechka brings the natural world into the Kirsanovs' manor house. As a member of the peasant class, she is closely identified with the natural order. When Nikolai first meets her (to remove a cinder from her eye), she has a tender, timid face; her hair is soft; her lips innocent and slightly parted; her teeth, moist and pearly white. She exudes both good health and erotic charm. In fact, not only does *Nikolai* love her, but both his brother Pavel and their houseguest Bazarov find her very attractive, virtually irresistible. Pavel sees a resemblance to his former love, Princess R., and refuses to let "that insolent fellow Bazarov" anywhere near her. Bazarov, meanwhile, falls prey to her charms, and flirts with her almost from their first meeting. Their prolonged kiss in the arbor eventually provokes the duel with Pavel, resulting in Bazarov's departure and Nikolai's decision to marry Fenechka.

At the end of the novel Fenechka is the woman who is most radically altered. Now called Fedosya Nikolaevna, she wears a silk dress, a broad velvet band in her hair, and a gold chain around her neck—all the trappings of her "office" as mistress of the house. Still, she sits in respectful stillness (very different from Odintsova's icy composure), as if "asking forgiveness . . . for her [own] happiness."[2] Meanwhile her young son Mitya is growing apace, and can be seen running around the house, talking nonstop. Fenechka has been transformed from "shy young thing" to "competent mistress"—but without losing her own sense of self or her grounding in cyclical time. In fact, Turgenev tells us that the two new "mistresses" (Fenechka and Katya) spend considerable time together. That makes sense—they share the same temporal modality— the one to which their husbands have submitted and the one that is clearly valorized by the narrator in that last scene at Marino.

Bazarov's mother, Arina Vlasevna, is yet another representative of cyclical time, but one who seems to have taken it to the extreme, almost

9. It has been suggested that Odintsova is also granted a glimpse of *monumental* time when she looks out the open window during and after her climactic interview with Bazarov; as appealing as that idea is, the textual evidence simply doesn't support it.
1. PSS, 399.
2. PSS, 398.

to the point of parody. Turgenev describes her as a genuine noblewoman of the old school, i.e., old Muscovy, who has somehow lived on into another age. She is devout, highly emotional, and believes in all sorts of bizarre omens, charms, dreams, and superstitions. She spends most of her time eating and sleeping, and has but one occupation—she runs their modest household with ruthless efficiency. She is absolutely devoted to her husband, and both loves and fears her son Bazarov.

The last female character in the novel, Avdotya Kukshina, is another representative of linear time, but clearly intended to serve as parody of that modality. She is described as a progressive woman, *"émancipée* in the true sense of the word."[3] She aspires in every way to participate in the "masculine" modality: her disheveled appearance, her slovenly study, her intellectual pretensions, her aggressive conversation, etc. She is a caricature of the new woman, aspiring to play some role in history such as she imagines Bazarov does. At the end of the novel, she is living in Heidelberg, locked into an endless pursuit of some new *telos*, studying architecture, yet still hobnobbing with students, especially young Russian devotees of the natural sciences (just like Bazarov).

The final chapter of *Fathers and Sons* (and Daughters) summarizes and restates the author's position. With the double weddings (Arkady to Katya and Nikolai to Fenechka), both men, father and son, have submitted to the mode of *cyclical* time espoused by their two women. (A discreet *private* toast is proposed by the victorious and magnanimous Katya to the memory of the erring and vanquished Bazarov.) In the follow-up, we are informed about Odintsova's recent marriage of convenience which reinforces her position in that time warp; Pavel Kirsanov is off in Dresden, now stuck in his own time warp, associating with the English and visiting Russians; and Kukshina is in Heidelberg, still pursuing linear time, with little chance of success.

The last page of the novel shows Bazarov's elderly parents kneeling and weeping at their son's grave; this poignant scene occasions Turgenev's rhetorical eloquence in a famous passage, one just as intriguing as Bazarov's haystack rumination on time and space quoted at the beginning of this paper, and one closely linked to it in its theme:

> However passionate, sinful, rebellious the heart buried in the grave, the flowers growing on it look out at us serenely with their innocent eyes; they tell us not only of that eternal peace, that great peace of "indifferent" nature; they tell us also of eternal reconciliation and life everlasting. . . .[4]

In a letter dated April 9, 1862, Herzen wrote to Turgenev:

3. *PSS*, 257.
4. *PSS*, 402.

The Requiem at the end, with the further moving toward the immortality of the soul, is good, but dangerous: you'll slip into mysticism that way.[5]

Well, I guess that's one way of putting it. Perhaps if Herzen had been able to read Kristeva's essay on "Women's Time," he might have interpreted this passage somewhat differently. It seems to me that here at the very end Turgenev is looking beyond valorized *cyclical* temporality ("flowers growing" and "the great peace of 'indifferent' nature"), and is casting one last longing, almost nostalgic glance at *monumental* time ("eternal reconciliation and life everlasting"). I argued above that Bazarov peered momentarily into that particular mode of temporality as he tried in vain to locate himself existentially in the space/time continuum and managed, albeit fleetingly, to perceive his own insignificance compared not only to his parents', but to the infinity of space and the eternity of time. Now Bazarov is no more, his worthy and devoted parents kneel at his grave lost in grief, while the author in a final flourish casts his own penetrating glance into the great beyond.

GARY SAUL MORSON

Two Kinds of Love†

They discussed at length the question whether marriage was a prejudice or a crime (52 [54]).

"I [Arkady] want to devote all my powers to the truth; but I no longer look for my ideals where I did; they present themselves to me . . . much closer to hand" (144 [137]).

As the title *Fathers and Sons* seems to invite, this novel is usually treated as an examination of two opposite ideological camps—the "fathers" and the "sons." But it seems to me that there is really a "third ideology" working here, which the title—this time taken as a whole—also seems to adumbrate. I mean the prosaic set of values that center around the family and ordinary life, the life of "fathers and sons" (or "fathers and children," to translate the title literally).

Bazarov separates himself from ordinary life. Arkady is offended when Bazarov distinguishes between two sorts of people, the "gods" and the "dolts." "It's not for the gods to bake bricks, in fact!" Bazarov declares

---

5. Quoted in Ivan Turgenev, *Fathers and Sons*, ed. Ralph E. Matlaw, New York: W. W. Norton, 1966, 187.
† From "Genre and Hero" by Gary Saul Morson, *Stanford Slavic Studies* 4, 1 (1991) 367–79. Reprinted by permission of the author.
    Norton Critical Edition page numbers appear in brackets.

(86 [83]). Arkady, who at this point is just beginning to free himself from his discipleship to Bazarov, allows himself to challenge his friend:

> "Oho!" thought Arkady to himself, and then in a flash all the fathomless depths of Bazarov's conceit dawned upon him. "Are you and I gods, then? At least, you're a god; am not I a dolt then?"
> "Yes," repeated Bazarov gloomily; "you're still a fool" (86 [83]).

Bazarov engages in what might, somewhat anachronistically, be called incipient Raskolnikovism: he divides humanity into the ordinary and extraordinary people, which is one reason why, when Odintsova wants to flatter Bazarov, she tells him that he is not ordinary and therefore should not consider living an "ordinary" life. In a larger sense, the argument between the ordinary or prosaic and the extraordinary or dramatic pervades this book.

In this respect, the nihilism of the younger generation and the romanticism of the older generation are equally far from prosaic values. Bazarov and Pavel Petrovich, both distant from family life, argue over dinner, and we may, in the process of following the exciting and dramatic discussion, forget that a third set of values is tacitly present. These values may be found in the hospitality of the meal, in Nikolai Petrovich's attempts to be friendly with his son, in Fenichka's pride in her child, and in the warm and kindly traditions of the household itself. Throughout the novel, prosaic values constantly figure as a quiet background to the major ideological conflicts. By their very nature, they do not call attention to themselves.

The same set of values forms the background at the Bazarovs's: When Arkady and Evgeny talk on the haystack about ultimate questions, they are interrupted by Bazarov's father, who more than anyone (except, perhaps his wife) represents a devotion to home, to family, and to immediate neighbors, especially the peasants, whom he treats as part of his family. While Arkady and Bazarov argue, Bazarov's parents overwhelm them (and us) with the ordinary kindnesses they take to extraordinary degrees.

On the way to the duel, Bazarov notices a peasant, who has gotten up early to attend to his daily tasks. "He at least got up for work, while we . . . ," Bazarov reflects (125 [119]). They meet the same peasant after the duel, and Pavel Petrovich asks, "What do you imagine that man thinks of us now?" (128 [121]). Here Bazarov and Pavel Petrovich, the two ideologists, are linked in their foolish dramatic episode, while silently opposed to both are the rounds of daily life. In the presence of a person whose goals are "close at hand," Bazarov and Pavel Petrovich are not as different as they have imagined.

The same contrast between ideological argument in the foreground and a third set of values in the background quietly opposed to both camps is also written into the scenes at Odintsova's. Bazarov and Odintsova

argue about art and the ideology of love, about nihilism versus romanticism, but something else that they do not notice is happening. In the
background, Katya, with her quiet sensitivity, her appreciation of daily
rhythms, and her attentiveness to small gestures of sensitivity and kind-
ness, plays the key role. She has a wisdom that her sister does not sense
and which Arkady comes to learn only gradually. He does not "fall in
love" with her suddenly; he does not yield to "passion," as Bazarov does,
nor to a fascination with the mysterious and romantic, as Pavel Petrovich
once yielded to his "sphinx," the elusive "Princess R." Instead, Arkady,
who has absorbed much more of the homely prosaic values of his mother
and father than he realizes, comes to appreciate Katya bit by tiny bit,
while she is still in the background and his attention is focussed mainly
on Odintsova.

> They did not talk to each other in Anna Sergeyevna's presence;
> Katya always shrank into herself under her sister's sharp eyes; while
> Arkady, as befits a man in love, could pay attention to nothing else
> [but Odintsova] when near the object of his passion; but he was
> happy only with Katya. He felt that he was unable to interest
> Odintsova. . . . With Katya, on the other hand, Arkady felt at
> home; he treated her condescendingly, did not discourage her from
> expressing the impressions made on her by music, reading novels,
> verses, and other such trifles, without noticing or realizing that
> these *trifles* were what interested him too (72 [70]).

Two kinds of love are debated in *Fathers and Sons*. The passage immediately following this one is the paraphrase of Bazarov's contempt for
the "madness" of "Toggenburg and all the minnesingers," that is, it
deals with the romantic ideal of love as something transcendent, extraordinary, fatal, mysterious, poetic, and infinitely distant from ordinary
life. By contrast, Arkady and Katya learn a *prosaic* love, in which they
feel not transported but at home. It leads them to a love of ordinary,
daily, family life, the life that Arkady's father and mother lived, a life
as far from the mad pursuit of mysterious princesses as it is from nihilism.

In his interesting study of *Fathers and Sons*, David Lowe stresses the
importance of the Arkady-Katya plot—Lowe calls it the "comedic
plot"—as few have done.[1] If I differ from Lowe, it is in seeing this plot
not as another endorsement of romantic love, but as quite the opposite.
In this novel, romantic love is attacked openly by nihilism, and it seems
to triumph in that contest. But in its encounter with a quieter enemy,
prosaic love, romantic love meets a more formidable opponent.

Turgenev's novel, I think, participates in a long tradition of *opposing*
family love to romantic love; it is a document in the argument stated
so forcefully in Denis de Rougement's classic study, *Love in the Western*

---

1. David Lowe, Turgenev's "Fathers and Sons" (Ann Arbor: Ardis, 1983).

World.[2] De Rougement, it will be recalled, took his stand firmly on the side of ordinary, happy, family love, and against passion, romance, and the love of "troubadours and minnesingers," which leads to a pursuit of mystery and the mystical, of drama and Desire. In his opening chapter "Behind the Vogue of the Novel," de Rougement links this contest of loves to the very problematic of the genre. To the extent that the novel endorses "the divine rights of passion," he finds the genre pernicious.

"Happy love has no history," de Rougement's first page insists. Here he alludes to the very same saying—"Happy people have no history"— that appears in the notebooks for *Anna Karenina* and resulted in the most famous first sentence of any novel: "All happy families resemble each other; each unhappy family is unhappy in its own way." Happy, ordinary families resemble each other, because nothing dramatic happens to them and so they have no *story*; but unhappy families all have a story, and each story is different. And for de Rougement and Tolstoy, this means that plot is an index of error.

Romantic loves seeks events and obstacles, and imagines that real life is to be found in passion and struggle. "The prospect of a passionate experience has come to seem the promise that we are about to live more fully and more intensely" (*Love*, 16), de Rougement observes. By contrast, ordinary, family love seeks the quiet, uneventful chores of daily life; and it values not the ideal, but the present. Prosaic love thrives in a realm without drama, and therefore usually is, at best, the background to a novel's great events. Its lesson is perhaps summed up in that old Yiddish curse: "may you live in interesting times."

In *Fathers and Sons*, it is Katya who best understands prosaic love. What she values, and what she achieves with Arkady, is, as she puts it, the happiness of the "tame" and not the excitement of the "wild." It is a love that values most of all "confidential intimacy" (135 [128]). She loves music, but does not believe in romantic love songs (137 [131]). Above all, she deals with people by being quietly and constantly "observant" and sensitive.

Identifying love with romantic love, Odintsova, and the newly passionate Bazarov, never understand that Arkady and Katya have grown to love each other. The older couple believe that the younger pair treat each other as brother and sister. Odintsova and Bazarov are therefore shocked to learn that Arkady and Katya plan to marry. Recognizing only one kind of love, they are blind to the quiet signs of the other.

At first, Arkady thinks that "passion" most interests him, but he does not notice that really he is most occupied with prosaic love, a love that values "trifles"—that is, what appear like trifles from the perspective of

2. Denis de Rougement, *Love in the Western World*, revised edition, trans. Montgomery Belgion (New York: Harper and Row, 1974). Originally written in 1938 and revised in 1954, de Rougement's book is a classic text of "prosaics."

Romance. The prosaic love to which Arkady rises—one would not say "falls into"—is that love which cherishes the small things in life, the love of the "tame." One is moved here to think of that grand defender of the prosaic, Tolstoy, who, perhaps more than anyone else, appreciated that ordinary moments are what matter. In one of his most remarkable essays, Tolstoy illustrated his point by retelling the story of how the painter Bryullov once corrected a student's sketch.

> The pupil, having glanced at the altered drawing, exclaimed: "Why, you only touched it a tiny bit, but it is quite another thing." Bryullov replied: "Art begins where the tiny bit begins."
>
> That saying is strikingly true not only of art but of all life. One may say that true life begins where the tiny bit begins—where what seem to us minute and infinitely small alterations take place. True life is not lived where great external changes take place—where people move about, clash, fight, and slay one another—it is lived where these tiny, tiny, infinitesimally small changes occur.[3]

This line of thinking informs Tolstoy's great novels. In *War and Peace*, it appears in countless forms. Pierre at last learns not to seek meaning in the distance, but in the familiar people and small events always before his eyes. History, Tolstoy reiterates, is made without a system by countless small incidents of ordinary people at ordinary moments, and not, as most narratives tell us, by great men at important moments. Prosaics is one of the great "anti-Napoleonic" arguments of Russian literature. In *Anna Karenina* (as in *Family Happiness*), real love and the truly meaningful events of life are ordinary and lie within the family and the small community. At the beginning of *Anna*, a scene appears that recalls Arkady's hesitation between "passion" for the grand Odintsova and prosaic appreciation of Katya. Kitty has strong feeling for both Levin and Vronsky, and both feelings might be called "love." Kitty does not yet know whether both can be called "love" and cannot yet decide which to choose:

> When she mused on the past, she dwelled with pleasure, with tenderness, on the memory of her relations with Levin. . . . In her memories of Vronsky there always entered a certain element of awkwardness, though he was in the highest degree well bred and poised, as though there was some false note—not in Vronsky, he was very simple and nice, but in herself, while with Levin she felt perfectly at ease. But, on the other hand, as soon as she thought of the future with Vronsky, there arose before her a perspective of brilliant happiness; with Levin the future seemed misty.[4]

3. Leo Tolstoy, "Why Do Men Stupefy Themselves?", *Recollections and Essays*, trans. Aylmer Maude (London: Oxford UP, 1961), p. 81.
4. Leo Tolstoy, *Anna Karenina*, the Garnett translation edited by Leonard J. Kent and Nina Berberova (New York: Random House, 1965), pp. 51–52.

With Levin she is at ease, at home; with Vronsky there is the prospect of brilliance and adventure. Tolstoy soon makes it crystal clear that the better love lies in the familiar and in the family, and not in "brilliant happiness." Happiness—real, prosaic happiness—is never brilliant. Kitty learns this, and rapidly becomes wise in her prosaic love because she has absorbed these lessons from her own wonderful family, much as Arkady achieves a wise happiness when he trusts the truths he absorbed from the rhythms of life at Marino. Odintsova and Bazarov play a tragic scene about the impossibility of happiness, and, overhearing it, Arkady and Katya resolve on a happiness that the "extraordinary" people will never understand.

But Odintsova and Bazarov do, eventually, come to bless the ordinary love they can neither share nor truly appreciate. In the novel's last chapter, we learn that "in the small parish church two weddings had taken place quietly, and almost without witnesses—Arkady and Katya's, and Nikolai Petrovich and Fenichka's" (162 [153]). Small, quietly, without witnesses—this is how prosaic love expresses itself. Odintsova gives her sister and brother-in-law a handsome present, and even Bazarov—now dead—has earlier recommended that Arkady "follow the example" of the jackdaw, which is, as natural history instructs, "a most respectable family bird" (149 [141]). Pavel Petrovich, who was the obstacle to his brother's marrying Fenichka, has given his blessing to that marriage, too.[5] And so the novel sets up a parallel structure, with the proponents of great abstract theories and grand romantic passions yielding to those cherishing the quiet virtues of daily life.

Both sets of values, the romantic and the prosaic, have shaped the development of the novel, as both Tolstoy and Turgenev knew. (De Rougement, perhaps because he remembers the French tradition most, seems to forget this.) Tolstoy has Anna read—and not especially like— an "English novel" on the train ride during which Vronsky is pursuing her; the novel appears to be three parts Trollope and one part George Eliot, that is, it is a novel that deeply affirms prosaic values. "If we had a keen vision and feeling of all ordinary human life," wrote George Eliot, "it would be like hearing the grass grow and the squirrel's heart beat, and we should die of that roar which lies on the other side of silence."[6] Trollope's belief that goodness, meaning, and morality are to be found in small communities and daily acts of honesty, rather than in grand gestures, romantic choices, or great theories, is recorded in all his great novels. But Anna Karenina prefers French, romantic novels; she imagines herself a heroine of one and is pleased when her friends (for the time being) praise her as such. Anna chooses romantic over prosaic love and suffers; at the same time, Tolstoy chooses the prosaic

5. Lowe is quite perceptive about the roles of Bazarov and Pavel Petrovich as "blocking characters," p. 20.
6. George Eliot, *Middlemarch* (New York: Random House, 1984), p. 189.

English novel over the romantic French one. In the context of the genre's dialogue about love and daily life, *Anna Karenina* is an extreme partisan of one side.

Fathers and Sons is not. It is just as hesitant, ambiguous, and inconclusive about this *intra*-generic debate as it is about the *inter*-generic debate between the novel and the utopia or tract.

The subtlest critic of Turgenev's position in this debate, Elizabeth Cheresh Allen, takes as her starting point the difference between Turgenev and other novelists, such as Eliot, Trollope, and Tolstoy, with whom he is often grouped.[7] Allen calls the latter group Realists (in a narrow and specific sense; as distinguished from realists in a broader sense). Eliot, Trollope, and Tolstoy share an ethical sense foreign to Turgenev; for they see the ground of ethics in the activities of specific small communities and regard individual goodness as possible only in the realm of inherited customs. In the terms I have been using, Allen's Realists explore and endorse the prosaic view of life. By contrast, Turgenev sees communities, large and small, as a threat to an always precarious individuality and sense of identity. Individuals reach their greatest virtue and potential when they seek their salvation on their own.

Specifically, Turgenev believes in what Allen calls "composure," a word to be taken in two senses here: first, an ethics of calm and restraint, and second, an individually imposed discipline of aesthetic control over one's life, which must be carefully and tastefully "composed," like a work of art. Allen perceptively connects Turgenev's subtle use of metaliterary devices to his belief in composure. The very act of telling—composing—an artful story has moral value, and so Turgenev (as well as many of his characters who are great storytellers) calls attention to it. In portraying the storyteller, and calling attention to himself as storyteller, Turgenev gives us what Allen calls "the image of the individual exercising control over experience"; we see in art the successful attempt "to instill form where there was none. Turgenev's characters love narratives because they love the sensation of control over experience that the act of creation conveys."[8] If Allen is correct, then Turgenev's metaliterary devices work in the opposite way from Tolstoy's. For Tolstoy, they serve to discredit the artifice and illusoriness of aesthetic control in a world that is fundamentally messy and in which value is to be discovered only in aesthetically *im*perfect experience.

As we have seen, Turgenev's metaliterary devices are subtly omnipresent in *Fathers and Sons*, and they bespeak precisely the set of values that Allen describes. We sense those values above all in the voice that tells the story, with its cultivated taste and its refined sensibility. Not that this narrator is incapable of appreciating prosaic values, too. At

---

7. Elizabeth Cheresh Allen, *Beyond Realism: Turgenev's Poetics of Secular Salvation* (Stanford: Stanford UP, 1991).
8. Allen manuscript, pp. 55–56.

some points in his description of Fenichka, Arkady, and Katya, he seems not only to admire those values but even to be jealous of them. But that is just the point: he is jealous, because prosaic happiness is incompatible with his own most cherished beliefs. It must be sacrificed for something more important, namely sophistication, aesthetic control, *composure*.

The narrator admires prosaic activities as if such happiness were possible only to limited people. He is fully capable of treating Bazarov as an intellectual equal, but he writes from a position as far above Arkady and Katya as, let us say, Balzac's narrator is above Eugenie Grandet. He writes from afar. Katya understands family and "perfect peace"; the narrator gives her beliefs their due, but still seems to sense in them the air of rural sybaritism, of Gogol's "Old World Landowners" and, perhaps most of all, of Oblomovka, the vegetable idyll. *Oblomov*, which was published in 1859 and occasioned some remarkable criticism (especially Dobroliubov's essay on "Oblomovitis") is probably an important "subtext" for the prosaic plot in *Fathers and Sons*.

The narrator finds a life of small deeds distasteful; however wrongheaded, the noble Bazarov is more to his taste. We recall that Odintsova takes "aesthetic control" over life to almost pathological extremes ("order is needed in everything," she repeats). "Nothing was repulsive to her but vulgarity, and no one could have accused Bazarov of vulgarity" (61–62 [60]). The narrator feels the same way. Both fathers and sons believe in "great deeds," they merely disagree about what deeds are great. But Katya is equally far from both sides, because she prefers small deeds and a tame life. The narrator understands this position, understands above all the warmth of the life it makes possible, but clings unsurely to his disapproval of prosaic routine as deadening and lethargic. And he holds fast to his appreciation for beautiful forms and noble deeds, whatever their cost.

Just as Turgenev's narrator never resolves the quarrel between nihilism and the novel, so he never decisively chooses between the prosaic and the aesthetic ideals. Condescending admiration, ironic blessing, and ambiguous appreciation mark his tone. We might consider two passages in which he describes prosaic happiness, one at the very beginning of the book, and one at the very end. When Nikolai Petrovich is waiting at the station for his son's arrival, the narrator tells us of his marriage to Arkady's mother:

> Leaving the civil service in which his father had by favor procured him a post, [Nikolai Petrovich] was perfectly blissful with his Masha, first in a country villa near the Forestry Institute, afterwards in town in a pretty little flat with a clean staircase and a rather chilly drawing room. . . . The young couple lived very happily and peacefully; they were scarcely ever apart; they read

together, sang and played duets together on the piano; she tended her flowers and looked after the poultry-yard; he sometimes went hunting, and busied himself with the estate, while Arkady grew and grew in the same happy and peaceful way. Ten years passed like a dream (2–3 [5]).

In the epilogue, the dream has returned:

The Kirsanovs, father and son, have settled down at Marino; their fortunes are beginning to mend. Arkady has become zealous in the management of the estate, and the "farm" now yields a fairly good income. Nikolai Petrovich has been made one of the mediators appointed to carry out the emancipation reforms, and works with all his energies; he is forever driving about over his district; delivers long speeches (he maintains the opinion that the peasants ought to be "brought to comprehend things," that is to say, they ought to be reduced to a state of exhaustion by the constant repetition of one and the same words); and yet, to tell the truth, he does not give complete satisfaction either to the refined gentry, who talk with *chic* or with melancholy of the *emancipation* (pronouncing it as though it were French), nor to the uncultivated gentry, who unceremoniously curse "tha' *'muncipation.'* " He is too soft-hearted for both sets. Katerina Sergeyevna has a son, little Nikolai, while Mitya runs about merrily and talks fluently. Fenichka, Fedosya Nikolaevna, after her husband and Mitya, adores no one so much as her daughter-in-law, and when the latter is at the piano, she would gladly spend the whole day at her side (164 [155]).

A remarkable play of tones characterize these passages. We sense the narrator's perceptiveness of social forms, practices, and values at every moment; we never forget his sophistication, his infinite superiority over Nikolai Petrovich, to whom, however, he is indulgent. Nikolai Petrovich is "blissful with his Masha" and more than content with a life of duets and the poultry-yard; does the narrator's voice emphasize the value or the limitedness of this happiness? When he calls the life "a dream," is his point their happiness or the sleepiness of that way of living? In the second passage, we are also given a picture of bliss—family happiness at its best—tinged with patronizing irony, that at moments seems to verge on ridicule, for example, in the reminder that this is supposed to be an English-style "farm" and in the reference to the word-bludgeoned peasants.

Taken together, these two passages, from the first and last chapters, frame the novel with an ambiguous image of prosaic happiness. "The Kirsanovs, father and son, have settled in Marino" (162 [155]). This sentence not only alludes to the title and to the prosaic understanding of "generations" but also recalls Kirsanov's first wife, after whom he has named Marino. In this novel about "fathers and sons" (or "fathers and children"), this passage calls attention to the person left out of the title—to the *mother*, who also becomes identified with traditions, the land, and country mores that form the desired backdrop for a prosaically virtuous life.

The epilogue tells us next of Pavel Petrovich, and his fate, too, comments obliquely on the narrator's own values. For no one is so much the ideologue of the romantic and the aesthetic as Pavel. His life, wasted by his pursuit of a mysterious woman, of course resembles that of so many Turgenev heroes, if not of Turgenev himself. We do not need such references beyond the text of this novel, though, to recognize that Pavel Petrovich resembles its author. Both, for example, regard self-control as the mark of respect for human dignity and obligations. Of course, Pavel Petrovich is not as truly sophisticated as he thinks he is, and he lacks the narrator's real insight into people. He seems, in fact, to play the role of a caricature of the narrator and to serve as the author's honest attempt to concede what his own values often become in practice.

Those values turn Pavel Petrovich into a living corpse. "His handsome, emaciated head, the glaring daylight shining full upon it, lay on the white pillow like the head of a dead man. . . . and indeed he was a dead man" (134 [128]). This line has special irony because it takes place shortly after Pavel Petrovich has survived the duel with Bazarov. But Pavel is dead anyway, and we can say that this novel has two deaths. It also has two funereal closings. We have already discussed Bazarov's parents at his graveside. Just before, we are told how Pavel Petrovich lives abroad, impressing everyone with his fine aristocratic manners; how he lives pointlessly, lives posthumously. "One need but glance at him in the Russian church, when, leaning against the wall on one side, he sinks into thought, and remains long without stirring, bitterly compressing his lips, then suddenly recollects himself, and begins almost imperceptibly to cross himself . . ." (165 [156]). It is almost as if he is celebrating his own funeral service.

What survives at the end of this novel? Two things: the Kirsanov family and the story in which they appear; fathers and children and *Fathers and Children*; ordinary virtues and an extraordinary act of storytelling. Which one we are to value more highly remains entirely unclear.

KATHRYN FEUER

Fathers and Sons: Fathers and Children†

* * *

The social-political interpretation of *Fathers and Sons* has been widespread. It was most recently articulated by Isaiah Berlin in his Romanes Lectures, published as *Fathers and Children*, where he calls the "central topic of the novel . . . the confrontation of the old and the young, of liberals and radicals, traditional civilization and the new, harsh positivism which has no use for anything except what is needed by a rational man."[1] Ralph Matlaw, in his preface to the valuable Norton Critical Edition, explains that he has chosen the widely used English title "Fathers and Sons" rather than the literal "Fathers and Children" because " 'Sons' in English better implies the notions of spiritual and intellectual generations conveyed by the Russian *deti*." Matlaw, with the majority of non-Soviet critics, sees Turgenev as having drawn on the specific details and data of the debate between Russian liberals and radicals for the portrayal of a not merely political but universal theme, the eternal conflict of generations.

Yet can our interpretation of the novel stop here? Only, I believe, at the cost of ignoring its deepest layer of meaning and thus missing its consummate achievement. The most perceptive discussion of *Fathers and Sons* that I have read is also, regrettably, very brief, an "introduction" to the novel by René Wellek. Wellek begins by explaining and paying tribute to the admirable "concrete social picture" of an era and its disputes which Turgenev presents. Calling "the eternal conflict between the old and the young . . . one of the main themes of the book," nevertheless, he asserts, *Fathers and Sons* "goes beyond the temporal issues and enacts a far greater drama: man's deliverance to fate and chance, the defeat of man's calculating reason by the greater powers of love, honor, and death."[2] "Man's deliverance to fate and chance" is indeed, I would submit, one central theme of the novel, but to see this clearly we must go a step further in the rejection of traditional interpretations. We must dispense with the notion that the novel portrays the conflict of generations and recognize that instead it portrays love between generations, the triumph of love over tension and conflict; that its essential core is the intertwining of two great themes, affectionate continuity from parent to child and child to parent and "man's deliverance to fate and chance," that is, man's knowledge of his own mortality. It is to this novel that

---

† From *The Russian Novel from Pushkin to Pasternak*, ed. John Garrad (New Haven: Yale University Press, 1983) 68–70, 71–79. Reprinted by permission of Yale University Press.
1. Isaiah Berlin, *Fathers and Children* (Oxford: Clarendon, 1972), p. 25.
2. René Wellek, "Realism and Naturalism: Turgenev, *Fathers and Sons*," in *World Masterpieces*, vol. 2, ed. Maynard Mack (New York: W. W. Norton, 1956), p. 502.

Turgenev gave the title *Fathers and Children*, which is, moreover, a novel far more profound in its political implications than we have heretofore realized.[3]

This reading of the book can best be elucidated by beginning at its conclusion, at the almost unbearable closing picture of Bazarov's aged parents kneeling and weeping at his grave. Waste, futility, and anguish are overwhelming, but then comes a dramatic reversal, and the novel ends with a declaration of hope:

> Can it be that their prayers, their tears, will be fruitless? Can it be that love, sacred, dedicated love will not be all-powerful? Oh no! However passionate, guilty, rebellious the heart concealed in the grave, the flowers growing over it gaze at us serenely with their innocent eyes: not only of eternal peace do they speak to us, of that great peace of "indifferent" nature; they speak also of eternal reconciliation and of life without end. . . .   [chap. 28]

This passage is remarkable, almost incomprehensible as a conclusion to all that has gone before it in the novel; the incongruity has been described best by Wellek: "Turgenev puts here 'indifferent nature' in quotation marks, but as early as in A *Sportsman's Sketches* (*Zapiski okhotnika*) he had said: 'From the depths of the age-old forests, from the everlasting bosom of waters the same voice is heard: "You are no concern of mine," says Nature to Man.' " And he adds, with reference to *Fathers and Sons*: "There is no personal immortality, no God who cares for man; nature is even a disease beyond reason—this seems the message Turgenev wants to convey."[4] The contradictory quality of the last sentence of the novel has been noted by many readers, yet Wellek alone has commented on the particular peculiarity of Turgenev's having written " 'indifferent' nature" with the adjective in quotation marks, seeming to imply rejection of the idea of nature's indifference, an implication almost insulting to the reader, so opposite is it to the text of *Fathers and Sons* and to the major body of Turgenev's writings over the preceding quarter of a century.

The quotation marks can be read another way, however, as meaning not "so called" or "not really" but denoting—literally—a quotation, in this case a quotation from Pushkin, from the last lines of one of his best-known poems, "Whether I wander along noisy streets" ("Brozhu li Ya vdol ulits shumnykh"):

> And let indifferent nature
> Shine in her eternal beauty.

3. I consider a literal translation of the Russian title to be significant and to have a bearing on my argument, but I will continue to use the generally accepted translation for convenience.
4. Wellek, "Realism and Naturalism." I think the pronouncement of Potugin, in Turgenev's *Smoke*, best expresses the author's essential message: "Man is weak, woman is strong, chance is all-powerful. . . ." And in Turgenev's writing, all-powerful indifferent chance is represented again and again, through imagery or fact, as nature.

That Turgenev could have had the poem in mind is not difficult to suppose. For most writers there are other writers whose lines, paragraphs, works, exist as part of their consciousness, touchstones which may only occasionally be specified but whose presence is constant. For Turgenev, Pushkin was such a writer. The last stanza of the poem, indeed, is a major passage in the conclusion of one of Turgenev's most important early works, "Diary of a Superfluous Man" ("Dnevnik lishnego cheloveka"). Moreover, Pushkin's poetry is an important presence in *Fathers and Sons*: as a thematic element, as an emotional vector, as an emblem for the existence of beauty.

*   *   *

Pushkin's poem is about death and about the poet's morbidly haunted awareness of the random uncertainty of the time when it will come and the utter certainty of its coming. What we find in *Fathers and Sons*, I suggest, is the onset of Pushkin's malady in Bazarov, as a direct consequence of his love for Odintsova. Once this love has infected him, he becomes haunted by the knowledge of his own mortality. It has always been recognized that Bazarov's love crippled him, although some readers see Odintsova's rejection as the decisive event. I am proposing here that the effect of love on Bazarov was not some sort of general demoralization coming from a recognition that his nature does not correspond with his ideology, but a specific effect, the one I have called Pushkin's malady: an obsession with the knowledge of his own mortality.[5]

Throughout the first fourteen chapters of the novel Bazarov is a triumphant expression of the life-force, a man exuberantly intelligent and supremely self-confident, caring for no one's good opinion but his own. He is liked by the peasants, works assiduously, takes pride in being Russian, exhibits a zest for life in a variety of ways: his pleasure in Fenichka's "splendid" baby, his eagerness for a visit to town, his appreciation of pretty women. His serious concerns are positive. He scorns upbringing or the "age we live in" as excuses for weakness: "As for our times—why should I depend on that? Let my times depend on me" (chap. 7).

In chapter 15 the crucial transition occurs. When Bazarov and Arkadi first call on Odintsova, Arkadi sees that "contrary to his habit Bazarov was talking a good deal and obviously trying to interest" Odintsova. Then, as they leave, when Odintsova expresses the polite hope that they

5. Hjalmar Boyeson records Turgenev as saying (originally in *The Galaxy* 17 [1874]: 456–66): "I was once out for a walk and thinking about death. . . . Immediately there rose before me the picture of a dying man. This was Bazarov. The scene produced a strong impression on me and as a consequence the other characters and the action began to take form in my mind." Quoted from the Russian in "K biografii I. S. Turgeneva," *Minuvshie gody* 8 (1908): 70, in Richard Freeborn, *Turgenev, The Novelist's Novelist* (Glasgow: Oxford University Press, 1960), p. 69.

may visit her estate: "Bazarov only bowed and—a last surprise for Arkadi; he noticed that his friend was blushing." Shortly after, when Arkadi comments on Odintsova's beauty, Bazarov agrees: "A splendid body! Perfect for the dissection table." And three days later, as the friends are driving to Odintsova's estate: " 'Congratulate me,' Bazarov suddenly exclaimed, 'today is June 22nd, my guardian angel's day. Well, we'll see how he'll take care of me.' "

What has happened here? Bazarov has called on his "guardian angel"; whether he realizes it or not he is aware for the first time of his vulnerability to death; he is subconsciously asking Pushkin's question: "Is the hour already near?" He will continue to ask the question until he dies, and his preoccupation, usually just below the surface though sometimes bursting forth in bitter outrage, will be expressed in the imagery of disease or death, which first enters his consciousness and conversation in the moment we have witnessed: "A splendid body! Perfect for the dissection table."

In chapter 16 he illustrates a nonmedical argument to Odintsova by an analogy with "the lungs of a consumptive." In chapter 17, when he has acknowledged his passion to himself, this love "tortured and possessed him," for he regarded such feelings "as something like deformity or disease." In chapter 18, when Odintsova asks whether happiness exists, Bazarov can answer only: "You know the proverb: it's always better where we don't exist." A little later, when she tries to question him about his plans and ambitions, he answers ominously: "What's the point of talking or thinking about the future, which for the most part doesn't depend on us?"

Immediately after this exchange come Bazarov's declaration of his love and Odintsova's refusal. Now the images of disease increase: in Bazarov's speech there is a movement from the sense of vulnerability to that of fatality. Moreover, new motifs appear: insecure megalomania supersedes self-confidence, hostility to Arkadi replaces condescending but genuine friendship. In chapter 19 he agrees to Arkadi's accusation of elitism: " 'Is it that *you're* a god while I'm just one of the blockheads?' 'Yes,' Bazarov repeated weightily, 'you're still stupid.' " Besides increasing in number, Bazarov's images of disease and death are now applied to himself: "The machine's become unstuck." Then, still in chapter 19, Bazarov articulates the first unequivocal statement of his intimation: "Every man hangs on a thread; the abyss can open up beneath him at any moment. . . ."

Soon after, his preoccupation with his "approaching . . . anniversary" breaks forth more explicitly:

> "I think, here I am, lying under a haystack . . . the tiny, cramped spot I occupy is so minute in comparison with the rest of the universe, where I don't exist and where I don't matter; and the

space of time allotted for me to live in is a mere moment in that
eternity of time where I was not and will not be. . . . And in this
atom, in this mathematical dot, the blood circulates, the brain
works, there's even a desire for something. . . . How outrageous it
is! How petty!"   [chap. 21]

Bazarov now gives way to impotent fury, vindictiveness, malice:

> "Ha! There's a fine fellow of an ant, dragging off a half-dead fly.
> Take her, brother, take her. It doesn't matter that she resists, make
> use of her as you will."

When Bazarov lauds hatred, "How strange!" Arkadi observes, "why I
don't hate anyone." "And I hate so many," Bazarov replies:

> "Hatred! Well, for example take yesterday—as we were passing our
> bailiff, Phillip's cottage—and you said that Russia will attain per-
> fection when every last muzhik has such a place to live, and that
> every one of us ought to work to bring that about. . . . And I felt
> such a hatred for your every last muzhik. . . . Yes, he'll be living
> in a white cottage, while the nettles are growing out of me. . . ."
>   "Ah, Arkadi, do me a favor, let's have a fight, a real fight, till
> we're laid out in our coffins, till we destroy each other."

This attack on Arkadi has been triggered by his comment on a dead leaf
falling to earth, fluttering like a butterfly: "Gloom and death," he remarks, "and at the same time gaiety and life!" What seems to enrage
Bazarov is that Arkadi can accept the unity of life and death, can see
death as a part of life rather than as its negation.

Bazarov's bravery during the duel with Pavel Kirsanov only underlines
the depth and inner intensity of his preoccupation with death. It is not
the concrete incident in which his life is endangered which obsesses the
death-haunted man; it is the subliminal question, when and where,
which accompanies him whether wandering noisy streets or lounging
beneath a haystack.

After his departure from the Kirsanovs Bazarov pays a brief visit to
Odintsova; once again the imagery of death is related to himself. When
Odintsova tells him that he is a "good man," he replies: "That's the
same as laying a wreath of flowers on the head of a corpse" (chap. 26).
Is there also a presentiment of fatality in Bazarov's parting words to her?
When she tells him she is sure they will meet again (as of course they
do, at Bazarov's deathbed), he answers: "In this world, anything may
happen!" Such an interpretation of his words is prepared by the grim
pun with which he has just before informed Arkadi that he is stopping
by at Odintsova's on his way home: "Well, so I've set off 'to the fathers.' "
As Matlaw points out, Bazarov here "mockingly (and ominously) recalls
the 'ad patres' used by Bazarov's father earlier [in chap. 20] as an expression for death."

Bazarov goes home for six weeks to settle down to work. Are the lethargy and melancholy that soon overtake him further evidence of his morbid preoccupation? It hardly matters. Soon, whether by accident or suicide, he *is* dying and, as when he faced death in the duel, his behavior is calm and courageous. The fear has dissolved, once it has become recognized reality. On one occasion he does rebel: he takes hold of a heavy table and manages to swing it around: " 'Strength, real strength,' he murmured. 'It's all still here, and yet I must die! . . . Well, go and try to refute death. She'll refute you, and that's that!' " (chap. 27). Bazarov is no longer haunted by wondering: the question of the date of the "approaching . . . anniversary" has been answered and we have come to the scene of Bazarov's grave, to the grieving parents, to Turgenev's assertion that the flowers speak of eternal reconciliation and not just of " 'indifferent' nature," and so back to Pushkin's poem.

The poet is haunted by the question of when death will come and then proceeds to a corollary question; *where* will it come? But this question is not obsessive; rather it provides a transition to the one consideration which can make the question of "when" bearable, for it allows him to imagine the grave in which—since there must be one—he would choose to lie. He has spoken of "moldering" or "decaying," but now he writes of "the place where I shall rest." It is, he hopes, a nearby valley, radiant with the beauty of "indifferent nature" but also alive with "young life at play." Death is bearable because life goes on. Pushkin has prepared this final statement in stanza 4: "As I caress a sweet little child." He speaks, moreover, of the continuity of generations not only for the future but from the past; in stanza 3 he writes of the oak tree which will outlive his age as it has outlived those of his fathers. (The force of the juxtaposition is vitiated in translation; in the original, "fathers" is the last word of stanza 3 and "child" is the first word of stanza 4.)

Once again the poem sheds light on *Fathers and Sons*. At Bazarov's grave are only his aged parents, grieving for the worst thing that can happen to parents, for the most unnatural pain which Nature can inflict, to outlive one's own child. Despite the birds and flowers and young pine trees there is no "young life at play;" Bazarov has been denied the single solace Pushkin offers to the man beset by the knowledge of his own mortality. This solace not only sheds light on the novel's closing scene but also states its second, inextricably related theme: love and continuity between generations.

Sharp conflict in the novel there is, but it is not between fathers and sons: it is between two men who dislike each other because they are fundamentally so much alike, Pavel Kirsanov and Bazarov. Were they contemporaries they might find different things to quarrel and duel over, but quarrel and duel they would. The father-son and son-father relationships are, on the other hand, respectful, affectionate, and deeply loving, despite the faint note of menace at the very outset, on the ride home after Arkadi's father has met him and Bazarov at the station. Arkadi and his father, riding together in the carriage, are renewing their acquaintance with affectionate sympathy when Bazarov, from the other coach, interrupts to give Arkadi a cigar. Arkadi lights the cigar, and it emits "such a strong and sour smell of stale tobacco that Nikolai Petrovich . . . could not avoid averting his face, though he did so stealthily so as not to offend his son" (chap. 3). But the threat of estrangement dissipates; it is never more substantial than cigar smoke in the breeze.

Arkadi's father defers to him on occasion after occasion and tries hard to adopt his attitudes and opinions. When he cannot, it is himself he considers inferior, as, when musing in the garden, he reflects:

> "My brother says that we are right, and putting aside any element of vanity, it does seem to me that they are farther from the truth than we are, but at the same time I feel that behind them there is something that we don't possess, a kind of superiority over us. . . . Is it youth? No, it's not just youth. That's not the source of their superiority; isn't it that in them there are fewer traces of the slave owner than in us?"   [chap. 11]

At the end of this remarkable scene Kirsanov is called by Fenichka, and he answers her more offhandedly than he would a woman of his own class: "I'm coming—run along!" And yet throughout the novel, although she is the housekeeper's daughter, both Nikolai and his brother treat her with perfect courtesy: Pavel Kirsanov, for example, always addresses her formally. It is only Bazarov who, having no right to do so, uses the familiar form of her name. And it is only Bazarov who flirts with her as with a servant girl, who behaves as he does not and would not behave with Odintsova. It is only Bazarov, in fact, who displays "the slave owner's mentality."

Bazarov's mother beatifically adores him, while his father does not merely defer to his son's views, he suppresses some of his own deepest feelings. The love of the fathers for the sons, however, hardly needs demonstration; instances can be found in every scene in which they appear together. The interpretation of the novel as a depiction of the conflict of generations rests rather on the attitudes of the sons toward the fathers. Where are these conflicts to be found? In a few moments of condescension or irritation or even unkindness by the sons, in Nikolai Kirsanov's hour of melancholy in the garden, in the disappointment of Bazarov's parents that his visit is so short. One can apply the term *conflict* to such moments only under the assumption that gentle condescension, slight irritation, unkindness, sorrow, and disappointment are not normal components of all human relations, under the assumption that we are living on the planet of Dostoevsky's Ridiculous Man before he visited it.

From the outset Arkadi is glad to be hugged and kissed by his father and hugs and kisses him in return, calling him "daddy" (*papasha*); even Bazarov's presence is only faintly inhibiting. The one feeling Arkadi has toward his father that could be called critical is that of condescension; it occurs on three occasions. First, when Arkadi, smiling "affectionately," tells him that his shame at his relationship with Fenichka is "nonsense" . . . "and his heart was filled with a feeling of condescending tenderness toward his good and soft-hearted father, combined with a sense of a certain secret superiority" (chap. 3). Second, when he displays conscious magnanimity in paying a formal call on Fenichka. Third, when Arkadi agrees to give his father *Kraft und Stoff* to read, approving this choice because it is a "popularization" (chap. 10). Not only does Arkadi never once manifest hostility or irritation toward his father, there is even no friction between them. On the three occasions when he condescends to him he does so tenderly, with affectionate respect, with embraces, with loving compassion and gentleness.

Perhaps even more significant is Arkadi's behavior to his uncle. Their mutual affection is open, and for a man of Pavel Petrovich's deep reserve, even demonstrative. When Pavel criticizes Bazarov (and on this occasion unjustly) Arkadi's response is the one with which we are acquainted— a silent look of compassion for his uncle's noncomprehension. When Bazarov criticizes Pavel (both wittily and aptly) Arkadi attempts a weak rejoinder, then deflects the attack: "Maybe so, only truly, he's a fine, good person" (chap. 4). Most important is that, despite his imitation of Bazarov's opinions, awe of his powers, and fear of his disapproval, despite, in short, Arkadi's schoolboy crush on Bazarov, he never wavers in his defense of his uncle.

Bazarov can be brusque to his parents but never treats them with the rudeness with which he treats everyone else. He submits to their repeated embraces ("Just let me hug you once more, Yenyushechka"), and he willingly kisses his mother (chap. 20). He is perfectly good-humored about having the priest to dinner, understanding what this means to his mother and father. When he decides to leave—abruptly and even cruelly after a visit home of only three days—part of his motivation is, in fact, love for his parents:

> "While I'm here, my father keeps assuring me: 'My study is all yours; no one will bother you there'; and he can't keep a foot away from me. And it makes me feel guilty to shut myself away from him. And it's the same with mother. I hear through the wall how she's sighing—and so I go out to her—and then I have nothing to say to her."   [chap. 21]

Though he tells himself, "never mind, they will get over it," all the same it takes Bazarov a whole day to bring himself to inform his parents that he is leaving, and having gone: "Bazarov was not altogether satisfied with himself" (chap. 22). At the one place in the novel where he exposes his inner feelings with ruthless honesty, the scene beneath the haystack, there is the following solemn exchange:

> "Do you love them, Yevgeni?"
> "I love them, Arkadi."

The supreme expression of Bazarov's love for his parents comes with his ultimate sacrifice for their sake. He is willing to receive extreme unction, though "at the sight of the priest in his robes, of the smoking censer and the candles before the icon something like a shudder of horror passed for a moment over the death-stricken face" (chap. 27). This is for him a final negation of all that his life has meant to him.

May it not even be said that Bazarov, who loves his parents and understands their love for him, has intimations not only of his mortality but also of the despair that will surround his grave, where there will be no "young life at play"? Consider his final parting with Arkadi:

> "There is, Arkadi, there is something else I want to say, only I won't say it because it's romanticism—and that means soggy sentiments. You get married, as soon as you can, and you build your nest, and you have lots of children. . . ."   [chap. 26]

I began with the thesis that *Fathers and Sons* is a novel with two entwined themes: "man's deliverance to fate and chance" and the love between generations, the continuity of generations as man's only consolation for the knowledge of his inevitable mortality. The political details of the debate between the men of the forties and the men of the sixties, I suggested, were only the temporal, particular setting for Turgenev's eternal and universal theme. Yet the implications of this theme are profoundly political, for the good pragmatic reason that it is the continuity of generations which is probably the most counterrevolutionary force in the world. On some level of consciousness, I would suggest, the real import of *Fathers and Sons* was sensed by Chernyshevsky when he set out to reply to Turgenev in his novel *What Is to Be Done?* (*Chto delat?*)[6] Doubtless there were other contributing factors: his desire to present his social theories in popularized form, his belief that Turgenev had slandered the radicals by portraying Bazarov in an alien environment, his conviction that Bazarov was a deliberate caricature of his recently deceased comrade, Dobrolyubov. Chernyshevsky's novel was indeed a successful manifesto; it recruited countless thousands into the radical movement and led Lenin (who is known to have read it at least five times) to declare, "[it] profoundly transformed me" and "created hundreds of revolutionaries."[7] It played this role not only because of its

6. N. G. Chernyshevsky, *Chto delat?* (Leningrad: Khudozhestvennaya literatura, 1967). The English translation by Benjamin R. Tucker is both inaccurate and incomplete.
7. Nikolai Valentinov (N. V. Volsky), *Encounters with Lenin*, trans. Paul Rosta and Brian Pearce (London: Oxford University Press, 1968), p. 73.

idyllic prophecies but because of its reply to the affirmation in *Fathers and Sons* of love and continuity between generations.

What, after all, is the usual experience of youthful political idealists? They rebel against their parents and against Society, which they seek to remake, often with a partner. Time passes, children are born to them, and their concern for the future becomes personalized, for it is hard— and abstractly inhuman—to pit one's own child's welfare against humanity's, and these are not always in self-evident accord. Having children of one's own has a further effect, that of placing the young rebels in the role of parents themselves. Other factors enter in: compromises of principle come to be accepted as expansion of experience, as recognition of life's ambiguities; more specifically, those who have created life and come to love what they have created are less willing to contemplate its destruction in the name of some abstract goal.

Chernyshevsky understood this process well; moreover, he knew from his own experience in the radical movement that rebellion against parents (and their surrogate, Society) was in fact a primary factor in many young revolutionaries' act of commitment. Given the widespread phenomenon, in Russia at that time, of youthful departure from parents' homes and ways for progressive activity, it is not difficult to suppose that Chernyshevsky's anger at *Fathers and Sons* was at least partially fueled by Turgenev's portrayal of these relationships as loving and positive. In *What Is to Be Done?* he provides in answer an effective presentation of life which fixes and crystallizes youthful rebellion, a program which substitutes for love between the generations a whole other world of affections and loyalties among peers.

This vision of a future with no bothersome babies or bothersome old folks, of a way of life in which revolutionary commitment can escape transformation into generational continuity reaches its apogee in Vera Pavlovna's "Fourth Dream" in the description of man's life in the Crystal Palace, where all social problems have been rationally solved, where there is prosperity and pleasure for all: "Everywhere there are men and women, old, young, and children all together. *But mostly young people: there are few old men, even fewer old women, there are more children than old men, but still not very many*"[8] (italics added). It is significant, I think, that when Dostoevsky sat down to answer *What Is to Be Done?* in *Notes from Underground* (*Zapiski iz podpolia*) (begun as a review of the novel), he ended:

> We even find it a burden to be men—men with *our own* real flesh and blood; we are ashamed of it, we consider it a disgrace and strive to be some sort of imaginary men-in-general. We are still-born and indeed not for many years have we been conceived by living fathers,

8. N. G. Chernyshevsky, "Excerpts from *What Is to Be Done?*," in *Notes from Underground and the Grand Inquisitor*, ed. Ralph E. Matlaw (New York: E. P. Dutton, 1960), p. 169.

300 DAVID A. LOWE

and this pleases us more and more. . . . Soon we shall contrive somehow to be born of an idea.[9]

We know that Dostoevsky admired *Fathers and Sons*, at least that he wrote to Turgenev about it in terms of appreciation which Turgenev said "made me throw up my hands in amazement—and pleasure."[1] We do not know what Dostoevsky wrote about the novel; we can be sure that he would not have been impressed by the notion of conflict between the men of the forties and the men of the sixties because he argued explicitly, in the first two chapters of *Notes from Underground* and throughout *The Possessed (Besy)*, that the men of the sixties are not the opponents but the direct descendants, the necessary offspring of the men of the forties.

Many speculations are possible, but it seems to me likely that Dostoevsky, the great poet of the "living life," would surely have responded to Turgenev's portrayal of Bazarov the nihilist as a man doomed by his preoccupation with death. And it seems even more likely that Dostoevsky, author of the magnificent birth scene in *The Possessed* and of the unforgettable burial scene in *The Brothers Karamazov (Bratia Karamazovy)*, understood Turgenev's affirmation of the reconciliation and continuity of generations, his affirmation of "young life at play" as that which makes bearable the inevitability of the grave.

DAVID A. LOWE

The Dialectics of Turgenev's *Ottsy i deti*†

In a review of my monograph on Turgenev's *Ottsy i deti*, Edward J. Brown remarked rather cryptically that on the pages of his greatest novel Turgenev had "breathed new life into Hegel's dusty triads."[1] To my knowledge, the only person besides Brown to mention Hegel in connection with Turgenev's novel is Octave Thanet (pseudonym of Alice French). In an article published over a hundred years ago, Thanet writes

---

9. Ibid., p. 115.
1. Letters to F. M. Dostoevsky, March 18 (30), 1862. The text may be found above, p. 172. Dostoevsky responded warmly to the work of the philosopher N. F. Fyodorov, *The Philosophy of the Common Task*. Konstantin Mochulsky, Dostoevsky's great biographer, says that according to Fyodorov, "All living sons will direct their forces to a single problem- -the resurrection of their dead fathers. 'For the present age,' writes Fyodorov, 'father is the most hateful word and son is the most degrading.'" Konstantin Mochulsky, *Dostoevsky, His Life and Work*, trans. Michael A. Minihan (Princeton: Princeton University Press, 1967), pp. 567–69.

† From the Kennan Institute's Occasional Paper #234. Reprinted by permission of the author and The Woodrow Wilson Center.
1. Edward J. Brown, review of David Lowe, *Turgenev's "Fathers and Sons"* (Ann Arbor, 1983), in *Washington Post Book World*, July 3, 1983, p. 5a. [*Ottsy i deti* translates as *Fathers and Sons*—Editor.]

of Turgenev the artist and moralist: "Tourguéneff has adopted Hegel's philosophical method. He assumes as true everything asserted of his subject, and then by its self-contradiction evolves the truth."[2] In the present paper, I propose first of all to follow Brown's and Thanet's lead by examining *Ottsy i deti* in light of the Hegelian dialectic and then to speculate on the actual source and significance of the dialectic patterns to be observed in Turgenev's novel.

A few fundamental observations about the Hegelian dialetic are in order.[3] The Hegelian dialectic employs series of triads to describe evolution of thoughts or ideas as they move from a lower level of perception to a higher one. At the lower stage, which Hegel calls *Verstand* (understanding), contradictions, divisions, oppositions, antinomies, and so on give the impression of chaos. Hegel maintains that at this level any given phenomenon necessarily implies its opposite: complementary abstractions depend on each other for either of them to lay any claim to validity.

The Hegelian dialectic explains the movement to overcome basic oppositions and dichotomies. Through the prism of *Vernunft* (reason) dichotomies reveal a hidden identity that manifests itself in the recovery of unity. The key concept here is *Aufheben*, Hegel's term for a transition wherein contradictions from a lower stage pass into each other and are simultaneously annulled and preserved in a higher stage. Since at the higher level unity embraces contradiction, that is, both preserves and abolishes distinctions, Hegel often uses the word *Versöhnung* (reconciliation) to describe this phenomenon. In essence, then, through the dialectic, chaos metamorphoses into cosmos, duality into unity.

The same patterns at work in the Hegelian dialectic may be perceived in *Ottsy i deti*. To begin with, the dialectic neatly describes the shift in the alignment of characters that occurs in the course of the novel. Joel Blair, perhaps not realizing that he was describing a dialectical pattern, has noted that "the principle of composition operating in the novel is the grouping and regrouping of characters: our understanding of the novel develops as we observe the initial groups of characters dissolve and perceive the formation of new pairs. Eventually, those characters who seemed most unalike are aligned; their similarities become more important than their initial differences."[4] This movement leads to the

---

2. Octave Thanet, "The Moral Purpose of Tourguéneff," *The Journal of Speculative Philosophy*, vol. 12 (1878), p. 429.
3. For my remarks about the nature of the Hegelian dialectic I am indebted to J. N. Findlay, *Hegel: A Re-Examination* (London, 1958), pp. 58–82; Martin Malia, *Alexander Herzen and the Birth of Russian Socialism, 1812–1855* (Cambridge, Mass., 1961), pp. 231–233; Walter Kaufmann, *Hegel: A Reinterpretation* (Garden City, New York, 1966), pp. 153–162; Charles Taylor, *Hegel* (Cambridge, England, 1975), pp. 224–231; and Clark Butler, G. W. F. *Hegel* (Boston, 1977), pp. 22–24.
4. Joel Blair, "The Architecture of Turgenev's *Fathers and Sons*," *Modern Fiction Studies* 19, no. 4 (Winter, 1973–74), p. 556.

discovery that similarities or dissimilarities in character and worldview cut across notions of class, ideology, and chronological age.[5] As the action of the novel progresses, attentive readers come to the recognition that the seeming antipodes Bazarov and Pavel share an outlook on the world and their fellow man that sets them apart from their apparent confederates, Arkady and Nikolai, respectively. The revelation that oppositions mask an identity is profoundly dialectical in the Hegelian sense.

At the point where we recognize the formation of new pairs of characters, however, we have not moved beyond the level of Hegel's *Verstand, for oppositions have dissolved, merely to reemerge in new form. One set of polarities has replaced another. By the conclusion of the novel, however, we approach the stage of Vernunft*, where unity embraces dichotomies without destroying them. Arkady turns out to be a competent estate manager: he has learned something from Bazarov's gospel of utility and practicality. Pavel, presumably as a consequence of his encounter with Bazarov's contempt for aristocratic social conventions, overcomes his inborn snobbishness at least long enough to urge his brother to marry Fenechka, a serf. Finally, on his deathbed, Bazarov abandons his hauteur and displays traits early associated with Arkady—humility and the recognition of beauty. Thus, on the level of characterization, *Ottsy i deti* proceeds in a manner entirely consistent with Hegel's dialectic: polarities and similarities shift and finally pass over into each other.

The movement of the plot is dialectical as well, pitting tragedy and comedy against each other. The observation that *Ottsy i deti* is at least in part a tragedy will hardly strike anyone as original. It is worth noting, however, that few commentators depict *Ottsy i deti* as an unqualified tragedy. Characteristic of such hesitation is Helen Muchnic's remark that although the novel's implications are tragic, its tone is not.[6] That *Ottsy i deti* is in any way a comedy may seem a curious notion, yet such an approach is implicit in as early a suggestion as the late Viktor Shklovsky's that "in *Ottsy i deti* Turgenev understood the love story as the confrontation of new people with a world built on old principles."[7] More recently, Alexander Fischler has written that the epilogue of *Ottsy i deti* transforms the drama of the novel into "*prostodushnaia komediia.*"[8] As I note in my monograph, what Shklovsky and Fischler have in mind, I think, is Aristotle's concept of comedy.[9]

The most brilliant modern recapitulation of Aristotle's notions about

5. For a discussion of the limitations of narrowly socio-political interpretations of the characters in *Ottsy i deti* and of the novel as a whole, see Yu. M. Lebedev, *Roman I. S. Turgeneva "Ottsy i deti"* (Moscow, 1982), pp. 4–5, and Lowe, *Turgenev's "Fathers and Sons,"* pp. 28–54.
6. Helen Muchnic, *An Introduction to Russian Literature* (New York, 1947), p. 118.
7. Viktor Shklovsky, *Zametki o proze russkikh klassikov* (Moscow, 1955), p. 221.
8. Alexander Fischler, "The Garden Motif and the Structure of *Fathers and Sons,*" *Novel* 9 (1976), p. 146.
9. Lowe, *Turgenev's "Fathers and Sons,"* pp. 15–27.

comedy belongs to Northrop Frye.[1] According to Frye, the standard comedic formula involves a young couple—the technical hero and heroine—whose marriage is blocked by other members of the cast (society). The hero and heroine tend to be dull but decent people, while the blocking characters are the truly interesting types. These blockers are normally but not necessarily parental figures. Moreover, they are likely to be impostors, as Frye calls them, people who lack self-knowledge. At the conclusion of comedy the blocking characters are either incorporated into or expelled from the given society, and as a result the hero and heroine are free to wed. Thus, comedies often conclude with a wedding and the birth of babies, often as not in a rural setting. The rustic locus represents an escape to a simpler, less corrupt society. At the conclusion of comedy the audience feels that justice has triumphed, that some sort of evil spell has been broken, that a higher, natural law has worked its will, and that everyone will live happily ever after in a freer, more flexible society.

The brief reduction of Frye's Aristotelian treatise should make it plain that one of the compositional patterns in *Ottsy i deti* is comedic. Arkady and Katia, along with Nikolai Petrovich and Fenechka, are the technical heroes and heroines, the paths to whose marriages are obstructed by Bazarov and Pavel, respectively. It is precisely Bazarov's magnetic influence that for a while prevents Arkady from coming to terms with his true, non-nihilistic self, after which recognition he proposes to Katia. Similarly, it has been Pavel's unspoken antipathy toward the idea of his brother's marrying a peasant girl that has caused Nikolai to wait so long before regularizing his liaison with Fenechka. The general movement toward these final, inevitable pairings is the stuff of comedy, and the double wedding noted in the epilogue comes directly out of the traditions of classical comedy.

Ottsy i deti is thus modelled on two structural principles that seem antithetical but which in a dialetical manner actually represent reverse sides of the same coin: the question of how a viable society is created. In comedy, the villains, the blockers, are laughed off the stage, while in tragedy the people who do not belong come to a more frightful end.

Understanding the relationship between comedy and tragedy in *Ottsy i deti* helps us understand in formal terms the initial and continuing furor created by the novel. In "Neskol'ko slov po povodu *Ottsov i detei*," Turgenev writes that he has an interesting collection of documents and letters from readers who accuse him of doing totally contradictory things in his novel.[2] This is hardly surprising, since Turgenev is in fact doing

1. My discussion of comedy is drawn from Northrop Frye, *Anatomy of Criticism* (Princeton, 1957), pp. 43–53, 163–185.
2. I. S. Turgenev, *Polnoe sobranie sochinenii i pisem v 28-i tomakh* (Moscow-Leningrad, 1960–1968), vol. 14, p. 104.

what seem to be contradictory things within the work. By combining the tragedic and comedic modes he seems to stand behind two diametrically opposed views of life at one and the same time. If we take the novel's comedic structure out of context, we conclude that life is triumphant, rewarding, and meaningful. Such is the conclusion that comedy forces on its audience. And in *Ottsy i deti* the portraits of the Kirsanovs, their babies, their joyous participation in the natural cycle, all lead us to infer that all is right with the world. On the other hand, if we take the novel's tragedic side out of context, we are led to the view that life, ruled by fate and the irrational, is essentially meaningless: death is triumphant. Sooner or later, of course, we end up asking where Turgenev stands. After all, it is precisely this point that divides the critics and scholars who have written on *Ottsy i deti*.

In a recent article on *Ottsy i deti*, James Woodward neatly sums up the two contrasting views of the novel that typify Turgenev scholarship.[3] The major disagreements concern the questions of which characters actually represent the novel's heroes and with which characters and ideologies Turgenev's sympathies lie. Commentators who interpret the novel primarily as a tragedy see Bazarov as a commandingly heroic figure, a rebel whose tragic demise shows that Turgenev's sympathies lie entirely with his Promethean protagonist. Readers attuned to the novel's comedic implications, however, argue that Turgenev's novel exposes the limitations in Bazarov's character and worldview, and elevates Nikolai and Arkady to the status of heroes of the golden mean.

Various attempts have been made to render compatible the two opposing views regarding Turgenev's intentions in the novel. Woodward suggests that such a synthesis can be achieved through approaching the novel as a study of the Schopenhauerian struggle of wills. On a less rigidly philosophical plane, Lebedev argues that the portraits of Bazarov and the Kirsanovs, *père et fils*, are linked by Turgenev's attempt to describe contradictory aspects of a single phenomenon, the Russian type.[4] Several critics and scholars who have written about *Ottsy i deti*, myself among them, feel that Turgenev sympathizes with all sides in the conflict he portrays, whether one conceives that conflict as narrowly Russian and socio-political or universal and a matter of personalities. Thus, Turgenev seems to argue in his novel that both sides, the gentry of the 1840s and the *raznochintsy* of the 1860s, are right in some ways and wrong in others. The truth rests on both sides, but neither side has an exclusive claim to it. The nobility, with its reforms and commitment to civilization, and the radicals, with their rejection of reform and tradition, are equally right and equally wrong. Turgenev's socio-political stance in *Ottsy i deti* dovetails with his dualistic view of life and human

---

3. James B. Woodward, "*Aut Caesar aut nihil*: the 'War of Wills' in Turgenev's *Ottsy i deti*," *Slavonic and East European Review*, vol. 64, no. 2 (1986), pp. 161–188.
4. Lebedev, *Roman I. S. Turgeneva*, p. 28.

nature. The Kirsanovs and their wives are limited, but limitlessly happy and fruitful; Bazarov is dramatic, intense, and barren. The Kirsanovs' love of life is justified, as is Bazarov's rage against Russian society. Nikolai and Arkady's ability to deal with the social problems of the day is limited but need not give cause for despair; Bazarov's disgust with the gentry and with limited, gradual reform is understandable, but his solutions are wrongheaded.

One cannot discuss *Ottsy i deti* within a Hegelian framework without speaking of reconciliation. That reconciliation, or at least the attempt at reconciliation, occurs on at least three levels. The first is the thematic, where one of the major themes in the novel, if not in fact the major theme, is that all children rebel against their parents, thus embodying a principle that Russian Hegelians would identify as negation. With the passing of time, though, children surrender—willingly or not—to the world of their parents. That world, after all, represents life's mainstream.[5] That movement toward a reconciliation between the generations stands out most obviously in Arkady, whose relationship with Katia manifests exact parallels with that between his father and mother.[6] By becoming a father at the same time he remains a son, Arkady encapsulates that Hegelian unity which would embrace contradictions without erasing them. Even in Bazarov, however, we observe a retreat to the family estate and to something resembling his father's way of life. Note, for instance, that Bazarov tells Arkady: " '*Ia otpravilsia k 'ottsam.'* '"[7] The plural emphasizes the universal implications of his action, and the transition from contradiction to reconciliation is entirely consonant with the logic of the dialectic.

The second level at which Turgenev attempts a dialectical reconciliation lies within the plot, where comedy and tragedy coexist and interact to produce a monistic view of life. In the final analysis, the monism that Turgenev projects in *Ottsy i deti* rests on man's mortality. As Turgenev wrote to his friend Annenkov, "I know that in nature and in life everything is reconciled one way or another . . . If life cannot [do the reconciling], death will."[8]

The mention of mortality leads to the third level of attempted reconciliation, the metaphysical. In the passage that closes the novel, as Bazarov's parents weep at their son's grave, the narrator asks: "*Neuzheli ikh molitvy, ikh slezy besplodny? Neuzheli liubov', sviataia, predannaia liubov', ne vsesil'na. O net! Kakoe by strastnoe, greshnoe, buntuiushchee serdtse ne skrylos' v mogile, tsvety, rastushchie na nei, bezmiatezhno*

5. For the clearest statement of this position in Turgenev criticism, see Nikolay Strakhov's classic article, "Ottsy i deti," *Vremia*, 1862, no. 4.
6. For details on these similarities, see Lowe, *Turgenev's "Fathers and Sons,"* p. 49. For a brief description of other situation rhymes in Turgenev's novel, see Lebedev, *Roman I. S. Turgeneva*, pp. 14–16.
7. I. S. Turgenev, *Polnoe sobranie sochinenii i pisem*, vol. 8, p. 370.
8. I. S. Turgenev, *Polnoe sobranie sochinenii i pisem*, vol. 2, p. 144.

*gliadiat na nas svoimi nevinnymi glazami: ne ob odnom vechnom
spokoistvii govoriat nam oni, o tom velikom spokoistvii 'ravnodushnoi'
prirody; oni govoriat takzhe o vechnom primirenii i o zhizni beskon-
echnoi . . ."*[9]

The choice of the word *"primirenie"* strongly suggests a Hegelian
subtext, and the entire passages attempts to create harmony out of dis-
cord. Whether the attempt is successful is another question, but the very
fact of the narrative intentions here, i.e., to reconcile tragedy and comedy, grief and joy, sterility and fruitfulness, and all the other contradictions and polarities in the novel, argues for the notion of an all-embracing
dialectical framework within which Turgenev created his masterpiece,
Ottsy i deti.

The question remains of Turgenev's conscious debt to the dialectical
notions so dear to German idealism. Twentieth-century commentators
on Turgenev's life and writings generally agree that one cannot come
to a satisfactory understanding of the man and his works without taking
into account his philosophical interests.[1] Turgenev's background in German idealist philosophy, especially Hegelianism, is quite well docu-
mented and requires only the briefest summary. As an educated Russian
coming to maturity in the late 1830s and early 1840s, Turgenev was
virtually fated to pass through the crucible of Hegelianism. With few
exceptions—Mikhail Lermontov perhaps the most significant of them
—young Russians of Turgenev's generation and station lived and
breathed philosophy, meeting in unofficial student circles to apply German idealism to the "cursed questions" that have never ceased to occupy
the Russian intelligentsia. Turgenev became attached to the most famous
of the philosophical circles, Stankevich's, in 1840, just a few months
before its leader's death. At that time the thinker most responsible for
shaping Russian intellectual discourse was, of course, Hegel.[2]

Even for an age in which almost all self-respecting members of the
Russian intelligentsia drank deeply from the font of Hegelianism, Turgenev's interest in the German master represented an unusual degree of
intellectual commitment. As is well known, Turgenev spent the winter
of 1840–1841 in Berlin, where he shared quarters with a fellow Hegelian,

9. I. S. Turgenev, *Polnoe sobranie sochinenii i pisem*, vol. 8, p. 401.
1. The most outspoken statement of this position belongs to Eva Kagan-Kans, who in *Hamlet and Don Quixote: Turgenev's Ambivalent Vision* (The Hague, 1975), p. 7, asserts that a philosophical substructure is always present in Turgenev's works and that one must approach him as a philosophical writer in order best to appreciate his art.
2. For general background on the philosophical circles of the 1830s and 1840s, see Edward J. Brown, *Stankevich and His Moscow Circle, 1830–1840* (Stanford, 1966) and Martin Malia, *Alexander Herzen and the Birth of Russian Socialism, 1812–1855* (Cambridge, Mass., 1961). For information on Hegelianism in Russia see the preceding two items as well as Boris Jakowenko, *Untersuchungen zur Geschichte des Hegelianismus in Russland* (Prague, 1937); Dmitry Chizhevsky, *Gegel' v Rossii* (Paris, 1939); and the collection *Gegel' i filosofiia v Rossii: 30-e gody XIX v.–20-e gody XX v.* (Moscow, 1974). Jakowenko and Chizhevsky have chapters devoted specifically to the topic of Turgenev and Hegel.

Mikhail Bakunin, and attended lectures on Hegelian philosophy given by the latter's Berlin disciples and interpreters. One can find evidence of Turgenev's thorough study of Hegel's most important writings in the well-annotated copies of *Enzyklopädie der philosophischen Wissenschaften*, *Geschichte der Philosophie*, *Wissenschaft der Logik*, *Phänomenologie des Geistes*, and *Vorlesungen über die Philosophie des Geistes* contained in the writer's personal library.[3] Upon his return to Russia, Turgenev prepared for a career as a professor of philosophy, taking and passing the master's examination at St. Petersburg University in May 1842. At that point, only the writing of a master's dissertation stood between Turgenev and a career in academia. He soon found a purely literary career more appealing, however, and the rest, as they say, is history.

Existing scholarship additionally suggests, however, that Turgenev's youthful immersion in Hegelianism left hardly any traces in his *oeuvre*, where one nevertheless often encounters allusions to other philosophers or reflections of their teachings. Chizhevsky, who studied the question of Hegel's influence on Turgenev more thoroughly than any other scholar, isolates only a very few examples of Hegelian moments in Turgenev's writings. They include a review of Vronchenko's translation of *Faust* (1845), an article about Ostrovsky's play *Bednaia nevesta* (1851), the classic essay "Gamlet i Don-Kikhot," and two or three letters.[4] In essence, Chizhevsky argues that Hegelian philosophy contributed hardly anything to Turgenev's works. Batyuto, who has also devoted considerable attention to the examination of Turgenev's use of philosophy, sees even less evidence of Hegelianism in Turgenev's *oeuvre* than does Chizhevsky.[5]

The traditional explanation for the perceived lack of correspondence between Turgenev's formal education in Hegelian philosophy and his literary activity is that like many other men of the 1840s, Turgenev soon rejected German idealism. His turning away from his former passion finds affectionate but mocking reflection in *Rudin* and *Dvorianskoe gnezdo* and becomes the subject of bitter denunciation in *Gamlet shchigrovskogo uezda*. Moreover, Turgenev also attacked German idealism vigorously in private correspondence, where he proclaimed more than once his implacable hostility toward any and all systems.[6]

Turgenev hardly lost his interest in philosophers and philosophy, however. Modern scholarship has frequently noted Turgenev's debt to Schopenhauer, for instance. Schophenhauer's influence on Turgenev's thought dates from no later than 1855,[7] and scholars have singled out the great pessimist as the inspiration for at least certain aspects of *Poezdka*

3. See V. N. Gorbacheva, *Molodie gody Turgeneva* (Kazan', 1926), pp. 13–14.
4. Chizhevsky, *Gegel' v Rossii*, pp. 162–63.
5. A. Batyuto, *Turgenev-romanist* (Leningrad, 1972), pp. 43–47.
6. See, for instance, Batyuto, *Turgenev-romanist*, pp. 47–48.
7. See Batyuto, *Turgenev-romanist*, p. 116.

v Poles'e (1857),[8] *Prizraki* (1863), *Dovol'no* (1865), and *Senilia* (1882).[9]
Quite recently James Woodward offered a provocative reading of *Ottsy
i deti* as Turgenev's depiction of two contrasting aspects of Schopenhauer's "war of wills."[1] Other philosophers whose voices scholars have
detected in Turgenev's fourth novel include Marcus Aurelius and Blaise
Pascal.[2] As I have tried to show here, however, the Hegelian dialectic
has no less relevance for the novel.

   Although *Ottsy i deti* invites the application of the Hegelian dialectic,
and despite Turgenev's demonstrated acquaintance with Hegelian philosophy, the question of influence remains neither soluble nor vital.[3]
Insurmountable methodological hurdles often stand in the way of prov-
ing a philosopher's influence on a poet or novelist, and Hegel's debt to
Fichte and Schelling in the matter of the dialectic further exacerbates
the difficulties in the present instance.[4] None of these considerations
vitiates the case for a dialectical reading of Turgenev's finest novel,
however. The notion of polarities representing complementary aspects
of a higher or broader unity underlies all kinds of systems of thought,
whether one calls the various aspects of that integral vision two sides of
the same coin; the Father, Son, and Holy Ghost; yin and yang; or thesis,
antithesis, and synthesis. However one chooses to label the dialectical
thought at the heart of Turgenev's novel—Hegelian, Schellingian, or
simply *palka o dvukh kontsakh*, Turgenev's dialectical intentions show
themselves in the work's very title, which links the generations even as
it seems to set them apart. Recognizing the dialectical patterns embedded
in Turgenev's novel in a myriad of ways, both large and small, will help
eliminate the sorts of simplistic, one-sided interpretations that too often
mar discussion of *Ottsy i deti*, Turgenev's novelistic vision of a complex,
dialectical unity.

8. See A. Walicky, "Turgenev and Schopenhauer," *Oxford Slavonic Papers*, vol. 10 (1962), pp.
   2–3.
9. See, for instance, L. V. Pumpyansky, "Turgenev-novellist," in I. S. Turgenev, *Sochineniia*
   (Moscow-Leningrad, 1929), vol. 7, p. 11.
1. Woodward, "*Aut Caesar aut nihil*: the 'War of Wills,'" pp. 161–188.
2. See Batyuto, pp. 63–82 on Pascal, and pp. 102–112 on Marcus Aurelius.
3. At this point I am happy to acknowledge Yury Mann's contribution to the present paper. In
   response to an earlier redaction of it, read at the American-Soviet conference on Turgenev
   held in Moscow in June 1987, Mann voiced two important considerations: (1) the manifold
   dangers inherent in attempting to prove any specific philosopher's direct influence on any
   given writer and (2) Hegel's debt to earlier German philosophers in the matter of the dialectic,
   especially Schelling.
4. For more on the precedents for Hegel's dialectic, see Karl Dürr, "Die Entwicklung der Dialektik
   von Plato bis Hegel," *Dialectica*, vol. 1 (1947); Z. A. Kamensky, "O razvitii dialekticheskikh
   idei v russkoi filosofii nachala XIX veka," *Voprosy literatury*, 1964, no. 8; and Z. A. Kamensky,
   Russkaia filosofia nachala XIX veka i Shelling (Moscow, 1980).

MIKHAIL BAKHTIN

[On Characters' Language]†

* * *

The next form for incorporating and organizing heteroglossia in the
novel—a form that every novel without exception utilizes—is the language used by characters.

The language used by characters in the novel, how they speak, is
verbally and semantically autonomous; each character's speech possesses
its own belief system, since each is the speech of another in another's
language; thus it may also refract authorial intentions and consequently
may to a certain degree constitute a second language for the author.
Moreover, the character speech almost always influences authorial
speech (and sometimes powerfully so), sprinkling it with another's words
(that is, the speech of a character perceived as the concealed speech of
another) and in this way introducing into it stratification and speech
diversity.

Thus even where there is no comic element, no parody, no irony
and so forth, where there is no narrator, no posited author or narrating
character, speech diversity and language stratification still serve as the
basis for style in the novel. Even in those places where the author's voice
seems at first glance to be unitary and consistent, direct and unmediatedly
intentional, beneath that smooth single-languaged surface we can nevertheless uncover prose's three-dimensionality, its profound speech diversity, which enters the project of style and is its determining factor.

Thus the language and style of Turgenev's novels have the appearance
of being single-languaged and pure. Even in Turgenev, however, this
unitary language is very far from poetic absolutism. Substantial masses
of this language are drawn into the battle between points of view, value
judgments and emphases that the characters introduce into it; they are
infected by mutually contradictory intentions and stratifications; words,
sayings, expressions, definitions and epithets are scattered throughout
it, infected with others' intentions with which the author is to some
extent at odds, and through which his own personal intentions are
refracted. We sense acutely the various distances between the author
and various aspects of his language, which smack of the social universes
and belief systems of others. We acutely sense in various aspects of his
language varying degrees of the presence of the author and of his *most
recent semantic instantiation.* In Turgenev, heteroglossia and language
stratification serve as the most fundamental factors of style, and or-

† From *The Dialogic Imagination: Four Essays* by M. M. Bakhtin, edited by Michael Holquist,
translated by Michael Holquist and Caryl Emerson. Copyright © 1981. By permission of the
University of Texas Press.

chestrate an authorial truth of their own; the author's linguistic consciousness, his consciousness as a writer of prose, is thereby relativized.

In Turgenev, social heteroglossia enters the novel primarily in the
direct speeches of his characters, in dialogues. But this heteroglossia, as
we have said, is also diffused throughout the authorial speech that surrounds the characters, creating highly particularized *character zones*
[*zony geroev*]. These zones are formed from the fragments of character
speech [*polureč*], from various forms for hidden transmission of someone
else's word, from scattered words and sayings belonging to someone
else's speech, from those invasions into authorial speech of others' expressive indicators (ellipsis, questions, exclamations). Such a character
zone is the field of action for a character's voice, encroaching in one
way or another upon the author's voice.

However—we repeat—in Turgenev, the novelistic orchestration of
the theme is concentrated in direct dialogues; the characters do not
create around themselves their own extensive or densely saturated zones,
and in Turgenev fully developed, complex stylistic hybrids are relatively
rare.

We pause here on several examples of diffuse heteroglossia in
Turgenev.[1]

> (1) His name is Nikolai Petrovich Kirsanov. Some ten miles from
> the coaching-inn stands a respectable little property of his con-
> sisting of a couple of hundred serfs—or five thousand acres, as
> he expresses it now that he has divided up his land and let
> it to the peasants, and started a "farm." [*Fathers and Sons*,
> ch. 1]

Here the new expressions, characteristic of the era and in the style of
the liberals, are put in quotation marks or otherwise "qualified."

> (2) He was secretly beginning to feel irritated. Bazarov's complete
> indifference exasperated his aristocratic nature. *This son of a
> medico was not only self-assured: he actually returned abrupt
> and reluctant answers, and there was a churlish, almost insolent
> note in his voice.* [*Fathers and Sons*, ch. 4]

The third sentence of this paragraph, while being a part of the author's
speech if judged by its formal syntactic markers, is at the same time in
its choice of expressions ("this son of a medico") and in its emotional
and expressive structure the hidden speech of someone else (Pavel
Petrovich).

> (3) Pavel Petrovich sat down at the table. He was wearing an elegant
> suit cut in the English fashion, and a gay little fez graced his
> head. The fez and the carelessly knotted cravat carried a sug-

1. Citations from *Fathers and Sons* are from: Ivan Turgenev, *Fathers and Sons*, tr. Rosemary
Edmonds (London: Penguin, 1965).

gestion of the more free life in the country but the stiff collar
of his shirt—not white, it is true, but striped *as is correct for
morning wear*—stood up as inexorably as ever against his well-
shaven chin. [*Fathers and Sons*, ch. 5]

This ironic characterization of Pavel Petrovich's morning attire is
consistent with the tone of a gentleman, precisely in the style of Pavel
Petrovich. The statement "as is correct for morning wear" is not, of
course, a simple authorial statement, but rather the norm of Pavel
Petrovich's gentlemanly circle, conveyed ironically. One might with
some justice put it in quotation marks. This is an example of a pseudo-
objective underpinning.

(4) *Matvei Ilyich's suavity of demeanour was equalled only by his
stately manner.* He had a gracious word for everyone—with an
added shade of disgust in some cases and deference in others;
he was gallant, "un vrai chevalier français," to all the ladies,
and was continually bursting into hearty resounding laughter,
in which no one else took part, as befits a high official. [*Fathers
and Sons*, ch. 14]

Here we have an analogous case of an ironic characterization given
from the point of view of the high official himself. Such is the nature
of this form of pseudo-objective underpinning: "as befits a high official."

* * *

MICHAEL HOLQUIST

Bazarov and Sečenov: The Role of
Scientific Metaphor in *Fathers and Sons*†

Valentin Kataev tells a marvelous story of how the great Mejerchol'd
once developed a plan for putting *Fathers and Sons* on the screen: "The
film was to have begun with a diagram of the human chest—white ribs
and, behind them, as if behind dungeon bars, a human heart, beating
at first steadily and rhythmically as the law of blood circulation demands,
then fluttering and leaping until it stops in a last convulsion . . . Bazarov
draws a charcoal circle on his chest around the place where his heart
beats. With horror he notices that it is love, passion, desire that makes
his heart contract. . . ."[1]
Mejerchol'd's interpretation of the novel refuses to take Bazarov's

† From *Russian Literature* XVI, no. 4 (1984) 359–74. Reprinted by permission of Elsevier
Science Publishers.
1. Valentin Kataev, *Trava zabven'ja* (Moskva 1967), 170.

Nihilism seriously: "Bazarov a Nihilist? Nonsense [*vzdor*]!"[2] He sees
Bazarov not as an ideologue but as a poet; and he even planned to have
Bazarov's role in the film played by Majakovskij himself. The film was
never made, which is unfortunate because it might have helped to clear
up a certain ambivalence that has grown up around Turgenev's reputation. I believe Mejerchol'd was absolutely right in perceiving that
Bazarov is more poet than scientist, a position I wish to extend in this
paper, in the hope that it not only will provide yet another interpretation
of *Fathers and Sons*, but will in some small measure add to the growing
body of work that seeks to offset the currently reigning clichés about
Turgenev's status as a writer in the distinctively Russian literary tradition.

As Isaiah Berlin made clear in his 1970 Romanes lecture, Turgenev's
"artistic reputation is not in question; it is as a social thinker that he is
still today the subject of a continuing dispute."[3] The most serious charge
against Turgenev of this kind would seem to have been made by D. S.
Mirsky: "There had always been in Turgenev a poetic or romantic vein
. . . his attitude to nature had always been *lyrical* . . . even in his most
realistic and civic novels the construction and atmosphere are mainly
lyrical."[4] What this vision of Turgenev's achievement results in is the
ineluctable conclusion that ". . . In his day Turgenev was regarded as
a leader of opinion on social problems. *Now* this seems strange and
unintelligible. Long since the issues that he fought out have ceased to
be of any actual interest." And then comes the inevitable and invidious
comparison: "Unlike Tolstoy or Dostoevsky," or virtually any other important figure of nineteenth century Russian literary culture—"Turgenev
is no longer a teacher . . . his work has become pure art. . . ."[5]

Not only is Turgenev not a novelist, he is more precisely not a *Russian*
novelist. I take this to mean that he is unlike Tolstoj or Dostoevskij
insofar as he is not a *thinker*: he is precisely what the most characteristic
strand of Russian criticism would have most vigorously objected to, i.e.,
someone who is *only* an artist, someone who provides merely aesthetic
pleasure. And insofar as this is true of Turgenev, he will be perceived
as not doing the work of Russian literature as defined by the great
Belinskij, whose views continue to shape ideas about the extra-aesthetic
importance of the artist.

The irony of such a view will become apparent if we remember facts
so familiar that their importance is often overlooked. Not only is *Fathers
and Sons* dedicated to Turgenev's old friend Belinskij, the still-invoked
conscience of the Russian intelligentsia, but it was as well a central
document in the intellectual—not *only* the artistic or political—life of
Russia during one of its most formative periods.

2. *Loc. cit.*
3. Cited by V. S. Pritchett, "Turgenev," *The New Yorker* (August 8, 1983), 90.
4. D. S. Mirsky, "Turgenev," Critical Edition of *Fathers and Sons*, ed. Ralph Matlaw (New
   York 1966), 249.
5. *Op. cit.* 250–251.

The conception of Turgenev as exclusively an artist of a particularly refined sort is usually combined with an indictment of him as a failed man of action. The implication of such a view is that the only area other than literature itself for such a lyricist to demonstrate his seriousness was politics, an area in which Turgenev clearly did not excel. Mirsky in a rather curious echo of Vulgar Sociologism, sums up this view by suggesting that in political importance, Turgenev was "representative of his class . . . and of his generation, which failed to gain real touch with Russian realities . . . and which, ineffective in the sphere of action, produced one of the most beautiful literary growths of the nineteenth century."[6] Finding in Turgenev "merely" beauty, it is inevitable that Mirsky concludes by saying, "We do not seek wisdom [in Turgenev]."[7] Turgenev, in other words, is the literary equivalent of the proverbial dumb blonde.

To dispute the Mirskian view of Turgenev as an ineffectual aesthete would require a principled study of the kind only a thoroughly trained Turgenev scholar might carry out. I am not in the position to make such a study. Nevertheless, I would like at least to hint at a relation between Turgenev and *one* of the major intellectual currents of the modern period, the mind/body duality that has haunted us since at least Descartes. My purpose will be to suggest the further point that Turgenev may be perceived not only as an artist, but *in* his artistry, as a certain kind of *thinker*. A thinker not so much about politics as such, but about the politics competing discourses represent as they express competing social currents in the history of the Russian language. In what follows, then, I will try very quickly to sketch two arguments: Turgenev *is* similar to other novelists and in particular to those Russian novelists from whose company Mirsky would exclude him, in that he uses the medium of the novel to think through important extra-literary problems. One reason we so often fail to see the intellectual, analytical side of Turgenev is because it is assumed the only scope for such activity was the immediate political situation of nineteenth century Russia. But there were other and arguably much more historically important trends of thought—and action—abroad in the same period, and it is in at least one of these, in at least one of his works (*Fathers and Sons*) that Turgenev's importance both as a thinker and as a figure whose work had consequences in real life should rather be sought.

The particular debate in which Turgenev played such a role is the one concerning the relation between the science of physiology, on the one hand, idealistic concepts of personhood and individuality, on the other. This is a problem that occupies some of the best minds—both scientific and literary—throughout the late eighteenth and all of the nineteenth century, indeed up to the present time. My argument

6. *Loc. cit.*
7. *Loc. cit.*

may be stated in a number of theses, which I will first list, and then go on to specify.

1) Turgenev occupies a distinctive place in the history of nineteenth century European literature insofar as certain of his works (particularly *Fathers and Sons*) mark a crucial stage in the movement toward a new perception of nature (and therefore of the place of man in nature) that begins to manifest itself in the middle decades of the nineteenth century, a movement charted in literary history between the poles conventionally called Romanticism, and, at the other extreme, Naturalism.

2) His place in that movement, in order to be appreciated, must be calibrated not only within the closed system of literary history, but rather as a border incident between literary and extra-literary discourses (particularly those of the body sciences).

3) The extra-aesthetic language which is most helpfully invoked if we are seeking Turgenev's unique place in the history of the novel is, then, *scientific*, not, as is so often assumed, political; and more specifically it is the language of a physiologically grounded *psychology* that was in the process of formation during the early and middle years of the nineteenth century.

4) The specific way Bazarov and his famous frogs are used in *Fathers and Sons* is as a means for testing what was this new scientific psychology's major claim, i.e. that thinking is an illusion based on an erroneous division between mind and body. This view held that all aspects of human existence previously ascribed to the individual person's intentions, to his unique soul or psyche, were merely extra-individual manifestations of physiological processes in the human organism. As Bazarov tells the little peasant boys in Chapter V, when they ask him why he is catching frogs: "I shall cut the frog open and see what's going on in his inside, and then, as you and I are much as frogs (only we walk on two legs), I shall know what's going on inside us too."

5) *Fathers and Sons*, then, is a kind of literary laboratory for testing certain nineteenth century claims of science. But since Turgenev is a much subtler thinker than, let us say, Zola, Turgenev's version of the *roman expérimental* is not a laboratory modelled on those in the Rue Gay-Lussac, with their electrical generators and Bunsen burners, but rather a *language* laboratory. What we get is not a naive application of methods in physiology, nor do we get an equally naive attempt to "attack" such methods. No, Turgenev sees that at the heart of the new somatic definition of man lurks a theory of language—an attempt to get out of words and to the *things themselves*. What he does is to translate the latent content of scientism into a set of discursive practices which he then tests against other forms of discourse in his novel.

6) Finally, Turgenev may indeed have been ineffectual in the realm of politics. But in the realm of science he was to have at least one important actual consequence: By raising certain questions about Ba-

zarov's physiological theories *in* his novel, *outside* the novel he caused Bazarov's double, the great physiologist Ivan Sečenov (1829–1905) to ask certain questions whose answers were to have a powerful and lasting effect on later concepts of the somatic structure of the brain and the way that structure relates to human psychology. Although Sečenov is precisely Bazarov's contemporary, then, I shall be arguing that if we were to apply Turgenev's own symbolic genealogy, it could be said that Sečenov is son to Bazarov's father.

But before we can see the relation between Turgenev and Sečenov —and the implications of such a relationship for ány attempt to assess Turgenev's role as novelist—we must deal with a few preliminary considerations.

At a merely anecdotal level, nothing could be simpler than to define relations between Sečenov and Turgenev: each respected the other; both at one time or another belonged to the circle around the journal *Sovremennik*; both spent great stretches of time in Germany and France absorbing the very latest ideas across a broad spectrum of interests, and both shared an almost British liberalism that made their politics appear slightly unreal or wildly eccentric to their more millenarian fellow Slavs. The connection between the two appears even more ineluctable to anyone who has seen the famous photo of Sečenov, taken in 1861, the year Turgenev completes *Fathers and Sons*: we see a fierce-eyed, hirsute young man sitting at his work table in the Medico-Surgical Academy, complete with Bunsen burner, electrical charging mechanism and a laboratory clamp from which are suspended—of course—three frogs. It is less the portrait of an individual man than it is the icon of an era, one of those rare instances that let us actually *see* the otherwise invisible historical forces shaping whole eras.[8]

But if we reach for the deeper meaning Sečenov and Turgenev had for each other, we shall have to go beyond their merely personal associations and look (very briefly) into the way each responded to the new challenges raised by Nineteenth Century science to traditional assumptions about man's place in nature. It is the cognitive revolution that took place between a time when nature was felt to reflect *man*, and a later time in which man was conceived as little more than a reflection of *nature* that makes the local relationship of Turgenev and Sečenov of particular interest.

Of all the pejoratives Bazarov uses, none in his eyes is more damning than "romantic." He means by this not merely that Romantics are old-fashioned because they prize the past: as a naturalist, he seeks as well to invoke by this term the particular romantic sense of *nature* that dominated Europe in the late eighteenth, early nineteenth century.

* * *

8. See: *Classics in Psychology: Biographical Sketch and Other Essays*, no. tr. (New York 1973), 19.

In March of 1860, at the very time Turgenev was at work on *Fathers and Sons*, Sečenov began a series of lectures at the St. Petersburg Medico-Surgical Academy. These lectures produced a sensation among not only the students, but all Petersburg. As the historian M. N. Šaternikov puts it: "Both the form and the contents of Sečenov's lectures produced an immense impression, not only on the academic world, but also on intellectual society in general. [His] manner of speaking was simple and convincing; his method of exposition was absolutely new. With youthful enthusiasm and deep faith in the all-conquering power of Science and Reason . . . he spoke not only of what had already been achieved, also of what was yet to be done . . . [he produced a large number of students and] we may confidently assert that Sečenov is the initiator of the Russian school of physiologists."[9] (I should add that Sečenov's work continues to be ranked very high, even in the West: in Boring's definitive *History of Experimental Psychology* it is said that Sečenov was "far ahead of West European thought," and the eminent cyberneticist Walter Rosenblith has called Sečenov "a too little appreciated forebear of Norbert Wiener.")[1]

But the aspect of Sečenov's achievement I wish to stress has less to do with his specific work on the brain. What I wish to emphasize, rather, is what Šaternikov has in mind when he says "The remarkable demonstration with which [Sečenov] illustrated his lectures acquainted students with the most recent techniques of scientific experiment and *taught them to use the language of facts*."[2] It is not Sečenov as a kind of *Urfigur* for Bazarov, but rather Sečenov's "language of facts" that is significant for understanding Turgenev's novelistic practice. It is Scientism as a *language*, as a discursive practice claiming a unique relation to truth that Turgenev will test in his fiction.

In order to proceed with this argument, we shall want to keep two prior assumptions in mind. First, that an interplay between science and literature is possible because both are, in the end, exercises in language. Secondly, that the novel is preeminently the literary genre whose constitutive feature is an artistically organized diversity of social speech types, particularly *Fathers and Sons* in which the major thematic and structural emphasis is on the ideology of Scientism as it is expressed in the speech practice of the Nihilists.

Turning to the text of *Fathers and Sons*, we will notice first of all the most *obvious* level at which Turgenev contrasts different languages. These would include the large number of what might be called *phatic* scenes: those encounters in which characters explain to other characters the peculiar meanings of their different idiolects. In Chapter XV we are aware of the growing differences between Arkadij and Bazarov when the

9. M. N. Šaternikov, "The Life of I. M. Sečenov," in *Classics in Psychology*, xvii.
1. Cf. Loren Graham, *Science and Philosophy in the Soviet Union* (New York 1972), 356.
2. Šaternikov, *op. cit.* xvii.

latter reproaches the former for interpreting literally his statement about Odincova's situation to the effect that "something is wrong here." Bazarov must explain to his young friend that "something wrong" (*ne ladno*) means "something *right* in my dialect and for me. . . ."[3] In the following chapter, Bazarov, impressed by the haughty demeanor of Odincova's butler, says to Arkadij, "What *grand genre*! . . . That's what it's called in your set (*u vas*), isn't it—."[4] When Odincova invites Bazarov for a walk she says "I want you to teach me the Latin names of the wildflowers." And Bazarov seeks to mark off the difference between them by insisting on the fact they speak different languages: "What use are the Latin names to you?"[5] he asks with his usual rudeness.

* * *

We could go on with this demonstration that self-conscious speech patterns that mark off distinct ideological positions are important building blocks in Turgenev's novel, with the corollary that when differences in *language* are dramatized, it is to dramatize *ideological* differences.

* * *

He [Bazarov] is convinced his own truth is timeless because it is extralinguistic, scientific. What scientific means in his value system can be gathered from its opposite, the set of conventions and beliefs Bazarov castigates as Romantic: Romantic means Puškin, it means literature, it means metaphors. It means, in other words, inaccurate or deceptive *language*. Poetry can become outmoded because it is in a language that is false. Bazarov holds that science is a system that is true to the extent it is free from the confusions of language. It is he, the polar opposite of the underground man, who holds up the extralinguistic proposition that $2 \times 2 = 4$ as the ultimate argument for the truth of science.

What he fails to perceive, of course—what the whole *movement* of scientism failed to perceive—was that the extension of purely intrinsic scientific laws to *extrinsic* considerations such as ethics or politics—*was itself a metaphoric move*. It was an attempt to organize *social* life by *scientific* principles, i.e. to translate one system of signs into another: same but different, the classical definition of metaphor. In translating the laws of science into ideological practice, Scientism gives up the extrahistorical claim to truth attaching to mathematical signs. Their extra-scientific claims for science become subject to all the confusions and historicity of natural languages, the limitations of which for anyone seeking to express extrahistorical, ultimate truths are all too obvious.

3. *Otcy i deti; Sobranie sočinenij v 10-i tomach* (Moskva 1961), t.3, 178.
4. *Op. cit.* 182.
5. *Op. cit.* 186.

Bazarov, like the underground man, is sick, and Turgenev is extremely acute in diagnosing Bazarov's disease: he is suffering from an illness that is the opposite of Dostoevskij's anti-hero, who suffered from an excess of "consciousness"; Bazarov, on the contrary, suffers from an *un*consciousness of the metaphoric nature of language. Speaking of his blindness as a disease is a metaphor, but so is Bazarov's sickness in the novel: the great proponent of the concept that men are no more than the sum of the cells and chemicals of their physical bodies is himself brought down by an illness contracted from his dissection of a corpse, i.e. a body that is *indeed* no more than its physical makeup. But the truth—the non-scientific truth—which this metaphor points to, is that Bazarov's disease is blindness to the metaphoric heart of his scientific ideology.

One way this is made apparent in the novel is in Bazarov's use of scientific metaphors. As the science he feels to be most scientific is physiology, it is not surprising that body imagery dominates his rhetoric. For instance, Arkadij—in defending his uncle—tells the story of Pavel Petrovič's hopeless romance for Princess R—: Bazarov answers with an uncharacteristically long speech:

> And what about all these mysterious relations between a man and a woman? We physiologists know what these relations are. Study the anatomy of the eye a bit, where does the enigmatical glance you talk about come in there. That's all romanticism, nonsense, rot, and artsy nonsense [*chudožestvo*]. Much better if we go and look at a beetle.[6]

What he's saying, of course, is that physiological mechanisms are *true*, but they may become layered over with false metaphors, especially the kind to which lovers are notoriously drawn. There is a truth of the physical on the one hand, and the fiction of a self that is more than sum of its cellular activities, on the other.

The interesting thing, of course, is that Bazarov's example of a bodily organ is precisely the one that constitutes the novel's most obsessively recurring metaphor: everyone in the book is characterized by the quality of his eyes. The only place where there seems to be a one-to-one fit between appearance and reality is in eye metaphors. The bailiff at Mar'ino is a cheat so his eyes are of course "knavish" [*plutovskie*].[7] When Katja is confused by Arkadij's blurted declaration of his love, her eyes accurately reflect that confusion: "her dark eyes had a look of perplexity."[8] The constantly flustered and anxious-to-please Sitnikov's eyes are "small and seemed squeezed in a fixed and uneasy look."[9] Eyes, as a Romantic would say, are the windows of the soul, external physical

6. *Op. cit.* 147.
7. *Loc. cit.*
8. *Op. cit.* 250.
9. *Op. cit.* 169.

signs accurately reflecting internal psychological truths. What Turgenev is doing here (as he does in his treatment of other parts of the anatomy, such as Kukšina's nose, Katja's feet, or Odincova's shoulders) is using the human body as lyrical poets had earlier used *landscape*. It is a selfconscious and highly sophisticated variant of the somatic sympathetic fallacy: instead of merely the landscape of nature reflecting inner psychological states (spring/young love), the whole body becomes such a metaphor (a lesson that will not be lost on Tolstoj).

The greatest twist on this metaphoric use of metaphor is Bazarov's own use of metaphor: as he lies dying, he metamorphoses into a romantic of the kind his Scientism previously had caused him to scorn. He spouts nothing but metaphors: a naturalist might explain away his reference to himself as a worm "half crushed but writhing still" as a last attempt on Bazarov's part to deny the difference between animals and humans. But only a poet would exploit light imagery as Bazarov does in his final speech: He says to Odincova, "be good to my parents, you'll not find any like them in your world even if you look by daylight with a candle. . . ." Turgenev as author quite wickedly conflates his own imagery in his authorial voice with Bazarov's imagery: Turgenev as author says Bazarov's eyes "gleamed with their last light," but has Bazarov say in his own voice, "Goodbye . . . breathe on the dying lamp and let it go out . . . Enough . . . Now, Darkness."[1] It is a poet's death: Mejerchol'd was quite right to want Majakovskij to play the role in his projected film of the novel.

Bazarov reverses in his biography the direction taken by the movement from Romanticism to Naturalism: he is a naturalist who metamorphoses into a romantic poet.

Does Turgenev's treatment of Bazarov mean that Turgenev is so completely "lyrical" that everything he touches turns into a kind of poetry (which seems to be what Mirsky is saying)? I have tried to argue that Bazarov's transformation is rather the result of an *analytical* process: it is the gradual revelation of the inescapability of metaphor, even in science, a fatedness the implications of which dominate current philosophy of science.

Finally, I wish to dispute the claim Turgenev had no extraliterary effects; not only did he force the fictional physiologist Bazarov to rethink language, but he forced the actual physiologist Sečenov, to do so as well. *Fathers and Sons* created in Bazarov not only a general iconic image of the Nihilist that immediately passed into use, he created as well an image of the extrascientific implications of physiology.

And it was this image of the physiologist as destroyer of human morality that was superimposed on Sečenov when, in the year following publication of *Fathers and Sons*, he sought to publish his "Reflexes of

1. *Op. cit.* 271.

the Brain" in *The Contemporary* and was refused by the censor (who did clear it for an obscure professional journal called *Medicinskij vestnik*). Persecution from the government reached a climax in 1866 when the book version appeared. Its sale was forbidden by the censor, and the High Court of St. Petersburg began an action against Sečenov in which he was charged with attacking the "natural order of things." *"Reflexes,"* it was said, "is directed to the corruption of morals: it is indictable as dangerous reading for people without established convictions and as such must be confiscated and destroyed under Article 1001 of the Penal Code."[2]

The book finally was allowed to appear, but the hullabaloo created around it utterly confounded the author, who merely had sought to say something about a topic in physiology. In his autobiography he writes "I was accused of proposing a Nihilist philosophy [he writes in obvious bewilderment] . . . Unfortunately the censorship rules of the time prevented me [from defending myself against such a charge] . . . such an explanation would have at once put an end to such misinterpretations. . . ."[3]

What had happened, of course, is that Sečenov was perceived in the light of Bazarov. Far from actually being a Nihilist, he was nevertheless accused of being one under the impact of surface similarities he bore to Turgenev's fictional hero. What we get is a reverse of the process by which a living figure becomes the basis of a fictional character. Turgenev may have indeed modelled Bazarov on a young provincial doctor, as he maintained in 1868.[4] But the ultimate irony is that Sečenov was in fact modelled on Bazarov.

DONALD FANGER

The Influence of Dostoevsky and Chekhov on Turgenev's *Fathers and Sons*†

I

The title of this paper as originally announced ("The Influence of Chekhov on Turgenev") expanded in the process of writing, but the theme remains the same: to consider afresh (if cursorily) the poetics of *Fathers and Sons* in historical context—with emphasis on the fact that the

2. Šaternikov, *op. cit.* 23.
3. *Op. cit.* 25.
4. "Apropos of *Fathers and Sons*," Critical Ed., *op. cit.* 169.
† From the Kennan Institute's Occasional Paper #234. Reprinted by permission of the author and The Woodrow Wilson Center.

historical context is not something fixed once and for all but, on the contrary, constantly changing.

The novel appeared exactly a century and a quarter ago, and it was appropriate that its contemporary readers should have taken as central what was most topical in it: nihilism (defined in Dahl's dictionary as "a monstrous and immoral teaching that rejects everything that cannot be palpated"), together with the revolutionary temperament of Bazarov. Even today these aspects of Turgenev's book are unquestionably useful and valuable for anyone who is concerned with the social history of Russia. For anyone concerned with the development of fiction in Russia, however, a contemporary understanding of *Fathers and Sons* requires seeing it in other, comparative contexts. For "the contemporary reader" is not only Pisarev, Herzen, Chernyshevsky, Annenkov, Strakhov, and company; in view of the ambiguity at the heart of the adjective, "the contemporary reader" may be with equal justice construed as the reader of the late twentieth century, Russian and non-Russian alike. It is precisely the latter reader that I have in view. In what way does he (or she) differ from that other contemporary reader? Principally, I will argue, in *the theoretical assumptions* he (or she) brings to the reading of the novel. I will confine myself to three examples, under the headings of "idea," "realism," and "tradition."

Idea

The now-familiar thesis, first elaborated by Chernyshevsky (in his *Sketches of the Gogol Period in Russian Literature*), that literature played a special role in nineteenth-century Russia by comparison with its role in the other countries of Europe turned quickly, in the minds of the intelligentsia, into a conviction that literature was important to the extent that it contained ideas of a sort that could not be discussed in print in any other form. Here the concept of "an idea" was simply transferred, unchanged, from the sphere of life to the sphere of art—and the transfer involved a relative neglect not only of the presence of art in a given work, but of the radical difference between "idea" inside and outside a work of art.

The difference in question was most succinctly formulated by Kant in the previous century when he defined "an aesthetic idea" as one that could only be grasped intuitively, in contradistinction to "a rational idea," to which no intuition could ever be adequate. In our time, this distinction was developed by Lionel Trilling in his article, "The Meaning of a Literary Idea" (1950). There Trilling insists on the special nature of literary ideas. It is not adequate, he insists, to think of ideas only as being "highly formulated"; they need not be "pellets of intellection or crystallizations of thought, precise and completed." Quite the contrary:

"*Whenever we put two emotions into juxtaposition we have what can properly be called an idea*" [my italics—D. F.]. Moreover, "the very form of a literary work, considered apart from its content, so far as that is possible, is itself an idea"![1] It is evident that such a viewpoint presupposes the possibility of many "correct" interpretations of any genuinely artistic text—for, as Frank Kermode has written recently, any such text may be considered as "a system of signifiers which always shows a surplus after meeting any particular restricted reading."[2]

From this it follows that neither the author's own interpretation nor his announced intentions are necessarily to be taken as authoritative— a point we find made by Turgenev himself in connection with *Fathers and Sons*. "I am not surprised," he writes Saltykov, "that Bazarov has remained a puzzle for many people; *I myself cannot clearly account for the way I created him*. There was some sort—don't laugh—of fate involved, something stronger than the author himself, something in- dependent of him. . . . I wrote naively, as if marveling myself at what was coming out."[3] And in a letter to Annenkov Turgenev generalizes the point, suggesting that "no author knows very well what he is doing."[4]

From this it follows that if an author doesn't know with any certainty what he is doing, it is quite possible that he may not know better than others *what he has done*. Thus Herzen had every right to claim that "Turgenev was more of an artist than people think in his novel, and so lost his way—happily, from my point of view: he was heading for one room but wound up in another and better one."[5] By the same token, over the century that separates us from Herzen, it has become quite legitimate to consider still other rooms as the best; i.e., to disagree not only with Herzen's analysis of the novel, but with the assumptions that underlie it. It may well be the case that Turgenev's artistic instincts led him not to confuse the rooms, but to construct a new house, on a new and separate model.

The form of the novel is its idea. Being an aesthetic idea, it embodies an intuition that could not adequately (i.e., fully) be expressed in "ra- tional" (i.e., critical) terms; that idea, of course, contains a series of "rational" ideas, but it uses them to its own ends and thereby relativizes them.

"Realism"

Thanks in part to the function of Russian literature in the nineteenth century as pointed out by Chernyshevsky, and in part to the spirit of

1. Lionel Trilling, "The Meaning of a Literary Idea," in his *The Liberal Imagination: Essays on Literature and Society* (New York, 1950), pp. 302, 296, 303.
2. Frank Kermode, *The Classic: Literary Images of Permanence and Change* (Cambridge, Mass., 1983), p. 135.
3. Letter of 3 January 1876, in *Pis'ma* 11, p. 190–91 (my italics).
4. Letter of 20 December 1869, *Pis'ma* 8, p. 147.
5. A. I. Gertsen, "Eshche raz Bazarov," *Sobranie sochinenii*, 20, p. 339.

the age, the poetics common to the novels of the time came to be called realism, and it became customary to judge novels in terms of the relative accuracy and the relative fullness of their "reflection" of social and psychological phenomena that were observable outside literature and testable in life. The consequence was that in writing about literature oftener than not "the object of analysis was not the artistic work itself, but rather whatever it was that the analyst found it 'reflecting'."[6] Only in time did other, more flexible approaches to the notion of "realism" become possible. Thus, V. V. Vinogradov found a whole multitude of realisms in the Russian nineteenth century:

> Our great writers did not hold to any single and exclusive system of realistic depiction. Turgenev wrote L. N. Tolstoi (in a letter of 3/15 January 1857): "Systems are valued only by those who can't get a grip on the whole truth and try to grab it by the tail; a system is like the tail of the truth, but the truth is like a lizard; it leaves the tail in your hand and escapes, knowing that it will soon grow another."
> Realism as a method of the artistic depiction of reality in the history of Russian nineteenth-century literature not only develops but stratifies. While preserving certain of the internal bases for the embodiment and representation of real life in verbal art, it at the same time gives rise to a whole series of literary-artistic systems in Russian nineteenth-century literature, not infrequently opposed to each other in particular, very important structural elements. . . . It goes without saying that to label all these systems or forms of realism "critical realism" is too general and calls for concrete historical differentiation. The study of the mutual interaction, struggle and succession of forms and types of realism, together with their interrelations with other methods and systems of artistic representation in the history of Russian literature in the nineteenth and the first half of the twentieth centuries is one of the central problems of the history of the Russian literary art. . . .[7]

Even if one were to speak of realism as the single, fundamental method of the classical novel, one might do that basing one's construction of the term on other considerations; e.g., on the position and viewpoint of the reader. Such an approach is taken by the American Hispanist Stephen Gilman when he writes:

> The novel may be defined as the kind of literature which presents a fictional world not necessarily resembling our own, but in a

6. B. M. Eikhenbaum, *Molodoi Tolstoi*, (Wilhelm Fink Verlag, München [reprint], 1968), p. 8.
7. V. V. Vinogradov, *O iazyke khudozhestvennoi literatury* (Moscow, 1959), pp. 506–07.

fashion resembling the way we experience our own—thus its natural realism less of mirrored content than of unfolding process.[8]

Like the reconstruing of the concept of "idea" in the novel, such a reconstruing of the concept of "realism" can lead to a new understanding of Turgenev's novel, one that would take it out of the literary museum for fresh inspection—in order to re-situate it there, perhaps in a new room, under different illumination.

Tradition

A reviewing of the notion of tradition may serve the same end; it is precisely with this point that the title of my paper is connected.

The present-day reader differs from Turgenev's contemporary reader principally in the fact that his awareness includes a whole series of writers who came after Turgenev (not to mention critics and theoreticians), with the result that the framing of any Turgenev text is inevitably different today. The best discussion of this phenomenon is T. S. Eliot's, in his 1917 article, "Tradition and the Individual Talent":

> No poet, no artist of any art, has his complete meaning alone. His significance, his appreciation is the appreciation of his relation to the dead poets and artists. You cannot value him alone; you must set him, for contrast and comparison, among the dead. *I mean this as a principle of aesthetic, not merely historical, criticism.* The necessity that he shall conform, that he shall cohere, is not one sided; *what happens when a new work of art is created is something that happens simultaneously to all the works of art which preceded it.* The existing monuments form an ideal order among themselves, which is modified by the introduction of the new (the really new) work of art among them. The existing order is complete before the new work arrives; for order to persist after the supervention of novelty, the whole existing order must be, if ever so slightly, altered; and so the relations, proportions, values of each work of art toward the whole are readjusted; and this is conformity between the old and the new. Whoever has approved this idea of order, of the form of . . . European literature *will not find it preposterous that the past should be altered by the present as much as the present is directed by the past.*[9]

8. Stephen Gilman, "The Novelist and His Readers: Meditations on a Stendhalian Metaphor," in Charles S. Singleton, ed., *Interpretation: Theory and Practice* (Baltimore, 1969), pp. 157, 160.
9. T. S. Eliot, "Tradition and the Individual Talent," in his *Selected Essays, 1917–1932* (New York, 1932), pp. 4–5 (my italics).

II

What is common to the points of view sketched above is an orientation toward poetics which in its turn allows us to approach two specific aspects of Turgenev's poetics of the novel—the first through the example of the "aesthetic idea" of *Fathers and Sons*, the second through a juxtaposition with the poetics of Dostoevsky and Chekhov.

The idea (i.e., the form) of *Fathers and Sons* is biographical. V. S. Pritchett is on record as having declared of Turgenev that "he writes [I would amend this to read "constructs"—D.F.] novels as if he were not a story-teller but a biographer."[1] Moreover, Turgenev's preference (as S. E. Shatalov points out) was for "depicting characters that were already formed. . . . One can consider as a distinctive sign of his artistic world the writer's tendency to tell how fully formed characters enter into relations with each other, and to show how their characters determine these relations and at the same time reveal the essence of themselves."[2]

Here Bazarov must appear as an exception, being the only character who manifests dynamism, and the only one who is not provided with the usual dossier. As Yurii Mann observed twenty-one years ago in an unusually interesting article in *Novy Mir*:

> In reflections on Bazarov two questions arise with increasing insistence. What has he done in the past beyond studying in medical school? And what does he intend to do tomorrow beyond completing his training as a doctor and working in the area of medicine? . . . The context in which we see him explains Bazarov's reserve, but not the reserve with which his image is presented. . . . Bazarov is the rare example of a Turgenev character who lacks not only a pre-history, but to whom the writer never applies introspection (i.e., an authorial explanation and testing of his subjective world) at those points where Bazarov's position—his past and future—is in question (yet such introspection is applied to his experience of love!).[3]

We see Bazarov only in the last weeks of his life, and this is crucial in light of Walter Benjamin's comment on the assertion that a man who dies at 35 is at every moment of his life a man who dies at 35. It would be more accurate, Benjamin writes, to say that a man who dies at 35 *will be remembered* at every moment of his life as a man who will die at 35, and he concludes: "The nature of a character in a novel cannot be presented any better than this statement, which says that *the 'meaning' of his life is revealed only in his death*."[4]

Turgenev, condemning Bazarov to an early death, said of his hero

1. V. S. Pritchett, "The Russian Day," in his *The Living Novel* (London, 1954), p. 223.
2. S. E. Shatalov, *Khudozhestvennyi mir Turgeneva* (Moscow, 1979), p. 302.
3. Iu. Mann, "Bazarov i drugie," *Novyi Mir*, No. 10, 1966, pp. 238–39.
4. Walter Benjamin, "The Storyteller," in his *Illuminations*, trans. Harry Zohn (New York, 1968), p. 100. (My italics.)

(in a letter to Katkov) that he was "empty and sterile."[5] Let us leave for a moment the question of his emptiness; I will return to it later. For now I would stress that the "meaning" of Bazarov's life evidently rests on his "sterility," which is to say, on his early death.

Why does he die? Turgenev's own statement on this score is well known: "I saw as in a dream a large, gloomy, wild figure, half grown out of the soil, strong, bitter, honest—and all the same doomed to die because he stands only on the threshold of the future. . . ."[6] All the same, more than one reader, captivated by the dynamism of Bazarov's character, has ruminated on how his life might have continued. Strakhov, for example, writes: "Bazarov's credo, nihilism, . . . I have adduced as an effort of thought to free itself from old concepts, as a coherent quest for a new path for life and mental activity. However, . . . this quest is only a transitional moment, an incomplete process. . . . Bazarov's whole depiction in this novel is only the beginning, the embryo of some future figure. . . ."[7]

Similarly, Herzen—though he praised Turgenev's art—found it easy to imagine a different ending for the novel:

> What if he had sent Bazarov to London? . . . We might have proved to him on the banks of the Thames that it is possible, without working up to the rank of department head, to be no less useful than any department head; that society is not always unresponsive and implacable when protest finds the right tone; that the cause can sometimes succeed. . . .
>
> The worst service that Turgenev rendered Bazarov consists in his having punished him with typhus because he didn't know how to come to terms with him. That is the sort of *ultima ratio* that no one can withstand. Had Bazarov recovered from typhus, he would surely have developed beyond Bazarovism, at least in the science which he loved and valued, and in physiology which doesn't change its approaches, whether it is dealing with a frog or a human being, redividing embryology or history. . . . Science would have saved Bazarov, he would have stopped looking down on people. . . .[8]

Even Nabokov could not resist the temptation to follow Turgenev's hero beyond the limits imposed on him:

> Bazarov is a strong man, no doubt—and very possibly had he lived beyond his twenties . . . he might have become, beyond the horizon of the novel, a great social thinker, a prominent physician, or an active revolutionary. But there was a common debility about Turgenev's nature and art; he was incapable of making his mas-

5. Letter to Katkov, 30.11.61, *Pis'ma*, vol. 4, p. 303.
6. Letter to Sluchevsky, 26.4.62, *Pis'ma*, t. 4, p. 381.
7. N. N. Strakhov, "Predislovie," *Kriticheskie stat'i ob I. S. Turgeneve i L. N. Tolstom*, SPb, 1887, p. V.
8. A. I. Gertsen, "Eshche raz Bazarov," *Sobr. soch.*, 20, pp. 339, 345.

culine characters triumph within the existence he invents for them.
. . . Love turns out to be something more than man's biological
pastime. The romantic fire that suddenly envelops his soul shocks
him; but it satisfies the requirements of true art, since it stresses
in Bazarov the logic of universal youth which transcends the
logic of a local system of thought—of, in the present case,
nihilism.[9]

This common tendency to extrapolate Bazarov's story, it seems to me,
points to a certain contradiction between the novelty of Bazarov's "emptiness" (i.e., his openness, his capacity, like the heroes of the late Dostoevsky, to change sharply and abruptly) on the one hand, and that
characteristic framework in which it is confined. The words of Bakhtin,
inspired by the heroes of the late Dostoevsky, apply fully to Bazarov:
"So long as a man is alive, he lives by virtue of the fact that he is not
completed and has not yet said his final word." That appears to be
something felt by all readers—and one might add that, like the heroes
of Dostoevsky, Bazarov does not so much proclaim his views—he speaks
of them unwillingly and rarely—as incarnate them.

So, from this point of view, *Fathers and Sons* turns out to be both
atypical and typical with respect to Turgenev's novelistic poetics. The
protagonist is atypical, being far from "already formed." He alone grows
as we read. But it turned out to be too much for Turgenev (or for his
poetics) to do what the late Dostoevsky did in *The Brothers Karamazov*;
that is, to finish the novel, leaving the young heroes alive and their fates
open, to call the novel in question "only a prehistory"—or to refer to
that "new story" that begins after the downfall of the hero, as Dostoevsky
does at the end of *Crime and Punishment*.

Turgenev himself admitted as much. To the observation that Bazarov
dies "an accidental death, as if you didn't know yourself what to do with
him," he replied: "Yes, I really didn't know what to do with him. I felt
then that something new had come into existence; I saw new people,
but how they would act or what would come of them, I could not
imagine. So it remained for me either to write nothing, or to write only
what I knew. I chose the latter."[1] In other words, Bazarov (in Yurii
Mann's phrase) "had to die in order to remain Bazarov."[2]

In this truncation we see not only a sign of what might be called
Turgenev's novel manqué (by comparison with the Dostoevskian novel
which he seemed to be approaching in *Fathers and Sons*), but also
(though in a less extreme form) one feature of Chekhov's future poetics.
I cite the article of Harai Golomb; though it deals with Chekhov's plays,
his words are applicable to the mature work in general.

9. Vladimir Nabokov, *Lecture on Russian Literature* (New York, 1981), p. 71.
1. Iz "Vospominanii o Turgeneve N. A. Ostrovskoi," *Turgenevskii sbornik.*, pod red. N. K.
Piksanova, Pg, 1915, p. 80.
2. Op. cit., p. 249.

Since Chekhov equally stresses both the existence-and-worth of the human potential and the inevitability of its non-realization, he can be sharply and equally distinguished on the diachronic axis from two groups of authors: (a) his predecessors (and many contemporaries) in literature and drama, who share with him only the high valuation of human potential, and (b) his successors (notably the "absurd" playwrights and authors), who share with him only the sense of its inevitable non-realization. It is this uniquely Chekhovian combination which makes him too complex for some reductionist critics (in the East and the West alike), who perpetuate the futile controversy about whether Chekhov's view of reality and mankind is "positive-optimistic" or "negative-pessimistic." Those critics, no matter whose side they are on, oversimplify the picture by failing to reconcile Chekhov's genuine respect for the great potential of the human mind, spirit, talent, compassion, etc., with his uncompromising, often relentless pursuit of his characters on their flight into illusion and self-deception, and the false hope of realizing those potentials. [3]

One might similarly apply to Turgenev's novel Isaiah Berlin's gloss on Strakhov's words about Turgenev's "poetic and truthful genius." Berlin speaks of the writer's capacity, "undistorted by moral passion," [4] for rendering "the very multiplicity of interpenetrating human perspectives that shade imperceptibly into each other, nuances of character and behavior, motives and attitudes. . . ." [5]

That feature, I submit, is one that we perceive, inevitably, through the prism of Chekhov—thus "the influence of Chekhov on Turgenev"—since, as a result of Turgenev's own definition of his novels, together with the response of his contemporaries to them, a tradition was formed that neglected precisely such nuances. By way of example one might analyze the remarkably subtle structure of the third chapter of Fathers and Sons, underscoring the nuanced modulation of feeling and perspective, the art of implication, and the way that these recall (for us, today) Chekhov, particularly in his plays. The chapter in question contains a delicately managed series of interchanges, in which Nikolai Petrovich speaks warmly of his future work in running the estate together

3. Harai Golomb, "Music as Theme and as Structural Model in Chekhov's Three Sisters," in Herta Schmid and Aloysius Van Kesteren, eds., Semiotics of Drama and Theatre, Amsterdam/ Philadelphia, 1984, pp. 174–175.
4. An example of such "distortion through moral passion" can be seen in the words of I. S. Aksakov about Fathers and Sons: "The novel is remarkable for the social problem it treats, but the artist n'est pas la porte du sujet—and the result is a monstrous enough work. Turgenev is a very intelligent man, and a very benevolent one, but as the daughter of the poet Tiutchev (who is bringing up the Empress's children) said of him with remarkable perspicacity and truth: il lui manque l'epine dorsale morale. Indeed, he has no bones in him at all; it's all cartilage." Quoted in N. P. Barsukov, Zhizn' i trudy M. P. Pogodina (St. Petersburg, 1888–1910), 19, p. 169.
5. Isaiah Berlin, "Fathers and Children: Turgenev and the Liberal Predicament" in his Russian Thinkers (London, 1978), p. 293.

with Arkady; Arkady switches the subject to the beauty of the day; Nikolai
Petrovich, agreeing, declaims Pushkin (an indirect lyrical confession)—
only to be interrupted by Bazarov's voice asking for a match; Arkady
himself then lights up to show his solidarity with Bazarov, thereby ex-
cluding his father and banishing (by polluting) the fresh spring atmosphere. Precisely like Chekhov, Turgenev "rel[ies] fully on the reader,
assuming that he will supply the subjective elements that are missing in
the account."[6]

Signs of such a reliance in both writers are the frequent pauses and
ellipses[7]; and particularly the eloquent gestures, quite as telling as words
(e.g., the way on first meeting Bazarov Nikolai Petrovich "firmly grasps
. . . the uncovered red hand, which [the former] hesitated to extend to
him").

III

(Conclusion)

Just as Odintsova finally rejects the temptation of Bazarov's passion and
strength in order to remain herself, so Turgenev rejected the temptation—evidently a serious one—of the kind of large novel that Dostoevsky
was shortly to begin writing. Because what he understood best of all (in
life and in art) were personal relations, the complexities of feeling and
nature, he was more drawn to the kind of inner dynamics which Chekhov
was later to develop and which, once developed by him, would allow
a clearer and fuller appreciation of the main aspect of the art of the
author of *Fathers and Sons*.

Turgenev's essential gift was that of a dispassionate and penetrating
observer; his genius lay in his rendering of character—not developing
but rather revealing itself in the humdrum interactions of everyday life.
That this was by no means the sign of an intellectual or artistic insuf-
ficiency but quite the opposite becomes irresistibly clear to generations
that have undergone the "influence," among others, of Dostoevsky and
Chekhov.

---

6. A. P. Chekhov, letter to Suvorin of 1.4.1890, *Polnoe sobranie sochinenii i pisem v tridtsati
tomakh, Pis'ma*, 4 (Moscow, 1976), p. 54.
7. Cf. A. Batiuto, *Turgenev-romanist* (1972), pp. 201–02: "The text of Turgenev's novel literally
swarms with pauses and ellipses. The device of the long pause or the suppressed statement
after which the train of thoughts, feelings, and experiences not always even named but understandable to the alert reader is hidden—this is a favorite means of psychological characterization for Turgenev and one he employs frequently."

ROBERT L. JACKSON

The Turgenev Question†

The tradition of all dead generations weighs down the brain of the living.

—Karl Marx

"People say that Turgenev has become obsolete," observed Dmitri Merezhkovsky in 1908, the twenty-fifth anniversary of Turgenev's death. Tolstoy and Dostoevsky have overshadowed him. "But forever? For how long?" asked Merezhkovsky. "Are we not destined to return to him through them?" Merezhkovsky's idea of a return to Turgenev was premature but perspicacious. In his memorial speech he was one of the few major Russian critics in the early twentieth century not only to challenge the notion of Turgenev as out of date but to pose what may be termed the Turgenev question in broadly aesthetic, cultural, and historiophilosophical terms.

"In Russia, in the land of all kinds of revolutionary and religious maximalism, a country of self-immolation, of the wildest excesses," Merezhkovsky declared, "Turgenev—after Pushkin—is almost the sole genius of measure and, therefore, a genius of culture. For what is culture if not the measuring, the accumulation and preservation of values?" To Russia's maximalists—Tolstoy with his cultural iconoclasm, his desire to save Russia "peasant style, holy fool style," and Dostoevsky with his contempt for the "godless, rotten west" and his conception of Russia as "the only God-bearing people"—Merezhkovsky opposes the "minimalist" Turgenev, Russia's "true conservator," Pushkin's legatee who first revealed to Europe that "Russia is also Europe." If the Russian revolution of 1905 went awry, Merezhkovsky argues, it was because there was "too much of Tolstoy and Dostoevsky in it, and too little of Turgenev."

Tolstoy's artistic genius was acknowledged early by writers and critics. Dostoevsky himself observed that "in all of world literature, throughout all of world history there never was a greater artistic talent than that of Leo Tolstoy." Yet the twentieth century indubitably belongs to Dostoevsky: it recognized itself in the man who observed: "Everywhere and in everything I go to the limit. All my life I have crossed the last boundary." What Dostoevsky saw in himself, he found in the world. "Reality strives toward fragmentation," remarks the narrator of *House of the Dead*. "There are no foundations to our society," Dostoevsky wrote in his notebook in 1875. "A colossal eruption and all is crumbling, falling, being negated, as though it had not even existed." Dostoevsky's

† First published in the *Sewanee Review* 93, no. 2 (Spring 1985) 300–09. Reprinted with the permission of the editor.

art, governed by principles of form that were in accord with his perception of reality, gave expression to eruption.

Turgenev, no less than Dostoevsky, was aware of the destabilizing forces in the individual and society, yet nothing was more nearly anathema to him in art and culture than "maximalism." He found his commanding poetic in the "life of nature": "a quiet and slow animation, a leisureliness and restraint of feelings and forces, an equilibrium of health in every individual creature—that is nature's very foundation, its unalterable law, that is what maintains it and keeps it going." Turgenev's poetics of nature, which conflicts with his tragic vision of human existence, did not lead him away from turmoil, conflict, ambiguity, but it led him to depict reality differently from Tolstoy or Dostoevsky. The art of Turgenev is in restraint, understatement, the capacity to perceive and embody the greatly significant, whether social, psychological, philosophical, or historical, in the everyday text and subtext of character and moment. "A poet must be a psychologist, but a secret one," Turgenev wrote in a letter to K. D. Leontiev in 1860 in one of his most revealing statements about his own artistic method. "He must know and feel the roots of phenomena, but represent only the phenomena themselves in their flowering and fading. . . . Remember that however subtle and complex the inner structure of some tissue in the human body, the skin, for example, nonetheless it is comprehensible and homogeneous." To present the appearance of simplicity and homogeneity, yet in fact reveal the full complexity and variety of individual and social consciousness: herein lies a cardinal feature of Turgenev's art.

Turgenev's artistic method derives in part at least from his heightened awareness of the usually concealed relationship between surface manifestation and internal reality in the life and consciousness of people. In remarks that anticipate Chekhov's understanding of the tragic, Turgenev writes to the Countess Lambert in 1859:

> It recently occurred to me that there's something tragic in the fate of almost every person—it's just that the tragic is often concealed from a person by the banal surface of life. One who remains on the surface (and there are many of them) often fails even to suspect that he's the hero of a tragedy. A woman will complain of indigestion and not even know that what she means is that her whole life has been shattered. For example: all around me here are peaceful, quiet existences, yet if you take a close look—you see something tragic in each of them—something either their own, or imposed on them by history, by the development of the nation.

Turgenev's "close look" is focused on meaning in image and gesture, character and action. The social and topical, too, which forms the surface attention of his major novels, always is rooted in deeper psychological, psychohistorical, and philosophical concerns. Turgenev said in 1856: "[Johann Heinrich] Merck puts his finger on it when he says, 'With the ancients everything was local and topical and so became eternal.' We write in some hazy, distant spot for everyone and for posterity and hence for no one."

The art of Turgenev, like the camouflage of mind and nature, conceals its deeper intent and emphases. *Rudin* (1856), explicitly concerned with the Russian idealist of the 1840s, is a profound study of the "relation between language and reality," as Jane Costlow has recently demonstrated in "The Death of Rhetoric in *Rudin*." Turgenev's "The Inn" (1852), at first glance a simple anecdote, is a philosophical novella centering on Russian man and history, a work (like *On the Eve* or "A King Lear of the Steppes") that reveals Turgenev's affinity with the tragic outlook of the Greeks. *A Nest of Gentryfolk* (1859), referred to by Dostoevsky as "an eternal work belonging to world literature," constitutes a rich tapestry of speculation on man, history, and freedom. *First Love* (1860) is not merely a lyrical evocation of first love but an acute revelation of the crossing of boundaries in psychosexual consciousness. Yet it is impossible to reach the rich levels of these and other works without bearing in mind the seriousness for Turgenev of his injunction that the artist's "task is . . . understanding in imagery and the representation of what exists, and not theories about the future, not sermons, not propaganda."

"You have grasped so well what I wished to express through Bazarov . . . you have got to the heart of things and have even sensed what I thought unnecessary to express," Turgenev wrote Dostoevsky after he read *Fathers and Sons*. "May God grant that this is not just the acute sensibilities of a master but that it can be understood by the ordinary reader." Turgenev, of course, had expressed the things that he had thought "unnecessary to express," but he spoke through tropes with an artistic ambiguity that baffled his ordinary readers. "Only after pondering every epithet chosen by him, every color he lays down, every thought he expresses will you discover the concealed riches of that devilishly light and musical prose," wrote S. A. Andreevsky in 1902. "This prose resembles the verse of Pushkin the profound inner content of which only a handful of people were able to disclose, and then very late."

For Turgenev truth was multivalent, complex, not easily accessible. "There's more than one side to Truth," he wrote to A. V. Druzhinin in 1856 concerning the radical democrats. "For you, all this present trend is a delusion which has to be rooted out, while for me it is part of the Truth which will always find (and must find) followers at those periods in human life when the full Truth is inaccessible." Turgenev later parted company with the radical camp of Chernyshevsky and Dobroliubov, but as an artist he remained faithful to his concept of truth— a fact that the diverse readership of *Fathers and Sons* and other works could not and would not grasp.

For all the breadth of his vision and characteristic ambiguity of his artistic design (in which, as the noted critic M. Gershenson noted, he resembles Dostoevsky), there was nothing cool or detached about Turgenev's relation to life or art. He expressed his paradox-laden idealism in his brilliant address "Hamlet and Don Quixote" (1860), a programmatic piece not only for his own writing but for Russian literature in general. It is no surprise to hear him complaining in a letter to S. T. Aksakov in 1857 of "a lack of any sort of faith or conviction, even artistic conviction," among the younger French writers he was encountering in Paris. Nor did his sense of multivalent truth and personal liberalism blind him to the indispensable role of conflict in the life of the individual and society. It is high time, he wrote P. V. Annenkov in 1870, for the French people "to take a look at themselves, inside their own country, and to see their own ulcers and try to cure them. . . . Without serious internal upheavals such self-examination is impossible; it cannot occur without causing deep shame and serious pain. But true patriotism has nothing in common with this arrogant, conceited aloofness which leads only to self-deception, ignorance and irremediable errors." Turgenev's words could have been directed at Russia as well.

In general there is a sobriety to Turgenev's approach to Russia and the Russian people that is absent from the utterances of so many of his peers, radical and conservative alike. "Perhaps in my opinion Russia is more misanthropic than you suppose," Turgenev wrote the reactionary journalist M. N. Katkov in 1861 in regard to his portrayal of Bazarov in *Fathers and Sons*. A year later he wrote to the populist and radical Alexander Herzen: "An enemy of mysticism and absolutism, you mystically worship the Russian sheepskin coat and see in it a great blessing and the novelty and originality of future societal forms—in a word, *das Absolut.*" Turgenev warns against "the danger of groveling before the people at one moment, distorting them the next, then crediting them with sacred and high convictions, and then branding them unfortunate and insane." Turgenev noted the people's "repugnance to civic responsibility and to independent initiative." "Take science, civilization and gradually cure [the people]," he wrote again to Herzen. The Russian people, he wrote later to another correspondent, need "helpers not herders."

Turgenev does not glorify the Russian people or its past. "I see the tragic fate of a tribe, a great societal drama," he wrote K. D. Aksakov in 1852, "where you find reassurance and the refuge of the epic." Ten years later, at the time of the emancipation of the serfs, Turgenev, anticipating Dostoevsky's skepticism about Russia's "foundations," asks in a letter to the Countess Lambert:

> Has history made us as we are? Are there elements in our very natures of all that we see around us? We, of course, in the sight

of heaven and aspiring to it, continue to sit up to our ears in the mud. . . . The general *gaseous* nature of Russia upsets me and forces me to think that we are far from the *planet* stage. Nowhere is there anything firm or solid; nowhere is there any core. I am not talking about our institutions, but about the people themselves.

Nearly a half century later, on the eve of the Russian revolution of 1905, the liberal historian of literature D. N. Ovsyaniko-Kulikovsky, confident that Russia was marching boldly along the progressive path of Western European social development, scolded Turgenev for the "pessimistic" and "skeptical" attitude he had displayed in his correspondence with Herzen toward "Russian reality, the Russian people, our history, our whole past and, at least, our near future." He found "simply absurd" Turgenev's admittedly disturbing historical-philosophical judgment that "of all European peoples precisely the Russian people are least in need of freedom." Yet Turgenev was absolutely correct in doubting that Russia could or would overcome its historical ailments at least with respect to *its near future.*

Chekhov, recalled Russian theater director Nemirovich-Danchenko in his memoirs, cried out almost in despair that "Russia must pay for its past," that "colossal sufferings" "will accompany the birth of the new Russia, and they are inevitable. Colossal illnesses go with a great people." Chekhov tempered his melancholy prognosis with the faith that "we [the Russian people] will hold out. Russia will endure." Here Chekhov only echoes Turgenev's Potugin (*Smoke*, 1867), who, despite his mordant skepticism, is confident that what happened with the Russian language (its capacity to absorb the violent impact of "alien forms") "will take place also in other spheres. The whole question is this: is there sufficient strength of character? Well, our character is not to be worried over, it will endure. . . . Only nervous, sick, really weak peoples can fear for their health, their independence."

Turgenev's view of Russia, like Chekhov's, is nonetheless sadly relevant to twentieth-century Russian history, particularly in the years of the development of the Bolshevik revolution. Epic design quickly passed into tragic reality, a crash of illusions, and a recognition among many Russian thinkers that the principal task of Russian society lay in the recovery of middle-of-the-road culture. The "crisis of culture," wrote the Russian philosopher Nikolai Berdyaev in 1923, reveals itself in "a longing to escape from the middle course into some sort of all-resolving end. There is an apocalyptic tendency in the crisis of culture. It is present in Nietzsche and it is present in the highest degree in Dostoevsky." Turgenev's art, his aesthetic and social thought, involved as they are with limits and compromises in all areas of human existence, constitute a powerful counterweight to the utopian and the apocalyptic in Russian social and political thought and ideology. Professor Marc Raeff, noting the dominant influence of the excited moral and religious thinking on social culture in the immediate decades preceding the Russian revolution of 1917, has written of the Russian intelligentsia's "cultural flight before the catastrophe." It seems likely that a reawakened Russian intelligentsia after the catastrophe will view Turgenev, the artist and thinker, in an entirely different light.

The reviewer of the Knowles and Lowe translations of a selection of Turgenev's letters—236 in Knowles's collection and 334 in Lowe's, out of more than 6,000 extant letters—immediately confronts a paradox that adds contemporary flavor to the Turgenev question. On the one hand, two scholars, independently of one another, conscientiously and skill-fully have devoted themselves as editors and translators to making a small but vital part of Turgenev's correspondence available in English. On the other hand, in their brief introductions to their collections they respond to Turgenev the man and writer so indifferently and tritely as to make the reader wonder what drew them to their enterprise in the first place.

Lowe sees Turgenev as one of the "literary giants" of the nineteenth century seemingly destined for "a permanent position in the pantheon of literary greats," yet with each passing year Turgenev's "literary stock slips a little lower." He has become an icon. "By and large, the vast body of Turgenev's prose fiction, not to mention his poetry and dramatic compositions, strikes us as singularly dated. The poetic sensibility at work in Turgenev's tales of destructive passion evokes ennui in the modern reader." Even if *us* can be construed as the modern reader, Lowe does not indicate that his views of Turgenev differ from those held by *us*. Yet Lowe finds it "highly unlikely that Turgenev will be forgotten." He will be remembered for his "enigmatic personality," his role as "a spokesman for his age," and for his position as "cultural intermediary between Russia and Western Europe." So much for Turgenev the writer.

Knowles, equally pessimistic about Turgenev, is a good deal more patronizing: "Turgenev's novels and stories have sometimes been criti-cized for their concentration on social problems of which he had little understanding or their doubtful characterization." Yet "very rarely has their style been regarded as anything but exemplary. While his letters clearly do not show the same care in composition his facility for writing is notable." Knowles concludes with a report-card assessment of Tur-genev's character: he was "politically naive," "weak-willed," "found it difficult to make up his mind," was "generally lazy," and was "a man with strong views on many subjects, but very few convictions; an agnostic and a lover of individual freedom." "It is nevertheless the more positive sides of his character that must have impressed those who knew him well," concludes Knowles in a more consoling spirit, "for almost every-one liked him and children adored him."

These dismal introductions to Turgenev (and a fascinating correspondence) would not be worth dwelling upon did they not constitute in their own way a treasury of the clichés that have cluttered a good deal of the criticism about Turgenev in the past one hundred years: Turgenev's novels are period pieces; he is a conduit only for studying his class and culture; he was indecisive and weak in character; he is a writer with poetic sensibility and style, but with nothing to say. In *Turgenev's Russia* (1980) Victor Ripp brings this line of thinking to its last stop: "The meanings of Turgenev's fiction are so accessible, the questions his characters raise and the values they endorse are so easily comprehensible, that commentary seems superfluous."

Turgenev's prose (he began his career as poet and dramatist) was received positively in Russia in the 1840s and 50s, though his *Sportsman's Notebook* and his early novels evoked interest largely for their topical content. Through the 1860s and 70s Turgenev held undisputed sway in Europe, England, and the United States as Russia's leading writer. Western educated, a master of four or five western languages, an inveterate traveler, and a friend of major European writers, critics, publicists, and translators, Turgenev represented Russian culture abroad. He was Russia "in a large measure," Henry James wrote in *Partial Portraits* (1884). "His genius for us is the Slavic genius." "When I think of Russia," H. G. Wells wrote in 1910, "I think of what I have read of Turgenev." Wells speaks of the "realist" Turgenev, the writer whose *Sportsman's Notebook* was presented in English in 1854 and 1855 under the naive titles "Photographs of Russian Life" and "Russian Life in the Interior." Appreciation of Turgenev's art by writers such as Flaubert, James, or Howells could be subtle, yet the general and popular view of Turgenev was limited. James himself saw in Turgenev a class of very careful writers whose "line is narrow observation," and whose manner is that of a "searching realist . . . a devoutly attentive observer." Such a critical assessment, echoing Russian and European views, had its severe limitations—and even severer consequences. As Liza Cherezh Allen observes in a forthcoming study of Turgenev, the Russian writer's reputation has been closely and fatally linked with a brittle nineteenth-century notion of "realism." "The critical term has fallen out of favor, but so have the works it once billed as providing 'an objective representation of contemporary social reality.' "

Russian critics set the stage for the downgrading of Turgenev in the 1880s and 90s. "There is little of genuine artistry, that is, creativity in the real sense of the word, in Turgenev," wrote the important conservative critic N. N. Strakhov. Without any "profound task" to fulfill, Turgenev is only the "singer of our cultured stratum, and then only of its last formations." Arguing for the relevance of Dostoevsky's work for modern times, the influential Russian critic and thinker V. V. Rozanov maintained in 1894 that "Turgenev's characters responded to the interests of their moment, were understood in their time, but now have left behind an exclusively artistic attractiveness." This naive assumption that the *form* of Turgenev's work can be separated from a consideration of the inner content of his work is one of the most persistent and flawed notions in Turgenev criticism.

The shift away from Turgenev was as noticeable in Europe as in Russia. "One is . . . still accustomed to view Turgenev as the representative of literary Russia," wrote the twenty-three-year-old German writer Paul Ernst in 1889, "but the Russia which Turgenev represented is dead; the new young Russia is represented by people like Tolstoy and Dostoevsky." Praising Turgenev for his "absolute sanity and the deepest sensibility," for an "unerring instinct for the significant, for the essential in the life of men and women," Joseph Conrad nonetheless wrote to Edward Garnett that with the year 1899 "the age of Turgenev had come to an end, too." George Moore, who had written with admiration of Turgenev's "unfailing artistry" in the 1880s, later complained of a lack of "psychological depth" in him. "He has often seemed to us to have left much unsaid, to have, as it were, only drawn the skin from his subject. Magnificently well is the task performed; but we should like to have seen the carcass disembowelled and hung up." The now forgotten Maurice Baring brought together in his *Landmarks of Russian Literature* (1908) the strands of Russian and European criticism. He praises Turgenev as a "great poet"—time can never take away the "beauty of his language and the poetry in his work"—but finds his "vision weak and narrow." Turgenev has "recorded for all time the atmosphere of a certain epoch." Baring relegates Turgenev's "magical" but now "useless" language to the Russian classroom. In his *History of Russian Literature* (1926) Dmitry Mirsky, a sometimes subtle critic, faithfully repeats well-worn clichés when he writes that Turgenev was "representative only of his class—the idealistically educated middle gentry" of the latter part of the nineteenth century. "Long since the issues that he fought out have ceased to be of any actual interest. . . . His work has become pure art." Such criticism has long ceased to have any intrinsic value, yet it serves well to define the heavy weight of tradition still bearing down on much of Turgenev criticism and scholarship, particularly in the West.

Rising to the defense of Turgenev in 1917, Edward Garnett sought to counteract "the disease, long endemic in Russia, of disparaging Turgenev." Yet despite his earnest efforts Garnett's criticism was as flawed as that of his opponents. He speaks of Turgenev's "exquisite feeling for balance" which is "less and less prized in modern opinion," of his "grace of beauty" and his "harmonious union of form and subject." Yet while complaining that "far too little attention has been paid to [Turgenev] as an artist," he insists that the "discussion of technical beauties . . . is not only a thankless business, but tends to defeat its own object. It is better to seek to appreciate the spirit of a master, and to dwell on his human values rather than on his aesthetic originality." T. S. Eliot rightly faulted

Garnett's approach to Turgenev when Eliot wrote in 1917: "A patient examination of an artist's method and form (not by haphazard detection of 'technical beauties') is exactly the sure way to 'human value', is exactly the business of the critic."

Eliot's observations, reflecting a new orientation in English and American literary theory and criticism, were not followed in the West by intensive critical analyses of Turgenev's language and text. Virginia Woolf would write warmly and sympathetically of Turgenev—but necessarily from a distance. The Russian Formalists, from whom one might have expected important critical studies, generally ignored Turgenev. An exception was Boris Eichenbaum, who dismissed Turgenev in a two-thousand-word essay for a class-oriented *"artistizm."* Turgenev's "every word" was mannered; he contributed no new word to Russian literature. He was simply "out of date."

Russian and Soviet academic scholarship on Turgenev, of course, has been abundant and fruitful, particularly in the literary-historical sphere. Yet Turgenev has evoked few critical or scholarly studies that can match the powerful work done on Pushkin or Dostoevsky. In the West Turgenev has had ardent defenders: Flaubert, Henry James, Howells, Conrad, Thomas Mann, Virginia Woolf, Louis Aragon, and others have written or spoken sensitively about Turgenev. Important critics such as Edmund Wilson, Isaiah Berlin, and George Woodcock have written intelligently about him, yet none of these critics or writers wrote intensively or extensively about Turgenev.

Recent Soviet, European, and English scholarship has begun to make major contributions to the study of Turgenev. Yet ultimately only the kind of intensive analyses envisaged by Eliot, along with a thorough reexamination of the historical roots, cultural context, and traditions of Turgenev criticism and scholarship in the East and West, will bring to Turgenev the appreciation and understanding that have hitherto been reserved for Pushkin, Tolstoy, Dostoevsky, and Chekhov.

The reasons for the cooling of interest in Pushkin in Russia during the mid-nineteenth century, Turgenev observed in his Pushkin speech in 1880, lay "in the historical development of society, in the conditions giving shape to the new life." While attempting to show "why this neglect was inevitable," Turgenev at the same time pointed to the renewed interest in Pushkin, a poet whom people had become accustomed to think of as a kind of "mellifluous singer, a nightingale." But those who had forgotten Pushkin could not be blamed entirely, Turgenev maintained. Even such a keen person as the poet Baratynsky, called upon to look over the papers of Pushkin after the latter's death, could not help exclaiming in a letter: "Can you imagine what amazes me most of all in these works? The abundance of thought! Pushkin—a thinker! Could one have expected this?" The same words could be uttered about Turgenev by anybody who has come into close contact with his fiction, essays, and correspondence. And what Turgenev said of the renewal of interest in Pushkin may also be said of the rediscovery of Turgenev: "Under the influence of the old, but not yet obsolete master . . . the laws of art . . . will again exert their power."

Ivan Turgenev:
A Chronology

1818	Born on vast manorial estate in the province of Orel in central European Russia.
1833	Enters Moscow University.
1834	Transfers to University of St. Petersburg. Father dies.
1837	Receives degree.
1838	Sets out to travel and study in Europe. Attends University of Berlin.
1841	Returns to Russia.
1843	Publishes first literary work, a narrative poem. Meets the young critic Vissarion Belinsky. Enters into liaison with French operatic singer Pauline Viardot.
1847–50	Publishes A Sportsman's Sketches.
1850	Writes drama A Month in the Country. Mother dies.
1852	Arrested for commemorative article on Gogol. After serving one month in the guardhouse, confined to his estate for one year.
1856	Publishes Rudin, the first of six novels.
1859	Publishes Nest of the Gentry.
1860	Publishes On the Eve.
1862	Publishes Fathers and Sons.
1863	Settles in Baden-Baden with the Viardots. Makes numerous trips to Russia during the next eight years.
1867	Publishes Smoke.
1875	Purchases an estate together with the Viardots in Bougival near Paris.
1877	Publishes Virgin Soil.
1879	Receives honorary degree from Oxford University.
1880	Participates in the dedication of the Pushkin statue in Moscow.
1882	Publishes Poems in Prose. Prepares new collected edition of his works. Becomes ill.
1883	Dies (of cancer) in Bougival.

Selected Bibliography

This bibliography does not include those works from which the excerpts above have been taken.

Brumfield, William C. "Bazarov and Rjazanov: The Romantic Archetype in Russian Nihilism," in *Slavic and East European Journal*, vol. 21, no. 4, 1977.

Freeborn, Richard. *Turgenev: The Novelist's Novelist*. London, 1960.

Gifford, Henry. *The Hero of His Time. A Theme in Russian Literature*. London, 1950.

Lowe, David. *Turgenev's Fathers and Sons*. Ann Arbor, Michigan, 1983.

———, ed. *Critical Essays on Ivan Turgenev*. Boston, 1989.

Magarshack, David. *Turgenev, A Life*. New York, 1954.

Mersereau, John. "Don Quixote—Bazarov—Hamlet," in *American Contributions to the Ninth International Congress of Slavists*, Columbus, Ohio, vol. 2, 1983.

Ripp, Victor. *Turgenev's Russia: From Notes of a Hunter to Fathers and Sons*. Ithaca, New York, 1980.

Schapiro, Leonard. *Turgenev, His Life and Times*. New York, 1978.

Schefski, Harold. " 'The Parable of the Prodigal Son' and Turgenev's *Fathers and Sons*," in *Literature and Belief*, vol. 10, 1990.

Seeley, Frank F. *Turgenev: A Reading of His Fiction*. Cambridge, 1991.

Wasiolek, Edward. "Bazarov and Odintsova," in *Canadian-American Slavic Studies*, vol. 17, no. 1, 1983.

Woodward, James B. *Metaphysical Conflict: A Study of the Major Novels of Ivan Turgenev*. Munich, 1990.

Yarmolinsky, Avrahm. *Turgenev: The Man, His Art and His Age*. New York, 1959.

For further suggestions see *Turgenev in English: A Checklist of Works by and about Him*, compiled by Riss Yachnin and David Stam, New York, 1962; and "Ivan Turgenev: A Bibliography of Criticism in English, 1960–83" in *Canadian-American Slavic Studies*, vol. 17, no. 1, 1983.